Universe Idol
A Sci-Fi Romance

P. Srigley

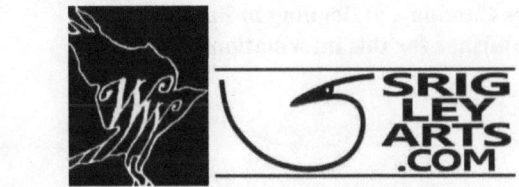

WigglesWorth Press & SrigleyArts.com

Library and Archives Canada Cataloguing in Publication:
Please contact the publisher for this information

ISBN 978-0-9810435-1-7

Published by:
WigglesWorth Press & SrigleyArts.com
Montreal, Quebec, Canada

Additional Titles

All Planetary Shipping
Fire-scape
Scarecrow in the Graveyard
Storyteller's Curse
Storyteller's Quest
The April-May June Series
Deeply
Unreal Estate: One Crooked House

WigglesWorth Press & SrigleyArts.com
Montreal, Quebec, Canada

Contents

1 Antor - Restricted Planet

"We will find out who our lucky finalist is …" Chrome Boreal, the host of Universe Idol, let the moment of suspense drag on and on and on. The last two contestants stood on the glittery stage, clutching each other like best friends, even though their respective planets were presently at war. The tall skinny Scarnivore and the short round Mannireplian were waiting, along with the rest of the civilized Universe, to hear who the winning finalist from the Double Dwarf Star Constellation would be. "… right after this commercial break," Chrome finally orated.

Antor slammed a hand down on the ship's console in front of him. "Another commercial! No wonder I hate this show."

Zenga leaned back in her chair. "You do not hate this show. You love this show. I do, too. I just wish a true humanoid would win for once, or even make it to the finals. Why don't you try out?" She was teasing.

"Too shy." But Antor wanted to, with all his heart.

"You don't have to tell me you're too shy. You won't let me, your best friend, hear you sing. I've never even heard you practice, and not for want of trying." Zenga frowned when the deck underfoot vibrated. "What was that?"

Antor scrolled through his sensors, checking every last one. "Nothing is showing up. All normal in Outer Space. We probably just passed through a gas pocket. Oh, the show is back on."

The vibration was forgotten. Chrome Boreal's face filled the viewing screen that dominated the main wall of the bridge. He flashed his good-natured smile to brighten the dingy gray room. At least the host was humanoid, even if the finalists never were. "Are you ready to find out who your next Universe Idol finalist will be?" he asked the stellar audience.

"Get on with it," Antor growled. The deck vibrated harder. Both Antor and Zenga pretended not to notice.

Chrome Boreal held up a ring-sized disc. He put it in his mouth to access the information and said, "Seedry Tupelo Nug …" Again, he let the moment stretch. The camera zoomed in on the four judges; only one was humanoid. The ship shook. At any other time, it would have generated a reaction. During the climactic end of Universe Idol, it was ignored. The

1

camera cut back to the two finalists. "… you are not the winner. Eenway Frakk, you will be moving on to the finals of the Universe Idol contest!"

Eenway Frakk, the Scarnivore, strode forward on her long skinny legs, beaming as brightly as the three combined suns of Gehenna. It helped that she was orange. The green Mannireplian could be seen in the background, flapping her four arms and starting to swell with distress. Antor hoped she didn't burst, as Manni's were prone to do under extremely stressful circumstances. There was nothing grosser than an explosion of Manni guts.

The deck trembled hard.

"Uh, Zen, I think we better check that out," Antor said, properly concerned now that the program was no longer distracting him.

"I knew Eenway Frakk was going to make it into the finals. The Scarnivores own the whole Universe, don't they? So they probably own the judges and the show!" Zenga turned off the viewing screen with a jab of her finger.

Antor performed a complete sensor sweep of the outer hull. Zenga came to stand behind him, reading the data-stream as it scrolled down the left side of the consol. "Everything looks fine," she said, patting Antor on the shoulder.

"It does," Antor agreed. "Nothing out there, nothing to worry about." He shouldn't have said that. It was inviting trouble.

Trouble arrived in the form of Hampelle. The official Captain of their All Planetary Shipper/Transport stormed onto the bridge. He was new to the position and had only been their Captain for one month. They were still getting to know each other, but Antor didn't think he liked his new boss. In fact, he was pretty sure he didn't like Hampelle even slightly, and he certainly didn't trust him.

The vibrating had disturbed Hampelle's rest cycle, his third one that day. The Captain slept more than he waked. Antor was just glad that Universe Idol was turned off. They weren't supposed to watch any entertainment broadcasts while on duty.

"What the black hole is going on?" Hampelle barked. He was only a small part humanoid, if that. The rest of him was something hairy, dark, and foul-tempered. Not to mention odorous.

"We are trying to determine that very thing," Zenga said crisply. "The sensor sweep confirms no problems outside the ship. All is normal in Outer Space."

Hampelle elbowed her aside as if he didn't think she knew how to do her job. The deck trembled on cue. Hampelle cocked his head, listening hard. He had big blue-black, sharply pointed ears, and exceptional hearing. "The problem is inside the cargo area, not outside the hull," he snapped, then muttered something under his breath about how hard it was to find good help. Even with his much smaller pinkish ears, Antor had no trouble hearing that.

All three of them went off to investigate, single file along the narrow dented corridor, and down the curved slide to reach the lower cargo area. In addition to dozens of secure lockers, the small ship had ten cargo bays of varying sizes. It was obvious which cargo bay was the source of the problem, because the door was dented outward, almost off its sliding track. Under normal conditions, it was dent-proof.

"Cargo 2. What's in there?" Antor asked Zenga. She was in charge of the shipping manifests.

"I don't know." She shot Hampelle an accusing glance, not bothering to hide it.

"But you always know what we're shipping," Antor said. "Have you forgotten?" It seemed unlikely.

"No, I haven't forgotten. He wouldn't tell me and A-1 didn't send any data." The *he* was Captain Hampelle.

"Uh, Captain Hampelle?" Antor said. "What's in there?"

"The contents of C-2 are a confidential matter, my private shipment. Not your business. My business." Something impacted against the door with force. Zenga leaped back into Antor, who hit the Captain. Hampelle was heavy and stocky with a low center of gravity. He didn't even sway.

"I think the contents of C-2 have become our business, since the contents are about to escape." Zenga didn't even try to sound respectful.

Hampelle released a hefty snort of disgust. "Nothing is about to escape. Everything is under control. I'll increase the sedation in the breathing mixture, fix everything." He pressed buttons on the control panel outside the wrecked door. He frowned and began turning the knobs that manipulated the temperature, humidity, and gases inside the storage chamber. Antor tried to peer around a wide hairy shoulder to see exactly what the Captain was doing. There was another thud and another dent appeared in the metal.

The Captain turned knobs more urgently. The door vibrated again. "Damn, I think the panel is disabled, maybe all the smashing ..." Hampelle trailed off, eyes wide and showing their whites. He was scared now.

"Captain Hampelle, what's in there?" Zenga demanded.

"Nothing. That's all I'm saying and all you need to know. Don't open this door under any circumstances. I'm going to get a dartgun." He jogged away. Antor had never seen the Captain move at any pace faster than a slow waddle. He wondered why the emergency blaster than hung in plain sight wouldn't do the job, unless Hampelle didn't want to kill what was about to escape, only knock it out.

Antor and Zenga shared a concerned glance. The door shook again. A little hole appeared in the metal, as if it was corroding from the inside out.

3

White frosty air began to leak into the corridor, through that little hole. They backed up, all the way to the base of the slide. Antor made sure the gravity flow was still reversed, just in case they had to make a run for it— or a reverse slide for it.

It was lucky he did. There was a tremendous impact and the door buckled outward, proving exactly how corroded the metal had become. Antor caught no more than a fleeting glimpse of something huge, hulking, hairy and purple, before he and Zenga dove into the slide-tube and slid upward. As soon as they reached the top, Zenga restored the normal gravity flow so nothing could follow them.

Antor was manually sealing the emergency hatch at the top of the slide when Hampelle appeared with the dartgun. "Did you fools open the door?" he bellowed.

"No! And we're not fools!" Zenga shouted back. Antor wouldn't have yelled at the Captain like that, not when he was holding a weapon. "Whatever that thing is, it broke through the door and got out all by itself. Something compromised the metal. What was in the cargo bay?" Zenga demanded, as if she was the Captain in charge. Antor had no doubt that, given a few more years, she would be a Captain, and a much better one than Hampelle.

Hampelle clawed the wall with an angry swipe, leaving deep scratches behind. "I guess you have to know now. And it's not one, it's two. A breeding pair."

"A breeding pair of what?" Zenga asked.

"Gorka."

"A breeding pair of Gorka?" Antor echoed, sure his ears had misheard. "But there's no such thing as a breeding pair of Gorka, unless they're on Wardangia."

"Why don't you glide on down to the cargo deck and have a look, Antor, if you doubt me." Hampelle curled his upper lip in challenge.

Antor knew he wouldn't be coming back if he tried that. He decided to take the Captain's word for it, as unbelievable as it was, that a breeding pair of Gorka was aboard the shoddy little Comet Tail—and in the process of destroying it.

Zenga gasped. "But ... but ... it's impossible to get a female Gorka, even a male costs a fortune, and requires certified ownership papers and ironclad travel documents." Every being knew that, including the Captain.

The creatures had the unique ability to scent out veins of blackworm oil, even when those veins were deep underground. It was the only lubricant in the Universe that could withstand the stresses of manufactured wormholes, and every ship with worm-hole capability needed a supply of the oil, not to mention periodic oil changes. There was an endless demand for the costly oil, and Gorka were the only creatures that could pinpoint it.

4

Unfortunately, Gorka were also vicious and uncontrollable, which made using them a highly risky affair. Add to that, their caustic saliva, and most beings were smart enough to avoid them.

The keepers of the Gorka were the Gorwargans, who ruled the planet of Wardangia. To guard their monopoly, they had slaughtered every last wild Gorka on their planet, and caged the rest.

Under cosmic contract, for every trace of blackworm oil discovered by their Gorka, they were paid a tariff. The Gorwargans were also savvy enough to only sell the males, never the females, so no-one else could breed them illegally. The Gorwargans tended to kill off the females, only keeping enough of that gender alive to breed. It ensured that the demand for Gorka stayed high, and had made the Gorwargans both rich and powerful, even by Universal standards. So who had gotten their hands on a breeding pair? And entrusted Hampelle to transport them across space? It was a question that begged asking, but Antor didn't dare to ask it.

"To the bridge!" Hampelle ground out, spinning on his heel.

Zenga shot Antor a wild-eyed glance and followed, saying, "Should we call the rest of the crew?" The rest of the crew numbered only one, and it was an auto-mate. The Comet Tail was a small ship. Under normal circumstances, four bodies were enough to pilot her and manage her planetary ports of call.

"No, we'll take care of this. Don't want to have to erase Willy's memories again. Already had to do it when he helped me bring the Gorka aboard." The Captain flung himself into the command chair and accessed a chart of the galaxy they were detouring through. He brought the map up on the main viewing screen, the same screen that had last imaged Universe Idol. Now, it showed a big, two-armed spiral galaxy that was about 100,000 light years across, and only 1,000 wide. "I need to land and get the beasties off the ship, before their spit eats a hole through the rear hatch and kills us all," the Captain said. The Gorka were on a tearing rampage below. The deck was vibrating as if it was having a seizure.

"Why not simply seal the level and open the rear cargo door? They'll be sucked into space. It would be quicker," Antor said.

"Quicker, yes, but I can't lose them or I'll lose my head. They're worth a bloody fortune. I'll have to pick them up again once they've run off some steam, killed some prey. We'll have to repair the ship first, and reinforce the cargo bay door ..." The Captain was muttering to himself. "Where can I put them?" He studied the galactic map and scanned the data-stream for information on the nearest solar systems. He zoomed in on one small blue orb, the third from an unimpressive sun. On the screen, a red line was superimposed on the planet.

"Restricted world," Zenga stressed when the Captain looked at it for too long. The red bar identified it as a planet that hosted life, but that life had no idea that the Universe was a highly populated place. Such primitive cultures often believed in the naïve notion that they were the only sentient life in existence. Such worlds were off-limits to all visitors. Ships weren't even allowed to crash on those planets. They were supposed to self-destruct first.

"Restricted planet is the best type of planet," the Captain said. "I don't want anyone to find out about this, especially not the UGS." If the Universal Guard Ships discovered what the Comet Tail was carrying, or that they had visited a restricted planet, the entire crew would be sentenced to Gehenna. Time on that prison planet was the very worst fate. Prisoners died slowly and painfully. Execution was considered the kinder penalty.

"Captain Hampelle," Zenga said, "we can't land on a restricted planet. We can't release the Gorka on a restricted planet. You know the beasts will kill every living thing they meet, and without natural predators -"

"Do I look like I give a crap?" He accessed more details about the small planet. "Habitable for the Gorka, primitive humanoid. Less than ten light years away. Perfect." He kept scrolling. "And look here, latest scans reveal that they survive in a near toxic environment. The air, the water, the soil, all of it is tainted. And look at that gaping hole in their ozone layer! Not to mention a plague of overpopulation. Six and a half billion humanoids crowd that shrunken planet—can you believe it? Temperatures are rising steadily. Except for the primitive humanoids, everything else is dying off. Polar caps are melting at an exponential rate, probably because of that hole. There is very limited volcanic activity ... I wonder what caused it." He didn't wonder for long. "And there's a sizeable meteor headed their way. It will impact in about eighteen years. It's a doomed world, so a couple of Gorka aren't going to matter one way or another." He began punching in a course.

"Captain Hampelle! We could divert the meteor's trajectory on a quick flyby, and save the planet! And you can't leave the Gorka on a world where they don't belong," Zenga said sternly. "We will report you, won't we, Antor!"

He knew she was right. "Uh, we should, I guess."

Zenga shot him a look of disgust, or maybe it was disappointment. She said forcefully, "We will. We will have no choice."

"Then you'll both take the blame and the punishment for me." Hampelle kept on plotting the quickest route. "Zenga, you signed for the illegal cargo. And Antor, you brought the Gorka aboard while they were sedated."

"We did not," they both cried.

"But that's what the ship's records say. I didn't even know the beasties were on board, did I? I must have been sleeping when you snuck them onto my ship." With a flourish, the Captain pulled the main lever fully back. The ship bucked and spun sharply left into a tight coil as it formed its own little wormhole for the short hop over to the restricted planet. "We'll be there in a blink. Whether you agree or not, I am the Captain and you will do as I say. You will help me save this ship."

"We can save it without causing harm to an innocent world," Zenga said, still trying to reason with him. "Jettison the Gorka!"

"That would cost me my head, and I'm not willing to give that up."

Short of blasting the Captain and taking over the ship in a full mutiny, there was nothing they could do to stop him. The ship was sucked into the wormhole to the sounds of the lower deck being battered. The Comet Tail was going to be in a mess of trouble, even if they could offload the Gorka and escape the restricted planet without being detected by the UGS.

The ship stretched out of its wormhole. For a moment of suspended time, the ship was impossibly long. The hole shrank and closed up with a snap. The Comet Tail's passengers made the physical and mental adjustment back to real time and space. Antor yawned, trying to pop the pressure that had built up in his ears.

"There she is," the Captain announced and switched the imaging screen to a live feed of open space. Dead ahead, their destination planet looked quite beautiful. It was blue and green, and white with clouds. It didn't look toxic. It looked like a rare gem of a green, garden world. Very few planets had enough water, Antor had never seen one with more water than land, like this one.

The Captain had chosen a landing site on the dark side of the orb, in a mainly unpopulated northern area. It wasn't a garden, it was frozen white. Here, it looked like an ice planet, and there were plenty of those dead frozen worlds scattered throughout the Universe.

"Temperature is cold enough for the Gorka. They'll be fine until I can come back for them," Hampelle said, as if Zenga and Antor cared. "They're already tagged with tracer chips, so they'll be easy enough to locate."

He landed the ship by himself. The Captain's good character might be lacking, but he was a gifted pilot. His skill had them setting down with a delicate thump on the snow. It was much smaller than the thumps and bangs being caused by the rampaging Gorka.

2 Holly - Stranded

Holly Noel Tate officially hated her boyfriend's truck. The hunk of junky metal had just ruined her life, and maybe ended her life. She banged the dashboard as hard as she could, but that didn't magically restart the engine or free the tires from the field of deep snow where they were trapped. All it did was make her hand hurt like hell. Life was so unfair!

For months, Holly had been planning to attend the singing auditions in the city. She couldn't wait to be on TV. She had practiced all the hit songs from the radio, until even her best friend, Fiona, was sick of hearing her voice. She had worked every Saturday, saving up the money for an audition outfit. Not to mention makeup, shoes, jewelry and awesome streaks in her hair, and a hotel room in the city. And then everything went wrong.

At the last minute, Holly's Mom had forbidden her to go, saying it was too far for Holly to drive alone, especially in the winter. And she didn't want Holly to miss even a day of her final year of school. Holly would have missed the whole boring year to audition to be a singing idol! She would have driven through a war zone in a blizzard to reach the tryouts.

Daniel, her boyfriend, hadn't approved of her going to the city alone either. And he wasn't about to miss school to go with her, proving he didn't love her as he claimed. So what if he was vying for a scholarship to university. A couple of days off wouldn't have ruined his chances.

Even Fiona wouldn't go with her. She claimed she couldn't get off work. In Holly's opinion, Fiona was just making lame excuses, but Holly wasn't sure why.

It was as if everyone in her life was conspiring against her. Another girl might have given up, or postponed her dream. But not Holly. Life was too short. She wasn't going to miss her chance at fame. And so, Holly had been forced to take drastic action. She had borrowed her boyfriend's truck, without actual permission, and skidded out of town in the middle of the night in a snowstorm.

A big chunk of the drive to the city was through a desolate wilderness of forest called a national park. The park was bigger than some countries. There were no houses, no stores, no towns, not even a gas station. You had to fill up your tank before you entered that stretch of wasteland or you

8

were doomed, especially in frozen winter in the dead of night, when no-one else was stupid enough to be on the curvy little country road that was laughingly called a highway.

Holly had topped up the tank, feeling optimistic because the snow had almost stopped falling. She'd made it halfway through the park before the truck started shaking and coughing as if it was a heavy smoker. Steam began spewing out of the front. Holly had thought the vehicle was on fire. She'd slammed her foot down on the brake—not the smartest thing to do on an icy road. The truck had fishtailed and spun in a circle, before it bounced right off the pavement and down an embankment. It sank into the snow and the engine died with a hacking wheeze. Just like that, Holly was stranded.

That's when she assaulted the dashboard, which didn't help her situation at all.

In hindsight, her determined plan to reach the city seemed nothing but reckless. She was probably going to freeze to death in the park. And if another car happened along, it would surely be driven by a serial killer/rapist, which would be much worse than freezing to death.

Holly checked her cell phone. It didn't have a single bar of reception, and hadn't for the last hour. "Dead zone," she whispered fatally. The radio was still playing, and as if to torment her, the song she had planned to sing for the idol judges came on. Tears filled her eyes. Her dire situation simply couldn't get worse.

When a light appeared in the sky overhead, Holly blinked to clear her vision. She leaned against the steering wheel, squinting up. The golden light kept getting lower. She knew it wasn't a plane from the way it was floating straight down. She cracked her window and couldn't hear a helicopter. She couldn't hear any engine sounds at all, even though the light was almost on top of her truck. It swirled like a whirlpool, with brilliantly sparking particles and an impossibly black center that seemed to suck up the light. As it got closer, she could tell that the ship had a hole through the middle. It was like some giant doughnut that glowed in the same manner as a firefly's abdomen. Holly had never seen anything remotely like it in her life, and she knew her situation had just gotten much, much worse. A spaceship was landing beside the truck. She was about to be abducted by aliens, there was no doubt!

Holly switched off the headlights and edged down in her seat, in case she hadn't been spotted yet.

The gigantic doughnut coasted to Earth ever so gently. It landed slightly downhill from her, on a flat white field. The beautiful golden glow faded until the ship began to look dull and kind of rusty, then even the residual radiance blinked off, leaving nothing but a dark still world of shadowy silhouettes against snow.

9

3 Antor - Release of the Gorka

Antor glanced through the viewing window at an icy field of smooth, unbroken white. It was bordered by a scraggily wall of trees. It looked like an isolated wasteland, not somewhere that primitive humanoids could thrive, or even survive. Perhaps there would be no killing rampage for the Gorka.

"Now to release the buggers," the Captain roared, making Antor jump. Hampelle punched two buttons, to open the inner and outer seals of the main loading hatch at the rear end of the cargo corridor. One of the buttons flashed orange, signaling a malfunction. The Captain pressed it again and again, almost pounding it through the consol. It wouldn't stop flashing.

"Inner hatch jammed?" Zenga asked, with smug satisfaction.

"Looks that way, doesn't it. Outer one opened fine. Antor, Zenga, you'll have to open the inner hatch manually from outside the ship." He pressed two more buttons and the bridge's double-hatched doors slid upward. A wave of frigid air flowed inside.

"We're not going to help you." Zenga crossed her arms and stood firm.

Hampelle surged to his feet, picked Zenga up and tossed her outside. He was much stronger than pure humanoids. He slammed the outer door down, locking her out.

"Uh, Captain Hampelle, she'll freeze to death," Antor mentioned, staying out of arm's range of the Captain, and keeping a chair between them.

"Yes, she will, but I'm not letting her back onto the ship until she releases the Gorka. You can tell her that. With her thin furless skin, I'd say she has about ten minutes before she turns to ice, maybe less."

"You want me to go out there?"

"Yes, Antor." The Captain sounded suddenly tired. "If you care for your friend, you will go out there and deliver my message. You will help her release the beasties." He was talking to Antor as if he was a tot, and not a bright tot at that.

Antor hesitated. "Can I have a blaster? In case we need to defend ourselves?"

"No blaster. I can't have the Gorka harmed."

"Uh, how about a dartgun?"

"You might use it on me, so no." The Captain opened the door again and lunged around the chair toward Antor, who opted to dash outside, rather than be tossed. The hatch slammed closed behind him.

"Zenga, Zenga!" Antor called. He couldn't see her.

"Over here." She was huddled against the scarred hull, somewhat sheltered from the icy wind. Antor joined her. The hull was warm from the stressed coils that generated the wormhole, and the descent through the planet's atmosphere. They pressed against it and each other, conserving meager heat. "Is he going to let us back in?" Zenga sobbed.

"He says he will, once we release the Gorka." The beasts' banging could be heard, even outside the insulated hull.

"What a mess." Zenga shivered hard. Antor hugged her closer, sharing body heat. They had been more than friends once, but it hadn't lasted long. They were simply too different. Zenga was decisive and strong. Antor was anything but.

"If we let them out, they'll attack us, you know," Zenga said against Antor's chest.

"I know."

"If we don't let them out, we'll freeze to death."

"Ya." He sniffled hard. The cold was making his nose run.

"If we let them out, we're helping to kill humanoids. Even if they are primitive, they're still humanoid, like us."

"It might be okay. This zone is barely populated. Maybe we'll be back for them before the Gorka can track any of the natives. Let's go have a look at the cargo hatch. Maybe it won't even open and we won't have any choices to make." Taking the easy way out was something of a habit with Antor.

"Fair enough. We can look." Huddled together, Zenga and Antor skidded on powdery ice to reach the back of the ship. The warm hull was melting into the snow, creating runoff and an eerie steam. His space boots were thin and Antor's feet were soaked and stinging with cold, before he reached the tail end of the sphere. The inner hatch door wasn't nearly as dented as C-2's door had been, but it was dented, proving the Gorka's acid spit was eating into it from the other side.

"Gorka are so savage and fast and strong," Zenga cried through chattering teeth. "If we let them out, they'll kill us before we can get back to the bridge." And Gorka didn't think twice about killing. Actually, they did. It was all they thought about, since it was their born nature. On the Gorka's best day (or worst day), a single pair could rip apart the population of a small settlement.

Antor and Zenga were standing half-frozen, gazing up at the rear hatch, when a pair of bright lights blinked on, illuminating their ship. They weren't alone.

11

"Uh-oh. I think we're about to meet a primitive," Zenga gasped, facing the lights.

"Not so primitive if they have lights. They're supposed to be using fire," Antor muttered.

The situation was going from bad to worse. A door pushed outward on a flimsy metal canister, and a third light went on. It highlighted the humanoid that emerged. Incredible music floated through the air. The most beautiful voice Antor had ever heard was cut off when the door was pushed shut. Antor spotted wheels, proving the metal can was some sort of vehicle, which was as unexpected as the lights.

A two-legged, two-armed being walked toward them, crossing in front of the vehicle's lights. Definitely a humanoid, and walking fully upright. It was hard to tell more, since the figure was covered in thick red cloth, patterned with a border of wavy stripes. It either had enormous feet, or the puffy padded boots it wore were huge.

"Where are the fur pelts?" Antor murmured. Zenga simply gawked.

A high-pitched voice called out a few short words.

Antor said to Zenga, "Communication could be a problem. I think it's a female."

"I think so, too. Our universal translators won't have any dialects from a restricted planet." Zenga smiled at the girl, who kept talking, rapidly.

"What do you think she's saying?" Antor asked, and then he understood her words. His universal translator transmitted an unlisted linguistic code into his brain, proving the dialect was already registered in the universal data-stream. The dialect shouldn't have been there at all, given that it was from a restricted planet. The fact that it had an unlisted designation was equally puzzling. In his twenty years of living on spaceships and visiting countless worlds, Antor had never heard of an unlisted planet, restricted or not.

"I wasn't going to get out of the truck until I saw other people here. Did you see the spaceship land?" The planet's inhabitant motioned at their vessel. Her voice was beautifully melodious. Zenga's eyes widened dramatically, and Antor knew her universal translator had just kicked in with the same information he had received.

The native kept speaking. "Why are you dressed like that?" She looked them up and down. "Aren't you cold? You must be frozen. Where's your car?" She squinted around before she backed up a step. "You didn't find the spaceship, did you? You were on the spaceship!" She turned to run, and in spite of her big feet, or big boots, she slipped on the icy snow. She went down hard.

Antor extended a hand to help the girl up. It wasn't appreciated. She screamed, slapped his hand away and kicked him in the shins. Her boots were a lot harder than his. He jumped back from the savage when she tried to kick him again.

Zenga spoke slowly and clearly to the girl. "Hello. There is no need to be afraid."

The girl lurched to her feet and looked back and forth between them. "Hey, you speak English. Did you or did you not arrive on that spaceship?" She pointed directly at their vessel, as if there were other spaceships in the vicinity that she might be referring to.

Zenga frowned and murmured near Antor's ear, "This is a restricted planet. How does she know about spaceships? And why is her language already registered, while the planet is unlisted?"

Before he could propose a wild theory, the girl interrupted. "I can hear you." She must have had excellent hearing for a humanoid. "What's a restricted planet? And why is Earth one? Did you get off that spaceship or not? I mean, it is a spaceship, right?" She asked a lot of questions, and seemed less skittish now that she could communicate with them.

The face under the hat was as pretty as the voice. As far as humanoid species went, it was exceptionally lovely, with pink cheeks and blue eyes. Blue eyes were more than rare throughout the Universe. Her nose was on the small side, and red and leaking, but that was probably from the cold temperatures. Antor's nose was stinging and leaking, too.

"We did arrive on the spaceship and it is a spaceship," Zenga confirmed. It was kind of hard to deny the enormous metal sphere. Although Antor wished his ship didn't look quite so pitted, rusted and dented, sitting there in the rapidly melting snow.

"Imagine! I thought spaceships would look spacier, more futuristic, although the flying lightshow was awesome. What are you doing here? Did you crash? Because it didn't look like you crashed. I watched you come down and it looked like you landed." The girl had turned awfully matter-of-fact if this was her first alien encounter, which it certainly should have been. And she talked a lot.

"Problems with the cargo," Antor said shortly. As if to prove his words, the hatch banged and another little dent appeared. The locking mechanism also started clicking away, which meant that Captain Hampelle had started pounding on the release button again.

The girl looked properly scared. "What's in there?"

"Some animals. They're a bit stirred up," Zenga said, trembling hard now. Antor kept shuffling his feet, so they wouldn't turn into blocks of ice. It felt like his toes were already getting frostbite.

The native glanced down at his soaked boots and shook her head. "You're not dressed for the weather at all. Have you never seen snow before?" She sounded patronizing, as if she thought she was the superior being in this first contact.

13

"Of course we've seen snow. Lots of worlds have snow," Antor informed her, trying to establish his superiority over the native. He never felt anything but lesser in the greater Universe that was his home, so he certainly didn't want to feel inferior to a primitive, even a beautiful one.

"We are cold." Zenga's voice quivered, her lips were turning blue. The primitive being did something really stupid then. She slipped off her warm coat and draped it over Zenga's thinly clad shoulders. Antor got the primitive being's scarf and hat. She had no survival instinct whatsoever. Most surprising of all, her hair was almost white with blue streaks. Anton had never seen a humanoid with such hair.

"Why don't you go back on your ship?" she asked.

"The Captain won't let us in until we release the cargo." Antor wound the long scarf all around his neck and shoulders. It smelled like sweet flowers in the middle of the icy wasteland. The girl must smell like flowers too. It was a delectable scent.

She pointed to her vehicle. "Come sit in the truck then, it's still warm. You can tell me where you're from. You seem like real people. I'm so glad to not be alone out here anymore. My truck broke down, well—my boyfriend's truck, and then it skidded off the road and got stuck in the snow. Maybe your ship can transport it back onto the road."

Antor didn't have a clue what she was talking about, since his ship couldn't transport anything except cargo. Regardless, he went without a second thought—it was that or freeze to death.

The truck was a lot warmer than outside. They all squeezed onto the padded seat. The music was still playing, except it was a different singer, who was every bit as good as the previous one. They were two best voices he had ever heard in his life. Both would have won Universe Idol, if the singers had been entered in the contest.

Zenga was thinking the same thing. "That is the most fantastic singing," she said in awe.

The primitive humanoid frowned rather fiercely. "She's okay, I'm better."

"You can sing better than that?" Antor gasped.

"Yes. I'm Holly, by the way. Holly Noel Tate. Do you have names?"

"Of course we have names," Antor snapped. "We're advanced beings, not primitives."

Zenga shot him a quelling glance. "I'm Zenga and the grumpy one is Antor. He's not usually grumpy. He's upset by the trouble we had on our ship."

"I am not upset." Antor really wished Zenga would stop talking about him as if he was five years old.

"Pleased to meet you, both of you." The girl pressed a button and a light went on inside the vehicle. She studied them. "You look a lot like me. Are you human? Are you from Earth originally?"

"No," both Zenga and Antor said.

"But you look human."

They did look human, because they were. Zenga and Antor could have walked among this planet's population as if they were part of it. There were small differences, but nothing that would have caused panic. Many pure humanoid species had a common enough appearance.

Zenga explained. "We are human, half of the Universe is humanoid, because of the Spread."

"The Spread?" Of course the girl didn't know what that was.

Zenga provided the short version. "Some species call it a plague, a plague of humans. Ages ago, humans were seeded throughout the Universe on worlds habitable to their kind. Usually only one world per galaxy. Anyway, many of them thrived, and now there are more humanoid species in the Universe than anything else. Your world would have been part of the Spread."

"Imagine that." The primitive opened her mouth to ask more questions. She screamed instead when the Comet Tail fired on the truck with a destructive laser beam. The light and the music died. "Did your Captain just shoot my truck?" Holly asked, as if she didn't believe what had just happened.

"Yes," Zenga confirmed.

"But … why? Is he crazy? Is he trying to kill us?"

"No. I think he wants us to get back to work and release the cargo," Antor said, finding his voice again. Something about sitting close enough to press against the girl's leg had frozen his brain, and his tongue. Or maybe it was the subzero climate.

"We have a new Captain. We don't like him." Zenga was being awfully forthcoming with the primitive.

"I don't like him, either. He wrecked my truck—my boyfriend's truck. Daniel is going to kill me." The girl was properly upset, with good reason.

"That's disturbing. How will he kill you?" Antor was curious. Most humanoid species didn't kill their friends over damaged possessions.

"What? No. He's not really going to kill me. It's an expression. It means he's going to be very upset, and super mad at me. I even took his truck without permission, which is kind of like stealing, and now -"

The front window shattered in a blast of light, spraying them with glass. The girl screamed again in the purest pitch Antor had ever heard. Even her scream was a musical delight.

"I think we better get out of the truck or Hampelle might kill us!" Zenga shoved Antor into Holly, which felt nice, until they bailed out and

15

stood again in the frigid air. The ship's cargo door was shaking under the force of repeated blows, and the lock was still clicking. Now that the Captain was finished laser blasting them, he was back to hammering the release button.

Uneasy, Antor suggested that they move closer to the bridge hatch, in case the Gorka freed themselves, with the Captain's help.

Zenga agreed. "If the Gorka vibrate the door at the same time the Captain clicks the button -" She didn't get any further. The rear cargo door shook and crawled up its track. Enormous furry purple feet with long black claws were revealed, then thick calves and black knees. The door kept creeping upward. The Gorka were almost free.

"Run!" Antor grabbed the native's small, cold hand and dragged her toward the bridge hatch. It was still sealed. Zenga pounded on the metal. If the Captain hadn't needed them to fly the ship, he probably would have left them outside to play with the Gorka, but he did need their help to fly the ship, because he liked to sleep most of the time. The hatch opened.

Grunty howls drew close and everyone tumbled inside. Both doors slid shut and the inner one almost amputated Antor's foot. He jerked it out of the way at the last second.

"Hang on." Captain Hampelle shoved a lever. The ship shot straight up and stopped dead. Everyone fell down, except the seated Captain. He barked, "Antor, go close the rear hatch! Now! Button won't work, we're losing pressure." He banged the button again and the ship stopped shaking. "Oh, there, that seems to have sealed the outer door. It should hold for the time being." He leaned back in his chair. "Whew, close call."

Hampelle didn't look nearly as human as Antor or Zenga, yet the girl didn't let his hairy, blue-black appearance stop her anger. "You wrecked my truck! You shot at me! On my own planet! Who the hell do you think you are?" she demanded.

The Captain still had the long dartgun propped against his chair. Clearly, this race of primitive human lacked even a trace of survival instinct. It was hard to believe that six and a half billion of them had survived to throng the world below.

Zenga volunteered the linguistic code that would allow the Captain to understand their visitor. Hampelle accessed the information and frowned, trying out the language. "Huh. We have a record of the exact dialect, yet the planet is recorded as unlisted?"

"Right," Antor confirmed.

"How very peculiar. Unlisted? An unlisted restricted planet. That can't be, yet it is. And you've captured a primitive."

"We didn't really … uh, capture her," Antor said. He preferred to think of it as rescuing.

"Of course you did. The primitive is on my ship, isn't she?" Hampelle snarled and showed his pointy teeth to the girl.

She stepped back into Antor, but her mouth kept working. "Hey, I'm not the one kidnapping innocent bystanders or shooting up people's trucks for no reason. That's primitive. I would never do those things, so I'm not the primitive one here." Even outraged, her voice was enchanting.

Captain Hampelle cocked his head and his ears wiggled. "I do what is necessary. The ship has been saved. Do you have a name?"

"Of course I have a name—Holly Noel Tate. And I want to know what you released on my planet. What are those purple animals?"

Zenga opened her mouth to reply. Captain Hampelle stopped her by jerking a lever. The ship tilted sharply and they all fell down again. While they were getting up, Hampelle answered the question. "We had to release a few livestock that broke containment. Tropical beasts, the cold will soon kill them if it hasn't already. No danger to your world," he lied glibly.

"Oh, well … that's good." Blue eyes darted around the bridge. "I'm not really captured, am I? You were joking, right? I want to go home now. Can you take me down? Or beam me down or something?"

The Captain looked confused. "Beam you down? What is that?"

"Don't you have a … a transporter, so you can drop me off at my house, beam me home since you've destroyed my truck—Daniel's truck."

"Drop you on your house? From up here?" the Captain asked incredulously.

"No! Drop me off at my house, not on my house. Deliver me to my house. Take me home! Nobody is going to believe that an alien craft destroyed Daniel's truck, not unless they see your ship, so I need them to see your ship, and I need a ride home." The girl gestured with her hands, as if they could speak. "When Nicole said she saw a flying saucer with flashing blue and purple lights, everyone thought she was nuts. I sure didn't believe her even though other people reported seeing the ship, and I don't want everyone to think I'm nuts, so I want you to show them your ship before you fly away."

The girl really did babble, and much of what she said was alarming.

"A flying saucer with flashing blue and purple lights has visited your world? A Scarnivore Disc," Antor said, wondering if the universal translator was simply confused, or malfunctioning.

"But this is a restricted planet. No ships are allowed to land or even orbit," Zenga said.

"You're here," the girl pointed out with straightforward logic. "And the flying saucer was seen at least three different times by three different people. Or maybe it was three flying saucers. And there were strange marks, like crop circles in the snow, left when the ships landed here. Or maybe they never landed, maybe it was a hoax. I always thought those crop

17

circles were hoaxes and it would be even easier to make the marks in the snow, than in a wheat field. Although I think your ship is going to leave one heck of a big crop circle in the snow."

The Captain shook his head as if to clear it. Antor felt the same way.

"And there was some alien with blue blood attacking people, at least that's what the story in the newspaper said. I didn't believe it was true until now. Do you have blue blood?" The girl stopped talking and actually waited for an answer.

"Blue blood? No, we don't have blue blood," Antor replied. "Are you sure that's what this newspaper story said?" Blue blood was universally rare. Catalysts were the only species of part humanoid reputed to have blue blood, but Antor had never met a Catalyst, and he'd certainly never stabbed one, so he really couldn't say.

"Three Scarnivore Discs landing here? And a Catalyst? No wonder the language is registered. This planet is far less restricted than the data-stream would have us think. I foresee myself on Gehenna, and that prison planet is far too hot for the likes of me." The Captain growled low in his throat and thrust the main lever fully forward. The ship spun into space and through a mini-wormhole with screaming coils. And then the mysterious restricted planet wasn't even a blot on the viewing screen. It was so far away, it was gone.

The native wasn't stupid. "This isn't the way to my house," she said faintly.

"We are not going to your house," the Captain told her.

"I really am being abducted by aliens?"

"Yes."

"Oh." The girl turned even paler than she was naturally and collapsed to the ground.

"Is she dead?" Zenga asked.

Antor laid a hand over where her heart should be. It was there, thumping strongly. "No, she's alive."

"Captain Hampelle," Zenga said, "we have to take her back."

"Not a chance. I can't have her reporting what she saw. Too many ships visiting the planet to hear the news. We'll have to jettison her into space so no-one will ever know we were there, then I'll be safe to revisit the planet and pick up the Gorka." He had it all worked out.

"No!" Zenga cried. "You are not going to jettison her! That's murder."

The Captain flapped a hairy hand dismissively. "She's a primitive."

"I don't care, I won't let you!"

"She doesn't seem that primitive," Antor murmured, his hand still on her heart. He liked resting it on her softness, and was in no hurry to move it. "And she can sing." He really wanted to hear her sing.

18

That piqued the Captain's interest. "Well, maybe I won't jettison her immediately. Her speaking voice was astoundingly musical, so maybe I will hear her sing before she leaves. Take her to the cargo deck. Lock her in one of the livestock cages until she wakes up."

Zenga smirked. "Might not be anything left down there that locks."

"Find somewhere or I'll jettison her now!" the Captain roared in a burst of temper.

They had no choice but to follow his orders. Antor had bought the girl some time, nothing more. Between them, Zenga and Antor hauled her down to the cargo deck. It wasn't completely destroyed, although the walls were a lot more eroded than before the Gorka had escaped. The beasts had only broken into five of the other bays, after escaping their own large bay. It left four still intact.

"I'm going to take a quick inventory." Zenga dropped the foot end of Holly Noel Tate into the middle of the mess. Antor lowered the head end more carefully.

Zenga disappeared into the first breached cargo room. She was quick to scurry back out. "The Gorka broke into the barrels of brined mintentacles. They had a feast and a food fight."

"Is that what stinks?"

"Maybe." She stepped over a flattened door into small cargo 6. She came out of there even quicker. "It looks like they peed all over the priceless vermink pelts. Probably marking their territory."

"Maybe that's what stinks. I hope we're fully insured," Antor said, even though that was the least of their worries.

"Yes, those pelts were destined for the Ninth Ice Planet. The rightful Nomad Megal is finally ruling again, and he needs some new clothes and furnishings. They say he rammed his own Ice Palace with a spaceship, almost destroying it."

Every being had heard the legendary tale. "He'll have to make do with common fur." Antor wasn't being very helpful. "What else is ruined?"

Zenga checked cargo 8. She came out carrying a communicator. The wires were sticking out like gutted intestines. "The Scarnivore long-range communicators are ruined, the whole shipment."

"They wouldn't have worked anyway." Scarnivore goods had a well-deserved reputation for malfunctioning the week after purchase, or at the worst possible moment, whichever came first. Beings bought them anyway, they had no choice. The Scarnivores owned more product patents than any other race, even humanoids.

Zenga peeked into the breached cargo bay nearest to Antor and groaned. "I was afraid of that."

"Afraid of what?" Antor stayed beside the Earthling in case she woke up frightened. He was ready to comfort her, if she didn't hit him or kick him again. Most humanoids liked a warm hug to make them feel better. Antor really hoped that Holly's type of human had the same custom, because Antor had an overwhelming urge to hug the girl. He settled more comfortably and shifted her head onto his lap, to pillow it.

Zenga reappeared and frowned down at him. "The stupid Gorka got into our food stores. Looks like we'll be eating dried rations for the rest of the trip." It wasn't good news. Space fare was awful enough, dried rations were so much worse.

She walked a few paces down the corridor and looked through the last broken door. She giggled. Antor could guess why. "The Gorka had a party with the party-bots?"

"I think they did, probably served our food as appetizers."

"Zen, where do you think Hampelle got a breeding pair of Gorka," Antor said, turning serious.

"I have no idea. But if the Gorwargans find out what we were transporting, we'll be in more trouble than we can imagine."

"I can imagine it just fine," Antor said. "Where should we lock up Holly?"

"I'll check out what shape C-2 is in." Zenga bravely entered the former home of the Gorka.

Antor leaned his back against the wall. Holly looked relaxed in sleep. Sleeping beauty, he thought, and wondered if she could really sing as well as she claimed. He couldn't wait to hear her voice and watch her sing. He had a strange feeling inside, like he wanted to keep her on the Comet Tail forever. He stroked a lock of blue hair off her forehead and tucked it behind her ear. In spite of her exceptional hearing, she had small ears for a humanoid. They were cute, and decorated with metal. He peered closer and saw that her ear lobes had pierced holes to allow the jewelry to stick through. It looked barbaric, and painful.

Zenga came out of the bay, nausea twisting her face. "We won't put her in there. I wouldn't put a shedding Decomp in there. Thank Celeste we have an auto-mate to clean up that foul filth. Let's just stash her in the empty crew cabin, the tiny one over the coil exhaust. It's loud and kind of hot, but better than down here. You can disable the interior door panel and she won't be able to get out, unless we let her out."

"Better than locking her into a stinky cage," Antor agreed, shifting Holly's head so he could stand. He reversed the gravity flow and they slid her back up to the main level. The empty cabin was the very last berth in the small crew section.

Antor and Zenga swung Holly into the lowest hammock without dropping her. Zenga shed the girl's coat and laid it over her like a blanket. Holly sighed and settled into true sleep. Antor realized he still had on the cozy hat and flower-scented scarf. He returned the hat, but not the scarf. Zenga raised an inquiring eyebrow.

"Smells nice," he said, a bit embarrassed.

"The door panel, Antor," she said, very dryly.

"Oh, right." He opened the panel and yanked a wire out of the inner workings, disabling the panel's functions and locking the Earth girl inside.

4 Holly - The Comet Tail

Holly awoke slowly. It sounded like she was on a boat. She opened her eyes, hoping to find herself on a boat, or on a train, or in a box with a fox—anywhere but on an alien spaceship.

She was swaying in a silky hammock in a tiny room, staring up at a second empty hammock. The walls were dented dull metal, as was the ceiling and the floor. She might have been on a boat, except for the gigantic red star glowing outside the little bubble window. Earth didn't have any stars like that.

"Spaceship," she groaned. It hadn't been a bad dream after all. She checked her watch. She had been out of it for a long time. She had missed her chance to sign-up for the singing auditions, as if that mattered now.

When she had driven away from her home the previous night, she had never ever wanted to go back to a town that was so dead, it could have doubled as a graveyard. She had been mad at her Mom, and Daniel, and Fiona, for not supporting her. She had figured she was better off without the whole lot of them. But now she wanted to go home more than anything in the whole Universe, even though there was nothing to do at home except listen to other girls sing on the radio.

She missed her Mom and Daniel and Fiona. They would all be worried to death by now. Holly had left her Mom a note on the kitchen table, saying that she would phone. And she had intended to call Daniel in the morning, to tell him she had borrowed (or stolen) his truck. The calls were long overdue and everyone would be thinking the worst.

Holly tried to stand up. She flipped out of the hammock and landed on her butt. The cabin certainly wasn't luxurious. The floor was very hard scarred metal, vibrating from below, and it wasn't very clean. The walls and the ceiling looked exactly the same. Holly was in a claustrophobic metal box.

She shoved to her feet and pulled out her cell phone. Her iPod, with all her singing music, came out, too. She returned that to her coat pocket and focused on the phone. It was stupid to even try to use it, but she did. All she could hear was dead air, and there was no reception. Of course there wasn't. She giggled a bit hysterically and tucked the phone away again.

Holly tried to open the door. It wouldn't budge. She pressed every last button on the panel, which was a waste of time. And she really had to go to the bathroom, if they had one on the spaceship. Her prison room certainly didn't have one, unless aliens simply peed on the floor. In her opinion, they were uncivilized enough to do just that.

"Let me out, let me out!" Holly shouted and pounded on the metal.

When it slid upward, she screamed even louder. The thing that faced her certainly wasn't human, maybe it wasn't even an alien. It didn't look alive, not really. But the eyes did, they stared into hers, matched for height.

"It's an auto-mate," Antor said, from the side. She hadn't seen him there. He was still wearing her scarf, which seemed kind of weird, because the ship was plenty warm. The pink and purple stripes clashed with his orangey-brown hair, which was long enough to wear in a ponytail, except it was hanging free.

Antor looked different in the proper light, and taller. In fact, if he'd been from Earth, Holly would have thought he was hot. His eyes were dark brown and a bit puppy-doggish, with super long lashes. His high cheekbones were beautifully defined and his lips were shapely without being too full or girlish. His nose was strong and straight. There was a flawless symmetry to his face that was rather unearthly in its precision and perfection.

Holly stopped gawking at him and swallowed the hot panic that rose up in her chest. "What the hell is an auto-mate?"

"An automated worker, half-mechanical and half-biological parts. The bio-parts work more efficiently than a lot of artificial mechanisms, especially when they're Scarnivore." He smiled as if they were friends, not kidnapper and kidnappee. Holly didn't have a clue what he was talking about.

"Well, that is the grossest thing I've ever seen." Holly looked into the auto-mate's very real eyes. They were pale green with hardly any whites and set too far apart in a flat, seamed metal face. At least they weren't human eyes. The mouth was a segmented oval hole, yet the wiggling tongue inside looked real and wet, and pointy. She couldn't spot any teeth. The greenish hands were long and skinny, with only three fingers and a thumb. They weren't artificial, and were somehow fused to metal wrists. Had they been cut off a living being? Holly felt queasy enough to vomit, with good reason. "Where's the bathroom?" she gasped.

"You can't take a bath, water is rationed. Sorry." Antor hunched his shoulders and ducked his head. His hair fell forward to hide his eyes. He was certainly timid for a sexy, space-traveling, kidnapping alien.

"I don't want to take a bath! I want to go pee! And I want to go home!" Holly cried.

His cheeks reddened and he pointed. "Um, you can urinate next door. The going home …" He trailed off and stared at the tips of his boots.

Holly shoved past him and found the bathroom. The door slid closed behind her automatically. There was no bath or sink. The cubicle was as rudimentary as her prison room, but at least it was human-friendly, except for the lack of water and mirrors. She couldn't look at herself standing on a spaceship, and see that it was really happening. She couldn't even wash her hands. "And they call me primitive," she muttered. The door slid opened when she stood right in front of it. Antor and the auto-mate were waiting.

"Do you feel relieved?" Antor asked.

"What kind of question is that?" Holly avoided the auto-mate's strangely alive gaze.

"A courteous one."

Holly snorted. "You abducted me! You stole me from my planet, my home, my family! You don't have to be polite. Where's the girl, Zenga?"

"Monitoring the bridge. We want to talk to you while the Captain is sleeping. Willy, you can go recharge your power cell. We can't have any of this conversation stored in your memory-bank. You understand, don't you?" Antor was awfully considerate of the auto-mate.

Holly couldn't believe it when the machine-man spoke. "Yes, Antor. Shall I return to cleaning the cargo deck, after I am recharged?"

"Good idea. Thanks, Willy."

Willy walked away with a smooth gait. He wore pants, but the sharp angles within hinted that his lower half was mechanical. Holly certainly hoped it was.

She rounded on Antor. "You could have told me that Willy had feelings, before I said how gross he was! Right in front of him!"

"He doesn't really have feelings, but it kind of seems like he does, so I just act like he does. His brain isn't human, or alive. It's computerized." Antor began trying to explain computers.

Holly cut him off. "I know what a computer is."

"Really? You shouldn't."

"Well, I do." Holly crossed her arms and glared.

Antor flushed and backed away. "Zenga is waiting, follow me please."

"And what if I don't want to?"

Antor stopped moving and stood rather helplessly. "Uh, if you don't want to, I guess I could get Zenga and we could talk to you in your room. The bridge can be unattended for a short time. I don't think we'll collide with a comet or meteor or get sucked into an uncharted wormhole. This patch of space is pretty barren. Not even any white holes spitting stuff out at us."

"What? Oh, forget it." Holly went with him, down the corridor and into the same small dingy control room as the night before. There were four fixed swiveling chairs with stuffing poking out of holes in the shiny metallic cloth. What appeared to be paper-thin computer screens glowed red. The keyboard control panels had oversized buttons, and looked old-fashioned compared to Earth's technology. The buttons weren't only big, they were stained with grime and so worn, some of the symbols had almost rubbed off, not that Holly could have recognized even one of the alien letters or numbers or whatever they were. The gear shift between the two front chairs could have come straight out of a classic Chevy truck.

The bridge of the ship was as disappointing as her metal box of a room, and the bathroom without a bath. Holly had always pictured aliens and their ships as so much more exciting, not dilapidated with grimy, dented equipment.

This ship's crew didn't even wear uniforms, but casual clothes that wouldn't have raised an eyebrow on Earth. Antor wore a tunic-style top, and what looked like leather trousers, tucked into gray boots that ended mid-calf. Zenga had on green leggings, matched with a top that was short enough to show her midriff, and had a fringe around the bottom. It could have come from Earth in the sixties. She wore some sort of hybrid boot/slippers. Zenga looked comfy, lounging in one of the two front chairs, a leg draped over the armrest.

"Did you sleep well, Holly?" Zenga asked. She seemed a capable sort of alien, with her short brown hair and small, quiet features. Her face did not have the sculpted perfection of Antor's, and in that way she looked more Earthly, except for her ears. They were too big and flat, and sat too far back on her head. Longer hair would have hidden the only thing about her that wasn't Earth-normal to the eye.

Holly crossed her arms and scowled. She had been kidnapped and locked up. She shouldn't appear too cooperative.

"Are you feeling better? Did you sleep well?" Zenga repeated more slowly and clearly, and as politely as Antor.

"Oh, like a log," Holly said grudgingly. It was kind of pointless to not talk.

"A log? Is that good?"

"Yes." While the bat-eared, bear-faced Captain wasn't around, Holly appealed for her freedom. "Look, I really want to go home. Can you turn the ship around and take me back while that scary alien isn't here? I won't tell anyone about you, I promise. I'll never say a word, ever."

"I wish we could, I really do," Zenga said with sincere regret, "but we can't right now. We're too far from your planet. We've already travelled through five wormholes, three natural and two of our own, and generating our own uses a copious amount of fuel." It was said with a finality that was absolute.

Holly's eyes burned hot. "You mean I'll never go home?"

"No, I didn't say that. We do have to … return to your planet in the near future. On our return trip, we can try and get you home, but not right now. We need to talk to you about something else, something worse."

"Worse than being abducted by aliens?" Holly sank into the nearest chair. Her knees were too scared to stand. "Am I going to be probed or something? Have I already been probed?"

"Probed? What does that mean?"

"Oh, never mind. If you don't know, I'm not going to tell you." Holly didn't want to give them ideas. "So what is this worse thing?"

"The Captain wants to jettison you into open space, because you know we landed on your restricted planet. Space will kill you instantly, it's a frigid vacuum," Zenga said. Holly's knees had been right to be scared. They began to tremble.

Antor edged a bit closer. "We're trying to convince him not to do that. We have an idea. You said you can sing?"

"So?" Holly dropped her head into her hands, they were as trembling as her knees. She wanted to scream hysterically, but there was nobody to save her for billions or trillions of miles or light years or some impossible distance.

"If you're a good singer, Captain Hampelle might let you live for now," Antor said.

Holly swallowed and sat up, trying to show some spine, trying to find her spine. She knew it was there somewhere. "Sing for my supper? Are all aliens crazy?"

"You wouldn't be singing for your supper. We'll provide you with space rations. You would be singing for your life." Antor grabbed her hand, then dropped it as if it was on fire. He perched on the edge of the chair beside hers. Up close, his earnest dark eyes had bright orange flecks. "Our Captain might be a little bit crazy, but you'll have to sing for him if you want to live. Sing your very best. It will earn you some time, and we'll help you get home again."

Zenga nodded. "We will. We don't agree with his actions or decisions, but he is the boss. He can jettison us as easily as he can jettison you. He threatens to do it at least once a day."

"Nice boss." At least sarcasm seemed to be universally understood. Holly rested her head against the back of the chair. The ceiling of the bridge was stained with chilling splashes. It looked like this ship had seen more than one bloody battle, and no-one had bothered to wash the ceiling. "When am I supposed to sing for him?"

"When he wakes up. Probably tonight."

"Isn't it tonight? It's dark out," she said without thinking. It was a stupid thing to say.

"Space is always dark, unless you're passing a bright star, a sun, or a quasar. That's about the most luminous object in the Universe. A quasar can be trillions of times brighter than your little sun." Antor hadn't taken his eyes off Holly's face. She wasn't sure he had even blinked. Maybe alien humans didn't need to blink. "It's actually afternoon on our ship. You slept a long time. A sleeping beauty," he blurted out and turned red. "I checked on you, to make sure you were okay."

"Antor, stop blubbering." Zenga sounded mad.

He stood up and hunched, like a scolded puppy. He really had not one thing in common with the aliens Holly had seen in movies and on TV. They were usually confident and commanding, or at least murderous and evil. Antor had been grumpy and short with her on Earth, now he was simply timid and apologetic, and kind of bumbling. Both Antor and Zenga seemed as Earth human as Holly, except they weren't. She had to remember that.

Zenga asked if she was hungry. Holly shook her head, too upset to eat. Antor asked if she wanted a tour of the rest of the ship. She declined his offer. The rest was probably as lame as what she had already seen. Holly opted to return to the noisy prison cabin and curl up in a fetal position, until the Captain summoned her to sing or die. Or sing then die.

She lay in the hammock, flashing between cold terror and hot panic. She knew she was a good singer, a really spectacular singer, but what if she wasn't good enough for Outer Space? If her voice didn't please the Captain, she would die a gruesome death in a few short hours. Holly was even too scared to cry. Since it was the better place to be, she fell asleep and dreamed of home.

5 Antor - UGS

After Antor locked Holly in, he tidied up his larger cabin, in case she changed her mind and did want a tour of the rest of the ship. He wanted to make a good impression, if that was possible after being involved in her abduction, no matter how unwillingly. His personal space was a disaster. His few possessions were strewn about the floor and a heap of dirty laundry was spilling out of the spare hammock. He carted the pile to the galley where he stanislized his wardrobe, and folded it neatly. Back in his room, he put the stacks of fresh clothes in his duffle bag. There was nowhere else, except the hammock.

His plants were a little dry so he fetched water and dampened the soil. He talked to them a bit about his adventure on Earth, and Holly. He had once heard that plants liked to be talked to, so he did. And it's not like he had a lot of friends to converse with, or any, except Zenga. The plants kept the air in his room fresher than the rest of the ship.

Antor straightened the pictures he'd hung on the wall, even though they never stayed level. One showed the endless ocean of Calma Surfarian. Antor had visited the pleasure planet once on a delivery. He'd even enjoyed a half day in the sea, before his ship had taken him away again. The second picture showed him with Zenga, standing in front of her home. Last year, Antor had been invited there to celebrate Solaria. The holiday in a real home had been the first one he'd ever known, and Antor hadn't wanted it to end.

With his room tidied, Antor changed into his finest clothes and tied his hair back, hoping to make himself as presentable as his quarters. When he returned to the bridge, Zenga looked him up and down and smirked. "Did you get all dressed up for me, Antor?"

"I didn't get dressed up. I just changed, while I was doing my laundry," he said, embarrassed.

She snorted. "If you say so. But you have to stop making moon eyes at Holly. It's pathetic! You can't like her, she's a primitive. And take that silly scarf off."

"It's not silly."

"Yes, it is."

Antor wrapped it tighter. "Holly doesn't seem like a primitive. And what do you think she meant when she said 'probing'? Do you think that means - ?"

Zenga groaned with gusto.

"I'm not acting that moony," Antor said.

"You are so, and that's not why I groaned. UGS are showing up on the long range sensor, and they're coming after us." Zenga calculated their speed. "We've got about nine minutes before they intercept us. I'll summon the Captain, but I don't know how we're going to explain the wrecked cargo deck, or the girl." Zenga yanked on his arm, hard. "Antor! You have to tell her to hold her silence. If the UGS board us for an inspection, and she tells them that we've abducted her from a restricted planet, we'll all end up on Gehenna, including her. Make sure she understands that, and if she's not going to cooperate, knock her out and hide her. Go!"

Antor ran out the door. Zenga was already paging the Captain.

With fumbling fingers, he pressed in the code to open Holly's door. It slid up and the girl bellowed, "Have you never heard of knocking?"

"Knocking what? Never mind, you can tell me later. This is an emergency." He stepped into her room. "The UGS are after us."

"UGS?" The girl tried to stand and fell out of the hammock. Antor extended a hand to help her up. She slapped it away.

"UGS, Universal Guard Ships. One is after us. They keep order across the Universe, and tend to blast first and ask questions second. They'll probably board us for an inspection," he said in a rush.

"So they're the space police? Good. Great! I'll tell them I've been kidnapped from Earth and they'll take me home." She smiled with brilliant beauty. She would have lit up the stage of Universe Idol, if she had been standing on it.

"No, no, you don't understand. If the UGS find out what we've done, where you're from, they'll blast the ship and everyone on it, yourself included. Or we'll all get sent to Gehenna Prison Planet." Antor looked into her eyes, trying to communicate his fear. "You can't say where you're from or we're all dead. You, too. It would be best if you stayed hidden and quiet."

She planted her hands on her hips. "As a matter of fact, being blasted sounds a lot better than being jettisoned into open space, at least to me."

"Holly, you have to hold your silence." Antor sounded as desperate as he felt.

"I do not have to keep my mouth shut," she declared, as if she held the upper hand.

"If you want to live, you do. At least with Captain Hampelle you have a chance. You don't with the UGS."

"You're just trying to scare me and save your own skin. How do I know you're even telling the truth?" She crossed her arms and glared at Antor as if she hated him. She probably did, and she had good reason.

"I am telling the truth," Antor said. "And I'm trying to save your skin as well as my own. I still haven't heard you sing, and I really want to."

"What if my singing isn't good enough? What if I'm lousy? Then I'm going to die anyway, so I might as well take your awful Captain with me." At least she didn't name Antor as another who deserved to die.

"Sing something and I'll tell you if you have a chance. I'll be honest, I promise."

Holly rolled her eyes, opened her mouth and started singing. There was no warm up, no music, no costume, yet the song was magical. Her voice stopped Antor's breath and made time stand still. He could have listened to her sing forever. She was better than the two best singers he had ever heard in his life—and on her planet. Maybe the whole six and a half billion could sing so, but Holly was on his ship! Antor couldn't move until she stopped singing, and then he said, "Please, sing another song." His voice came out hoarse.

"Why? Wasn't that one good enough?"

Antor laughed. UGS were after the ship and there was every chance that he was about to die, but he laughed. Her music had lightened his heart and spirit. It had filled the emptiness that was so much a part of him. "Holly, you're the best singer I've ever heard. You could win Universe Idol."

"There's a Universe Idol? Earth has Idol contests, too, like Canadian Idol and American Idol, but … how can Outer Space have TV shows? And the same TV show as Earth?"

It was an intriguing question, one that Antor couldn't answer. "I don't know. How long has Earth broadcast the show?"

"About ten years, I think. What about Universe Idol?"

"This is the twelfth," Antor replied.

"So you had the show first. Then how did Earth get it?"

"No idea." Antor could only wonder who on Holly's Earth could possibly have the technology to eavesdrop on the cosmic entertainment broadcasts, and copy them for the restricted planet's audience. It was a riddle that would have to wait. "Holly, Captain Hampelle will never jettison you, not when you can sing like that." He smiled and might have tried to hug her, if she hadn't looked so hostile.

There was a thump that tilted the floor. "The UGS have docked. They're going to board, but you'll be safe, Holly, as long as they don't find you. Hide and be quiet, and we'll all be safe."

Without warning, she lunged for the door. Antor tackled her. They landed hard, flat in the corridor outside the small room. The girl fought like she came from a savage world and she believed she was fighting for her life. Antor took a punch to the eye, before he got a grip on her wrists. She also fought dirty and kneed him where it hurt the most. Antor cursed in a way he wouldn't usually. Holly squirmed with abandon and screamed as if she was being murdered. Antor released one of her arms so he could clap a hand over her mouth. She bit it, drawing blood, and yanked some of his hair right out of his scalp.

"I'm trying to save your life," he cried, still hoping to reason with her.

She banged her forehead hard against his, which he was not expecting. He saw stars inside the ship and everything faded away, long enough for Holly to yank free and run. Antor staggered to his feet and gave chase. He wasn't quick enough. He was on Holly's heels when she skidded onto the bridge.

Captain Hampelle was clearly terrified to see the girl. The whites of his eyes showed, all around. "You should have knocked the primitive out, or killed her," he raged at Antor. "Damn, too late now. The UGS are unsealing the hatch." He switched to Holly's dialect. "Keep your mouth shut, girl."

"Or what?" Holly's temper was proving to be as volatile as the Captain's.

"Or they'll kill us all." Hampelle's hands were shaking on the controls.

Holly looked to Zenga, as if she trusted her more than the rest of them. "Really? Me, too?"

"Yes. Didn't Antor tell you?"

"He did, but he could have been lying." Breathing hard, Holly focused on Captain Hampelle. "Well, it seems to me that your life is in my hands now, so you better stop threatening me—and you will promise to turn this ship around and take me straight home, or I will tell these UGS everything, and I mean everything," she stressed. "Promise to take me home or I'll see the ship destroyed!"

"I promise to take you home," the Captain ground out. His vow was worth as much as a shed flap of Decomp skin, but the girl didn't know that. She took him at his word.

"Good." She sat down in the back chair, her body tense.

Antor was dabbing at his stinging eye with his sleeve, when three UGS marched onto the deck, their boots polished and their buttons shiny. The trio of females was stern-faced and no-nonsense. Everyone on the bridge stood at attention. Holly jumped up again, following their lead.

Captain Hampelle bowed to greet the leader, who was identified by the extra metal rings that jingled around her wrist cuffs, and she carried the longest dartgun. "I am Captain Hampelle of the Comet Tail,

31

shipper/transport under contract with A-1 All Planetary Shipping." He was sweating under his fur, giving off a rank odor.

"Universal Guard Chief Zandee." The big-jawed female sniffed and surveyed the small bridge. "Destination? Cargo?" Universal guards were not known for their small talk.

Captain Hampelle illuminated their pickups and deliveries. Zandee read the data-stream. "Scarnivore communicators, cheap crap. Party-bots. And vermink pelts for the Nomad Megal." She actually cracked a smile. "I met him when he was on the run. Almost captured him, almost vaporized him. When you deliver his pelts to the Ninth Ice Planet, tell him Zandee sends her regards."

Captain Hampelle swallowed hard and sweated harder.

Zandee narrowed her eyes suspiciously. "Since we're aboard, we will make an inspection of the ship."

"Completely unnecessary," the Captain blustered. "We've had a bit of a problem down in the cargo area and -"

"Show me this problem." It was not a request, but a crisp order. Hampelle left the bridge surrounded by the three big guards.

As soon as they were out of hearing, Zenga hissed, "How do you think he'll explain the mess below?"

"I don't know, Zen. At least the Gorka aren't on board, that would have been a disaster."

"What's happening?" Holly asked. Without a Universal translator, she wouldn't have understood a word of what transpired.

"Hampelle is showing the guards the cargo deck," Antor said in her language, without volunteering more than that. He also judged it wise to hold his silence about the worthlessness of the Captain's promise. If Holly knew that truth, she would confess all to the UGS.

While they waited for Hampelle and the guards to return, Zenga tried to eavesdrop on what was happening below, by opening the communication channel to the cargo deck. It wasn't functioning, probably because of the Gorka's rampage.

When Captain Hampelle returned with his escort, it looked like things had gone well. He was smiling to show his pointy teeth.

Zandee said, "I must commend you and your crew for fighting off a pirate attack. I will include in my report that half of your goods were stolen or destroyed. The report will be filed, in case you need a copy for your insurance claim. I have the names of your crew as witnesses to the attack. If we catch the pirates, you will be asked to identify them. This is the entire crew?" Zandee motioned around the bridge.

"Yes."

"Your manifest lists only four, including the auto-mate. I count five. Who is not listed?" It was a simple question.

"The … the girl there." Hampelle motioned at Holly and came up with a creative lie. "One of my crew, Antor, snuck her aboard. She's his girlfriend, a stowaway I guess. By the time I discovered her, we had already left orbit, so she isn't listed. Anyway, she's been making herself useful, I never mind a pair of unpaid hands." The Captain was babbling in a manner not unlike Holly.

Antor found himself under silent scrutiny. He set his jaw and tried to stand taller, hoping he might look like a man who was worth following across the Universe, even though he wasn't. Holly kept her mouth shut, yet looked kind of frustrated that she still couldn't understand a word of the alien dialect.

She certainly didn't understand Zandee when the guard said to her, "I'll need your name and home planet, to include you in our records as a possible witness." Holly simply stood mute and blinked at the guard.

Zandee turned to the Captain. "Why is she not answering?"

"She speaks a different dialect, and not being part of my crew, she doesn't have a translator."

"Ah. What dialect."

With obvious reluctance, the Captain told her the linguistic code.

Zandee processed the information and raised her dartgun. "That dialect's planet of origin is unlisted. I've never encountered an unlisted planet in the Universal Guard data-stream before." She addressed Holly in the language Holly understood. "Tell me your name and your home planet."

Holly swallowed hard. Antor begged her not to with his eyes.

"Me? Oh, um, my name is Holly Noel Tate and I'm from Gehenna—no, I'm from …" She shifted from one foot to the other, as if she was going to make a run for it, as if there was anywhere to run to. She must have recalled that the Captain had mentioned the planet Gehenna, but it was the worst possible choice of a home world.

Antor stepped quickly to her side. "Holly's home is Ghaway in the Misshapen Galaxy. Same home base address as me and Zenga."

Zandee's distrustful gaze fixed on Holly. "Why did you name Gehenna Prison Planet? You are a criminal?" Holly shook her head, eyes huge. Antor put an arm around her, holding her against his side. It felt like she belonged there. "Antor, did you purchase her from the planet as a slave?" Zandee asked.

It was actually a good cover story. With no time to think about his answer, he said, "Yes."

"Then you will have the release papers?"

"Not on the ship." Antor's words sounded more like a question.

Zandee crossed the small deck in four strides. She jerked up Holly's sleeve. Antor guessed she was looking for the prisoner's brand. There was no burned scar to find.

"This girl was never a prisoner. Why are you lying?" Zandee stuck her prominent nose right in his face.

"Uh, because …" Antor was floundering badly. Singing was the first thing that popped into his head. "Because I don't want anyone to know about Holly yet. She's a big secret that we've discovered. She's going to be the next Universe Idol. We're taking her to the last round of auditions." Those words rang with conviction, because Antor knew Holly truly could be the next Universe Idol.

Zandee laughed with belittling humour. "Pure humanoids never win Universe Idol, ever. They don't even make it into the finals. Humans can't sing." She turned dangerously serious in a heartbeat. "Now tell me the truth!"

"That … that is the truth. If you heard her sing, you would believe me. We're taking her to the Lost Gaseous Galaxy for the auditions on Nightrous. We pass by there on our delivery route." Antor knew when and where all the auditions were held, since he still dreamed of competing himself, although he knew he never would. He was simply too shy to sing, unless he was alone.

Zandee pointed her weapon at Holly and said, "Sing."

"Me?" Holly asked.

"No, the auto-mate. Of course you! I will see this story proved true, or I will impound the ship and get the real truth." Zandee made that sound very threatening. Antor knew it was. More often than not, an impounded ship was never seen again, nor was the crew.

"Sing, Holly," Antor said, squeezing her shoulder. In his head, he thought *or we're all dead.*

6 Holly - Sing or Else

Holly heard the panic in Antor's voice. It was mirrored in his eyes. There was a different message in Zandee's eyes, a darkly ominous and deadly message. Holly had to sing, or it would be the end of her, and Antor and Zenga. She gulped hard and tried not to stare at the nozzle of the weapon that looked kind of like a miniature harpoon. The pointy projectile was aimed at her heart, and her eyes got stuck there. She'd never had a weapon pointed at her, except for a paintball gun. She didn't like it, not one bit.

"Holly!" Antor shook her. "You have to sing."

"I do, don't I? Okay. Now?"

"Now or never." Zandee was good with threats—low key, but not too low key.

"Okay, any requests?" It was a stupid question, since Holly didn't know any Outer Space top hits. Before anyone could suggest one, she plunged into the song she had practiced for her audition on Earth. It was a ballad about broken hearts that half the Earth's population could have hummed along to. It had both high notes and low notes and everything in-between. It was a song that allowed a singer to show off their range, if they had one to show off. Holly did, that's why she had selected it. And she liked the strong, uncomplicated beat of the music. She could feel the rhythm inside her. She concentrated on it, rather than the weapon that was primed to kill her.

Her small audience listened without interrupting, so Holly kept on singing, every last verse. When the final note faded, there was no immediate reaction to her spontaneous performance. She thought she was about to die, until she noticed the tears running down the tough Zandee's cheeks. Even Captain Hampelle dashed away a bit of moisture that had leaked into his fur. Aliens certainly seemed to be ultra-sensitive to music.

"Was it okay?" Holly asked.

"There are not words." Zandee yanked Holly against her hard chest in a bear hug. It felt like the woman wore a layer of armor under her starched shirt. "Antor, your unlikely story is confirmed. You are transporting the next Universe Idol to fame and fortune. What planet do you really come from?" she asked Holly.

Antor answered for her. "We aren't revealing that information. Holly prefers not to draw any attention to her home world or her family. You understand."

Zandee appeared to. "Yes, there is such frenzy over the finalists. Their families are harassed, or kidnapped or murdered. Some finalists have had to withdraw as the ransom to rescue their loved ones. Universe Idol has even spawned several planetary wars. You are very wise to keep your true identity a secret, Holly. I will ask no more questions, but I will be cheering for you when the time comes. My luck to you, not that you'll need it, not with that voice. Finally, a human that can win!" She turned to Captain Hampelle and said, "Make sure you get her to Lost Gaseous safely, or I will track you down."

"Of course, of course." Hampelle started to sweat again.

"Safe journey. If any more UGS delay you, refer them to me. I will clear your safe passage myself."

"Thank you, very gracious of you." The Captain bobbed his head.

Chattering about Universe Idol, Zandee and her officers marched off the bridge. There was a lurch when their ship separated from the Comet Tail, and then they were gone.

"We're safe?" Holly asked.

"We are, thanks to you," Zenga said. "And what a talent! If I hadn't heard it with my own ears, I wouldn't have believed it. You're ten times better than Eenway Frakk, the Scarnivore who just beat the Mannireplian to make the finals at Double Dwarf. And you're a pure humanoid!"

"Are humans really such bad singers? On my planet, I'm good, but so are lots of other singers," Holly said. "We have so many great singers on Earth, it's hard to even make a living as a musician."

"I would keep that a secret if I were you," Zenga warned, "or your Earth's citizens will be abducted and enslaved as singers. Some warrior races might even take over the planet to harvest and breed singers. And your planet lacks any sort of planetary defense."

"My lips are sealed," Holly said with a shiver. She couldn't believe how uncivilized these supposedly advanced beings sounded, and she didn't like how the hairy Captain's eyes had lit up when she'd talked about Earth's surplus of singers. "So, I'm not going to be jettisoned into space?" she guessed.

Captain Hampelle said, "No, you will not be jettisoned, but you will sing to earn your keep, and to prepare yourself for the competition."

"What competition?" Holly asked, fearing she already knew the answer.

"We are taking you to the auditions on Nightrous, so that you can win Universe Idol." The Captain spoke slowly and clearly, as if he was talking to someone very stupid.

"But you promised that you would take me home," Holly cried.

"And so I will, after you win this contest. The prize is one thousand bizoux."

"Is that a lot?" If it was equivalent to a thousand dollars, it wasn't much.

"It is a hundred fortunes. And you will win it, and then you will pay me all of it for your transport home." The Captain smiled and his teeth looked like they had gotten pointier, as if he had sharpened them inside his mouth.

Holly whispered, "But your promise."

"Will be kept, in time. Don't look so disappointed. You will enjoy fame, fortune and adulation that you could never know on your small doomed world. You are lucky we took you. By the time this is over, you may not wish to return to your planet ever again." The Captain sat down and studied the viewing screen. "Antor, when are the auditions on Nightrous?"

"Uh, in two weeks. They're the last round of auditions for this year, then the real competition takes place between the top ten winners." He glanced anxiously at Holly. "The finals last about a month."

Her face fell. "But everyone at home will believe I'm dead by then." Her mother would be brokenhearted. Daniel would be dating someone else, and believe her a car thief or a corpse. Her father might not even notice she was gone, since she hardly ever saw him. Her sister would have moved into Holly's room and taken all her stuff. Holly would have missed enough of her senior year to have to repeat it, for a second time. And she would have been fired from her part-time job. When she got home, she would have no life left. Maybe Hampelle was right, maybe she wouldn't bother going back if she was rich and famous.

"The time passes quickly in space," Antor said, trying to reassure. "And it's a lot better than being jettisoned or vaporized."

Holly scowled. "Do you always look on the bright side?"

"Toward a sun?" he asked.

"No. The positive side, the happy side."

"Not always, no, but I try."

"Well, it's annoying." Holly was the grumpy one now, worried about everyone back home thinking she was dead.

Captain Hampelle banged his consol. "You can be quite annoying when you're not singing. Go help Willy clean up below, all of you. Get out! Get off my bridge!"

The four of them tromped along a dark skinny passage that ended in a slide, of all things. Holly slid down the curved arc into a filthy, stinky mess. "Cargo deck?" she guessed.

"You've been here before, but you were fainted so you won't remember." Zenga flashed a friendly grin. Holly had saved her life, so she should be friendly.

"Glad I was fainted." Holly plugged her nose. "And this mess was made by the tropical animals that you released on Earth?"

"Yes." Neither of her companions met her gaze or volunteered information about the beasts.

"What kind of animals were they?" she asked.

"Oh, just ordinary beasties," Zenga said dismissively. "Big and purple, nothing special. So, what cargo bay should we tackle first?"

Antor sighed. "Let's start with C-8. The smashed, long-range communicators aren't as stinky as the mintentacles, or the fouled vermink pelts, or the rotting food stores, or the Gorka's home. And the party-bots, well, no rush to go in there." His cheeks turned pink, then red.

"C-8 it is," Zenga agreed.

"What shall I do?" Willy said in his flat, hollow voice.

"Do you want to clear up the mintentacles, since you don't have a nose?" Antor patted a mechanical shoulder as if the auto-mate was a buddy. "It's kind of hard for those of us who do have noses."

Willy's metal face somehow managed to look puzzled. He squeezed Antor's nose with his long-fingered green hand, then felt his own face. "I do not have a nose. Should I have a nose, Antor?"

"No. You don't need one. Your tongue does your smelling for you. You look good just the way you are."

Again, Willy's metal faced managed an expression, a pleased one. "I will clean up the mintentacles now, Antor, since I do not have a nose and do not need one." He walked off to do just that.

The rest of them tidied C-8. It wasn't so bad. It was just a lot of wrecked electronics. Antor had called the gadgets long-range communicators.

Holly picked a couple up and studied them. They looked sort of like old-school cell phones, with buttons instead of a touch-sensitive display screen. A few of them didn't look smashed at all. She glanced out of the corner of her eye. Antor and Zenga were scooping handfuls of the electronic ruins into a miraculously hovering waste bin. As quick as a cat burglar, Holly shoved one of the communicators into her sweatshirt pocket. To cover her larceny, she strolled over to help Zenga and Antor with the bulk of the wreckage.

It was really warm and she started to sweat. Antor said it was so hot because they were close to the coils. He must have been warm too. He took off her scarf, and his tunic-style shirt.

Holly almost dropped the handful of electronic waste she was scooping up. Antor's leather trousers hung low on lean hips, looking like

38

they were going to drop off at any minute, and Holly couldn't spot any trace of underwear. Maybe aliens didn't wear boxers, or briefs, or undergarments of any kind.

On Earth, Antor could have been one of the sexiest underwear models on the planet. He was perfect in a way that Earth humans could only manage in doctored and air-brushed photographs. His skin was taut, impossibly smooth and golden, and without a trace of hair. His lean muscles were so defined, they could have been sculpted, and they weren't in the least bit bulky. Wide shoulders tapered to a slim waist and below that … the pants that were barely holding position. The abdominal muscles that disappeared into the front of those pants were almost X-rated. Given how much Holly was enjoying the sight of his top half, she really wouldn't have minded if his pants fell off, so she could verify that Antor was Earth normal below the belt, and see if his nether regions were as sexy as the rest of him. When he walked out of the cargo bay steering the floating bin, his rear view was as mouth-watering as his front.

Zenga elbowed her. "Stop drooling."

Holly felt much much hotter than before Antor had shed his shirt and stammered, "I'm not drooling, am I? Are all Outer Space humans so … gorgeous?" The word seemed inadequate.

Zenga smiled affectionately. "Definitely not. Antor is pretty exceptional. He thinks he's pure humanoid, but sometimes I wonder if he doesn't have a trace of the Divine Race in him, or more than a trace. Anyway, in most ways, he's had an isolated life and he doesn't have a clue, so don't drool around him, just enjoy the sight. We don't want him to get a big head, do we?"

Holly didn't know how to answer that question without being X-rated, so she didn't even try. "How can he think he's pure human if he isn't? He must know by looking at his parents, and what is the Divine Race?"

"You never ask one question at a time, Holly. Antor doesn't know his parents, he's a spaceship orphan."

"A what?" Holly dropped another armful of ruined electronics into the second bin.

"A child born and abandoned on a spaceship. It happens sometimes. Most of the newborns go unreported and are jettisoned when they're discovered, but the crew that found Antor kept him. He must have been really cute and good-natured, even as a baby. Anyway, he was raised on spaceships, and has no true home world and no family. His name is taken from the ship he was found on."

"His name? Antor?"

"No, his full name. The ship was called the Falling Star, so he was registered as Antormand Falling Star. Antormand after the Captain of that

39

ship, and Falling Star after the ship. But Antor is less of a mouthful, so he's Antor."

Holly couldn't imagine not coming from any world at all. "It sounds like a lonely way to grow up. Is that why he lacks confidence?" Never having a family or a home could certainly have that result.

Zenga kept cleaning and said, "He never talks about it, so it doesn't seem to bother him, but I know he ended up on a few rough ships when he was younger. He's been kicked around some, but it hasn't changed who he is—a sweet guy with a big heart." Zenga talked about him as if he was her little brother. "Being raised on spaceships can be a pretty reclusive life, and I think that's why Antor is the way he is."

"Are you a spaceship orphan, too?" Holly asked.

"No, I just like to travel, I like space. And the pay is decent. My family and home base are on Ghaway in the Misshapen Galaxy. Antor uses my home base address as his own, since he doesn't have one." Zenga jostled the floating bin, encouraging the contents to settle.

"And what is the Divine Race?" Holly asked.

"The Divine Race is also called the First Race, but no-one knows what happened to them. They're reputed to have come from the lost Green World, and the ones responsible for the Spread, the first humans, or so one legend says. Supposedly, they were powerful and perfect beings whose very image struck awe in the hearts of lesser beings." Zenga pulled a face.

"They sound a little bit like some of Earth's mythological gods," Holly said.

"If you believe in gods, we share the same gods. You're part of the Spread as much as I am," Zenga reminded her. "And there are other, less inspiring legends about the Spread."

"Such as?"

Zenga wrinkled her nose. "Well, there's a rumour that just won't die, that humans were seeded across the Universe as a convenient food source for a nomadic race of brutish carnivores, who supposedly once ruled all the heavens. Instead of carrying their meat on ships, and having to feed and water it, they seeded their food across the Universe, so they could eat anywhere, anytime."

"Yuck, so we would have been like … cattle?" Holly much preferred the godly explanation for the spread of humans.

"Cattle? Cows?"

"Cows, beef, meat, food on Earth. Most humans eat a lot of meat on Earth."

"Then yes, we would have been like cattle." Their bin was full and Zenga motioned for Holly to help her steer. Together, they guided the overflowing container to the rear hatch. Antor was working there, trying to unstick the dented inner door. Holly tried not to ogle him, or drool.

40

"This jettisons waste into open space," Antor said, his muscles straining to force the door up, inch by inch. "I'll have to bang the dents out later."

When there was enough of a gap, they emptied the bins into the sandwiched space between the double-sealed enclosures. The trash all inside, Antor forced the inner door closed. He sealed it manually, and pressed a button. The outer door slid opened with a startling whoosh, and everything was sucked away. That door got stuck opened, until Antor banged the button a few times and it ground closed on its own.

"Would I have been stuffed in there to be jettisoned?" Holly asked, struck by the horror of it, imagining herself floating away, screaming her head off, although she probably wouldn't have lasted long enough to do even that.

"Probably. There's a smaller chute on the upper deck, but it would have been hard to stuff you in that one," Antor replied. Aliens seemed to lack the tact that was second nature to Holly, and most Canadians.

She shuddered. Antor put his shirt back on, and draped her scarf around his neck, so she opted to return to her room, to see if she could get the long-range communicator to work. If she was lucky, she could tap into the Universe's satellite network or something, and maybe reach Earth. She wanted to let her mother know that she was safe, sort of, and would be home in a couple of months, if all went well.

Antor escorted her back to her door and shut her in. "Bang and shout if you want out," he called through the metal. It sounded like a song. Holly liked to write her own songs.

"Bang and shout if you want out, bang and shout if you want out," she sang, trying for a tune. "Bang and shout if you want in." Holly groaned, she'd been thinking about Antor wanting back in, and letting him in to keep her company. Surely aliens kissed like humans, since they had lips like humans, right?

"Stop thinking about him that way. He's your kidnapper. You have to hate him, and keep fighting him," Holly told herself, wondering if she was already succumbing to Stockholm syndrome, to be so attracted to her abductor. Although technically, Captain Hampelle was her abductor, not Antor, who had been nothing but friendly and kind. He hadn't even mentioned the black eye she had given him. The longer they had cleaned together, the darker it had gotten. He had also been favouring the hand she had bitten, and not once had he complained.

She sat on the only seat in the room, a swing that dangled on string that wasn't any thicker than dental floss, yet it still held her weight. She took out the communicator and wondered just how long-range it really was. It looked like an old cell phone, but she didn't know the phone number for Earth. Maybe there was a cosmic operator who could connect

41

her to Earth. It was a long shot, but Holly was desperate enough to try anything.

She pressed the topmost purple button and the gadget hummed in her hand. Lights flashed along the top. She randomly keyed some of the other buttons. She almost dropped the device when a guttural voice blasted out of the thing. It sounded mad, as if she had called at three a.m. or something. When the voice finally shut up, she said, "Hello, I'm Holly Noel Tate. I've been kidnapped by aliens. I live on Earth and I want to tell my Mom that I'm not dead. Can you pass this message -" There was a loud click that sounded a lot like a phone being slammed down.

"Aliens are so rude," Holly fumed, and pressed in different buttons. She didn't get anyone or anything, only dead air. After about twenty more futile tries, she stuffed the communicator into her hoodie pocket and dropped into the hammock. She rocked back and forth, glowering at the dingy wall for a very long time before she fell asleep.

7 Antor - Call Home

Antor banged the worst of the dents out of both hatch doors, then sealed all the corroded spots with quick-metal. Zenga finished scraping up the foodstuffs. They were jettisoned out the waste chute, like the electronics. Two cargo bays were now cleaned, and Willy was scrubbing away the last of the mintentacles.

"That's three almost done. Does the air smell any fresher yet?" Antor sat down against the wall, hoping for a rest before Captain Hampelle ordered them to get back to work. Zenga joined him for a break.

"Maybe a bit. It's been an exciting trip, hasn't it," she said with a grin.

"Yes, but you like excitement more than I do." They both knew it.

"That girl can really sing. I can't wait to hear her again. The Earth song wasn't bad either. Broken hearts are certainly a Universal theme."

"Yes," Antor agreed, to everything. He wanted to hear Holly sing again, and he thought he might be getting a broken heart. There was something about the girl that tugged and twisted at his insides. When he wasn't fighting with her, he found himself yearning for her in the oddest way. He had never yearned for anyone before, not even Zenga. They were best friends, but she had never filled the lonely emptiness inside him. That feeling simply vanished when he was with Holly.

"You really like the primitive, don't you?" Zenga nudged him with an elbow.

"Please don't call her that. I know her planet isn't technologically advanced and they don't know that the Universe is full of life, but other than that, she doesn't seem primitive, except in how she fights." Antor shot Zenga a sideways glance. "Would you mind if I did like her?"

Zenga laughed. The hurt must have shown on Antor's face, because she linked their hands and said, "No, Antor, I wouldn't mind. You're a great guy and I love you, but you and I are too different to be more than friends. You're my best friend, but when we try to be more than that, we rub each other the wrong way."

"I thought we rubbed each other the right way, at least a few times." He arched an eyebrow and was elbowed even harder.

"We did, we certainly did. I'm not saying we didn't. Do you think Earth humans do it the same way as other humans? I think that's what Holly meant when she asked if she'd been probed."

"You think they call sex *probing*? And she accused us of probing her? Or me? I guess it would have to be me."

"I think that's what she meant. Maybe you should ask her." Zenga's grin was decidedly mischievous.

Even thinking about asking that question made Antor blush. He heard a thump inside the Gorka bay. "Is Willy in there?"

"No, he must have banged the connecting wall. He's still clearing mintentacles." She pulled a face. "I haven't eaten all day. I'm starving, but not for rotting mintentacles."

"Holly must be hungry too. We haven't fed her yet. Let's get her, and we can have lunch before we get back to work."

"More like dinner." It was that late.

They slid up the slide and woke Holly. She was sleepy and rumpled, but said she was kind of hungry. She came along to the galley. Like the rest of the ship, it was a small functional space. There was a counter to prepare meals, and a paper-thin plastic table to eat at. Zenga and Antor prepared three bowls while the girl watched.

She didn't look impressed and asked, "Is that human food?"

"Yes."

"It looks more like dog food." It sounded like an insult.

"It is human food—space rations. Unfortunately, most of our food stores were in one of the small cargo bays," Zenga said, brushing off her fingers. "You saw what happened down there." Holly nodded. "So we're left with dried rations, and nothing but."

Antor felt like he should add to the conversation. "But they are nutritionally complete and balanced for humans. The vitamins and minerals will provide you with everything your body needs, uh ... nutritionally." He slammed his mouth shut when he felt like he should stop talking.

Zenga bit her cheek, trying not to laugh. He scowled at her and carried Holly's bowl over to the table.

They all faced their food with a marked lack of enthusiasm. Holly considered the mound of white, green and brown lumps. The brown ones were the smallest and squarish, the white ones were bigger, airy and roundish, and the green ones were the biggest of all, and kind of flat and crispy.

"Are you sure this is food?" Holly dropped a white lump on the table and it bounced. Antor picked up a brown lump and ate it, to prove the point. "And you eat with your fingers?" Holly didn't seem clear on the concept of eating.

"If it's space rations."

"Ah," she said, as if she both did and didn't understand, all at the same time. She picked up a brown lump and tried to nibble a piece off. Her

44

teeth weren't as sharp as many humanoid races. They looked dull along the edges, not good for eating tough food. Antor ran a tongue along his own teeth. They were sharper than Holly's, but not as pointy as Captain Hampelle's. He was gripped by a sudden urge to run his tongue along Holly's teeth. The desire to do so left him quite breathless and overheated.

The girl struggled to bite the lump and finally popped the whole thing in her mouth, crunched with effort and swallowed. She looked a bit nauseous and sampled a softer white round lump and a green flat one. She preferred the green ones and picked those out to eat.

"Acceptable?" Antor asked, dragging his gaze from her mouth when she glanced up. Holly had the biggest blue eyes. Antor felt dizzy, like he was falling, when he gazed into them.

"I don't suppose you have ketchup of something, to make the lumps taste better?" she asked.

"Ketchup?" The translator came up with sauce. "Sauce?" Antor asked.

"Yes."

"No."

"No?"

"No sauce. Not on the spaceship," Antor said.

Zenga chewed a white lump thoughtfully. "Our next scheduled delivery of unspoiled cargo is on the planet Fursay. It's a safe enough world to visit. I'll see if I can persuade Hampelle to pick up some fresh food there, some ketchup, will that do?"

Holly nodded and said, "Thanks. I'm not being spoiled. Maybe food is more important on Earth than other places, planets. Um, do you have anything to drink? Like juice or milk, to wash this down?"

"We have drinking water." Zenga filled three wide bottomed cups from a bladder shaped sack that dangled down from the ceiling. Holly drank the water and refilled her cup twice more. She liked the water more than the space rations, it seemed.

The meal over, Zenga collected the bowls and placed them in the stanislizer. It zapped the bowls and she took them out, sparkly clean.

"That's washing the dishes?" Holly guessed.

"Yes."

"Easier than water," she said. "But how do I get clean if I want a shower? Do I go into a bigger one of those?"

Antor was beginning to understand that Holly really was uninformed about the basic things he took for granted. He felt it was time to add to the conversation again. "If you tried to clean yourself in the stanislizer, you would be fried alive. You'd come out all dehydrated and crispy and dead. On the spaceship, we clean our skin with a -" The translator had trouble coming up with the right word and settled on sponge-tongue. "With a sponge-tongue. We rub it all over our bare skin, everywhere, it licks the skin clean." Antor's hands pantomimed rubbing his chest. "I can show you, if you like?" Holly was looking at him rather wide-eyed, as if he was crazy. He stopped rubbing his chest, and talking.

There was a moment of awkward silence. Antor avoided looking anywhere near Zenga. "I'm going to the bridge now," he said and left quickly. If there was girlish giggling in his wake, he didn't hear it, but he was pretty sure it was happening.

Captain Hampelle was napping in his chair. Antor cleared his throat loudly, twice. The Captain didn't stir. Antor peeked over a hairy shoulder and verified that the ship was on course and not in any trouble. No warning lights were flashing, but a message icon in the corner of the viewing screen indicated that a communication had arrived.

Antor settled into the adjacent chair and rerouted control of the ship to his consol. He listened to the message on a low volume, so as not to disturb the Captain. It was lucky he did. An angry Zlogther wanted to know why someone from the Comet Tail was calling him on a long-range communicator in the middle of the hibernation season.

The only long-range communicators, aside from the Comet Tail's own ship circuitry, were the ruined Scarnivore shipment in the cargo hold. Or maybe not so ruined. Antor erased the message, returned control of the ship to the napping Hampelle, and went to find Holly. She was in Zenga's quarters being shown a sponge-tongue.

"Uh, Zenga, could you watch the bridge? Hampelle is sound asleep and he's got the ship headed for a cloud of asteroid debris," he said from the doorway. Both girls simply looked at him. He ducked his head. "And I need to talk to Holly."

Zenga raised one eyebrow and left.

"Let's talk in your cabin," Antor said.

"It's kind of loud in there." Holly rubbed the sponge-tongue up and down her arm, testing it. She moved it to her neck and giggled. "It tickles when it licks me." The scene was almost enough to make Antor forget why he'd come to talk to her. Almost, but not quite.

He glanced over his shoulder to make sure Willy wasn't around. "You made a long-range call," he said significantly.

Holly froze, the sponging forgotten. "Yes, I made a call," she said with defiance. "I have a family, you know. And they're going to think I'm dead when they find the wrecked truck, if they even find it. It's probably buried under a mountain of snow by now, and I'm missing in the frozen middle of nowhere. They're going to be sad, especially my mother. My sister might not care, since she'll get all my stuff, and my father is pretty well out of the picture, so he might not even notice, but Daniel, my boyfriend, will be really sad. He won't have his truck or me." Holly stopped for a much needed breath.

46

"Daniel is your boyfriend. Is that like a mate?" Antor didn't want her to have a mate.

"Not mate. A boyfriend is more of a date than a mate."

Antor didn't understand the distinction.

"Listen, my Mom, and Daniel, need to know I'm not dead. I don't want them to have a funeral for me when I'm alive." She started crying. She hadn't cried yet and she'd been abducted for two days. Antor didn't know what to do. He stepped inside Zenga's room and put a comforting arm around Holly's shoulder. It was a bit like a hug, or half a hug. "I'm sorry, Holly."

It must have been the wrong thing to say, and do. She shoved him away. She did that a lot. "It's your fault, so stop pretending to be nice. Stop pretending that you care that I'll probably never see my family again, and … and they'll never know what happened to me." She turned her back, as if she couldn't bear the sight of him.

"I'm not pretending, Holly. I do care. I would take you home now if it was up to me." Unfortunately, it wasn't, but perhaps he could help in another way. "Uh, Holly, maybe we can get a message to your home. I'll show you, in your cabin. Will you come with me?" He backed out of Zenga's room and waited to see if Holly would follow. She did.

When he opened the door to her cabin, a communicator was ringing inside. He traced it to her coat pocket. "Holly, shush. I have to answer this or you could be in a lot of trouble—we all could."

She sniffed and balanced on the edge of the hammock.

Antor pressed a button. Before he could say a word, he was shouted at by the same angry Zlogther who had left the previous message. Since the voice was automatically translated into Holly's language, it proved that she was the person who had made the first call. Antor listened for about ten minutes, then tried to get a word in. "Uh, the call was accidental. Dialect from an unlisted planet? Never heard of such a thing. Yes … yes, the communicator is Scarnivore. Yes … yes, they never do work properly. It must have rerouted the call from elsewhere. Yes, it could have been a prank call. So sorry your hibernation was disturbed … rest well." He pressed the button to end the transmission and sighed with relief.

Holly had sagged onto her hammock, crying without any sound. Her tears made Antor feel as sad as she looked. He perched beside her and said, "Holly, the communicator seems to be working. Do you want me to try and get a message to your family? Or maybe you could talk to them."

She scooted closer, her face brightening with hope. "Really? Could you arrange that? Is it possible?"

"It might be, I'm pretty handy with circuitry, well, I grew up on spaceships, and this is a powerful communicator, when it works. A web of communication networks link most parts of space through wormholes.

There are wormholes at or near the center of almost every galaxy, including your Earth's. Earth has radio waves?" Antor had heard the radio waves with his own ears, when he had listened to Earth's beautiful music.

"Yes, we have many advanced technologies."

Antor bit his lip, trying not to laugh. "I'll see if I can link with those radio waves." He removed the top panel and studied the guts, before he felt his top molar for his core-text connector. He gripped the end of the fine wire and pulled, lengthening it out of his mouth, until it was long enough to poke around in the communicator, telling him which parts did what.

Holly was gaping at him. "Why is that in your mouth?" She tried to look past his teeth, leaning against him warmly. If he wasn't mistaken, Earth humans had a slightly higher body temperature than most other humanoid species. Sharing Holly's body heat made Antor tingle from head to toe.

"I'll explain later." He gulped and tried to concentrate. It didn't take long to know that the communicator was not going to be able to meld with the radio waves. It couldn't even recognize the primitive signals. He retracted his wire and shook his head. "Sorry, Holly, it won't work with the radio waves."

"But what about the wireless internet for computers, or the cell phone towers? There's one near my town," Holly said.

"I didn't know your planet had those things." And it shouldn't even have radio signals, according to the UDS, or Universal Data-stream. "Our information about your Earth must be very outdated. Maybe the communicator can talk to a cell phone. Your mother has a wireless cell phone?"

"Yes, and so do I." Holly fished around in her pocket and produced one. "Will that help?"

"It certainly will." He lengthened the wire again.

"Why is that in there?" Holly demanded.

"For reading." He studied what should have been an archaic communication device. It wasn't. Even by Universal standards, the tiny communicator was progressive technology. Antor honestly didn't know what to make of that.

"Reading books?" Holly said.

"Huh?"

"The wire, is it for reading books?"

"Books?"

"You know, paper books?" Holly said.

"Oh. We don't have those. We have digital information streams, or UDS."

Holly frowned. "No books you can hold in your hand?"

"No."

48

"That's sad. So what do you read with that wire? And how?"

"The core-text uses the wire to absorb information rather than read it. It's a lot faster than reading with your eyes. The information goes directly into my memory, via the links in my brain, through my tooth." He jiggled the wire. "Similar to your computers, I guess, except my brain is the computer."

Holly gasped. "Are you not really alive? Are you like Willy?"

"No! I'm alive, very alive." Antor was feeling more alive by the minute, sitting close beside Holly, but he wasn't explaining things very well. He was trying to concentrate on the complex reconfiguring of the communicator and absorb a whole lot of new information. Not to mention the shock of discovering modern technology on a primitive planet. Perhaps, like the television shows, it had been imported to Earth, but by whom? "Let me finish this and then we can talk," he said.

"Okay." Holly didn't make a peep of sound, while Antor examined the cell phone. It didn't even use buttons. It had an amazingly miniature touch-sensitive screen. Antor couldn't figure out how to use it and was rather embarrassed when he had to ask Holly.

She demonstrated all the features, and even held the phone at arm's length, pointed at the pair of them. She clicked a button and returned the phone to him. Antor couldn't believe his eyes when he saw a picture of the two of them right there on the viewing screen. He thought they looked great together. He wanted to keep the captured image and hang it on his wall.

"Holly, your technology is far more advanced than it should be," Antor mentioned, hoping for some sort of explanation.

"Or Earth is much more advanced than you realize. And a lot of your ship's equipment is kind of old-school and dilapidated, for a spaceship," Holly said bluntly. "Even this communicator uses big, old-fashioned buttons."

"But we can traverse the heavens, and you don't even know there's life out here."

Holly quirked her lips in the cutest way. "It doesn't make a whole lot of sense, does it?"

"No," Antor agreed.

"So, can you fix it so I can call home or not?"

"I'll try, Holly." Antor opened up the cell phone. The inside of the device was as modern as the exterior. It was a challenge to even expose the innermost guts. In the end, Antor succeeded in conjoining the two technologies with some wire borrowed from the wall panel. What he created wasn't pretty, but he thought it would work. He pressed buttons on the Scarnivore communicator's keypad and asked, "What's your mother's identification number?"

"You mean phone number?"

"I believe so."

Holly provided it. Antor pressed more buttons. He needed to press one hundred and twenty-eight buttons, before he had Holly input her mother's phone number on her cell phone, because he didn't know the Earth symbols. He watched closely and memorized the sequence she keyed in. Nothing happened. Antor had to poke around inside the communicator once more and do it all again, because he hadn't gotten things quite right. Forcing the Scarnivore communicator and the Earth cell phone to understand each other, and work together, wasn't easy.

After Antor had to repeat the whole procedure a third time, he finally heard a bell ringing. "Is it supposed to sound like that?" he asked.

"Yes." Holly beamed at him. He felt a bit like a hero, even though he wasn't one, not by any standards.

He offered the assembly to her, saying, "Try not to jostle the wires, they're loose."

Ever so gently, Holly held it and leaned over to press her ear against the phone.

"Hello?" a woman said.

"Hello, Mom?" Holly shouted much louder than was necessary.

"Holly, Holly! Where are you?" The woman started crying. Antor could hear both sides of the conversation clearly, since Holly was holding the phone so close to his ear.

"Mom, listen, I don't have long to talk, but I'm okay, I'm fine, not dead. I'll be home in about two months, so don't let Sarah move into my room or take my stuff, okay?"

"No, it's not okay. Where are you?" the woman demanded.

"I'm on an adventure. You wouldn't believe me if I told you," Holly said, smiling.

"Well, you better tell me. I thought something terrible had happened to you!"

Antor shook his head warningly and whispered, "Don't say anything about a spaceship." He leaned closer to her free ear. "Others can pick up this transmission."

Holly nodded. Her ear brushed Antor's lips. He was sure it was her fault entirely, but he certainly didn't mind. He tried hard to think of something else he could whisper in her ear. He had nothing. She started talking again.

"Mom, I'm traveling with some friends, I'm seeing all kinds of new places and doing interesting things. I'll be home in a few months."

"You're pregnant, aren't you? It's Daniel's, isn't it?" the woman accused.

"No, I'm not pregnant, I'm not that stupid. I'm going to be in a singing contest, but I have to go now. I'll try and call again. I love you, Mom, and I'm fine. I'm not pregnant. Can you let Daniel know I'm okay? Tell him I'm really sorry about his truck. It got wrecked … No! Not when I was driving it." Holly was barely giving her mother a chance to say anything.

Antor signaled for her to end the call. The longer the channel was opened, the greater the risk it could be traced to Earth.

"Bye, Mom. I love you. I'll call again soon. Everything is okay. Bye." Holly handed the phone to Antor, while her mother was still talking. He pressed the blue button on the communicator to end the call. He stuck the makeshift assembly in his pocket. When he had a chance, he would firm up the wiring so Holly could call home again.

"Feel better now?" he asked.

"Yes. Yes and no. She thinks I'm pregnant. Better than believing me dead, I guess. Thank you, Antor." Holly gazed at him as if she didn't hate him anymore, and maybe even liked him. Too bad she had a mate.

He backed toward the door. "It's okay, it was nothing. Just don't tell Captain Hampelle."

"You would get in trouble?" she asked.

"I'd probably get jettisoned." In fact, he was sure he would.

"I won't tell." Holly kept looking at him warmly, and he got that dizzy feeling again. "I wouldn't want you to get in trouble for helping me talk to my Mom. Zenga said that you don't have any family at all."

"Zenga has a big mouth."

"It must be hard, to not know where you come from, for your life to be a mystery. I'd feel so lost if I didn't have my family. They're not perfect, far from it, and sometimes they're more of a pain than anything else, but I would be lost without them."

If Antor wasn't mistaken, Holly pitied him for being a spaceship orphan. He didn't want her pity. He was starting to realize that there was a whole lot he wanted from Holly, but not pity. "This is all I've ever known, Holly. I've never had a family or home so I can't miss what I've never had. At least I wasn't jettisoned as a baby. I was treated well enough on the ships I grew up on. I always had food, and I was tolerated as long as I helped out. I wasn't beaten or mistreated very often." Antor was the one with the big mouth now, and Holly was definitely looking at him as if she felt sorry for him. "Uh, I better get back to the bridge."

Holly stepped close and hugged him. Even though she didn't squeeze him very hard, he lost his breath. He couldn't hug her back, because she had his arms trapped against his sides. "Thank you so much, Antor." She rested her head against his shoulder as if it was a pillow.

"My pleasure." It really was.

51

She released him much too abruptly. "And now I'm going to freshen up with that tongue-sponge or sponge-tongue thing. Zenga let me borrow some clean clothes."

Antor backed toward the door. "Have a nice cleansing. You know how to use the …?" He motioned to the tongue-sponge with one hand and rubbed his chest with the other. "You just rub it on your skin …" He never knew when to shut up. Antor fled to the bridge.

8 Holly - Deal with the Alien

The next day, Holly was so restless that she volunteered to help Antor with the cleaning of the cargo deck. It wasn't just because she wanted to ogle him some more, she felt she owed him for his help. And maybe she wanted to get to know him better. His heart seemed to be in the right place, and not just physically. Since Holly had told her mother that she was okay, she felt happier—less kidnapped. Her Outer Space trip was starting to feel like an adventure. Holly had always wanted to travel, and now she was getting her wish, in a really big bizarre kind of way.

Antor smiled when she offered to work with him. He really had the most appealing smile, the way it grew and spread across his face, not fast, but slow. Even his eyes curved warmly into slight crescent moon shapes. He had tied his hair back again, probably to work, and Holly could see all of his face. It was as beautiful as his body, especially when he smiled.

Together, they slid down to the lower deck. Willy was already there. Zenga wasn't. She was in charge of the bridge, while the Captain slept in his quarters, instead of the command chair.

"Finished clearing away the mintentacles, Willy?" Antor asked, sniffing the air.

"Yes, Antor," Willy said, standing as still as a fashion mannequin.

"Have you been cleaning C-2? Home of the Gorka?"

"I have just begun."

"Great, we'll help you." Antor turned to Holly. "It's the largest bay, where the animals were kept, before we had to unload them."

Holly stopped in the doorway and surveyed the pigsty, and that's exactly what it was. Big balls of something that looked like teal coloured mossy hay were grouped in all four corners, and a thick layer of the stuff was spread across the floor. There were gnawed bones scattered throughout, and clumps of purple fur. And excrement.

"Can I clean a different room, since I'm a volunteer?" she asked. "What about the room with the party-bots?" Antor turned red and avoided eye-contact, making Holly ask, "What are party-bots exactly?"

"I would really rather not say." Antor's colour deepened.

An answer like that only made her curiosity grow wildly. She strode out the door to have a look for herself. Antor gave chase. "Holly, let Willy clean that room. You really don't want to see what's in there." He lunged around her and blocked the doorway into the cargo bay with his body.

"Oh yes, I do. I want to know everything about Outer Space. I'm only going to make this trip once, you know." Holly tried to peek around him. He stood firm. She would have expected him to back down. "Fine, if you really don't want me to go in there, I won't." She turned around and started walking. She could hear Antor's sigh of relief. He was quick to follow her back to C-2. As soon as he lifted a shovel off the wall and began scooping fouled hay, Holly took off running.

She beat Antor down the corridor and skidded into the off-limits cargo bay, and then really wished she hadn't. It was like stepping into the scene of a bloody mass murder, if the blood was oily and purple. Somehow that didn't lessen the sense of carnage. Ripped to shreds all around her, were robots that were kind of like Willy the auto-mate, except prettier, and some had lots of long hair. There were both male and female party-bots.

Feeling sick enough to lose her space rations, Holly turned around. Antor was frozen in the doorway, looking as guilty as if he had committed the mayhem himself. "Party-bots?" Holly said. "Does that mean sex-bots?"

"I guess you don't have things like this on Earth," he mumbled.

"Not ... exactly. Not made with real bio-parts like Frankenstein's monster, no. It's beyond perverted and creepy. This could be the set of some pornographic slasher flick." She convinced her feet to move and get her the heck out of there. In awkward silence, they walked down the corridor. Holly stopped. "What ... who ... is that how people have sex in Outer Space?"

"Some beings, space travelers mostly. On extended trips, the, uh, company is ... appreciated."

Holly really wanted to ask him if he had one of those things stashed in his room, since he'd spent his whole life in space, but she held her tongue. They barely knew each other. They certainly weren't close enough to share personal information. Even best friends might not disclose such intimate confessions.

"I don't feel like cleaning anymore," Holly said and went back to her room. She locked herself in and tried really hard to forget what she had seen. She fell asleep and had X-rated nightmares until Antor woke her for a late supper, or perhaps it was a bedtime snack.

They ate more awful rations on the bridge with Zenga, and watched Outer Space broadcasts that were like TV. It was kind of fun. It wasn't Universe Idol, because that show wasn't on, but a rather slapstick comedy about a group of gardeners that had all kinds of trouble with their plants. Apparently, in the rest of the Universe, plants were not as sedate and rooted as they were on Earth, and they were inclined to run amuck. Holly laughed along with Antor and Zenga.

Captain Hampelle turned up. He spoiled their evening by shouting at Antor and Zenga, for having the broadcast on when they were supposed to be monitoring the ship. Holly was ordered to sing for him and she did, which put him to sleep in his chair. Holly's voice was exhausted by then, and she sought her cabin. It looked like Antor was stuck watching the bridge, since Zenga had taken the day shift.

The next day was a repeat of the previous one. Holly offered to help with more cleaning, once Antor assured her that he and Willy had jettisoned all the party-bots' remains. It meant they were back to cleaning C-2, but given what was in the other cargo bay, the home of the Gorka no longer seemed so bad.

Antor got right to work and lifted the shovel off the wall. He began scooping fouled hay into one of the hovering bins.

"That will be jettisoned, right?" Holly said, hanging back.

"It will. I'll do the dirty work with Willy, if you want to pile all the hayballs in one corner of the room, or are they too heavy for you to carry? If they are, I can get the other bin to float them."

"How do those things float, anyway?" She pointed at the cart.

"The ship has an artificial gravity field, so we don't float, too. The bins have a gravity blocker on the bottom, so they float at the set height. More expensive models of floaters will block planetary gravity, too." Antor demonstrated by pressing buttons on the bin's side-panel. The bin sank to the floor. He pressed more buttons and it rose again.

"I wish I had a gravity blocker for my snowboard," Holly said.

"Snowboard?"

Holly described the sport, while she moved hayballs. They weren't as heavy as they looked. They were lighter than bales of Earth hay, and they smelled a bit like spicy grass. She kicked and rolled some of them. It felt good to move around. She wasn't used to being sedentary. One by one, she shifted the balls to the front corner of the room and lined them neatly against the wall, adding a second, then a third layer, as if she was making an army of mossy haymen instead of snowmen.

Antor and Willy made steady progress clearing the floor and dumping the mess into the chute for jettisoning. Antor took his shirt off again. It was the highlight of her day. Holly watched him work while she worked. She began to hum and then sing. She knew a lot of songs by heart, old songs and new songs and some of her own songs. She was always happier when she sang, unless it was for Hampelle.

Antor plunked down on a hayball to listen. Holly joined him to take a break. "Zenga said you sing, Antor. Why don't you sing with me?"

His head dropped shyly. "Not with my voice."

"Let me decide. Sing something for me. Please."

He shook his head, eyes fixed downward. He was starting to hunch. It was probably a habit from when he had been a little unwanted boy, who never knew when he was going to get kicked or smacked. Holly placed a hand on his back to straighten him. His skin honestly felt like velvet, only velvetier. He arched stiffly. He had been working hard. "I'll give you a massage if you sing," she proposed.

"A massage?"

"You know, I'll rub your muscles, your skin."

He leaped to his feet looking completely scandalized. "You want to rub my skin? Here? Now?"

"Massage your skin, it feels good."

He cleared his throat, twice. "I'm sure it would feel good, very good, fantastic, but ..." He stopped talking and cleared his throat for a third time, as if he was choking.

Holly began to suspect they weren't on the same wave length. They seemed to be having a miscommunication, in spite of his Universal translator.

She didn't want to embarrass him further and stopped talking about rubbing his skin. "Well, it's not fair if I have to do all the singing. I'd like to hear you sing. Come on, one song."

"I would be ashamed to sing for you." He picked up the shovel, a clear signal that he was getting back to work, and would not be singing.

"You'll sing for me one of these days." Holly returned to making haymen. She thought she heard a rustling noise inside the haphazard stack of hayballs in the very back corner of the bay. Maybe it was a space mouse. She ignored it. "What about dancing? Can you dance, Antor?"

"Not as well as I can sing," he said.

"Then sing."

"No."

Holly laughed. "Then dance." She strode across the room toward him kicking a hayball aside. He didn't make a run for it. When she reached him, she held out her arms. "Dance with me?"

He tossed his shovel aside. "What do I do?"

Holly positioned his hands on her waist and shoulder, then held him the same way. "Follow my lead."

She guided him through a few traditional waltz steps, moving slowly and turning circles. Antor smiled down at her and mirrored her movements. He had a natural grace, when he wasn't feeling shy and self-conscious. Holly began to sing, so they would have music. He moved her closer, then closer still, until their chests were pressed together. "Is it okay to dance like this, on your planet?" His voice in her ear was deep and husky, and rather breathless.

"Very okay." Holly sounded as breathless as Antor. They might have been in a romantic ballroom, not shuffling through stinky hay. Holly closed her eyes and rested her cheek on his bare skin. She forgot all about singing. She even forgot where she was, except in Antor's arms.

When Willy said, "The bin is full," Antor sighed. She heard it and felt it.

Holly released him, reluctantly, and went to get more hay. Maybe the interruption had been timely. She had a boyfriend and Antor was one of the aliens who had abducted her. It could never work out between them. She had to remember that and control the crush she seemed to be developing on him. So he was sweetly appealing, so he was too handsome for his own good, so he had arranged for her to call home—it didn't mean she had to like him.

Holly hauled another hayball into her arms. She froze when she definitely heard a noise. She dropped the ball and kicked others aside.

"What are you doing?" Antor asked, not yet out the door with the bin.

"I think there's something in the hay, it sounds alive." Holly shifted another ball and couldn't believe her eyes. There was a nest inside with five purple wolf-sized animals. They looked a bit like little miniature abominable snowmen, except they had long toothy snouts like crocodiles, and little horns beside their small ears. "Oh look, are these babies? They're big for babies and they aren't very cute."

Antor bellowed, "Get back!"

She skidded away when one of the purple pups snapped with lightning speed, and enough fangs to put a werewolf to shame. It came after her, its feet as fast as its mouth. It would have got her, too, if Antor hadn't hurtled in front of her and blocked the attack. He cried out when teeth ripped into his arm. He staggered and tried to pull the miniature monster off.

Holly screamed bloody murder, when a second beast leapt on him, knocking him flat. The animal sank its front fangs deep into his beautiful chest, while the remaining three closed in. Before they could rip into Antor, Willy grabbed a weapon from outside the door and started firing. Antor had said it was a blaster. It really did blast big holes with some sort of sizzling electrical bullets. And they were deafeningly loud, like contained thunder and crackling lightning all mixed together. The first shot downed the monster on Antor's arm, the second shot missed. The third stopped the one digging into his chest. Willy kept blasting until all the fiends were dead.

Holly stood frozen with shock, until Antor arched his back and cried out. She stumbled forward and pushed the purple bodies off him. His skin was shredded. The little teeth had done an incredible amount of damage to his flesh. "Oh, Antor. Oh god, Antor. Why did you jump in front of me?"

His eyes were opened, but glazed. "Think I lost my … survival instinct," he whispered. It looked like he tried to smile, but his mouth was too tight with pain. His lips were alarmingly white.

Holly tore off her sweatshirt and pressed the fabric on his chest, trying to stop the gurgling blood. There was too much blood. It was so dark red, it was almost black. "Willy, get Zenga!" she screamed.

There was no need. Zenga came skidding into the room. "I heard blaster fire. Did you blast him?" she accused Holly.

Holly shook her head, tears washing down her cheeks. "Willy shot those purple things, but they got Antor. He saved my life."

"Oh damn. Antor!" Zenga fell to her knees on his other side. "How bad is it, Holly?"

"I think it's bad." Holly lifted the shirt away and Zenga shut her eyes.

"Very bad," she agreed. "Keep pressing on the wound. Willy, bring me the medical kit, quickly." Zenga looked down into Antor's face. His eyes were still opened, staring blindly out of a gray mask of pain. She cupped his face with her hands and said, "Keep breathing."

"Breathing." His voice was without substance.

"I'm going to get you fixed up. We're only a wormhole away from one of the Castorian planets. I'll get you a surgeon, so you hang on. That's an order."

Antor's eyes drifted closed. Willy arrived with the kit. Zenga took out a canister and motioned for Holly to lift the drenched sweatshirt away. As soon as his chest was bared, she sprayed a clear mist over it. The bubbling blood stopped bubbling, and hardened as if it had frozen. It plugged the wound and stopped the rest of his blood from leaking out, if he still had any left. Zenga did the same for his arm, which was bitten halfway through. Lastly, she pulled some sort of thin membrane out of the kit and shook it. Holly helped her tuck it around Antor's body. It radiated heat, as if it had just come out of a dryer.

Zenga dashed tears from her eyes. "There, he should be able to hang on, I hope. I'll get the surgeon on board. Willy, jettison those Gorka carcasses before we have visitors."

Even the baby Gorka were monsters. It was lucky that the cold on Earth had killed the mature ones, otherwise a lot of people would be dead by now. Although, with all that thick purple fur, they looked more like northern animals than tropical beasties.

Zenga ran and Antor lay like death. Willy carted away the bodies for disposal. He returned to cleaning the floor as if nothing tragic had happened.

"Willy, why did you have to hide the bodies?" Holly asked.

In his flat voice, Willy said. "I know nothing about Gorka."

"But you just jettisoned five young ones."

He didn't respond and kept working.

Antor began to shiver. His shallow breathing faltered. "Hang on, Antor. Zenga's getting help." Holly stroked his forehead. His breathing

58

only got weaker. He was dying before her eyes. He was dying because he had saved her life. Holly didn't know how else to help him, so she sang to him, because he loved her voice. Softly, she crooned beautiful Celtic ballads that always made her think of angels. Antor rallied. His breathing strengthened and he stopped shivering. She clutched his hand tight under the warmed sheet, afraid that if she let go, she would lose him.

Holly sang until Zenga dashed. She was closely followed by a pair of aliens straight out of Earth's lore. The beings were small, skinny and white. Their bald heads were enormous with over-sized tilted yellow eyes. Their fingers were far too long. Holly had seen pictures of this type of alien, who were reputed to have crashed on Earth in the past. One of them carried a small metal trunk.

"This is the surgeon and his assistant." Zenga knelt beside Antor. "How is he?"

"Still alive, even though he doesn't look it," Holly said.

The surgeon didn't waste time on greetings. He peered under the blanket and motioned to his assistant. They discussed what they saw and spoke to Zenga in a fast hissing language. Her face fell and she hissed something back. They sounded like a nest of snakes.

Holly was frustrated that she couldn't understand a word. "What are they saying?" she asked Zenga, when there was a lull in the conversation. "Is Antor going to be okay? Can they fix him?"

Zenga translated. "His wounds are grave. He will die without immediate and extensive treatment." She shook her head hopelessly. "They want two bizoux to heal Antor. That's a fortune."

"Won't the Captain pay, or the shipping company?"

"Maybe," she said without conviction.

The Castorians' translators must have deciphered Holly's dialect. They began speaking it, like Zenga.

"We will need your Captain's promise of payment," the surgeon said.

"Worth a try, I suppose," Zenga said kind of hopelessly. She sent Willy to wake up the Captain and explain the situation. Holly couldn't believe that he had slept through the blasting, then again, he did sleep a whole lot more than most beings, so maybe he slept sounder.

While waiting for him to appear, the two Castorians unpacked the strangest medical equipment that Holly had ever seen. There were no metal scalpels or needles, only insect-like tools that looked partly artificial and partly biological, kind of like Willy, but much smaller. The tiniest ones had abdomens that were crystal clear and filled with pale blue liquid. Maybe they produced webbing, like spiders, and could stitch wounded flesh back together, inside and out. Or maybe it was super glue for skin. The largest ones had long needle-noses, like over-sized mosquitoes, perhaps to suck out blood or inject medicine. The mini-machines moved all by themselves, on legs that were as long and delicate as any daddy longlegs spider. The medical bugs looked like true advanced alien technology, the kind Holly had expected to see in Outer Space.

Captain Hampelle stomped in and surveyed the scene with his hairy brow so lowered, you could barely see his eyes. He listened to the Castorian's request for a payment of two bizoux to save Antor's life. He didn't even think about it. "No, too much. Let him die."

"May we claim the body? To cover the cost of our ship call?" the surgeon asked.

"Agreed. The carcass is of no use to me." Captain Hampelle waved a hand dismissively.

Holly couldn't believe how callously the Captain was acting, calling Antor a carcass when he was still alive.

The Castorian got chatty. "We have a need for limbs, as always, and internal organs, of course. None of the body will go to waste."

Holly stood dumbstruck, until Zenga rounded on Hampelle. "No, no! You will not let Antor die and sell him for parts. This is your fault. You brought those beastly Gor -"

"Enough," the Captain thundered. "Do not say that word. I do not have two bizoux. APS will not pay two bizoux when the accident cannot be explained. Antor will die without treatment, so he will die. Might as well get some benefit from his corpse."

The Castorian ghouls stood off to the side, discussing whether or not to repair Antor's arm before he died, so it would have value afterward. Holly felt trapped in a waking nightmare.

The deal was struck quickly. The Captain was offered a black medallion that hung from the Castorian's scrawny neck on a chain. Hampelle pressed his thumb to the medallion and the physician said, "As soon as the breathing stops, we will remove the body. It will not be long."

Zenga turned away, tears running freely down her pale cheeks.

Holly honestly couldn't credit what she was hearing. "Zenga, are they going to stand there and wait for Antor to die, so they can carve up his body for spare parts?" she asked, to be clear.

"Yes. They make a huge profit from harvesting and reselling humanoid bio-parts." Tears were welling in Zenga's eyes.

"But that's the most barbaric thing I've ever heard. They're just going to let him die, so they can chop him up? I can't believe anyone in this Universe would dare to call me primitive!"

Zenga made shushing motions.

Holly turned to the skinny aliens. "You, Castorians, would you accept three of these bizoux things to save Antor's life, if you'll wait a couple of months for the payment?"

The Castorians were interested. "Explain," they said in one voice.

"I'm the next Universe Idol. I'll be getting a thousand bizoux in the near future," she declared with supreme confidence. It was an act.

The surgeon shook his oversized head and actually smiled, his tiny lipless mouth stretched upward into a clown's grin. "Everyone thinks they are the next Universe Idol, and you appear to be pure humanoid. Humans can't sing. No deal."

Zenga dug her fingers into Holly's arm and shoved her closer to the Castorian. "She can so sing. Listen to her, before you decide," she implored. "Just listen, please."

"Sing while we repair the arm," the surgeon said with disinterest.

"Okay, okay," Holly gasped, her heart pounding with such fear that she could barely speak. Her voice could save Antor, if she could sing well enough. She took a deep breath and tried to settle her nerves.

"You can do it, Holly," Zenga said, with complete confidence.

Because Antor seemed to be fading fast, she repeated the last Celtic ballad that she had sung to keep him alive. The Castorians stopped preparing their equipment to listen. When the song ended, they requested another. Holly sang something upbeat and toe-tapping, a complete contrast to the first song. They seemed to like it, their toes tapped. When she finished, they requested another.

Zenga shouted, "No! Antor is dying. Do you agree to the new deal or not?"

There was no hesitation. "We agree, for five bizoux at the end of the Universe Idol contest."

"Thank you," Holly breathed. Captain Hampelle started to protest, until Zenga whispered something in his ear that sounded like 'Gorka'. He shut up then.

The Castorian wasn't finished. "If, by some misfortune, you do not win Universe Idol, the medical bill must still be paid."

"But how?"

"We will take three limbs at that time, if you cannot compensate us financially. Agreed?"

Holly glanced at Zenga in confusion. "Three limbs?"

"Universal law doesn't allow them to kill Antor, but they can take his limbs as payment, instead of the bizoux, if you don't win."

Holly decided that she didn't like the Castorian aliens at all. She loathed them. "What should we do?" she asked Zenga.

"Agree to the deal. Antor is dead otherwise. At least this way, he has a chance. I'll give one of my limbs in place of Antor's, if it comes to that." It was a tremendous sacrifice for a friend, but it was not accepted.

"The three must come from the same host for ease of removal and genetic matching. Do you still agree?" The Castorian extended the medallion to Holly. She pressed her thumb to it, as the Captain had done.

When the deal was finalized, the Castorian pulled a ring out of its mouth and strung it on the chain with the medallion. Holly had no chance to ask what it was, before the Castorian ordered everyone out, while the treatment was performed.

Zenga took Holly to the bridge and they settled in adjacent chairs. The Captain didn't make an appearance. Zenga muttered that he had probably gone back to sleep.

"Will Antor survive?" Holly asked Zenga.

"Celeste, I hope so. The Castorians possess very innovative surgical and medical techniques. It's one of their specialties. Well, they heal for profit, don't they? They do everything for profit. And they charge more for not reporting suspicious injuries." Zenga sagged into her chair.

"Can't they simply clone parts?" Holly asked.

Zenga looked at her oddly. "You know about cloning?"

"Yes. The Earth has cloned sheep. We've probably cloned people, too, since we've cloned sheep, but no-one will admit to that. Experiments like that are hushed up."

"The Earth has cloned sheep? Lambs?"

Holly nodded.

Zenga didn't look disbelieving, she looked astounded. "That is unexpected, but I doubt you've cloned humans. Pure humanoids don't clone, not properly. It's a Universal mystery, actually, why we don't clone with the ease of other organisms. Most attribute that to a god gene which goes back to the Divine Race and the original Green World. Anyway, that's why the Castorians harvest parts whenever they can."

Holly mulled that over. "Well, it explains why the Castorians visit Earth and abduct people. We're like a free supply of spare parts." She felt violated just thinking about it.

"Why would you think the Castorians abduct Earthlings?" This time, Zenga did look skeptical.

Holly had neglected to mention one important fact. "Because the Earth has pictures of Castorians."

"What? Are you sure?"

"Yes, I've seen them. They're not photographs, but the sketches are accurate. Castorians have been to my planet. There are rumours that one of their ships crashed on Earth, and that we keep it in a secret bunker. They must visit Earth to abduct people and probe them," she said.

Zenga gave Holly a very frank sort of look. "I don't think Castorians are interested in … probing. They are interested in profit, not probing, since they're not very emotional or physical. Now, the abductions, that I can believe. Free biological parts harvested from an unknown and unreported source, and an infinite source given the billions that overcrowd your world. Yes, vast profit in that."

"I bet the Castorians have been abducting Earthlings for years. People have had sketches of them since the 1960's, I think. In Earth years, that's more fifty years ago."

Zenga squirmed deeper into her seat. "It certainly looks like they can be added to the growing list of Earth's visitors."

Holly sagged back in her own chair. The conversation had helped to distract her from worrying about Antor, if only for a moment. When silence settled heavily on the bridge, a wave of anguish washed over her. The strength of it was unexpected. She hurt terribly inside, imagining Antor's suffering.

It seemed the same for Zenga. She began to sniffle. "Poor Antor, to be so savagely attacked, but at least he has a chance to survive now. You said he saved your life?" She turned her head to look at Holly.

"Yes, the purple things were going for me. He stepped between us." Holly bit her lip. "I was surprised, I mean, he's quite timid most of the time."

Zenga smiled sadly. "That's Antor. He is timid with people, or even talking to people, but when a situation is truly hazardous, he thinks nothing of himself and more of others. He's courageous when you least expect it. He totally lacks survival instinct, and he doesn't even realize it. He saved my life once, when I first started working on the ship."

"How?" Holly asked.

"I was young and foolish, well, younger and more foolish. I talked him into looking for excitement on a rather disreputable planet. He didn't want to go, I insisted. Anyway, we sure found excitement. A gang of illegal slavers tried to take us from this seedy bar. I didn't know Antor as well as I do now, and I think I was more astonished than the slavers when he leapt on one of them and managed to steal the lout's blaster. There was a wild firefight, we were so lucky to get out of there alive." She smiled reminiscently and shook her head. "I think we were both drunk. It was the first time Antor got drunk, thanks to me."

"How long ago was that?" Holly asked.

"Almost two years, that's how long we've worked together on the Comet Tail." She lost her sad smile and simply looked sad. "We've shared lots of good times, more so before Captain Hampelle came aboard, but still, there is no-one I would rather travel with than Antor. When I get to captain my first ship, he's promised to be my ... my first-mate. Is that the right word?"

"Yes."

"He's my best friend. Celeste, I hope he pulls through." Zenga dropped her head into her hands, sobbing as if there was no hope.

Holly was young enough to have avoided close contact with death or serious illness. She wasn't sure how to comfort, but she tried. She put an arm around Zenga and said, "Antor will recover. He will. You got the surgeon here in time. He's going to get better. Don't think that he won't."

Zenga rested her head on Holly's shoulder and seemed content to leave it there. It felt like they were friends, allied together. It wasn't the right moment to ask Zenga why she had ordered Willy to hide the furry purple corpses, and why the Castorians had to be paid extra to keep silent about Antor's injuries. So Holly didn't.

⁹ Antor - Preparations

Nothing was real or solid. Antor was floating. He couldn't quite remember where he was, or who he was, or what he was. He simply floated along as if he was riding the buoyant seas of Calma Surfarian.

A deep slow breath made his chest feel like it was ripping open. The pain triggered a distant memory of vicious teeth and razor claws, and shredded human skin—his. "Am I dead?" he asked the mist that pressed around him. It had no answer, except to wrap him tighter and smother him. He stopped floating and began to sink into black fog that was thicker than water.

The most beautiful singing in the Universe guided him out of the dark cloud into the light. He listened and tried to speak Holly's name with a mouth that was as dry as a Gehennan wind. His body felt like it had been crushed under a falling star that was still falling. He fought to stay with Holly, but he had no cohesion to that world. It faded away in the inky mist.

A cup touched his mouth, penetrating the haze. Water soothed his cracked lips. He sipped until it was gone and accomplished the great feat of lifting his eyelids. Zenga's face swam in and out of focus. She looked awful.

"What's wrong, Zen?" Antor asked. "You okay?"

"I'm okay," she said and started to cry.

He thought that meant he was dying. He tried to say goodbye. He didn't have the strength for more words. The fog pulled him away from her.

Holly's voice forced him back again and anchored him to his body, when he would have gladly left its pain behind. Her warm hand held his too tight. Antor tried to squeeze her fingers, he couldn't. "Water," he whispered. The cup brushed his lips and he drained it. His eyes opened, they saw Holly and didn't want to close again.

"Sing," he breathed. "Your voice keeps me here."

Holly sang for him with tears in her beautiful blue eyes and Antor knew he was finished dying, because he could never leave Holly.

It was two more days before he sat up, and three before he stood. Holly kept him company in his room, when she wasn't replacing him on the bridge. He kept falling asleep. When he could stay awake, they talked, although she did most of the talking. Antor preferred to listen, to hear about her life. It was so different from his own.

Holly had roots, she had grown up in one place. She told him about going to school and working at her part-time job and hanging out with her friends. She described her home and family in such detail, Antor could almost see them. He could feel how much she missed them. As a small boy, the daydream of an imaginary home and family had fortified Antor through many hard times, even though he'd known it wasn't real, and never would be.

Zenga claimed some of Holly's time and taught her the ship's basic controls. Holly was so thrilled and excited when she told Antor that she had piloted a spaceship, that he had limped to the bridge to watch her drive the Comet Tail. She was a natural pilot and said the ship's controls weren't that different from an old truck's.

Only when he was half himself again, did Zenga tell him the Castorians hadn't expected him to survive. And she revealed the bargain that Holly had made with the surgeon, so he could keep his life, and maybe lose his limbs. He knew a tracer chip would have been inserted somewhere on his person, probably inside his chest, before it had been patched back together. The Castorians would have no trouble finding him and his limbs, if Holly didn't win Universe Idol.

Hampelle complained a lot about the inconvenience Antor's injury had caused him, even though the fault was entirely the Captain's. He had brought the breeding pair of Gorka aboard. He should have figured out that the female had given birth. Hampelle went so far as to grumble about the costly loss of the five young ones, some of which had surely been female.

If Antor had had an ounce of strength to spare, he would have punched Hampelle right in his tough little black nose.

The ship settled into a comfortable routine, with Holly aboard and Antor recovering. The Comet Tail made a couple of routine pickups and deliveries. The Captain completed and filed a detailed insurance claim for the ruined cargo. And they got closer and closer to Nightrous.

When they were a few days away, Antor was feeling almost steady on his feet. The Castorians had worked miracles, and he didn't have a scar to show for his ordeal. Holly had examined his chest more than once, even touching it with her soft warm hand as if the feel of his skin pleased her. She was amazed that there was no visible trace of the extensive damage done to him.

With Holly's audition almost upon them, Zenga called a meeting in the galley during one of Captain Hampelle's rare bridge shifts. Over space rations, Zenga said, "Holly needs to start really preparing. She needs to choose and practice a song that will astound the judges. She needs a costume. She needs to do something about that hair."

"What's wrong with my hair?" Holly twirled a lock around her finger. "I mean, I know it's dirty because there's no water on the ship for washing, and that sponge-tongue isn't nearly as good as a proper shampooing. It leaves my scalp kind of itchy, but there isn't much I can do about that."

Zenga shook her head. "No! The blue is what's wrong with your hair! The blue will raise too much speculation about your home planet. I've never seen any other humanoids with striped blue hair."

"It's streaked, not striped. And my hair isn't really blue."

"Of course it is—I can see it. It's blue," Zenga said.

Holly explained. "The blue is dye, like hair paint. The blue will grow out."

"Why would you want to paint your hair blue?" Zenga asked incredulously.

Antor wisely kept his mouth out of the discussion about hair. And he was rather biased, he liked everything about Holly, even the blue hair. She was perfect in his eyes.

"It's just a … an Earth thing," Holly said. "Some people like coloured hair, or tattoos on their body or piercings—holes through various body parts, like ears and lips and eyebrows and bellybuttons and noses and … and nipples, stuff like that. I only have my ears pierced though, not any other parts."

"Crazy planet," Zenga said dismissively and got back to planning. "We could shave your hair off, then there would be no more blue. A lot of human races are bald. Do you think the judges would like Holly with a bald head?" she asked Antor.

"No!" both Antor and Holly shouted.

Zenga drummed her fingers energetically, studying Holly's hair. "What about if we only trimmed off the blue streaks and left the white-blond? You would still have half your hair."

"No!" It was unanimous, at least between Antor and Holly.

"How about a hat?"

"Maybe, if it's a cool hat," Holly said.

"Why would you want your head to be cold?"

"Not cold—cool. Cool means … stylish, trendy, fashionable."

"Oh, okay. We'll select your outfit first, then consider a hat to match," Zenga decided, as if she was in charge of Holly's cosmic makeover. She jumped to another subject—song choice. "I can't decide if you should sing a Universal hit or one of your Earth songs. They're good, and you know those already, except you won't have the music. That might be a problem."

"I do have all the music I need with me," Holly said.

"Where?" Zenga asked.

Holly dashed off. She returned with a tiny white rectangle in her palm.

"That's a song?" Antor guessed.

"It's the music for about a thousand songs. It's my practice music, and all the music I'll need as long as you can download it into your data-stream."

Antor picked up the little device. "Shouldn't be a problem, but are you sure there are a thousand songs on this?" He didn't think it was possible.

"Positive." She plugged a black wire into the white rectangle and inserted two rounded ends of the wire into Antor's ears. She pressed miniature buttons and suddenly, throbbing music filled his ears. The sound quality was impressive, especially in light of how small the whole assembly was. And it seemed Earth humans could create music with instruments. The music was every bit as remarkable as their singing.

Zenga had a turn next. She listened and her eyes widened. "This is Earth technology?" she asked, as if she didn't believe it.

"It is," Holly said.

"Imagine. It doesn't make sense for a primitive planet to have developed this, but I'm glad you have music."

"I also write songs myself. I have that music on there, too."

"Do you really write songs? And music? The judges are more receptive when the singer has written their own song. Have you written any about broken hearts?"

Holly nodded. "Quite a few, actually."

"Everyone likes songs about broken hearts. You should sing a song about that," Zenga decided on the spot.

"Do you want to hear my best ones? Then you can decide if they're suitable for the audition," Holly said.

"Yes." Antor always wanted to hear Holly sing. Nothing in the Universe made him feel so content.

Holly sang three songs about broken hearts. She had her own unique style. "I like the second one the best," Zenga said. "It has the catchiest tune, and it's the saddest."

Antor agreed. "They were all great, but I think the second one will appeal to the judges. It might make them cry."

"Is that good?" Holly asked.

"Very good."

"Okay, the song is decided, and you have the music." Zenga clapped her hands smartly together. "Now, about the costume, we have one more stop before Nightrous, to drop off a shipment of cargo that wasn't ruined." She glanced at Antor.

"Ja'Dorp?" he guessed.

"Yes. We could make a quick trip down to the surface, to the commercial port, and buy Holly an outfit."

Antor frowned. "I don't think that's a good idea."

"Why not?" Holly asked.

Zenga wrinkled her nose. "The trading port on Ja'Dorp, it's kind of dangerous."

Antor snorted. "Kind of dangerous?"

"Okay, it is dangerous. We usually don't go down there," Zenga admitted. "The cargo is normally transferred on or off the ship at a docking bay, above the planet. But if we take precautions, stay on the main streets, take Willy with us and a couple of blasters, I'm sure we would be fine to visit the port during daylight hours."

Before he could veto Zenga's suggestion, Holly said, "I would love to see another world. It would prepare me for the audition on Nightrous, wouldn't it? And it would be so exciting!"

Antor didn't want her at risk on Ja'Dorp and said, "Being abducted by aliens and taken halfway across the Universe isn't exciting enough for you?"

"Of course it is." It was obvious that Holly was simply placating him. "But I've only seen the ship, and the UGS and black Outer Space and wormholes and a quasar. This is the most exciting trip I'll ever take, and I want to see a lot more than the ship. I want to see as many planets and aliens as I can before I go home."

Antor didn't want to think about taking her home, any more than he wanted to think about taking her to Ja'Dorp. As always, Zenga held the opposing opinion. She stood up with enthusiasm. "I like how you think, Holly Noel Tate. Next stop—Ja'Dorp. I'll go arrange it with the Captain."

"He might not want to let us off the ship." Antor could hope.

"Of course he will. He wants Holly to win Universe Idol even more than the rest of us. Well, maybe not more than us, because we want your limbs saved, but you can bet he's dreaming about all those bizoux." Zenga looked awfully smug when she strode away.

Antor sat at the table, scowling at his space rations, until Holly gently touched his still tender arm. "Antor, please don't be upset. You'll come with me, you'll keep me safe," she said with a beautiful show of faith.

"If I can. I'm still not fully recovered." He hated how sulky he sounded.

"I know. Then I'll keep you safe. Can I carry a blaster?"

Antor couldn't tell if she was joking or not. "Maybe a small one."

"A small blaster is better than no blaster." She flashed him a warm grin and left her hand resting on his arm. Antor didn't dare to hope that she was flirting with him, even though she was acting as if she liked him. It was probably because he had saved her life. Maybe she simply felt indebted to him.

As happily as she had left, Zenga dashed back in. "Captain Hampelle has granted permission for us to disembark. He was actually enthusiastic.

69

He's contacted the port authorities for our landing passes, and ..." She let the suspense build, rather like Chrome Boreal.

Antor wasn't amused. "And what?"

"And he's chipped in a couple of coins for Holly's audition costume. I've got some savings I can add. What about you, Antor? You save most of your pay."

"I have some savings." He actually had a lot of coins on his money-chain, and he was very responsible with those coins. "You're welcome to what you need, but I still think it's a bad idea to visit Ja'Dorp."

"Of course you do." Zenga stopped behind him and ruffled his hair.

"I'm not two years old," he grumbled.

"Of course you're not."

Antor knew when he was beaten. "It's time for my nap," he said and marched out.

10 Holly - Ja'Dorp

Holly awoke filled with anticipation. It felt like Christmas morning. She was going to visit another planet! Not many Earthlings could claim that honour. Maybe none. But Holly Noel Tate was going to walk on a world halfway across the Universe from Earth. She was going to shop on another planet! She was so excited that she couldn't stay horizontal for another second. Her watch said that it was four in the morning, her time. It was morning enough. She rolled out of her hammock and landed on her feet.

Antor had repaired her door panel, granting her freedom to come and go as she pleased. She used the rudimentary facilities, cleaning up as best she could, before she woke Zenga and Antor. She didn't know the personal codes to open their doors, so she banged on the metal and shouted, "Meet me in the galley."

She served up three bowls of dog food, as she thought of the rations. Zenga had been too distracted by Antor's condition to seek out fresh food anywhere. Three cups of water completed the dreadful meal. There was no coffee or tea on the ship. Aliens didn't start the day with caffeine, or maybe they didn't have caffeine. Earth was clearly superior in that department.

Antor turned up first, looking exhausted and grumpy. He really could have used a coffee. "Breakfast!" Holly said. He grunted and slumped onto the stool.

At least Zenga was livelier. She strode in with a spring in her step and said, "I can't wait to get off the ship. I stopped at the bridge and Captain Hampelle had left Willy in charge, even though that is completely against APS regulations. Anyway, Willy has us right on course. The Comet Tail will be at the docking platform above the planet, by the time we've finished eating."

"So we don't just land, like you did on Earth?" Holly said.

"Oh no, that was an emergency landing. We almost always orbit or dock high above the planet, and take a small ..." Zenga hesitated as if the translator was slow to find the word. "... a small taxi down to the surface when we actually visit a planet."

"Why don't we land?" Holly asked.

71

"Because landing and launching stress the engine coils, especially in an old ship like this. It also burns too much fuel, which is really expensive, so we order a taxi."

"Oh." Holly could understand that. Gas on Earth cost a fortune just to power a car. "So the shuttle craft is on its way?"

Antor perked up. "Shuttle craft? The Earth sure has a lot of commonly used space words in its vocabulary, considering it hasn't even dunked a toe in the galactic ocean of Outer Space."

"The words must come from all those aliens that like to visit Earth and probe Earthlings," Zenga said with a gleam in her eye.

"Zenga!" Antor flushed as if he was embarrassed. "Don't talk about probing."

Holly was about to ask what they thought probing meant, when Zenga rose. Holly shoved her bowl away. She was finished eating. "Where are the blasters? Antor said I could have one."

"I did not," he groaned and dropped his head on the table. He left it there.

Zenga said, "I'll show you where the blasters are."

"Wahoo!" Holly hadn't felt so childishly excited in years. Shopping! And on another planet! At that moment, she was thrilled that she had been abducted by aliens. It was the greatest adventure ever.

They woke Captain Hampelle, before they departed the ship. Zenga escorted him to the bridge and sternly ordered him to stay awake. She sounded like his mother. He yawned and promised that he would. Holly now knew that his promises were merely empty words.

A dark gray planet was visible through the viewing screen—Ja'Dorp. The surface looked the same everywhere, a flat drab gray with no water or greenery. The Earth looked much prettier from space, not that Holly had had a chance to see her planet from above with her own eyes. The Comet Tail had departed too quickly for that. But she had seen pictures.

A blue button on the console started flashing. "Shuttle is here," Captain Hampelle said. "Off with you lot. Stay out of trouble. Why don't you have lunch on the planet? Our cargo won't be offloaded until noon, so you've got half a day." He was acting uncharacteristically generous and agreeable.

Zenga froze. "You're not going to do anything you shouldn't, while we're gone, are you?"

"Don't need to, not now that I'm coming into a fortune." Hampelle flashed his pointy white teeth. Holly was his fortune. "If you must know, I'm looking forward to having the place to myself for once. An old friend is dropping by to discuss some private shipping contracts, so don't come back early. If you do, you'll find the hatch locked up tight," he growled, his short-lived humour gone. "Clear enough?"

"Clear enough," they echoed and left the bridge. As soon as they were down the slide, Zenga muttered, "Private shipping contracts—does that sound like smuggling to you, Antor?"

"It does. Not much we can do about it though. He's the boss."

"Maybe we should hire on with another shipper."

"If I still have my limbs in a couple of months, let's look into that," Antor said lightly.

Their shuttle-taxi was waiting, docked against the undamaged side hatch. Holly had learned that the hatches were magnetic, and compatible with most other ships. She followed Zenga into a cabin that was about the size of the passenger section of a stretch limousine.

They had the compartment to themselves. The shuttle detached from the Comet Tail with a violent shake and sped away. The ride was much rougher than on the bigger ship. Holly felt like she was actually zipping through space. She had little sense of that on the shipper/transport. Even when the Comet Tail was going its fastest, the stars didn't zoom by like they did in the movies. Apparently, that aspect of warp speed was pure fiction.

As soon as they were settled, Antor wrapped a blue sash around his lean waist and tied a flashy purple sash onto Willy. It must have been an alien fashion, maybe an alternative to ties. He licked his thumb and rubbed a patch of oily dirt off of Willy's face, saying, "There, you look good for your day out, Willy. Very handsome." It was endearing how Antor took care of Willy, as if the auto-mate was truly alive.

Willy said, "Thank-you, Antor."

Zenga checked that the two blasters were fully charged. "Oops, better put the safety on this one." She clicked it into place. "Safer now. Okay Holly, there are some things you need to know. While we're on the planet, don't say a word about Universe Idol. Don't mention anything about coming from a restricted planet or being abducted or Antor's attack by Gorka or the Gorka themselves or -"

"I'm not stupid," Holly cut in, a bit exasperated. "But why can't I mention the Gorka?"

"Because Hampelle was smuggling the animals, so don't even say 'Gorka'. I'm starting to think he's a smuggler more than an APS Captain. Anyway, maybe you shouldn't talk at all when we're on the planet. And don't stare at anyone bigger than you. Don't stare at anyone at all. Much of the population will be humanoid or partly humanoid, but not all, and some aliens are really weird looking. Some have odd habits, like spitting and worse. Some are aggressive. Be warned." Zenga was fussing.

"Warned," Holly acknowledged.

73

Antor leaned forward. "Just follow our lead, do what we do and stick close, especially since you don't have a Universal translator. You won't be able to converse with anyone unless they have one."

Holly hadn't quite figured out the Universal translator business. "So as long as one person is wearing a translator, you can both understand each other?"

Antor nodded. "Because the being with the translator will speak the language of the being that doesn't have one."

"And if neither has one, no-one can understand each other?"

"Right, unless you speak the same language."

"What if you're both wearing translators?" Holly asked.

"Two isn't really any better than one. One is all it takes to communicate."

"Do most people … aliens … humanoids—whatever, do they have Universal translators?"

"No. Zen and I do because we work on a shipper/transport, and we're always loading and off-loading on different worlds, but a lot of beings never leave their own planet, and they don't need translators. Some cultures don't believe in them, and refuse to use them at all."

"More beings don't have translators than do have translators, unless they're travelers like us," Zenga summarized more succinctly.

"Should I get one?" Holly asked.

"Definitely. You'll need one when you're in the Universe Idol contest, because you'll be associating with multiple beings." Zenga stretched her legs into the middle of the compartment. "You can get one inserted on Ja'Dorp, if there's time after we shop."

Holly gulped. "Inserted?"

"It's a really tiny chip that communicates with your brain, vocal cords, mouth, everything necessary."

"Okay, I guess." It sounded straightforward, and appropriately alienish. "How long does this shuttle ride take?" There were no windows at all.

"Half an hour. Shuttles are much slower than real spaceships."

They were still leaps and bounds faster than Earth's lumbering space crafts.

Over the half hour, Zenga told Holly more about the various aliens she might encounter, and how she should and shouldn't behave. It got so confusing, Holly stopped paying attention.

The shuttle landed with a rough thump and skidded along the surface of the planet. As soon as they stopped moving, Antor slid the door upward and said, "Welcome to your first alien planet, Holly."

Her initial reaction was disappointment. The drab terminal they strolled through could have been mistaken for any bus station on Earth.

Their four passes were scrutinized by an ordinary looking human in a beige robe. She bit a perforated triangle off the top corner of each of their passes, before she returned them and allowed their party of four through a secure gate into the port city. She said something to them, but Holly didn't understand a word.

Everyone sealed their documents into their respective pockets and they exited the boring building.

Holly was further disappointed by her first sight of the city. It looked too much like Earth on an overcast day in autumn, and the people looked too much like people. Vegetation was sparse and scrubby, almost colourless. Beside the wide dirt path, gray mud puddles bubbled as if they were simmering. Small orange insects clouded the air, but stayed near the puddles.

When they got closer to the populated settlement, Antor reached for Holly's hand, saying, "I don't want to risk losing you." She didn't mind holding his hand. It felt nice—more than nice. Her hand felt super-sensitized to the feel of Antor's skin, and she found herself smiling for no reason.

Willy trailed behind with one of the blasters. Zenga led the way with the other. Holly felt secure, even though she hadn't gotten a blaster after all, not even a small one.

The deeper they penetrated into the settlement, the more interesting it became. Flat warehouse style structures gave way to brighter, more irregularly shaped buildings, with skinny pointy tops that jutted up into the gray sky. The smooth grayish ground became congested with more bodies, and some of them were not the slightest bit humanoid. Holly recognized a pair of scrawny pale Castorians, and Zenga pointed out a trio of tall skinny orange Scarnivores with stick-like legs, not unlike the legs of an Earth insect.

Holly tried not to gawk when Antor whispered, "Mannireplians," in her ear, and tilted his head at four round green beach balls with too many small arms and legs.

"Ugly," she grimaced.

"They don't think so. They think you're ugly."

"Thanks, thanks a lot." Holly was teasing, but Antor didn't realize.

"What? No, no, you're not ugly. You're, uh, quite the opposite," he stammered. "You're ..." He was lost for words and starting to look miserable.

Holly took pity on him. "Antor, I was just kidding, joking."

Zenga rolled her eyes at the pair of them. "Manni's think anyone with colourless skin is ugly. In their opinion, the more colour the better, unless it's Scarnivore orange."

75

Antor glanced all around, surveying the area. "The Scarnivores and the Manni's are presently at war, well, it's more of a skirmish, but I don't like them together in the same block, especially since a Scarnivore beat out a Mannireplian for the ninth Universe Idol spot in the Double Dwarf Star Constellation. Bound to be hard feelings."

"Antor, stop worrying and enjoy the day off the ship," Zenga chided.

Holly kept watching the passing aliens. None traveled alone on this planet. There were groups of hairy beings walking on two or four legs, and clusters of beings with patterns of colour on their skins, as if they had been tattooed from head to toe, and albino beings, and very small humanoids, and an alien with real wings, and one that levitated who didn't have wings at all, and one with eight glowing red eyes that looked like Christmas lights, and one pair of normal looking humans, except that they appeared to be joined by an umbilical cord and ...

Antor stopped walking. They had arrived at the shops. "Clothing stores are in this sector," he said.

Zenga moved to Holly's other side. "I've never shopped here, but there's an Arch-Essential outlet. They always have a wide selection for the human form, well, most stores do." She pointed to a symbol that Holly couldn't read. "We'll start there."

The front of the store was glass. Too-tall men and women paraded inside the crystal clear facade, their clothes changing as they walked.

"How do the models do that?" Holly asked.

"The models aren't real, they're three dimensional images."

"Holograms?" Holly guessed.

Antor grinned. "Yet another space word."

"Earth uses them."

"Shush," Zenga hissed. "You're not supposed to name your planet, remember. Some aliens can hear for miles, not that the name of your planet will mean anything to them. That's only what you call it, the rest of the Universe won't know that name. Your planet probably doesn't even have a Universal name, but don't say the E word anyway, just to be safe."

"Got it!" Holly pretended to zip her mouth.

"What are you doing?" Zenga asked.

"Zipping my lips."

"You have a zipper in there?"

"No." Sometimes Holly got tired of explaining useless things. "It's an expression, a pantomimed expression, for keeping your mouth shut."

"Oh, well make sure you do. Come on, let's get this done." Zenga had told Antor to relax and enjoy the day, but she didn't seem able to follow her own advice.

Inside the shop door, they were greeted by a woman who was disturbingly over-the-top. She was too tall and too slim and too plastic-

76

skinned. Her eyes were too big, as were her breasts. She resembled a Barbie doll crossed with an Anime character, and brought to life.

There was a brief exchange of words that Holly couldn't understand. Zenga nodded and stepped through the model, as if the model was a ghost. Holly really hoped she wasn't an alien ghost, but another hologram—one that could actually communicate.

They passed by a line of identical arched doorways and stopped at the seventh. Zenga posted Willy and his blaster outside. There was nothing in the little room except a couple of plain, paper-thin plastic chairs. Antor sat down immediately. He was still recovering his strength after the Gorka attack, and would have to miss his nap that day.

Zenga pointed to a mark on the floor and told Holly, "Take all your clothes off and stand still, right there."

"Stand there naked?" Holly said, sure she had misunderstood.

"Without clothing. Yes."

Holly was about to protest when Zenga pressed a button on the wall, isolating Holly inside a shimmering round privacy cubicle. She did as she was told, but felt silly standing stark naked on the mark. She almost screamed when strobe lights clicked on and off and shot up and down her body. It was kind of like having an x-ray while standing up, or maybe being a stripper in a club with futuristic lighting.

When the flashing stopped, Zenga shouted, "You can redress."

Antor said, "You don't have to."

Holly giggled and pulled on her borrowed clothes. Zenga's leggings and fringed top were actually really comfortable. When the privacy cubicle disappeared, she said, "What now?"

They relocated to a slightly bigger room. There still weren't any clothes, only a raised platform and half a dozen padded lounging chairs that faced it. "This is the worst shopping that I've ever done," Holly griped. "There are no clothes!"

"Sit," Zenga said. She and Antor settled with their feet up, so Holly joined them.

Each chair had a keypad on the arm. Zenga began pressing buttons. "Okay, we'll look at casual formal wear. Judges like it when you dress up, but you don't want to overdo it." After more button pressing, melodious background music started to play, similar to what you might hear in an elevator on Earth.

Holly almost fell off her chair when she saw herself walking along the platform with a graceful stride, getting closer and closer, wearing a spectacular red gown that appeared to be made of feathers. The illusion of distance was exaggerated, given the confines of the room.

"That's me!" she cried.

"A hologram of you," Antor corrected.

77

"It's still awesome. I look good! A little skinny because the food on the ship is so crappy, but good." Holly laughed at herself when she did a graceful model's spin and strutted away. "I wish I could walk like that."

Before the first illusion was out of sight, a second was approaching in a shimmering yellow gown that was very short. Holly's legs had never looked longer, at least to her eyes. The six inch heels helped. A third Holly wore mysterious iridescent blue. A fourth wore jeweled layers of leaves, like a millionaire forest nymph.

Holly changed her mind. "This is the best shopping I've ever done. Can I see me in a white dress, and a black dress?"

"No, the judges prefer colour." Zenga kept the colourful gowns coming.

"How about pants, can I see me in pants? And shorts? I want to see what my butt looks like from the back," Holly said.

"No, the judges like dresses."

"You can be really bossy, Zenga. Well, how about another short dress?"

Antor began pressing buttons on the armrest of his chair, and the next Holly Hologram to appear was wearing the shortest tightest skirt in the Universe. It was also see-through. At least she wore shimmering black tap pants underneath it, teamed with a shiny black corset. It was laced up so tight at the front, she had some impressive cleavage happening. Holly looked like a high-class hooker, and she could see way too much of her butt, and boobs.

"Stop that, Antor. Put some clothes on me. I need a trench coat over that outfit." Holly covered her eyes, then peeked through them. At least she didn't look bad, not bad at all. "Antor!" she elbowed him. He was staring, rather fixedly.

Zenga took control again.

The next Holly wore a dress with a short swingy gold skirt and a silver cape, and a chain hipster belt. It was very Earth sixties. "I like that one." Holly had liked all the dresses, but this one was more her. Even amid the alien designs, it was less traditional.

"It does suit you, but it needs more colour." Zenga turned a knob. The gold began to shimmer with red. The belt got brilliant green jewels.

"Super." Holly liked the green and red combination. She had been born on Christmas day, hence her name.

"Now, your head."

While the Holly Hologram stood posed in front of them, smiling vacuously, a turban-like hat appeared on her head. The real Holly grimaced. "No! I look like a genie with that turban on my head."

"A what?" Antor asked.

"A genie, a fictitious magical being that comes out of a lamp and grants three wishes."

The turban transformed into something that looked like a pope's hat.

"No!" Holly didn't try to explain religion and religious wardrobes. That would have taken two years.

Antor got busy with the buttons again. Holly expected her clothes to shrink, but only the hat on her head transformed into a wig of thickly braided silver and gold strands, in a sort of layered bob cut.

"Do you like it?" Antor asked.

Holly grinned. "I love it. It looks fabulous."

Zenga made it unanimous. "The wig suits the outfit. I think this is perfect for your audition." She added red platform shoes, saying, "You always want to look tall. It gives you more presence."

It was the same on Earth. The shoes were kind of clunky, but better than spiked heels. Holly tended to fall off of those. Zenga keyed more buttons and groaned. "You have expensive taste, Holly. The wig costs as much as the dress."

"But I'll repay you, if—when I win my fortune. I'm not giving Hampelle all my bizoux, that's for sure. I'll keep some for spending money, after I buy Antor's limbs back."

"Don't want to do without those." Antor leaned around Holly to see Zenga. "She does need to look good, as well as sound good, Zen, or I'll pay a price much higher than my life savings."

"I know, Antor. I hate even thinking about it." Zenga exhaled and pressed one last button. "There, it's done. Now let's get the Gehenna out of here and find some real food."

The exit door was a different one from the entrance. Zenga removed a chain from around her neck, strung with various coins that all had holes through their middles. She was carrying all the cash, it seemed.

Zenga handed about two dozen coins to a nondescript middle-aged humanoid woman. She was the first living person Holly had seen in the whole store, aside from customers. Zenga received a big silver balloon in exchange for her coins. The balloon floated as if it was filled with helium, and it was stamped with the same logo that had been on the façade of the store. It also had a dangling silver cord, which Zenga wrapped around her hand.

"Is my outfit in there?" Holly asked.

"Everything we ordered," Zenga confirmed. And it was weightless. It sure made shopping easier, if you didn't have to haul your packages around.

They walked outside, trailed by Willy. Ja'Dorp was still gloomy and overcast. "Is the sky always so dull here?" Holly asked.

"Yes, even the nearest sun never shines clearly. The atmosphere is permanently hazed." Antor looked up at the sky. "Many beings won't live on the planet, because they find it depressing."

"It is depressing."

"But they have food other than space rations." Zenga turned eagerly up the first cross-street. "We'll eat before we get you a Universal translator. The food sector is this way."

In the previous safety formation, they made their way through the press of bodies. Holly knew they were close to their destination when she could smell food. Space rations had no smell at all, which was probably a good thing given their stale taste.

She tried to enter the first eatery. Antor steered her away from the door saying, "That's not a place for us to eat."

"Why not?"

"The food would kill you. It would corrode your stomach. Compared to most species, pure humans have sensitive digestive systems. We'll eat somewhere that specializes in human food," he explained.

"Oh, okay." Every so often, Holly was forcibly reminded of how much she didn't know about the cosmos. This was one of those times.

Zenga suggested several eateries. Antor vetoed them. They finally agreed on one, after studying a hologram of food choices that were appearing and disappearing on a rotating pedestal outside the restaurant's door. The images came complete with delectable aromas. It was almost like 3-D scratch-and-sniff, without the scratching.

The eatery's sunny yellow façade was cheerful. The tunnel they passed through to enter the place was airy and fragrant, with the scents of more food. At the end of the tunnel, they descended into what appeared to be a drained swimming pool. It was crowded with tables and chairs. Half of them were occupied by tough-looking humanoids and tougher-looking aliens.

"Do they serve fish, or are we the fish?" Holly joked.

Her companions didn't understand her humour, or maybe it wasn't funny.

Holly explained about swimming pools. Zenga simply thought that swimming in artificially contained water was a flagrant waste of precious reserves. Holly didn't tell anymore jokes. She looked around at the plates of the other diners. She didn't recognize any of the food. It was to be expected, but she was still disappointed. She had been craving a simple cheeseburger and fries with a gigantic salad, and maybe a milkshake.

There were no menus, not that Holly could have read one, only a clear jar with small rings inside. Antor put one in his mouth and got a faraway expression on his face.

"Am I supposed to eat one, too?" Holly asked. "Are they appetizers?" Maybe the rings tasted better than they looked, and were a lot more filling.

Zenga laughed. "No, that's the menu. It's a ring disc, but it won't work for you. You don't have a core-text."

"That's that wire thing that Antor pulled out of his mouth, right? Should I get one of those when I get my Universal translator?"

"No, they're much more complex to install, since nano wires have to connect to all the different parts of your brain. It has to be installed by a licensed specialist. If you got one on Ja'Dorp, you would probably end up a drooling idiot. The translator will be fine for now. I'll tell you what the lunch specials are." She put a ring in her mouth and recited the menu.

Of course, Holly didn't recognize any of the dishes. She said, "You can order for me. I'm hungry for meat and veggies and fruits and dessert and a drink. Something with flavour that isn't water. Unless you have coffee, do you? I want all of it!"

"No coffee, whatever that is, but I can order the rest." There was a small panel set into the middle of the table. Zenga pressed buttons.

Antor said, "Willy, what do you want?" The auto-mate had joined them at the table.

"The usual," Willy said.

"The usual it is." Antor grinned as if it was a standing joke, and pressed buttons.

"What is Willy's usual?" Holly asked.

"Willy doesn't have a stomach. He runs on an organic power cell. I guess his usual would be a recharged power cell, but they won't have that here."

"Yummy. Zenga, what did you order for me?" Holly assumed the button pressing had been the food order.

"What you asked for."

"And where did the discs go?" Holly felt like a little kid, the kind that never stopped asking annoying questions.

"We eat them after we read them. They're edible, since this is a restaurant."

"Can I eat one, even though I can't read it?"

"Go ahead."

Holly put a ring in her mouth. It tasted like the dusty old candy in her grandma's candy dish. She swallowed it, because she didn't want to be rude and spit it out at the table. There were no napkins to spit into.

The meal arrived almost instantaneously, brought by a much more rudimentary auto-mate than Willy. It had the same non-human eyes, but it didn't have any arms, only a tray welded to its stomach. They had to lift their dishes off the tray themselves. The auto-mate wouldn't have gotten very good tips on Earth.

The food smelled great, even though Holly didn't know what anything was. The meat was recognizable as meat. It tasted fishy, but had the texture of liver. It came pre-cut into bite-sized cubes. The veggies were green and grassy. And there was a fruit salad, also in pre-cut squares. The fruit was much sweeter, tangier and denser than Earth's. Bread and water accompanied the meal. The bread was nearly Earth normal. There was no ketchup, but a bowl of lime green sauce for dipping. Everything was eaten with the fingers or a skewer—one pointy chop stick to stab through the cubes. Holly thoroughly enjoyed every single mouthful.

When the dessert arrived, it didn't look good. It looked like a pile of sand in a bowl. They each got one, except Willy. There were no spoons, only straws. Holly crinkled her nose and asked, "Do I suck up the … the sand?"

Antor demonstrated. As on Earth, the straw was used to suck. The sand flew easily up the straw and Antor got a euphoric look on his face.

"It can't be that good," Holly said. "It looks like beach sand." And then she tried a sip. It didn't taste like, or have the texture of, sand. It fizzed and melted on the tongue, releasing the best flavour that Holly had ever tasted in her life. She hadn't thought anything in the Universe could put chocolate to shame, but this did.

"Do you like it?" Zenga asked.

Holly nodded and sucked more of the ambrosia. She wasn't going to talk until she finished her dessert, and then she was going to order takeout, as many desserts as she could carry back to the ship. She had almost reached the bottom of her bowl when a violent cramp in her stomach had her bending double, her arms wrapped around her middle.

"Holly, what's wrong?" Antor asked.

"Don't know. I'm sick," she gasped, sweat beading on her forehead. "Where's the bathroom."

Zenga frowned. "You can't take a bath now, Holly."

"No—the facilities, the toilet!" She thrust urgently out of her chair when Zenga scanned the room. On Earth, most restrooms were at the back. Holly ran that way. Zenga followed. Down a short hall, there were two doors with indecipherable symbols.

Zenga opened the one with the spiral shape and Holly stumbled inside. It was a single facility. "You'll want to shut the door, with you on the outside," she moaned.

Wisely, Zenga did. Holly was sick, sicker than she had ever been in her whole life. It was torturous. She was sure that her stomach was corroding. Zenga knocked on the door, more than once. Holly told Zenga that she was dying, every single time.

Finally, she lay curled on the floor in a ball of pain. She must have passed out, because Zenga's urgent knocking woke her. "Holly, our

82

planetary visas are about to expire, we have to leave before they do. You have to come out. We'll give you some stomach medicine on the ship."

"I can't make it to the ship," Holly whimpered. "I'm dying."

"Willy can carry you, he's really strong. I'm opening the door," Zenga warned.

"You really don't want to do that."

Zenga opened the door anyway, and didn't comment on the offensive odors. She pulled Holly to her feet. "You can make it to Willy. He can carry you, if you really can't walk, but we have to go. This city is the last place we want to be when darkness falls, and it falls early."

Holly allowed Zenga to guide her out the door. "I think my dessert was bad, or poisoned, or I was allergic to it," she groaned, walking with support. "You and Antor didn't get sick?"

"No, we're fine. You'll feel better soon." Zenga kept a firm hand under her elbow.

Holly made it to the table. Antor was waiting, his face all worried. He stood up as soon as she reached the table, saying, "The bill has been paid. Willy, can you get the shopping?"

Willy held the balloon's cord in one hand, and his blaster in the other. The two objects didn't look like they belonged together. As always, Willy brought up the rear. They made it out of the restaurant and Holly didn't disgrace herself.

"Poor Holly." Antor rubbed her back.

She leaned against him. "I'm never eating dessert again."

"Don't think about it. We'll have you back on the ship in no time."

"I want to go back to the ship. I want my hammock." Holly was always a big baby when she was sick. She didn't handle illness as well as most people.

They were detouring between the warehouse style structures when darkness insidiously replaced the dusky gray light. Antor suggested Willy carry her. Holly tried to walk faster. There was something so creepy about Willy's living hands on metal arms that she didn't want him touching her. They were debating the issue when blaster fire sizzled through the air. It was dangerously close.

Zenga clicked the safety off her weapon. "I thought I saw Scarnivores lurking back there, I bet they've ambushed the Manni's. We're in the wrong place at the wrong time."

Antor took Willy's blaster and readied it, his jaw clenched. Holly felt like she was in the middle of an Old Western/Sci-fi movie, one that had a really bad ending.

"Holly, get down behind that wall." Antor pointed. She did, without hesitation. There was about four feet of space between the low wall and the building at her back, and she felt nicely sheltered.

She felt even more secure when Willy joined her as her personal guard, because Antor told him to. A second round of blue blaster fire was close enough to be seen. Holly quickly hauled down the big silver balloon that was floating over her head, and advertising her position. She was tying it to a rock when a chunk of wall came down almost on top of her. She lunged left. Something hit Willy and he fell right over. "Willy!" Holly screamed. She shook him. He was completely unresponsive, and she couldn't see Zenga or Antor anywhere.

Even worse, the battling aliens were coming down the road toward her. Holly wasn't going to sit like a sitting duck, waiting to get a big smoking hole blasted through her body. Crouched low, she scuttled between two buildings. She kept going into the next block, searching for somewhere safer to hide. Before she found anywhere, she turned a corner and came face-to-face with a trigger-happy bunch of Mannireplians. The green beach balls were waving around deadly black blasters.

One of them spotted Holly and aimed the business end of his weapon at her head. Her hands shot up in the air, like an actor in an Old Western. Through the rushing in her ears, she could hear a cowboy drawling, 'Reach for the sky, pardner.'

Her stomach chose that moment to spasm, as if it had been stabbed with a knife. Holly dropped to her knees, bent double. Her timing was perfect, a blaster charge whizzed over her head from behind, sizzling hot. She didn't know if she was the target, or the green beach balls. The Scarnivores were closing fast and Holly was stuck in the middle, in no alien's land.

Since the ground was safer, she stayed where she was and prayed for all she was worth, while a fireworks display of destruction arced overhead, coming from both sides. There was no sheriff in this town to stop the gunfight.

Or maybe there was. When a shrieking wail almost split her skull in two, the adversaries ran in opposite directions. Holly thought she was safe, until two of the beach balls detoured and stopped their flight right beside her. They spoke rapidly. It was obvious they were talking about her, but Holly couldn't understand a word of the guttural harsh dialect. One of the beach balls started to get bigger, like an inflating balloon. The other one extended his four small arms and bent to pick her up.

Holly screamed and squirmed. One of the hands clapped over her mouth, the rest of the arms took care of her squirming. The beach ball was stronger than it looked. It took off running, with her in its clutches.

Holly was being abducted by aliens for a second time, and these aliens *looked* like aliens. She kept fighting until the Mannireplian dodged around a building, cutting the corner a little too close. Holly's head whacked a stone wall, and the world turned off.

84

11 Antor - Lost in Space

As deafening as it was, the shrieking siren was a welcome sound. Antor clapped his hands over his ears and watched a parade of fleeing Scarnivores race by. They could move fast with their long stick legs. As soon as they were out of sight, the siren stopped. The warning had done its job. No local security-mates would be sent in to stop the scuffle, because the scuffle was over.

Antor stood up and scanned for Zenga. She stepped from behind the corner of the nearest building. "Antor, are you okay?"

"Fine. You?"

"Not a scratch. Let's check on Holly."

They went to find Holly behind the wall. Antor was thinking about how scared she must be, when he looked over the low barrier. Willy was unmoving on the ground and Holly wasn't there at all. Time seemed to stop for Antor.

Zenga crouched beside the auto-mate. "Oh no, Willy!" She turned him over. His shutter eyelids were closed, protecting his fragile organic eyes.

"Are you okay, Willy?" Antor asked, touching the dent in his metal head.

The shutters opened. "I am fine, Antor. How are you?" Willy's voice sounded normal.

"Not so good." Antor helped him up. "Do you know what happened to Holly?"

"I do not know, Antor. My memory is incomplete." Willy untied the balloon from a rock and stood, awaiting instructions.

"Where is she?" Zenga turned in a circle, scanning the area.

Antor tried to be optimistic. "She can't have gone far. Holly! Holly!" he called. There was no response.

They split up to search for her, ignoring the danger of that action. They met back at the wall, without Holly. Together, they widened their search, covering three radial blocks. There was still no sign of the girl, or any clue as to what had become of her.

At that point, Zenga said, "Maybe she traced her way back to the departure terminal. She does have her pass. She might be waiting there for us, or on the Comet Tail."

Antor liked both possibilities. "I bet you're right." And then another idea struck him. "Unless she's run away from us. We did abduct her. Do you think she's taken off?"

"No. That would be really stupid and Holly isn't stupid. She knows we're her only way home."

"Then we better go find her." They weren't that far from the terminal and Antor managed a steady pace. A different attendant at the gate gave them an earful about staying past their scheduled time, before she allowed them through, for a reasonable bribe.

"Did a human girl with blue streaked hair enter the terminal alone?" Antor asked. He didn't see Holly waiting inside.

"I just came on shift. I have no idea," the woman said, with a distinct lack of helpfulness, despite the bribe. Perhaps it had been too reasonable.

"Thanks anyway," Antor said. They searched the terminal. Holly wasn't there.

"Let's try the ship." Zenga started for the line of shuttle-taxis.

Antor shook his head. "We should call Captain Hampelle. If Holly isn't on the ship, we're just going to have to come back down and search again."

"True. A call could save us a whole lot of time." Zenga scanned the terminal. "Public communicators are over there. Willy, go ask the shuttle drivers if they saw Holly. Remember to say she has blue hair."

Willy went in one direction and they went in the other, to where a couple of grimy communicators were affixed to an even grimier wall. Zenga crinkled her nose before she popped in a coin and keyed the Comet Tail's identification code. She spoke into the wall. "Captain Hampelle? Captain Hampelle?"

There was no answer. She tried again and asked urgently if Holly was aboard.

"Still nothing," Zenga bit out. "I bet he's sleeping, and Holly was really sick. If she is aboard, she won't be hanging around the bridge. So do we go up or not?" She was leaving the choice to him.

Antor was standing indecisive when Willy came back with news. "A girl with blue streaked hair left the planet in a shuttle with five Mannireplians," he reported.

"Five Manni's?" Antor gasped.

"Who saw her?" Zenga asked at the same time.

Willy led them over to the shuttle driver who was first in line. He was a short humanoid, his eyes level with Antor's chest. His nametag read Griff.

"You saw the girl with blue hair?" Zenga asked without preamble.

The fellow tilted his smallish head to look up. "Hard to miss. I've never seen a human with blue hair before."

"Did she go with the Manni's willingly?" Antor didn't think Holly would do that.

"Willingly enough. She was unconscious." Griff cracked a smile as if he had made a joke.

Antor didn't think he was funny, not at all. He wanted to strangle the bearer of the terrible news. "Unconscious?"

"Bloody bump on the head." Griff tapped his own forehead. "Dead to the world, she was. Manni's carried her into a shuttle, took off with her." He pointed up to the night sky, as if they couldn't have figured that part out for themselves.

"Do you know the name of their ship?"

"How would I know that?" Griff asked. He leaned against his vehicle. "There was a real rush around that time, lots of beings leaving the planet because of the blaster fight. Lots of Manni's, lots of Scarnivores, lots of humans. I thought there was going to be another battle right here." Griff clicked his tongue in regret. "Happens every other day lately. I'm risking my skin to work here."

"What about the shuttle driver? Do you know who it was?"

Griff closed one eye and squinted, thinking. "No, sorry. I didn't notice, so I probably didn't know the driver."

Antor gazed up at the vast black sky and felt defeated. There was simply too much space in Outer Space.

Zenga took his hand and squeezed it reassuringly. "We'll find her, Antor. We'll call the port authority from the ship, and get the names of all the Mannireplian ships that were here this afternoon." Zenga turned to Griff. "Can you take us to the Comet Tail? Quickly?"

"You got it." Griff had them there in twenty minutes. Zenga tipped him extravagantly with Antor's money, and they rushed to the bridge. Captain Hampelle was soundly asleep in his chair.

"He's useless," Zenga fumed. "We would be better off without him."

"And a lot less likely to get jettisoned," Antor added.

They didn't bother to wake the Captain. He would have been a hindrance more than a help. They worked around his hairy body, checking for messages from Holly or the Mannireplians. There were none. Nor was the port authority willing to help. Apparently all such information was classified, except to the UGS.

That gave Antor an idea. "Let's call Zandee. She can find out which ship took Holly, and I bet she'll be willing to tell us."

Zenga bit her lip. "I hate to involve the UGS, but I guess we have no choice. And we better do it before Hampelle wakes up. He might not like the idea. Stop pacing, Antor. Sit down and rest."

Antor kept pacing. Zenga tried to contact Zandee. She had to go through channels and leave a message. It was frustrating. The disappearing minutes were too precious to squander. At least Zandee was quick to call back.

Her stern voice was immediately recognizable, filling up the bridge. "Comet Tail, I got your message. You've lost your very important passenger? You say she's been taken by Manni's off of Ja'Dorp, sometime this afternoon?"

"That's right." Zenga glanced sideways. The Captain was stirring.

"What were you thinking, taking such a special humanoid down to that hole?" Zandee demanded, her opinion crystal clear.

"She needed a costume for her audition," Zenga said lamely.

Critical silence filled the channel.

Hampelle sat up, rubbed his eyes and said, "What's going on?"

Zenga shushed him with a raised hand and asked Zandee, "Did you get a list of the Mannireplian ships that left in the last hour or so?"

"I did."

"How many?" Antor interjected.

"Six owned by Manni's. But your suspects could have been on another ship with a mixed crew," she pointed out.

"How many other ships left at that time?" Zenga asked.

"About fifteen, if you have the time right, if the ship left. You do realize it could still be parked over the planet." Zandee was just full of bad news.

Antor leaned around Zenga and asked, "How many ships are presently holding orbit?"

"Counting your own, thirty-eight."

Antor sat down heavily, doing the math in his head. Fifty-six ships, although they could probably rule out any Scarnivore owned ships. He asked Zandee how many of those there were.

"Four," she replied.

"That still leaves fifty-two ships, fifty-one not counting ours," Antor said. "Uh … I don't suppose you could contact them all? Ask if they have Holly?"

"Do you really think they would tell me if they did?" Zandee snapped, losing patience. "That would be admitting to participating in an illegal firefight on a populated planet, and there is a hefty penalty for that. No crew is going to volunteer that information."

"True. If they have her, they're not going to admit it." Antor rubbed his head. It was aching. He had lost Holly, Holly was gone. Inside, his chest felt as mauled as after the Gorka attack.

Zenga thanked the Universal Guard for all her help.

"I'll keep my ears alert for news. I'll let you know if I hear any," Zandee said and ended the call.

"You lost the girl? You lost my fortune?" Captain Hampelle bellowed, as soon as the channel was closed.

"We lost Holly," Zenga said, tragic eyes on Antor. She didn't mention that he was in danger of losing a whole lot more than money. They both knew it. "But we're going to find her. We'll keep trying."

"You have two days! If you haven't found her by then, you're both fired, and by fired, I mean jettisoned." Hampelle's clenched fists banged buttons brutishly. The old ship was too worn to withstand such harsh treatment, and one button embedded itself within the consol. "Might as well get out of here while you track her down. We've still got some deliveries to make." Hampelle kicked the console, trying to free the button. It did pop up, but only because he split the whole panel casing. Antor absently noticed some fresh drilling in the panel, and a row of shiny new buttons that hadn't been there before he left for Ja'Dorp.

At any other time, he would have asked questions. As it was, Antor was simply glad it wasn't his face being pounded by Hampelle's fists. He didn't care what mischief Hampelle had been up to while they were gone. He only cared about finding Holly.

12 Holly - The Universal Language

Holly opened her eyes to half-mast. For a lovely hazy moment, she thought she was in her own bed on Earth. Her pounding head and burning guts reminded her that she wasn't even on the Comet Tail anymore. She had been abducted from her abductors. Her body was so stiff, it felt like she had been asleep for a very long while.

She peeked through cracked eyelids and discovered she was alone. The room was deluxe, compared to her previous accommodations. It was double the size, with smooth lime green walls and lots of leafy plants in sconces. They made the air smell forest fresh. Holly was cozily installed in a round nest-like bed, under soft green blankets. An archway even hinted at an ensuite bathroom.

With a groan, she rose and limped across a carpet of grass to investigate. The bathroom wasn't as human-friendly as the Comet Tail's, but it was still perfectly usable. There was even water. It was only a trickle that dribbled out of a miniature nozzle, when Holly pressed a button, but it was water. She rinsed as best she could, especially her mouth. The water tasted kind of funky, so she didn't risk swallowing it.

There was no mirror, and Holly was thankful for that. If her bloodied, filthy clothes were anything to go by, she was not looking her best. Far from it.

She was settled back in the nest of a bed when the door disappeared into thin air. One of the green beach balls scurried in on four thick short legs.

"Hello," Holly said carefully, hoping for a *hello* back. There was no return greeting, so no Universal translator.

The Mannireplian had close-set yellow eyes, a bulbous nose, and a wide lipless mouth. There was no visible neck on the round body. In a lot of ways, it looked like a puppet. The four bendy arms and four legs added up to eight appendages. The clothing was a sort of draped toga, green again. Holly honestly couldn't tell if the being was male or female. It began talking fast and loud, and harshly. The noise hurt Holly's head. Of course, she didn't understand a word.

"Could you talk a little quieter?" she asked, covering her ears.

The Mannireplian stopped blabbering, sniffed wetly, and turned to leave.

"Wait. Can I come with you? Can I see the rest of the ship? Does anyone onboard have a Universal translator?" Holly stumbled up and tried to follow her captor. The door reappeared between them. Holly slammed into hard metal.

"Ouch. Thanks, thanks a lot!" She stomped in a frustrated circle, then rapped on the metal. It sounded as solid as it felt, even though it could disappear like a hologram.

Frustrated, Holly kicked at the door. When it disappeared without warning, she ended up kicking a different Mannireplian. This one was significantly bigger, and she guessed it might be a male. She fell back. "Sorry, so sorry. I didn't see you there. Do you have a Universal translator?"

What was surely a reprimand for the kicking assaulted Holly's ears, but it wasn't in any language she could understand. After the scolding, Holly was motioned to follow the alien. She went willingly, hoping to find someone who could understand her words.

Everything about the ship was bigger than the Comet Tail. The corridors were wider and taller, no doubt to accommodate the bigger bodied Mannireplians, who were a million times more alienish than Antor and Zenga. Holly was still a bit dazed and decided the Western theme had run its course. She now felt like the star of a sci-fi movie, as she followed the green blobby body down the corridor. She ended up in a small, bare room, with one hovering stretcher. She was pointed to lie down.

Another big Mannireplian approached with a floating tray of implements and Holly knew she was about to be tortured, probably probed. She screamed as long and loud as any worthy actress in a cheesy movie. Both Mannireplians backed off and looked at her like she was nuts. Neither made any move to pick up the scary tools, or do anything aggressive at all. They simply talked to each other rather quietly, so maybe it was their version of whispering. It was pretty obvious that they were discussing about her.

"Aren't you going to torture me now?" Holly asked, when they gazed at her impassively, giving nothing away.

There was no verbal answer, but the second green blob touched his forehead significantly and pointed to Holly's head. She felt in the same place. There was a wound, it felt like there were already stitches in it. "Oh, you want to check my head? You're a doctor?" she guessed, feeling foolish and distinctly embarrassed about all the screaming.

He stepped closer and she decided to cooperate. She lay back on the stretcher. The Manni did some pretty normal medical stuff, like cleaning and nodding his approval at her healing condition, before he stepped back and raised his arms. It looked like a motion for her to stand.

"All done? Well, thanks, thanks a lot. Sorry about the noise." Holly rose, bowed respectfully, and followed the first green blob. He didn't take her back to her room. He escorted her to a crowded cafeteria-style galley. It was full of the green blobs. She was the only non-green blob in sight, and felt a bit conspicuous, although no-one did more than glance at her with disinterest. From what Antor had said, humanoids were a dime a dozen in the vast Universe. Maybe the Mannis didn't want to look at her, because they thought she was hideous with her pale skin.

Her guide prodded her to move it along, up to the front of the room where a long table was lined with big bowls. The largest held squirming snaky worms. They were swimming in red sauce, and it wasn't ketchup. The other bowls held better food, like salady green leaves, and some big red berries.

Holly was leery of space food after her last experience, yet starved enough to taste. She picked up one leaf and the Mannireplian slapped her hand. "What? Isn't this food?" she asked.

He pointed to tongs and a stack of clean empty bowls.

Holly blushed. "Sorry, forgot my manners. I've gotten used to eating with my hands on the Comet Tail." She served herself a few leaves with the tongs and a slice of what she hoped was alien bread. It looked like bread, except for the moldy green colour and the blackish spots that resembled raisins. She added one of the red berries. Her escort didn't take any food. He wasn't eating, at least not with her.

"Can I eat here?" Holly pointed to an empty table. It would be more interesting than eating alone in her room. And the Mannireplians were being so nice. They had provided medical care and a buffet lunch, not to mention the comfy room. Aside from the abduction, she felt like a guest.

Her guide gestured to the same table, and Holly assumed she could stay. She sat down awkwardly in a chair that was much too big and round for her body. She kept sliding down and back into its bowl shape, too far away to eat her food. She ended up sitting cross-legged with her bowl in her lap.

While she nibbled cautiously, testing the fare, she chatted to her companion as if they were friends, as if he could understand her. She christened him Mars, even though he didn't come from that planet or even her galaxy.

The salady greens went down a lot better than her last meal, so Holly tried the bread. It was actually really good, with a salty seaweedy flavour and a dense texture. The black chunks were meaty and chewy. When she nibbled on the red berry, Mars made a hand motion that she didn't understand.

She looked at him blankly. "What?"

He got up and served himself a couple of berries. As soon as he sat down again, he picked one up and broke it in half with his fingers. Inside, a thick yellow larva squirmed around. Mars slurped it up and discarded the berry. He looked at her and smiled encouragingly.

Holly's stomach clenched. Any desire for second helpings vanished. She put her plate on the table and pushed it away, trying not to think about the black chunks in the bread. She really did not want to know what she had just eaten.

She sipped from a glass of flavoured water, rinsing her mouth and teeth as best she could, and trying not to feel nauseous. Over a second glass of the sweetish, green-tinged minty water, she mulled over her situation. It was better than dwelling on what was digesting in her stomach.

She was safe, that was obvious. Based on how she was being treated, it was entirely possible that she had been taken from Ja'Dorp for her own safety. Maybe the Mannireplians hadn't wanted to abandon her on the dangerous dark planet, and she had appeared to be injured and alone. But Antor wasn't safe. If Holly missed her audition chance, he would pay a most dreadful price.

Holly had to find a way to get to Nightrous. If she could have communicated with her new hosts, she would have begged them to take her to Nightrous, but she couldn't—at least not in a traditional way. But perhaps in an untraditional way?

Holly toyed with her glass and pondered how best to proceed. Zenga had told her not to sing or mention Universe Idol under any circumstances, but surely she hadn't meant *these* circumstances. If the Mannireplians heard her sing, Holly knew there was a risk that they might enslave her on their ship to sing to them forever, but hadn't Zenga and Antor mentioned that in the last auditions, a Scarnivore had beaten a Mannireplian finalist? A Scarnivore who was not nearly as good a singer as Holly? If that was the case, the Mannireplians would want the Scarnivore to lose, since they were kind of at war with the skinny sticks. If the beach balls believed Holly could beat the Scarnivore contestant, maybe they would zip her across space to Nightrous.

It was a long shot, yet it was the only shot she had.

Holly had no idea how long she had been asleep, but she didn't think she had any time to waste. "No time like the present," she said to Mars and stood up. Mars thought they were leaving and rose to clear their dishes. Holly pointed him back into his seat. He plunked down, holding the bowls. She clapped her hands to draw the attention of all the eating Manni's. They glanced up curiously. Holly waved and announced, "I need to go to the Universe Idol tryouts, so I'm going to sing you a song and hope you figure that out."

Deciding that she might as well perform with flare, Holly used the chair as a step to get to the tabletop. Mars looked outraged. Before he could haul her off the table, Holly burst into a lively song that had a Western flavour. She thought the Manni's might appreciate that type of toe-tapping ballad, since they had so many extra toes to tap.

The beach balls stopped looking mad and started clapping their many hands in a rhythmic beat. Holly finished that song and segued into one of her own, about broken hearts.

Mars tossed the bowls aside and ran from the room. Holly kept singing and no-one stopped her. When Mars returned, he wasn't alone. A swelled-up green beach ball came, too. Holly was belting out a rock and roll classic, at that point. She was even strumming an air guitar.

The swelled Mannireplian watched from the doorway. He had authority scribbled all over him. Holly guessed he was the ship's Captain. She slid into one last tune—the beautiful Celtic angel music that she had sung to Antor to keep him from dying. She felt like she was trying to save his life all over again and put her whole heart into the performance. She held the final note, as long and pure as ever before, and then there was silence. Holly bowed and waited for some sort of reaction.

The Captain, if that's who he was, shouted at Mars. Mars shouted back and pointed directly at Holly. The Captain pointed at Holly. Mars approached and said something to her. She wished to understand his words, but wishing didn't do a darn thing. She said, "I need to go to Nightrous, to the Universe Idol auditions."

Mars answered with his own song. It sounded like he was trying to copy the first Western ballad that Holly had performed. He was an awful singer, he couldn't carry a tune to save his life.

"Do you want me to sing that one again?" she guessed. He stopped singing, thank goodness. Holly repeated the Western ditty, adding a second similar tune for good measure. And then she waited again.

The Captain said something to Mars and left. Holly jumped off the table and went after him. Mars came along, staying on her heels. She followed the Captain to a bridge that was bigger, cleaner, and more modern than the Comet Tail's. The Captain's chair had no stuffing popping out. None of the chairs did. All the seats were occupied by green bodies, eight in total, focused attentively on their duties. None of them were slumped in sleep. And they wore uniforms! Identical green togas with a black symbol over the chest.

The Mannireplian Captain barked an order and his crew got busy with their many arms. The ship banked sharply and picked up speed.

"Does this mean we're going to Nightrous?" Holly asked, filled with hope.

Mars stepped up and tried to sing again. Holly really hoped that meant *yes*. She patted his sloping, green, non-existent shoulder and said, "I hope you don't think we're doing this as a duet, because I really need to win."

She was fairly certain she was on her way to Nightrous. She was almost sure that she had managed to bridge the communication gap. And from the extreme pitch of the ship's engines, they would be lucky to arrive in time.

"I need some sort of costume," Holly told Mars, plucking at her bloodstained and filthy top. The blood must have come from her head.

He looked her up and down and his face squinched inward like a foam puppet's. He motioned for her to follow and took her to someone's cabin, it might have been his. He pointed at a line of hanging clothes, all togas in various hues of green. Some had green spots and some had green stripes, but everything was some shade of green.

Holly selected a plain one and dropped it over her head. A half dozen of her could have had a party inside the slime green toga. "No mirrors?" she asked Mars. He didn't have a clue what she wanted, and she didn't know how to pantomime mirror. "Maybe it's for the best. What do you think?" She twirled once and looked at him questioningly.

He yanked the toga off over her head and hung it back up on the hook.

"That's what I thought, too. Luckily it's my voice that counts, right?" She was ready to return to her cabin. She pointed to the door. Mars understood. He escorted her and made sure she found it.

It had been an exhausting morning. Holly checked her watch. It was barely noon, Earth time, yet she felt the need for a nap. "Probably the bump on the head," she mumbled and fell asleep.

Mars woke her and he had brought another costume choice. It looked like someone on the ship knew to sew. A toga had been tailored smaller, a lot smaller. It was an awful puke green, but it wasn't a tent anymore. Mars offered a belt and everything. The belt was nice, made of some sort of spotty fur. Holly tried the outfit on over her clothes and Mars adjusted the belt. It wrapped around her middle four times, creating a sort of belt-corset. Mars tightened it further. She thought that meant the outfit would suit.

"What about my head?" Holly held up some of her hair. "Should I wear a hat? I had a nice wig, but it's probably with Antor and Zenga, unless it got sizzled in the blaster battle. I hope Antor and Zenga are okay, and Willy." Holly sighed, missing her new friends, and that's how she thought of them now. Antor was certainly more than a friend. He had saved her life at great cost to his own health and future.

Mars touched her hair with surprisingly delicate fingers and frowned. The Mannireplian aliens didn't have any hair to speak of.

"I know my hair is probably a mess. It hasn't been washed in ages." Holly tried to pat it down and discovered something very disturbing. The hair on the crown of her head felt crunchy. She yanked out a shortened strand. It was burnt black and frizzled. The memory of blaster fire almost decapitating her, surfaced. She had been within an inch of dying, it seemed—and her hair had paid the price.

Holly groaned and walked her fingers around on her head, exploring how extensive the damage was. The fried hair began to fall out, leaving her with a bald streak, like a reverse Mohawk. "Damn, damn, damn! My voice better be good, or I'm going to get laughed off the stage—or off the planet!"

Mars could tell she was upset. He backed out the door, and Holly was glad to be alone. She hung the toga on a hook and felt her hair again. She was still groping her head when Mars returned. He'd been fashion consulting again. He was carrying a hat of sorts. It looked rather like a really ugly green helmet. It was rectangular, too tall, and the equivalent of a bunch of green grapes sat on the flat top.

"Where did you get that?" Holly asked in dismay.

The hat was held out to her, proudly.

"Uh, no thanks. As awful as it is, I'd rather stick with my hair."

Mars placed it on her head. It was so big, it slid down over her eyes. She yanked it off before she was trapped. "See, it doesn't fit. Maybe it will fit you." Mannireplian heads were rather pointy on top and wide at the bottom, compared to human heads. Holly put the hat on Mars and it sat there securely, looking ridiculous.

Holly smiled and said, "Suits you more than me. I'll stick with my hair. Or maybe Zenga is right and I should just shave the rest off, except I don't have a razor or scissors." She mimed snipping scissors with her fingers. Mars simply stared at her blankly.

"That's okay. Don't worry about it." She flopped down on her bed. Mars pointed at the toga, and then at the door.

"Oh, are we there?" Holly gasped. "Are we at Nightrous already?"

He motioned more urgently at the toga, and the door.

"Right, got it. Give me one minute." Holly held up one finger and hurried into the bathroom. She rinsed her mouth, face and hair, as best she could with the rationed water, before she shed her ruined clothes and donned the tunic. She wrapped her middle in too much belt and, feeling like a wreck, followed Mars along a different passage.

All the Mannireplians that they passed smiled at Holly and spoke the same guttural word to her. "Shazormpith!" She decided that it meant good-luck, or they were telling her to shave her armpits. She still didn't have a razor.

They ended up at an exit hatch. A pair of Mannireplians was waiting. Both were bigger than Mars and tougher looking. These two almost had shoulders, and they definitely had blasters. Maybe Mars wasn't a male after all.

Mars gestured through the hatch into a shuttle-taxi. Holly had been hoping that he would accompany her. That didn't happen. He stood firm and saluted over his head in a sort of farewell gesture.

"I guess this is goodbye, then. Well, thanks for all your help." Holly returned the salute and stepped into the shuttle with her two new companions. She thought they were bodyguards. She liked that idea. It made her feel important and she saluted at them. They didn't salute back.

In the shuttle, Holly perched on the edge of the seat, trying to control an attack of nerves. In her very wildest dreams, she had never imagined herself singing for a Universe filled with aliens. Her wildest dreams had shown her winning the Canadian contest—the minor league compared to being the star of Universe Idol.

The ride was long. Holly kept checking her watch, since she couldn't pester her escorts with questions like, 'How much longer?' or 'When will we get there?'

When she didn't think she could sit still for another second without exploding, the shuttle scraped land and coasted to a stop.

Holly cheered. Her bodyguards looked at her coolly. One of them said something to the other. The pair chuckled together in a grunty, snorty kind of way. Holly didn't have to be Einstein to know that they were laughing at her, but it was no matter. She was on Nightrous, or so she hoped.

She stepped out of the dark shuttle into a herd of similar vehicles. The parking lot seemed to be sitting in the middle of a prize-winning garden.

The sunlight on this world was tinged with red. The sun looked much closer than it did on Earth, yet felt no hotter. The ocean in the distance was glowing red-purple under a similarly hued sky, and the breeze smelled like no air Holly had ever breathed. It carried the scent of sweet water and flowers, tinged with something else that she couldn't even begin to describe. It made her salivate. The fragrance was so delicious, Holly wished it could be worn like perfume.

The bodyguards crowded her like bookends and set off, as if they knew exactly where to go. At the end of the parking lot, a path bisected the flowers, which up close looked less like flowers and more like crumpled balls of well-used wrapping paper.

The path led to a wider track. It actually moved, as if the ground was crawling. More humans and aliens were lining this route. The path crawled right into a tunnel, taking everyone along. The tunnel sealed itself at both ends and there was a whooshing sound. Holly suspected that the compartment was racing along, yet there was no real sense of movement.

There was nothing to hold onto. It was like everyone was standing in a stationary room. The lack of seats hinted that the ride would be short.

"Bit like an alien subway," Holly murmured. Before she could inquire if any of the other passengers had Universal translators, both ends of the tunnel opened.

Holly stepped out into a crowd, except it wasn't a crowd. It was a wide column of beings engaged in singing practice, and it was so long, it disappeared into the distance.

It could only be the line for Universe Idol. Holly had made it to Nightrous!

13 Antor - Against All Odds

A ntor sighed and slammed his hand down on the communication button, ending yet another futile cross-galaxy call. He had been contacting ships for two days, and there was still no trace of Holly. Not one single clue.

"Still at it?" Zenga asked, walking onto the bridge.

He shook his head hopelessly. "I'm done. No more ships to call. Poor Holly is probably dead or enslaved. We'll never find her. I'll never see her again and she'll never go home."

Zenga dropped into the adjacent chair. "We might still find her, Antor, but it will be too late for you. The auditions are over. They're broadcasting the results now. I guess you don't want to watch them?"

The last thing that Antor wanted to see or hear was Universe Idol. He would never be able to watch the program again. "How did it all go so wrong so fast?" he murmured.

"I believe it started with Captain Hampelle's vile Gorka. I didn't help by insisting we visit Ja'Dorp. I'm so sorry, Antor." Zenga touched his arm. She looked like she was going to cry.

"It's not your fault, Zen. It's Hampelle's. And I want to talk to you about something before the Castorians turn up to collect, when Holly doesn't make it into the finals. I'm not going to be able to work anymore and I don't want you to feel responsible for me. You know I'll manage, I always do." He projected a firm tone and avoided thinking about the horror he was soon to face—the horror he would soon become.

Zenga, being Zenga, opened her mouth to argue. She was distracted when an icon flashed that a call was coming in. Antor made no move to answer it. He was too disheartened to talk to anyone. Zenga pressed the button and said, "You've reached the Comet Tail, A-1 All Planetary Shipper."

The voice that filled the bridge was unexpected. "Zandee here. To whom am I speaking?"

"It's Zenga. Do you have news?"

"Are you watching Universe Idol?" the guard chief asked.

"No. That's the last thing we want to see. Why?"

"Turn it on. Zandee out." The call ended just like that.

"What's she about?" Zenga activated the viewing screen and switched on the entertainment broadcast. Antor rose to leave quickly. Zenga's shriek stopped him. Zenga never shrieked. He glanced at the screen and froze. Ten audition finalists were lined up on the glittery stage. Nine were beautifully turned out in colourful costumes and elaborate hairstyles. One was not. One was a disaster, draped in an ill-fitting green toga and strangled by a furry snake of a belt. A smile took over Antor's face. It was so big that it hurt, yet he couldn't stop smiling.

"She made it to Nightrous!" Zenga cheered and grabbed Antor to almost squeeze the life out of him. "And she's made the audition finals! You're saved, Antor. Oh, quiet! I want to hear this," she said, even though she was the one making all the noise.

Antor's joy was too deeply profound to release. He wanted to hold it inside and keep it forever. Holly was safe, and she was on Nightrous! He sank into a chair to watch the show.

The camera cut to Chrome Boreal's big white smile. "We're down to the top ten finalists from our auditions on Nightrous. One of these lucky ten will move on to the next and final round of Universe Idol. Let's meet them, shall we!"

Chrome Boreal introduced them one by one and shared a few words. Antor barely noticed the other contestants. When the host reached Holly and the camera zoomed in on her alone, Zenga winced. "Celeste, she's a catastrophe."

She was, with her bruised face and stitched forehead and … "Is her hair burnt off? On top?" Antor asked.

"Looks that way. She should have just shaved it all."

Chrome Boreal's smile faltered. "Here we have Holly Noel Tate, from the planet Ghaway in the Misshapen Galaxy. Holly is a full humanoid, we don't see many of those in the finals. In fact, we've rarely had a humanoid make it this far. And Holly's sponsors are Mannireplian. Curiouser and curiouser! So, Holly, if you don't mind me saying, it looks like you had a rough time getting to Nightrous for these auditions."

An amplifying Universal translator floated under her nose and waited for a comment. Holly was not shy to speak and snatched the device out of the air to move it closer. "Yes, I had an awful time getting here. I was almost blasted." She touched the top of her head with a rueful grin.

Zenga hissed through her teeth. "Close call."

"That's when I lost my hair and my audition clothes, so I've had to make do. I hope the judges will forgive my present attire. If I am lucky enough to make it to the next round, I promise I will clean up my act."

"I'm sure you will." Chrome Boreal tried to reclaim his amplifier. Holly jerked it away. There were chuckles all round. The camera cut to the four judges sitting in their elaborate throne chairs. There was a Castorian, a

Scarnivore, a Schwill and a Humanoid. Three were looking generally benevolent, the Scarnivore was not.

Holly kept talking. "And I would like to say a special hello to my friends in Outer Space. I'm going to make you proud. You know where to find me."

She released the host's amplifier and it floated over to him with an offended air. He closed the show and it was over. Commercials filled the viewing screen.

Antor snapped the screen off. He knew the program's formula. He had been a fan of Universe Idol since it first aired on the most popular broadcast network. This preliminary show was a build up to tomorrow night, when the ten singers would perform. Only one would win a place in the final round, to compete against the winners from the nine other galaxies.

"I'm going to alter course for Nightrous. There's a wormhole off our portside," Zenga said, already plotting the fastest route. She didn't even mention consulting Captain Hampelle. "And I'll try to get a message to Holly, that we'll be there as quick as we can."

"Can we make it in two days? Before she's moved to the main competition?" There was no doubt in Antor's mind that Holly would be the winner.

Zenga pursed her lips. "I don't know. Even at top speeds, it will be close."

"Top speeds usually make the power coils spiral too hot and stall," Antor added.

"True, but we can try. I can't believe Holly made it to Nightrous. She's pretty resourceful for a primitive."

"I think our concept of primitive needs some revising, or Earth is completely misrepresented in the Universal Data-stream." Antor was trying not to beam like a sun. Holly was safe, and she was singing her way to fame and fortune on Nightrous. He couldn't wait to see her again—in person.

14 Holly - Sabotage

Normally, Holly loved to be the center of attention. She had never had stage fright in her life, but she seemed to be suffering from it before the big show.

The audition process had been a hectic whirlwind that hadn't allowed her to think. She had sung for lesser groups of judges, moving her way up through the ranks until she reached the very top. And now she had to strut her stuff before an audience of zillions, competing against the nine other galactic finalists in this semi-round of Universe Idol.

As one of the top ten contestants, Holly had been given her own room. The first thing she had done was wash up properly with water, in a combination shower/steam bath, complete with sponge-tongue. It had felt so good to be squeaky clean after two weeks without a shower. Never in her life had she been as grimy as when she had landed on Nightrous.

Her temporary home was located on one of the top floors, in what would have been comparable to a five-star high-rise hotel on Earth. Holly had a spectacular view of a world filled with colourful crumply flowers and a red-purple ocean under a red tinged sky. The smaller surrounding buildings were laid out in decorative spiral patterns. The weather was perfectly temperate, and the delicious smelling breeze was a treat.

Holly's Mannireplian bodyguards were never far away. One of them produced a shiny blue mini-dress. It had a lot of frills, and green polka dots. Holly wouldn't have chosen the outfit herself. Still, it was a huge improvement over the puke green toga.

Hours before the show, she was picked up from her room by a Universe Idol assistant. The girl's name was Olliz. She was a humanoid, not much older than Holly, and she had a Universal translator. It allowed them to converse with ease. As she escorted Holly to be primped along with the other contestants, one of the first questions Holly asked her was, "Where can I get one of those translators?"

"I'm surprised you didn't have one inserted for the competition," Olliz said.

"I was going to, that's when I got blasted."

"Bad luck." Olliz took a ring disc off her baby finger and pressed it onto her tooth. She had about twenty discs on her various fingers. "Okay, you can get one here, but there's no time today. Your schedule is already full."

"Tomorrow?"

Olliz nodded and spat the disc into her palm. "If you're moving on to the next round, we'll make sure you get one. You will need it." The girl leaned close and whispered, "I think you'll be moving on."

"Thanks, thanks so much." Holly appreciated the support. She was missing Antor and Zenga, and her bodyguards weren't very good company, although they were protective, always sticking close. Sometimes too close.

Olliz didn't seem to appreciate the big green lugs breathing down her neck. She asked, "Why do the Mannireplians follow you everywhere?" They were scurrying along behind the girls.

"I assume they're guarding me, but I haven't been able to ask them. Maybe you could."

Olliz did, sounding very harsh. There was some back and forth dialogue and Olliz turned back to Holly. "They're protecting you while you're on Nightrous. They are confident that you will win here and move on to beat the Scarnivore contestant, Ahah, who is one of the present favourites. Since the Manni's are your sponsors, they're worried that the Scarnivores might try to harm you here, where the security is lax compared to Playara."

"Playara?"

"That's where the final competition takes place. Once you get there, you'll be inside a secure facility."

"Oh. Do contestants get harmed?" Holly asked.

"Sometimes," Olliz said candidly. "But if you make it to Playara, there is very little chance that you'll be assassinated."

"Assassinated?" Holly had already been on the wrong end of a weapon twice since she had left Earth. She did not want it to happen a third time.

Olliz smiled reassuringly. "There is no need for concern. On Playara, we have our own highly trained security team for the top ten finalists. A small army, really." She slowed and pointed left. "Turn here."

Holly entered the room where contestants were to be beautified. Her guards waited outside when Olliz growled something at them.

Five differently shaped chairs were lined up in front of a reflective wall, in a brightly lit room. The wall wasn't a mirror exactly, it looked truly three dimensional, as if Holly was wearing 3-D glasses. It was a shock to see how bad she looked in the brilliant light. Her shower might have cleaned her, but it hadn't undone any damage. Half her forehead was discoloured, and she was missing a whole strip of her hair. If she had passed herself on an Earth street, she would have thought she was a crazy homeless girl.

At least the room was empty. "Do they take us one at a time?" Holly asked.

"No, your beautician thinks you might need more attention than the rest of the contestants, so you're here a bit early."

Holly grimaced at her reflection. "No kidding. I think I might need a miracle, not more time and attention."

Olliz tapped the first chair, the one that fit human bodies. Holly sat down.

"Oh, and this is for you." Olliz handed over a ring disc from her baby finger. "Messages from all over the Universe wishing you luck. All the humanoid races are very excited that we have a human who might make the finals. You have a lot of support. It will be fantastic for the show's ratings."

It was nice to know, yet added to the pressure that Holly was already feeling. She studied the ring disc and said, "I can't read it, I don't have one of those core-text mouth thingies." From Olliz's reaction, Holly might have said that she didn't have a brain.

"But ... everyone has a core-text, absolutely everyone. How could you not have one?"

"Uh, I lost it," Holly joked, sticking the disc on her baby finger like a real ring, as Olliz did. It was a perfect fit, because it stretched like an elastic, even though it was clearly made of hard metal. Rubbery metal didn't exist on Earth, and Holly could imagine all kinds of uses for such a material.

Olliz didn't seem to realize Holly was kidding and said, "How is it possible to lose a core-text? It's part of you. If you've merely lost the wire attachment, I'll get you a replacement."

"Okay," Holly said, wanting to appear space normal. Before Olliz could respond, the beautician arrived.

A tall humanoid, he was dressed in stark black with skin as pale as snow. His long fingers were moving like restless spiders as he walked toward Holly. Olliz relayed Holly's language code before she left.

He sighed heavily and introduced himself. "I am Vorm. So, we begin with the challenge, Holly Noel Tate."

"Yes, we do. Can you make me look beautiful? That's what you do, right?"

"Such faith! You are beautiful, sweet little thing. It is simply the damaged packaging that needs my magical touch."

Long white fingers combed through Holly's ruined top hair. There was some *tsk-tsking* from Vorm. "Blaster fire you said?"

"Yes."

"At least the burned off portion runs almost symmetrically from front to back. Yes, I can work with this." He massaged a cream into her scalp, saying, "This will stimulate and speed up the new hair growth." Maybe there were miracles to be found in Outer Space.

"Now I must ask you about this blue. It does not look natural, nor have I ever seen a humanoid with blue hair." He fingered the blue strands and even sniffed them.

"It's not natural. I coloured my hair."

Vorm pursed full lips. "I am intrigued. Painting the hair? How original, how creative." He began to smile. "I think that you and I are about to start a new galactic fashion. Oh, I see fame and fortune for me! Painting the hair? Why have I never thought of this before?"

Vorm got busy, washing and trimming and styling, humming all the while. Holly watched in the 3-D mirror, fascinated by how her hair was being transformed. When he was finished, her hair looked spectacular—in a bizarre kind of way. Vorm had placed a small hollow cone on the top of her head, over the worst of her bald streak. He had spiraled all her remaining hair up and around the cone, hiding the exposed scalp completely, inside the twirling strands. It made her hair as tall as an old-school beehive, but not nearly as tall as Marge Simpson's blue hair. The spiraling blue and blonde emphasized her streaks. To complete the coif, he inserted blue feathers into the top of the hidden cone, as if her hair was a vase. The blue feathers matched both Holly's hair and dress.

When the last feather was placed just right, Vorm stood back and waved his hands like an Earth magician, saying something that sounded a lot like, "Ta-da!"

Holly clapped her hands. "Fantastic, Vorm. That is a very cool hairstyle."

"Cool? Your head is cold?" He wasn't sure about that.

"No, my hairstyle is wonderful. I love it," Holly stressed.

He relaxed. "Of course you do. Now for the face."

Before he could commence, a second finalist walked in. Holly had seen the alien on the stage, but they hadn't been introduced. The being had hard red skin and a segmented body. An exoskeleton. Stunted antennae jutted up from the bristling short hair on the flattish head. There was something very ant-like about the being, at least to Holly, who waved and said, "Hi."

Her friendly overture was ignored, and Holly didn't think it had anything to do with Universal translators. The new arrival sat in the most distant chair from Holly. "Do you style her or him next?" Holly whispered to Vorm, when he leaned closer to examine her skin. He even licked it.

"Lovely complexion, very soft, delicate. And no, each contestant has a beautician from their own race." Vorm was gently pinching her skin when another red-skinned ant person walked in. The being stopped behind Holly's chair and squeaked at her reflected image. Vorm's offended demeanor made it clear that Holly, or his attempt to pretty her up, was being insulted. He scowled and squeaked something back. The hostility in the air was palpable. Holly thought they might come to blows, until the ant person moved on, to get to work on his or her client.

With a disdainful sniff, Vorm moved to Holly's other side, so his back was presented to the pair. He leaned in again to rub her skin with a fresh smelling cleanser, and Holly whispered, "Vorm, what race are they? And are they male or female?"

"Gubbs." A resentful gaze was cast over his shoulder. "Gubbs are neither male nor female, they are both."

"Androgynous?" Holly guessed.

"Perhaps. Tilt your head back, close your eyes." Vorm smoothed something unpleasantly sticky on Holly's freshened skin. "How do you not know Gubbs? I thought you were from the Misshapen Galaxy? The Gubbs live right next-galaxy to you."

"Don't ask," Holly gasped, trying not to breathe. The fumes wafting from the sticky stuff were very strong. She fanned her face with her hands. It didn't help.

"Ah, a mystery." Vorm was silent for a minute, then he tapped Holly's cheek. The sticky stuff had hardened almost instantly. "I just consulted my language data base. Did you know that your dialect's home world is listed as unknown?"

Holly played dumb. "Is it?"

Vorm started cracking the layer off her face, as if he was peeling a hardboiled egg. "I've never seen a dialect from an unlisted world before. It is highly irregular."

Holly's exposed skin stung painfully where the air touched it.

Vorm inhaled sharply and cried, "Sit up and keep your eyes closed." The last of the peel came off in one big chunk. A wet cloth began scrubbing Holly's skin. It really hurt.

She jerked away. "Ouch."

"Don't move." Vorm spritzed her face with moisture and dabbed more gently. It still hurt. He repeated the spritzing and dabbing.

Holly squirmed. "Vorm, what are you doing? Can I open my eyes now?"

"No!" he shouted.

There was squeaky laughter from the Gubb corner. Holly couldn't resist a peek at her three dimensional reflection. She screamed bloody murder. Vorm burst into tears. Holly stopped screaming when her Mannireplian bodyguards raced into the room, blasters primed and glowing. As soon as they saw her face, they wailed and clapped their extra hands over their respective mouths.

Holly wanted to do the same, but she was afraid to touch the green field of pustules that her skin had become. One of the Manni's pointed his blaster at Vorm.

"Don't do that," Holly shrieked, even though they couldn't understand her. It was lucky for Vorm that Olliz turned up to take control of the situation. After a startled glance at Holly, she cleared the room of Mannireplians with the skill of a diplomat.

Vorm collapsed into a chair, still sobbing. Holly looked at Olliz helplessly, she looked anywhere but at her awful reflection. "What happened to my face?" she wailed. "Vorm, what did you do?"

Olliz thrust a handy towelette into his hand. "Vorm, stop crying and explain."

He mopped up and gained precarious control. "It is obvious that someone has tampered with my products. The peel, give me the peel." He pointed to the container in question.

Olliz handed it over. He applied a dot of the stuff to his hand. It dried in seconds. He peeled it off and one big green pustule was revealed.

"It is proved!" he declared. "Someone has sabotaged my products, someone who wants Holly Noel Tate to lose this competition." He sniffed the goop delicately. "I think maragoesy acid-root has been added. It grows in abundance on Scarnivia."

Olliz shushed him. "Don't say that. We'll have a full scale war between the Manni's and the Scarnivores. We can't have the competition disrupted. We'll have to say that Holly had an allergic reaction to something."

"And how is that supposed to help me?" Holly couldn't stand to look at her monstrous visage. No-one would want to watch her sing, yet she had to sing, for Antor.

Another contestant walked in at that moment. Holly knew it was a Schwill, because Antor had pointed one out on Ja'Dorp, and one of the judges was a Schwill. Antor had explained that the Schwill was a half-humanoid species that had evolved by mating with a winged race in the long distant past.

They didn't look very human. Their eyes were too big and their ears were almost nonexistent. Their noses were small and flat, over a fairly standard human mouth. Their skin, while the same basic hue as Holly's, was iridescent, as were the fine wings that draped down their backs, when they weren't in use. The wings weren't feathered. It looked like the beings were permanently attached to a small hang-glider. The species had no hair, only a thin dark exoskeleton where hair would normally grow.

This Schwill faltered in step when she caught a glimpse of Holly. It looked like she was going to run. "Tell her it's okay to come in, tell her I'm not contagious, and you might want to add that I'm not a monster, because that's exactly what I look like. You might even have to tell her I'm human. I certainly don't look human, not one little bit." Holly was babbling, she was verging on hysterical.

"I can understand you," the Schwill said. A hint of a smile indicated that she found Holly's rant amusing.

"Oh, well then you'll know I'm not a monster, but a human. You have a Universal translator?"

"I had it inserted for the competition." She stepped closer, as though fascinated. She was really very pretty, in a nonhuman way, and friendlier than the Gubbs. "What happened?" she asked.

"Product sabotage." Even speaking hurt Holly's face.

"Oh, that's not fair. I'm sorry, not for me, but for you," the girl said frankly, yet not meanly. "I'm Teef, by the way. When I heard you sing, I almost hopped the next ship home."

"I didn't hear you sing. I'm sure you're very good, Teef." Holly thought she liked the girl, if first impressions could be trusted.

The Schwill beautician came in and motioned the girl far away from Holly. Teef went where she was told. There was no more conversation.

"Vorm, is there anything that can make this go away?" Holly asked.

He shook his head. "Only time. It isn't permanent, or overly long-lasting, thank Celeste, but it will require a period of healing."

"So what can we do for tonight?"

"Nothing. I have failed you. I have ruined your chance to win Universe Idol." Vorm's eyes welled up with tears again.

"Stop that, Vorm! Crying won't help, and I have to compete. My voice still works, now what can we do about my face?"

The tears receded like a tide. "You will still perform? You will go on stage looking like ... that?"

"Yes. Now what can we do about my face? Olliz, any ideas?"

The Gubb beautician said something to Olliz, who snapped something back.

"What did the Gubb say?" Holly asked, not really expecting any assistance from that quarter.

"It said we should cut your head off. That would only make things worse." Olliz slumped.

"It certainly wouldn't help." Holly took a deep breath and looked at herself again, long and hard. She felt sick enough to vomit. No-one would be able to focus on her voice, if they had to look at her face. "Can I wear a veil to sing? Or a mask?"

"No," Olliz said. "It's against the rules to sing with a covered face, in case someone tries to cheat and not really sing live, or have a stand-in sing for them. All of that has happened in the past, hence the rule."

"What about makeup? Vorm, do you have any really thick cover up?"

"Nothing that would hide that." He shuddered. The pustules were very lumpy. "I could tone down the green colour, but not the bumps. And the cover up won't stay on for long, given the leakage." He grimaced.

Holly nodded sadly. The lumps were already starting to weep gross watery stuff. She kept thinking. "What about a hologram? You have the hologram of me yesterday, from my audition. Couldn't we use it as a stand-in while I do the singing? Still on stage, but unlit?" She knew she was grasping at straws.

Olliz said, "Holograms are against the rules."

Holly sagged into her chair. "Does anyone have any other ideas? Ideas that would work?"

Teef nudged her beautician aside. "Face the back of the stage. That's not against the rules, is it?"

"Face backwards," Holly murmured. "Is that against the rules?"

Olliz's expression brightened. "Nothing in the rules states how you stand on stage. That might just work."

It was a simple but effective solution. Holly smiled at Teef; it made her face sting fiercely so she stopped. Teef wasn't looking at her anyway, no-one would want to do that. "Thanks Teef, that's a great idea, but you shouldn't help me. You should try to win." Holly felt a twinge of guilt over using the girl's suggestion, yet she would, for Antor.

Teef waved a hand as if a mosquito was pestering her. "The best singer is the one who should win. And cheating ruins the contest, so I will help you if I can."

No question, Holly liked Teef. She liked her a lot.

"Holly, you need to get back to your room until the actual competition. You can practice there. We don't want anyone else to see you like this." Olliz urged her to stand and handed her a towel. "Keep your face covered. I'll lead the way, come on."

"Okay. And thanks again, Teef. See you on stage." Holly went with Olliz, blind under the towel. The Mannireplians followed as closely as shadows. Holly could hear their feet padding along behind, all the way back to her room.

With nothing to do except be depressed, she sat and gazed out the window, until Olliz turned up with a humanoid man. He could have been mistaken for an accountant on Earth, if his jutting Adam's apple hadn't been bright orange.

"Since you're restricted to your room, you might as well get the Universal translator today," Olliz said.

"Thanks for thinking of it, Olliz." Holly didn't attempt a smile. Her whole face was throbbing.

"It's my job. Jorne, this is Holly."

Instead of greeting her, Jorne grimaced.

Holly sighed. "My face is pretty awful, eh?"

"Indeed. I will need you to prostate yourself," Jorne said.

"What?" Holly didn't think she wanted to do that.

"Lie on the bed, face up."

"Wait." Olliz plucked the feathers out of Holly's hairstyle and said, "Now you can lie down. Try not to mess your hair up." She settled in the chair by the window, stroking the feathers absently. Holly was glad she stayed.

Jorne opened a satchel and Holly reclined on the bed. He unpacked a metal device that resembled long narrow pincers. A ridiculously elongated needle appeared next. Both looked dangerous. He put them on the bed beside Holly and stuffed a pillow under her neck, so her head was tilted back. She was starting to think that she definitely should have asked more questions about the procedure.

"Maybe I don't need a Universal translator after all," she said.

"Of course you do." Jorne stuck the pincers in her right nostril and twisted them. The device blossomed in all directions and stretched her nostril as much as it could, without tearing. He locked it like that and lengthened his core-text wire out of his mouth. He threaded it into the needle somehow.

"I don't think I want a Universal translator anymore," Holly cried, her voice so high, it squeaked. She didn't like needles, especially not really really long ones.

"It is important that you don't move at all." Jorne wasn't taking her seriously and had the needle inside her nose before she could escape. Holly froze. The needle punctured through her sinus membrane and it hurt like hell. She could feel it poking deeper and it started to tickle. She was overwhelmed with sensations that made no sense. Jorne frowned and lengthened his core-text wire, inserting it deeper into the needle. It went so deep, it must have been probing Holly's brain. She was actually being probed by an alien, although it wasn't at all what she had expected.

Jorne began speaking. Holly didn't understand the language, and then suddenly, she did. With no forewarning, Jorne depressed the plunger end of the needle. That really stung, until he pulled the needle back out. The pincers followed. His core-text was retracted from the needle and he wiped it off with something that smelled like vinegar. The wire must have had her brain goo all over it, and brain goo probably tasted nasty.

Holly sat up carefully and cupped her nose. It was hard to see, because her eyes were watering as if she was crying. Jorne handed her a towelette. "All done. That wasn't so bad, was it?"

Tempted to tell him where he could stick his pincers, Holly wiped her eyes and nose, which was bleeding. "It's all done?"

"Yes, the chip is in your brain. Now we'll test it," he said.

She sniffed and sneezed. Maybe she was sneezing her brains out. Holly wiped more blood and Jorne said, "I wish you luck in the contest."

"Thank you. I'll need it."

"I never thought I would see the day when a humanoid would make it to the final round." His mouth moved differently, but Holly understood him perfectly.

"A lot of people have said the same thing."

He nodded sagely. "Because it is the truth. Your Universal translator is working perfectly. I have just spoken to you in three languages."

"Really?"

"Four now, and now I will be on my way. The bleeding will stop soon. You might notice a bit of brain fluid seeping out, as well. It is nothing to be alarmed about."

Holly didn't believe him, and she was alarmed. Very alarmed. "What if too much brain fluid leaks out?"

"That hardly ever happens. And the brain does have fluid to spare. I had one unfortunate client lose a quarter cup, and he was perfectly fine." Jorne gave a funny little bow and picked up his satchel.

Holly scooted to the edge of the bed, not quite ready to stand. "Well, bye, and thanks, I think."

Olliz handed Holly her feathers, as well as a coil of hair-fine wire, saying, "For your core-text."

"Oh, okay." Holly stayed where she was. They saw themselves out the door. She was glad to be left alone and blew her nose. There was a lot of blood, and another fluid that wasn't mucus. Brain brine. So far, she wasn't impressed by the so-called superior medical practices of Outer Space. It was as if they had never heard of painkillers or sedatives, or a comforting bedside manner, or not amputating perfectly healthy limbs.

Feeling sleepy, Holly decided to have a nap instead of getting up. She would need all her energy for what was sure to be a difficult and trying evening. Plus, her brain fluid was less likely to leak out if she remained horizontal.

15 Antor - The Finalists

"**Z**en, the show is about to start. Where are you?" Antor broadcast the message throughout the ship. He had the viewing screen on and all systems running smoothly.

"I'm here, I'm here." Zenga rushed onto the bridge with a little bowl of space rations. "Hampelle is going to watch it in his cabin. I don't think he likes us any more than we like him." She flung herself into the chair beside Antor's. "Did I miss anything?"

"No. Perfect timing."

The intro music began to play. Chrome Boreal's smiling face flashed across the screen in a sparkle of lights and stars, followed by a slideshow of previous winners, all smiling or crying or doing whatever their race did to express exultant joy and/or supreme victory over others. "Soon that bunch will include a real human," Zenga said.

"Our human," Antor added with satisfaction.

The intro ended with an eruption of exploding stars. After a commercial about the latest updated model of Scarnivore stanislizer, Chrome Boreal welcomed the audience with his usual enthusiasm and recapped what had come before this show. He finished with, "And tonight, the judges will decide which of these ten finalists from Nightrous will move on to the Universal Idol final!" The camera panned the line of competitors. Holly mustn't have been expecting it, because she was facing the back of the stage.

Zenga cheered and Chrome went on about how this was the most exciting year yet, and then there were more commercials.

Before the show got to the singing, Chrome Boreal introduced the judges, who were more famous than the contestants. The Scarnivore, Ruce Burny, was a snappy dresser who was known for his frank, but fair critiques. Flieda Egga, the Castorian, always wore the white robes of her race. Her words were generally encouraging to the contestants, mainly commenting on the positive aspects of their performances. She only mentioned the negative if the contestant was really awful. The Schwill was just plain quirky, some called her flaky. X-Orgon usually focused on the creative aspects of the singing. Her critiques were not always understood by the viewers, or the contestants, or the other judges. It was rumoured that she had severed all relations with her family and home world when she immersed herself in the entertainment industry. And last but not least was the humanoid, Cowbell Cumin. He was the most entertaining of the judges. He didn't sugarcoat anything. His brutally honest and cutting comments were usually right on target. He made more aspiring singers cry than all the other judges combined.

"Get to it," Antor growled impatiently, even though he knew they would drag it out as always. There were more commercials.

When Chrome Boreal returned, he introduced the first contestant to sing. It wasn't Holly, it was Beedotte Slanch. The Gubb sang well. The race was known for hitting the high notes, but Antor found their vocals too screechy for his ears or taste.

The four judges found the performance competent but uninspiring. The hard exoskeleton made Gubb emotions impossible to read, and it was hard to tell if Beedotte was disappointed.

With commercials in-between, four more singers took their turns, and then the Schwill sang. Teef Mosh performed beautifully. She had one of the best voices that Antor had ever heard, not counting the ones on Earth, and not counting Holly's, of course.

Zenga grimaced. "Teef is really good."

"She is, and she's pretty. Seems nice. I think the judges will like her."

They did. She got glowing reviews all round, even from Cowbell Cumin.

Three singers followed Teef, and they weren't nearly as good as the Schwill. And then there was only one singer left. Holly got to go last. Antor paced through the next annoying batch of commercials, too wound up to sit still. "I wish Holly could have performed first," he grumbled to Zenga.

"Relax, she'll be fine."

But Holly wasn't fine. That was obvious as soon as Chrome Boreal introduced her as Holly Noel Tate from Ghaway in the Misshapen Galaxy. Holly sidled to the center of the stage keeping her back to the audience. Her hair was spiraled high with blue feathers sticking out the top. She wore a frilly short blue dress that showed off her legs, but she didn't turn around.

Zenga groaned. "What is she doing?"

Chrome Boreal nudged the floating amplifier/translator closer to Holly while staying at arm's length. The thing seemed reluctant to go any nearer to her. Chrome vacated the stage as if he was fleeing a rampaging horde. Recorded music began to play—Holly's music. She must have been carrying her little music player when she was taken from Ja'Dorp.

She started singing a bit timidly, but she didn't turn around. Her voice gained confidence as she moved into the chorus and by the second verse, her voice had wrapped Antor in its spell. He listened with deep pleasure, while he longed to see her face.

"What is she doing?" Zenga repeated. The camera panned to the judges, who were looking baffled. Holly's behaviour was distracting them from her voice.

"Turn around, Holly," Antor breathed. She didn't. She sang the whole ballad facing away from her audience, swaying in time with the music. And when the last note faded to silence, she bowed to the back of stage and walked backwards to stand before the judges, awaiting her critique.

Cowbell Cumin cleared his throat and spoke first. "Holly Noel Tate, while your voice was spectacular, I did not enjoy the performance, because of your bizarre behaviour. If you do not face me immediately and explain yourself, I will not be casting my vote your way."

Holly spoke into the floating amplifier, which had followed her. "Do I have to?"

"If you want any chance to advance in this competition, you do."

Holly's shoulders slumped. "The audience might want to close their eyes then," she warned, before she turned around.

A gasp like a gale came from the live audience. It was echoed on the bridge of the Comet Tail. Holly looked like a monster, her face was a field of bloody lumpy yellow-green pustules.

"Ah!" Zenga cried.

Antor didn't want to look, yet he couldn't seem to look away. "Poor Holly."

"You can turn back around now," Cowbell said. Holly started to do just that. "No, no, I'm kidding. Holly, what happened to your face since we saw you yesterday?"

"I had a … a bad reaction to a skin cleanser. I didn't want my appearance to detract from my song, so I faced away, sparing everyone," she said, plucking some feathers from her hair and holding them like a fan in front of her face.

"Well, Holly, I am impressed that you would appear on this stage at all, looking as you do. That took courage," Cowbell Cumin said very sincerely. "Now, to get back to your singing, your tone is absolutely superb, as is your range. I've never heard a humanoid sing with such richness and clarity, and rhythm." He paused and X-Orgone, the Schwill, jumped in.

"Such a voice, such a voice. Celeste in the heavens would sing with such a voice. Magnificently done," she gushed.

"I wasn't finished." Cumin scowled playfully at X-Orgone.

"You sounded finished to me. And I think we've run out of time."

Chrome Boreal was making urgent hand motions. "Ruce, Fleida, anything to add?" he prompted.

The Castorian said, "A voice to enthrall anyone in the Universe with ears."

Ruce Burny, the Scarnivore, was less complimentary. "For a humanoid, it was not a disappointing vocal performance."

Zenga gasped indignantly. "There's something wrong with his ears, that's for sure."

"He's biased because the Manni's are listed as Holly's sponsors," Antor said absently, watching as the camera showed the contestants one last time. All of them were giving Holly a wide berth, except the Schwill.

Chrome Boreal ended the show by reminding everyone to watch the results broadcast, same time tomorrow. Before more annoying commercials aired, Antor clicked off the viewing screen.

Zenga said, "That didn't look like a skin allergy to me. It was too extreme for that. It looked more like a skin poisoning." She nibbled her fingernail thoughtfully. "I bet the Scarnivores are already trying to ruin Holly's chances."

"She went on stage anyway," Antor said. Had she done it for him? The possibility made him feel warm inside. "Do you think her face did spoil her chances, Zen?" he asked, in need of some reassurance.

"I really don't think so. You heard Cowbell, he was impressed. How could they not vote Holly on?"

"The Schwill was really good, and there is a Schwill judge. The Scarnivore isn't going to vote for Holly." Antor was trying to be realistic. "The contest isn't only about singing. The politics come into it, don't they?"

"I suppose." Zenga checked the ship's systems again.

"Still, it could have been worse." Antor was trying to feel positive, and not think about losing his limbs, or worry about Holly being harmed by something more lethal than skin poisoning.

"It definitely could have been worse." Zenga tried to cheer him up by saying, "We're making good speed. We might be there in time for the results show tomorrow. And Holly will have entry passes waiting for us, if someone passed our messages on to her personally, as I asked. She should be expecting us."

The thought of seeing Holly the next day made Antor's heart feel bigger inside his chest than it normally did. It didn't matter to him that her face resembled the bumpy, cratered terrain of Ghaway's nearest moon. She was still Holly—his Holly. Missing her rather badly, he went to his cabin to get her scarf.

115

16 Holly - Teef

For obvious reasons, Holly spent the day before the results show in her room. Olliz visited and Holly requested some sort of veil to wear for that evening's program. "That's allowed isn't it? Since I'm not singing?" she checked.

"Yes, and a good idea. We don't want to make our audience sick." Olliz left immediately to find one.

"No tact, no sense of humour, no painkillers, and aliens call me primitive," Holly muttered and dropped back onto her bed, moping. Her greatest moment as a singer had been spoiled entirely. Well, she was going to watch her own back from now on. She was going to keep both eyes on those Scarnivores. They weren't going to hoodwink her again.

Olliz returned with a purple veil that Holly adjusted to fit the lower half of her face, under her eyes. With her bangs pulled down over her forehead, hardly any of the pustules showed. Olliz nodded her approval and ran. Her job kept her super busy.

In the late afternoon, Teef dropped by. An older female Schwill accompanied her to the door, but didn't come inside. Holly was happy to see Teef, and glad she was wearing her new veil. Her face felt disgustingly scabby. At least the sores were drying up quickly, which meant they were healing.

"Hi, Holly. How are you feeling?" Teef perched on the edge of a chair. Her wings seemed to get in the way.

"Fine, I guess. You? Are you nervous about tonight?" Holly knew she was.

"Not really. I've sung my song. The results have been decided. Nerves will serve no purpose." Teef had a placidity about her that Holly found soothing.

"I wish I felt the same way." Alas, there was too much at stake in Holly's case. "Your singing was fantastic, Teef. I thought you were the best contestant, and the prettiest. I was really impressed. I would sing a duet with you anytime, not that I've ever really sung a duet, but it might be fun to try one." As always, when Holly was nervous, she rambled. Even with both feet stuck in her mouth, she could still go on and on and on.

Since she couldn't talk about her own planet or life as an Earth teenager, Holly asked Teef questions. "What's your home world like, Teef? Is it far from here? And can you really fly?"

Teef tilted her head as though puzzled, and Holly realized that she should probably know the answers to all those questions. "I talk when I'm nervous," she said, trying to explain her lapse. "I say anything, even nonsense. You can talk now if you want."

Teef giggled and did start talking about her life. She was betrothed to be married, even though she wasn't any older than Holly. She said Nastos Roth came from an upper caste family, who didn't fully approve of Teef's lower caste roots. They had signed the betrothal bond regardless. Teef said they had even initiated the match, and she wasn't sure why. Her parents were thrilled to be moving up in Schwill society, which pleased Teef.

Holly frowned. "Do you even know this guy?"

"I have met him twice now. He is very presentable." Teef didn't seem at all bothered by the arrangement, so Holly kept her mouth shut. She had no right to judge a culture she knew nothing about. And Earthlings, who, for the most part picked their own mates, had a ridiculously high divorce rate, so that system couldn't be called a success.

Holly kept asking questions and learned a lot of fascinating information about Teef's culture, species and home planet. Teef left before dinner, saying she would see Holly on stage. The same older Schwill was waiting in the corridor for Teef, as if she had never left. Holly had forgotten to ask Teef who she was, and Teef hadn't mentioned the woman at all.

Dinner was delivered to her room by an auto-mate. Holly picked at her food, her stomach so knotted, she could barely eat. And then it was time to prepare for the results show.

Holly wore the same blue dress as the previous night, because she had nothing else. Normally, she wouldn't be caught dead in the same dress two nights in a row, especially on TV, but she really didn't have a choice. The puke green toga wasn't an option, nor was going on stage stark naked, although Holly had spotted a few beings walking around in public without a stitch on, so maybe clothes were optional in Outer Space.

Her face didn't hurt nearly as much as the previous day, so she smiled, imagining the Universe as a giant nudist colony. Her thoughts shifted to Antor, as they were prone to do, not because she was thinking about nakedness. She wondered where he was now. Surely he had seen the show and knew she had made it into the finals. She really hoped that he and Zenga were zooming across the Universe to Nightrous, or already sitting in the audience, unless the awful Captain Hampelle had jettisoned them for losing Holly.

It was a terrifying possibility and made her heart cramp. There was no denying that she missed her new alien friends more than she missed her boyfriend, Daniel. The longer and farther she traveled from Earth, the more his memory faded. Holly was beginning to suspect, and admit to herself, that she didn't really love him after all. Absence was supposed to make the heart grow fonder, as the saying went, and her heart hadn't grown fonder, except for Antor.

Olliz came to get Holly personally and escorted her backstage. They were followed by Holly's green blobby shadows. Teef was already there, appearing as calm as earlier. Holly felt anything but. There was a brief wait before the ten contestants paraded onto the stage together.

Since she wasn't facing backwards or distracted by her face, Holly had a proper look at the audience. She hadn't processed quite how big it was the previous night. There were tens of thousands of spectators out there in a sea of seats, or maybe hundreds of thousands. Trying to spot Antor's carroty-brown hair was impossible. And Holly could only see the first hundred or so rows clearly. The rest were a blur.

The audience started clapping and the show was underway. Chrome Boreal did his thing. He was a good host, lively and enthusiastic, with an innate sense of timing. He introduced the ten contestants again, and each stepped forward and bowed or waved or did something. Teef opened her wings. The applause for her was strong.

Holly was simply glad she was wearing a veil, and when Chrome called her name, she stepped forward and waved with both hands. She got as much applause as Teef, maybe more. None of the other contestants received the same level of enthusiasm. Chrome said he liked her veil.

Gigantic screens replayed highlights from the previous night's performances, before Chrome got down to business. Eliminating contestants was done in reverse order. The singer with the lowest judges' rating was sent off first. Holly was pleased it was the snotty Gubb. One by one, singers left the stage, until there were only two left—Holly and Teef.

Chrome Boreal announced yet another commercial break. Holly wanted to grab the floating amplifier and whack him over the head with it. The suspense was killing her, almost literally. She thought she was going to have a heart attack right there on the stage, at eighteen, and create yet another spectacle of herself.

Teef squeezed her hand, saying, "Not long now." She didn't release Holly's hand. The contact helped to steady Holly's nerves. She took a deep breath and exhaled some of the tension out of her chest.

Chrome resumed orating. It was the moment of truth. "And now, we will find out the name of tonight's winner, our last lucky finalist!" With a showy gesture, Chrome raised a little gold ring and placed it in his mouth. There wasn't a peep of sound from the audience.

When the suspense had built to breaking point, Chrome flashed his smile and said, "Well, this is an unexpected turn of events. Teef Mosh ... you will be moving on to the next stage of the competition."

There was a stunned silence from the audience. Teef looked more surprised than anyone. Holly closed her eyes in pain. She had failed Antor. Tears burned behind her lids and she had to bite her lip hard to keep from breaking down in front of the whole Universe. She was barely listening when Chrome began talking again. She only paid attention when she heard her name. "Holly Noel Tate ..." She opened her eyes. Chrome smiled brilliantly. "You will also be moving on to the final round of the Universe Idol competition."

"Huh? Me?" she said stupidly. She didn't understand. There was only supposed to be one finalist from Nightrous.

Cowbell Cumin took over. "Teef and Holly, you will both be moving on. We were unable to eliminate either of you based on your impressive performances. And our audience wants to see more of both of you, and so they shall. This is their show."

An explosion of applause almost brought the roof down. Holly beamed and cried, all at the same time. She hugged Teef and Teef hugged her. They were both moving on. It was the best possible result.

Before the show ended, Chrome made a brief and somber announcement. The finalist from the Freeform Nebula had been arrested and sent to Gehenna for murdering the finalist from the Orglop Star System, so the competition had been down two finalists. The judges had chosen the runner-up from the Orglop Star System to fill the murdered winner's spot. The Freeform Nebula's contestant would not be replaced, given the crime of murder. Holly couldn't help but think that was the real reason that both she and Teef had been promoted.

The slate of the ten top finalists was read one more time. Holly was proud and thrilled to hear her name included in that number. The bright lights turned off and the show was over. It had only lasted an hour, yet it had felt much, much longer.

After the hubbub died down, and before Holly and Teef left the stage platform, Olliz rushed up with instructions. As finalists, they were told that they would be leaving the next day for the Pac System where Universe Idol was filmed. A ship would be provided to transport them to their new location.

They could expect to be there for one month, if they weren't eliminated. "And I think you two will make it all the way," Olliz said. Holly wondered if she said that to all the finalists. And she wondered how she could get in touch with Antor and Zenga.

"Will you travel with us?" Holly asked. She had gotten used to depending on Olliz.

"No, I'll meet you there. I have to wrap things up on Nightrous, while you need a couple of days to practice with the other contestants, to prepare for the first show."

Before Olliz rushed off, Holly said, "I've kind of lost touch with the friends that were bringing me here originally. Is there any way I can call their ship, the Comet Tail?"

Olliz looked at her oddly. "Of course. You can contact them from your room, or is your long-range communicator malfunctioning?"

Holly guessed this was basic information that she should know. "Uh, no, the communicator is working fine. I'll do that, contact them from my room, of course. Thanks, Olliz."

She strode away with Teef, closely followed by the Manni's. They kept congratulating Holly, now that they could communicate with her. Teef was just as closely tailed by the older Schwill woman, although they did not speak one word to each other.

Both girls were in a mood to celebrate and Holly invited Teef into her room to do just that. Before she agreed, Teef glanced at her shadow. The woman nodded as if in permission. Teef came inside.

"Who is she?" Holly asked, as soon as the door closed.

"My chaperone, provided by the Roth family, to ensure my loyalty and fidelity to my intended," Teef said, as if it was no big deal.

"Oh." Holly kept her thoughts about the archaic practice to herself. She was preoccupied anyway, she wanted to talk to Antor and Zenga without delay. She scanned her room and spotted what was probably the communicator attached to the wall. "I'm just going to try and call my friends," she said, approaching the panel. She pressed the top left button, hoping that would turn the thing on. Instead, all the lights in the room went off. "Oops, sorry." Barely able to see the panel, she pressed what she hoped was the same button, to restore the lighting. Instead, the room filled with wind.

Before she could press more buttons, Teef reached over her shoulder. The button she pressed made the wind stop and the lights brighten. She turned to study Holly, tapping the panel. "This is basic, standard technology. Why don't you know how to use it?"

Holly shrugged. She didn't have a ready answer.

Teef said, "Are your shoulders itchy?"

"No. Why?"

"You twitched them."

"That means 'I don't know'."

Teef tilted her head, puzzled. "You don't know how to use basic technology? Or you don't know why you don't know how to use basic technology?" Their conversation was getting confusing.

"I just want to call my friends. I guess I pressed the wrong buttons."

"That's not even the communicator," Teef pointed out.

"Oh. What's the wind for?" Holly was too curious not to ask.

"It cleans the room—vacuums, dusts and refreshes the air, all in under a minute."

"Efficient. And where is the communicator? I don't see it."

Teef pointed at what strongly resembled a flat-screen TV hanging on the wall, except that it was paper-thin.

"Isn't that the television? Or the viewing screen?" Holly had assumed it was.

"It is the viewing screen, and the screen to watch entertainment broadcasts, and the communicator. Do you want me to call your friends on the Comet Tail for you?" Teef offered, without asking more of the questions reflected in her eyes.

"Please, yes, and thanks." Holly watched carefully while Teef pressed buttons on a little handheld device that looked a lot like a remote. With no forewarning, Antor's face filled the viewing screen.

"Holly!" He smiled brilliantly, looking like a hot young Earth actor on the broadcast screen. And he could see her, too. She was glad she was still wearing her veil.

Zenga appeared beside him. "Holly! Congratulations!"

"You're both unharmed? You didn't get blasted or jettisoned?" Holly asked straight off, even though she could see that they were safe with her own eyes.

"We're fine, we're both fine. We watched the show! We had some bad moments, but you made it to the finals! That's fantastic." Zenga cheered.

"I did, so did Teef. She's here, she helped me make this call." Holly pulled Teef closer, in case they couldn't see her and thought Holly was alone. She didn't want her friends to reveal something they shouldn't.

Greetings were exchanged. As soon as she could get a word in, Holly asked, "Where are you?"

"The Comet Tail has almost reached Nightrous," Zenga said. "We thought we would make it in time for the show, but we had a little breakdown. Antor has managed to get the coils spiraling at speed again, so we'll be there soon. Did you get our message?" Antor just kept smiling, as if he was as happy to see Holly, as she was to see him.

"Uh, no. What message?" Then Holly remembered the little ring. It was still around her baby finger. "Oh, I was given a ring of messages, but I couldn't read it, could I? No mouth thingamajiggy and no-one relayed the actual messages."

Teef shot her another disbelieving glance.

Zenga said, "We'll arrive in about an hour. Can you arrange a landing pass so we can come and see you in person?"

121

"Sure. How do I do that?"

Teef said, "I'll arrange it." She told them Holly's room number and floor level and wing name. Holly had no clue where she was, other than on Nightrous.

"See you in an hour," Holly said and blew them a kiss before they signed off.

Antor's jaw dropped and Zenga's eyes got almost as big as Teef's, which were the size of an anime cartoon character's. Zenga gasped, "Holly! What the Gehenna?"

"What?" Holly asked, clueless.

"Don't you know what that means?"

"Uh, no. I guess not. I thought I was blowing you a kiss, you know …" She repeated the innocent gesture.

Antor covered his eyes, Teef turned red. Zenga said, "Stop doing that. Never do that again."

"But … what does it mean?" Holly said, glad she hadn't done it on stage.

Not one of the three would tell her. Teef pressed buttons and the viewing screen went blank. Holly missed seeing her friends' faces. She couldn't wait for them to arrive. Teef used the same viewing screen/communicator to arrange the two passes for Antor and Zenga.

While the girls waited for them, they chatted about the show. After they had rehashed everything, Teef said rather shyly, "You and Antor certainly seem to have moon eyes for each other."

"Do we?" Holly hadn't realized it was so obvious.

Teef nodded. "I thought the screen was going to melt. He is very handsome, for a humanoid."

"He is, isn't he? Problem is, I have a boyfriend back home. I'll be going home again and Antor will keep traveling with All Planetary Shipping, so there really can't be a future between us." And then there was the little matter of coming from different galaxies. As far as star-crossed lovers went, Romeo and Juliet had nothing on them.

Teef's eyes lit with laughter. "Forget the future, enjoy the now. You have the freedom to do that, and the future is so nebulous, it may never unfold as you foresee it. Life is merely a series of uncontrollable accidents. You have to embrace the happy moments when you are offered them, since they can be few and far between."

It was the last thing Holly expected to hear from the Schwill, who had let her parents choose her future husband, and had a chaperone following her around. "What about you, Teef?"

"I am content with my arrangement, so I have no desire to look elsewhere. I do hope to find happiness with Nastos."

"That's good, I guess." Holly didn't know what else to say. She was having a hard time wrapping her head around that aspect of Teef's life.

"If I am not eliminated from the competition, Nastos will come to be with me for the finale, and you can meet him for yourself." Teef smiled serenely. "I will get to know him better here, since I can spend more time with him."

Before Holly could stick her foot in her mouth, Antor and Zenga arrived. There was some confusion at the door, with the Manni guards trying to pat down the new arrivals for weapons, and Holly trying to hug both Zenga and Antor—Zenga first and Antor second, so she could hold him a little longer. He didn't seem to mind and didn't let go until a Mannireplian guard groped his butt.

Teef introduced herself in living person, then said, "I should go. I'm sure you three have a lot to talk about."

"No, stay," Holly protested. "We have to celebrate our win."

"As you wish." Teef stayed long enough to share the snacks that Zenga ordered, the second she stepped into the room. The girl was petite for a human, yet seemed to eat more than anyone Holly had ever met.

Teef barely spoke a word now that she wasn't alone with Holly, and didn't linger long.

"She's quiet, but sweet," Zenga said, as soon as the door closed after Teef.

"She is great, and she's been a big help. It was her idea for me to sing backwards after my skin was sabotaged." Holly felt her veil to make sure it was still in place. "Hopefully my face will be back to normal by the time the real competition starts."

"How did it happen?" Zenga asked.

Holly explained, and then brought them up to date on her adventures, since they had lost each other on Ja'Dorp. Zenga burst into laughter when Holly described singing and dancing on a table in a room filled with Manni's, to convince them to take her to Nightrous.

Holly's still tender nose reminded her to say, "I had a Universal translator inserted, so now I understand everyone perfectly. How come neither of you mentioned how much it hurts to have a hole poked through your nasal passage and into your brain?"

"Pain is always worse if you're expecting it," Zenga said, "so it's best not to expect it." There was some truth in that. On Earth, Holly preferred to forget she had a dentist appointment, until the day of.

"Sorry about that," Antor said, as if it was his fault.

"It's okay, Antor. I survived and only a little bit of my brains leaked out."

"That shouldn't happen," he said worriedly. "Maybe you should see a physician."

"I'm joking! And to tell you the truth, I'm not at all impressed with Outer Space doctors." Holly changed the subject, and asked about all that had happened to them, in the days they had been apart.

Zenga went on to describe how they had searched for her, and how Zandee had called, telling them to watch Universe Idol. By the time they ran out of words, the night was half over.

The room was plenty big so they had a sleepover. Both Zenga and Antor enjoyed a proper cleansing. The planet Nightrous had a surplus of water, and the shower/steam bath was one of the perks offered by the luxury hotel complex.

It had been a long and exhausting day. Holly fell asleep while Antor was still in the bathroom getting steam-cleaned. When she woke up, he was on one side of her, and Zenga was on the other. She had assumed he would use the couch, but he hadn't. He had cuddled up to Holly. She smiled, feeling all warm and fuzzy (or maybe it was hot and tingly) to be horizontal with Antor.

She studied his tranquil face in the rosy morning light. His long lashes fanned his cheeks. His mouth curved as if he was smiling just a little bit, or having a lovely dream. Maybe alien humans were superior sleepers compared to Earth humans, because he didn't snore or drool or do anything disgusting. He looked quite angelic in repose.

Before she gave into temptation and woke him with her lips, she slipped quietly off the foot of the bed. She had another steamy shower, just in case the next spaceship rationed every molecule of water like the Comet Tail. The heat stung her face and when she looked in the little 3-D mirror, her skin didn't look improved, not one bit. In fact, it looked like she had an extreme case of chicken pox, with the pox being at the scabby stage. Her skin was healing, but maybe it had to look worse before it looked better.

She checked her head and the cream that Vorm had applied was indeed making her hair grow much faster than normal. It was already about an inch long. Holly smiled and bunched her damp hair together on the top of her head. She tied it there with a blue elastic ribbon left over from Vorm's hairstyle. With the ponytail jutting straight up and the purple veil back in place, she looked like a genie, and not a pretty genie. It was the best she could do, until more of her hair grew back and her skin cleared.

Antor and Zenga were awake when she finally vacated the facilities. Someone, probably Zenga, had ordered a huge breakfast. Holly sat down and helped herself to more unfamiliar foods. Zenga grinned and said, "All this is paid for by Universe Idol, now that you're one of the ten finalists. Did you know?"

Holly raised her glass of juice in toast and said, "Fill your boots."

"Why would we want to put food in our boots?"

"It's an expression, it means 'eat a lot' or 'stuff your stomach'." Holly popped an orange grapey thing into her mouth. It tasted deliciously like candied fruit. "You should take a doggie bag with you, so you can have proper food on the Comet Tail, instead of space rations."

"A doggie bag?"

After Holly explained what that was, Antor said, "Good idea. Holly, what happens now, as far as the competition? Have you been told?"

"Briefly. A spaceship will take me to the Pac System, where the finals are held on a planet called Playara. If I last through the competition, I'll be there for a month, all expenses paid. I'll have a hotel room and be expected to make promotional appearances, and practice, practice, practice. It's supposed to be a very hectic month, if I'm not voted off the show."

"Of course you won't be voted off. You're going to win, Holly," Zenga said, with a confidence that Holly could only dream about.

"Will you be able to go with me? If it can be arranged? All the other contestants seem to have at least one friend or family member accompanying them. But I suppose Captain Hampelle won't give you that much time off, will he?" Holly ate another grapey thing.

"I think he'll want us to stay close, and keep you safe. He's drooling for you to win him a fortune," Antor said.

"A fortune to take me home," Holly murmured, definitely not ready to go home yet.

Zenga said, "As long as the Comet Tail can keep up, and doesn't breakdown completely, we'll follow your ship and meet you there. We don't have any more cargo to deliver, since the bulk of it was ruined by the Gorka and Hampelle hasn't picked up any more big shipments."

"Speaking of Gorka, are you sure the cold killed them on Earth? They had as much fur as a fur coat. They looked like northern animals, except for being purple." Niggling doubts had been camping in Holly's brain and wouldn't leave.

"It killed them," Zenga said, frowning.

Antor nodded, eyes evasive. He hunched a bit. He was probably recalling his own near-fatal encounter with the vicious monsters.

Zenga cleared her throat and said, "Holly, find out if you can list Antor and I as your companions, then we'll be able to stay with you in the Universe Idol complex. That's so much better than on the Comet Tail with Hampelle. It will be like a vacation, and we can help to protect you."

"Okay, I'll ask Teef if I can do that. She seems well informed about everything, so she'll probably know." As if Holly had wished her there, Teef arrived. She was welcomed in. Her chaperone waited outside, while she joined them for breakfast. There was still a lot of food left.

She confirmed that Holly could register two companions to stay with her. "I only have one, a chaperon provided by my betrothed's family," she told Zenga and Antor. It must have been a common practice in Outer Space, because they didn't even blink. As soon as Teef had finished nibbling, she rose, saying, "I have to pack. My shuttle taxi is departing at eleven o'clock."

"I don't know when mine is coming, I haven't been told," Holly said, wondering if she'd been forgotten.

Teef pointed across the room. "You have one message on the communicator. Do you want me to check it?"

"Yes please, and thank you."

Holly followed her, to learn how to retrieve messages. Teef simply touched a little flashing button in the corner of the viewing panel and a mechanical voice said, "Shuttle pickup for Holly Noel Tate, planetary eleven o'clock, passenger gate VX. Destination, the Solar Wind bound for Playara. Verify." Teef pressed a button to verify. Hearing messages couldn't have been easier.

Teef smiled. "We will share the same shuttle, and the same ship, of course."

"That's great. Thanks, Teef, for checking. I wouldn't want to miss my ride." Holly walked her to the door and hugged her, really happy aliens liked to hug.

Teef left with her unsmiling chaperon. Holly was glad to see the woman's back. She was inclined to glare at Holly when she thought Holly wasn't looking. Zenga left soon after Teef, carrying a doggie bag full of food. She said she had a bit of shopping to do, and that she would meet Antor in the main lobby.

And then Holly was alone with Antor in the privacy of her room. He cleared his throat nervously and said, "I guess I'll see you in the Pac System."

Given a choice, Holly would have traveled on the Comet Tail, but she couldn't. She was now under contract to Universe Idol and had to ride on their ship. "Yes, I'll see you there," Holly said, melting a bit inside when she looked into Antor's chocolate brown eyes. She was wondering if he was going to kiss her good-bye, when she remembered the veil, and her face. No-one in the Universe would want to kiss her now, and Antor certainly made no move to lift the veil and lean in for some hot lip-to-lip contact.

Instead, he pulled something out of his pocket and said, "I brought along the communication device, in case you want to call your mother again. You won't be able to call her from the Universe Idol ship."

It wasn't at all what Holly was expecting. "Thanks, Antor. That's really thoughtful."

"And maybe you want to call your mate, Daniel," he said hesitantly.

"Boyfriend," Holly stressed, more sharply that she intended.

"Boyfriend. He must be missing you. He must be really worried. I know I would be, if I was him and you were missing." Antor began pressing in the extremely long sequence of buttons.

"Don't you have redial? With your superior technology?" Holly asked.

"What's redial?"

"Just what it sounds like. The sequence of numbers is digitally stored in the phone's memory, and when you press redial, the numbers key themselves, or something like that. You only press one button instead of hundreds." Holly wasn't exactly sure how redial worked, but it did work.

"That would be a lot easier. I'll see if I can add a redial feature when I'm back on the Comet Tail." Antor kept concentrating on pressing buttons.

Holly packed up her meager belongings until Antor motioned her over. He had gotten the numbers right on the first try, and shoved the ringing phone at Holly. Her mother's sleepy voice answered on the third ring.

"Hi, Mom." Holly glanced at her still-on-earth-time watch. It was the middle of the night.

"Holly, I'm so glad you called. I've been so worried. I want you to come home—now!" Her mother sounded almost hysterical, and it took a lot to upset her. She was cooler than most moms. She even had a pierced bellybutton.

"What? Why? What's wrong, Mom?"

"Haven't you been reading the newspapers?"

"Not so much," Holly said lamely.

"Where are you?" It was a demand to know, rather than a question.

"Uh, I'm really far away, Mom. I'm … in Europe. I did really well in the singing contest, so they're paying my expenses to be in the final competition, in Europe. That's what I phoned to tell you."

There was a moment of silence, before her mother said, "I thought you were trying out for the Canadian show."

"I was going to, but I didn't make it in time because of Daniel's truck, and I heard about this other singing contest, so I tried out and won a place in the final, and now I'm in Europe. All expenses paid," Holly stressed. "This is an incredible opportunity, Mom, but I only have a couple of minutes on this phone -"

"Well, I guess you're safer there than here. There have just been so many animal attacks, and deaths. I was worried sick about you." Her voice ended in a sob.

"Animal attacks? Deaths? Mom, what are you talking about?"

Antor motioned rather desperately that she should end the call. Holly wasn't about to do that, not before she knew what was upsetting her mother so badly.

"They think it might be bears, or wolves, or wild cats. They're really not sure, but lots of people have been attacked south of here, in the park. It's unheard of for so many people to be mutilated by wild animals in such a short time period. No-one can figure out what's going on."

"Oh." Holly looked at Antor. He studied the tips of his boots. "That's awful, Mom, but I need to hang up now. I might not be able to call for some time, so please don't worry. I'll explain everything when I come home. Oh, and can you let Daniel know I phoned?"

"Holly, I hope this doesn't upset you, but you should know that Daniel is seeing Fiona."

"What?" The news caught Holly completely off guard. Fiona was her best friend. She shouldn't be dating Daniel. Holly had only been gone for a couple of weeks. It wasn't like she'd been away for years, or even months. So much for the loyalty of a best friend. She could understand Daniel dumping her, since she'd stolen and wrecked his truck, but Fiona's betrayal cut deep. They had been best friends since grade six.

"Are you okay, sweetie?"

"Yes, Mom. I'm okay, and it's okay. I'll deal." Holly glanced at Antor. He was still fascinated by his boots.

"I'm sure you will. I never really thought you and Daniel were made for each other, if you don't mind me saying so. Now, I want you to call at least once a week, and I want an address and phone number where I can reach you."

Holly ended the call abruptly, hoping her mom would think the line had gone dead all by itself. Antor took the device out of her hand and rushed for the door, saying, "I have to go."

Holly grabbed his arm. "Antor, those purple Gorka, they're attacking people aren't they? The cold didn't really kill them, did it?"

His cheeks turned a guilty red. "I don't know anything about Gorka, except what Captain Hampelle told us."

"You're lying!" Holly shouted, furious and disappointed. "You've been lying to me all along, and I thought we were … friends. People are dying on Earth because of what you let loose on my planet!"

Antor stopped hunching. He stood tall with his shoulders squared, and looked quite valiant. "I didn't let those beasts free to kill people. We tried to stop Hampelle, but we couldn't. You were there, he locked us out to freeze to death and shot at us. He released them. We couldn't stop him." Holly had never heard or seen Antor mad before, but he was mad now— mad that she was accusing him of murder.

She did remember every last detail of that night, and what he said was true in regards to how the events had unfolded, but still, he had lied to her, and people on Earth were dying. Even though she was officially unattached now and free to do so, Holly didn't want to kiss him anymore. She didn't even want to hug him. Holly opened the door, a clear hint for him to leave.

Antor paused in the threshold. "Captain Hampelle plans to pick the Gorka up on our return trip, when we take you home to your planet. He's got a tracer on them, so he can find them again."

Holly was too upset to talk to him. "Just leave, Antor."

"I'll see you in the Pac System? Next week?" he asked.

"I guess," Holly said, after a too-long pause.

He sighed, looking more hurt than angry now, like a wounded hero. He left without another word.

17 Antor - Space Pirates

Antor found Zenga waiting near the front of the lobby. She was digging into a little bag of candy. She took one look as his broody face and said, "Uh-oh. What happened?"

He shook his head. "I'll tell you when there aren't so many people around. Ready to go?"

"Yup." Zenga tucked a hand through his arm. She steered him onto a path that detoured through a flower garden saying, "I'm not ready to be cooped up again. So, you messed up with Holly?"

"She found out about the Gorka. She knows we lied to her, and that they're still alive, killing people on Earth."

Zenga plunked down on a handy stone wall. "How could she know all that?" She offered him the bag of candy. He selected a blue spotted one, before he confessed all. He even showed her the device he had rigged up, by linking the two very different technologies. If she was impressed, she didn't say so.

"Oh, Antor. That was a stupid thing to do, arranging for her to call home. You know the communication could have been overheard, or traced back to the restricted planet."

"I know. She was just so sad." Antor ducked his head and his hair blocked Zenga's reproving eyes. "Anyway, now she's really upset—with me for lying to her, and about what's happening on Earth. She'll probably never speak to me, to us, again."

"She'll have to, if she wants to get home. And I should think saving her life outweighs a lie of omission. She'll forgive you, Antor. She probably just needs time for her temper to calm. She'll have that on the other ship."

"Let's hope so, but she's really disappointed in me." Antor was used to being a disappointment. He knew he let Zenga down on a regular basis, by not standing up for himself or the things that mattered, yet being a disappointment to Holly felt worse. He longed for her to think highly of him. There was no way she could care about him, the way he cared about her, if she didn't respect him.

Antor vowed, then and there, to start standing up for himself and his beliefs. He wasn't a little orphan boy anymore, who had needed to hide and cringe to survive. It was time for him to give up those habits, to be the man that he knew was inside, although that man only showed himself when Antor least expected it, like when facing Gorka and blasters. That man was a man worthy of Holly.

Busy examining Holly's cell phone, Zenga was unaware he was soul-searching. "How does it work?" she asked. Antor demonstrated the touch-sensitive screen and showed her the photograph of him and Holly together. He looked at it a lot.

Zenga was as baffled as Antor had been, the first time he'd seen the device in action. "Antor, how is this possible? Earth isn't even capable of true space travel, yet they can invent this technology? And that tiny music player? And Holly said the Earth had successfully cloned complex organisms. It simply doesn't make sense."

"I know. It's as incongruous as cave dwellers having computers, and Earth does have computers. I don't get it either, Zen." But he had come up with a few theories. Either the technology was being imported to Earth in secret, by non-Earth humans, perhaps for profit. Or the data-stream was full of false information, to keep the planet segregated, and the Earth was not a primitive planet at all, except perhaps in lack of space travel. It was always possible that Earth's space efforts were being sabotaged by someone non-human, who wanted to keep the planet cut off from the rest of the Universe, for their own self-serving reasons.

Zenga returned the device. He stuck it in his pocket and they started walking. Captain Hampelle would be awaiting their return, and he never waited patiently.

Riding the shuttle to the Comet Tail, Antor shared his theories with Zenga. She came up with a possibility of her own. "Maybe Holly is right about the Castorians, and they keep the Earth isolated as a restricted planet, so they can harvest body parts. The planet is so overpopulated, it would never run out of parts."

"It's possible, I suppose," he said, and changed the subject. The last thing he wanted to dwell on was Castorian harvesting practices. He already had recurring nightmares about his limbs being hacked off, and him lying helpless on the ground as his limbs were carted away.

When they reached the Comet Tail, they informed Captain Hampelle that Holly was on her way to the Pac System. Hampelle agreed that the Comet Tail should follow along. He even approved their request to stay on the planet with her, to keep her safe and make sure she won the contest. Antor had his doubts that Holly would still want them as companions, but maybe Zenga was right, maybe a week would be time enough for her to forgive him for not telling her the truth.

Captain Hampelle went off to nap in his room. Antor and Zenga monitored the ships departing from Nightrous, until they located the Solar

Wind. It wasn't a big vessel, but it was sleek and sporty. It looked fast, and proved to be super-fast when it hurtled away from the planet as if it had been catapulted.

"Hang on," Antor warned Zenga, before he gave the Comet Tail full power. The little ship couldn't match the Solar Wind's speed, but she was steady enough when she wasn't laden with weighty cargo or breaking down.

They trailed at a distance, which increased with each passing hour, but Antor wasn't concerned. They knew the Solar Wind's destination.

For three days, all went well. The Comet Tail only required minor repairs to keep her coils spiraling at full power. They were within two days of the Pac System when all stopped going well. Antor was monitoring the sensors when he noticed something amiss. He called Zenga to the bridge, rather than the ship's Captain.

She turned up, drowsy and yawning. "I was having the best sleep. Why did you wake me up?"

"Look!" Antor pointed urgently at the viewing screen. It showed two purple dots closing in on a third purple dot—the Solar Wind.

Zenga's eyes flew opened. "Are the two ships attacking?"

"Well, they don't look like a welcoming party, do they? I think they must be attacking."

"I suppose it's not unexpected. The Solar Wind is carrying the two best Universe Idol finalists. I bet those two ships are Scarnivore."

"Makes sense." He watched the ships close the gap a little more. "Although the Solar Wind should be able to outrun them. It's not even trying."

Zenga dropped into the seat beside him. "We have to help. Top speeds, Antor!"

"We are traveling at our top speed," he snapped. "I'm not stupid."

"I know you're not stupid." Zenga dashed her hair off her face. "Have you tried to contact the Solar Wind?"

"You just said you know I'm not stupid," Antor reminded her.

Zenga flushed. "What did they say?"

"They're not answering."

"Really? That's odd."

"It's alarming. If we can get there in time, I don't know how much help we'll be. Our fire power is pretty limited." In truth, it was nonexistent. They would be useless in an attack, except as a target.

"Maybe a second ship will scare them off, you never know." Zenga chomped on her fingernail and stayed focused on the viewing screen. They both watched tensely as the two dots arrowed toward the Solar Wind, which seemed to be slowing, rather than speeding up to escape.

"Do you think they're having engine problems?" Zenga said.

"And communicator problems? Highly unlikely."

At least the Solar Wind's reduced speed allowed them to close the distance. Zenga tried again to contact the ship, which still didn't answer. When the Comet Tail was almost upon the Solar Wind, Antor pressed buttons and the viewing screen turned into a viewing window. They were near enough to see what was happening with their own eyes.

The Solar Wind was limping along, yet appeared to be undamaged. One black ship was docked against a side hatch, while a second glided overhead. Neither ship had an identifying mark on its hull.

"Pirates!" Zenga gasped. Space pirates were the bane of the Universe, attacking unsuspecting ships, stealing their cargo and then blowing them up, or commandeering them, depending on the ship's value. "What the Gehenna is going on? It doesn't look like the Solar Wind even tried to defend itself. And they didn't summon help." Zenga jabbed buttons and said, "Solar Wind, please respond. Have you been boarded by pirates?"

Finally, they got an answer, and it was the last voice Antor expected to hear. "Zenga, it's Holly. Where are you?" She was whispering and her voice shook.

"Right behind your ship. Where's your crew?"

Teef answered. "We think most of them are dead, and we think there must be a traitor aboard. Please help us."

"We'll try, but we're not a fighting ship," Zenga said. It was the biggest understatement in the Universe.

Antor nudged her. "I think the pirates have noticed us."

The hovering ship picked up speed. It looped around and shot toward them like an arrow. Zenga switched chairs to access their ship's blasters. She was a better shooter than Antor and began firing, before the other ship did. Antor did the only thing he could think of, he took evasive action.

The pirate ship cut left with them and fired. A hit shook the ship, but didn't penetrate the hull. Antor angled right, almost colliding with the Solar Wind. He hadn't meant to do that, yet it was effective. The pirate ship on their tail had to dodge away to avoid an impact.

When Captain Hampelle stormed onto the bridge, Zenga didn't give him a chance to shout at them. She screamed, "We're being attacked by pirates. They've taken over the Solar Wind." The black ship was on their ass, firing again. The blast just missed and sizzled past like a streak of red fire.

Hampelle took one look through the viewing window and snarled, exposing all his teeth. He looked both pleased and bloodthirsty when he said, "How fortuitous. We'll take care of the buggers, oh yes we will."

"How?" Antor steered erratically, zigzagging all over the place.

Hampelle lifted Zenga right out of her chair, and took over the ship's meager arsenal. "Antor, I need a target. We're going on the offense."

133

"We are? But -"

"Just do it," the Captain bellowed.

Antor banked the ship hard left, almost hitting the Solar Wind for a second time. He kept losing track of her position. Again, he was more lucky than skilled, the pirate ship spun away. Antor aimed the Comet Tail's nose straight at the vessel. He hoped the Captain knew what he was doing. They'd never fought together before. Shipper/transports rarely engaged in space battles, unless it was to defend themselves and their cargo.

"Keep her steady," Hampelle purred.

Antor managed to hold the ship's nose pointed straight at the pirate ship. The Captain depressed one of the newly added buttons on his consol. A sizzling green ring shot at the pirate ship, growing steadily larger as it neared the vessel, which passed through it like threading a needle. Its hull began to shake and glow, before the metal buckled inward on itself, again and again. The ship kept shrinking until it was as small as a compact shuttle.

Antor blinked and wondered if he was hallucinating. He had read about the experimental magnetic weapon that could compress a ship into a retrievable lump of valuable metal, ensuring a battle would turn out profitably for the winner, but he had never seen the technology with his own eyes. He certainly hadn't known the shoddy little Comet Tail boasted such a rare and destructive weapon. First a mating pair of Gorka, now this. Who was their new Captain?

Captain Hampelle laughed and focused on the viewing window.

"The … the second pirate ship is docked against the Solar Wind." Zenga eyed Hampelle with trepidation. "Holly is in trouble."

"Not for long," he growled. "Antor, turn us around. Aim at the ship."

Antor held position. "But they're linked. You can't destroy the pirates without destroying the Solar Wind."

Captain Hampelle reached over and smacked him on the side of the head, hard enough to rattle his brain and his teeth. "Do as I say! I'm not going to let any harm come to my fortune."

Ear ringing, Antor angled the nose of the ship at the Solar Wind, and awaited further instructions. He darted a glance at Zenga, who was standing with dropped jaw, as stunned as Antor by what had happened.

"This should take care of the pests," Captain Hampelle murmured, his hands a blur on the new array of buttons. He leaned over to Antor's console to adjust their heading by a fraction of a degree, before he pressed the same button as before. The sizzling green ring that shot out was much smaller than the previous one, and it didn't expand. It surrounded the pirate ship's side fin as if it had been tossed onto the jutting appendage like a gaming ring. The ship began to buckle inward toward the fin. In shrinking,

134

it detached from the Solar Wind, before she was downsized, too. In less than a minute, the second pirate ship was another unrecognizable metal lump. The battle was over, won single-handedly by the Comet Tail.

Zenga found her voice and communicated with the Solar Wind. "Holly? Are you still there?"

"Yes, but there are intruders roaming around the ship." She was still whispering. "There was a lot of shaking. What's happening?"

Antor wanted to deliver the good news and said, "We've destroyed both pirate ships. We'll dock against your hatch and help you get rid of any pirates that are left." He tried to sound confident and tough, even though he'd never fought pirates before. He'd never even met one.

"Do you know how many are on the ship?" Captain Hampelle asked. At least he seemed to know what he was about.

"At least four," Holly whispered.

"I think more than that, maybe five or six," Teef interjected.

"Stay hidden, we'll take care of them." Bloodthirsty grin back in place, Hampelle said, "Antor, dock against their hatch, nice and easy. Don't let them know we're coming. Zenga, Willy, let's get blasters."

"Get one for me," Antor called, wishing he had been assigned a more heroic role than driving the ship. He had to redeem himself in Holly's eyes, and saving her from space pirates seemed an ideal way to do it.

Antor concentrated on uniting the two ships as smoothly as possible. He managed the linking without so much as a rub or nudge. When the two ships were magnetized together, Antor left his post. He caught up with his crew, before they opened the hatch into the Solar Wind. Zenga was carrying an extra blaster. She handed it over, her face pale and determined.

"Thanks, Zen. Well, this is a first, fighting space pirates," he said, trying to ease the tension.

Hampelle told him to shut up, before he slid the hatch upward, slowly and quietly. The long corridor ahead was empty. The Solar Wind looked and sounded deserted. Hampelle led the way to where the passage forked, and peeked around the corner. He turned left and took Willy with him. Zenga and Antor were pointed down the right branch.

The ship had a completely different layout from the Comet Tail. Antor tried to deduce how to get to the bridge, which would be located at the front of the ship.

Stealth was forgotten when blaster fire sounded from Hampelle's direction. It was still reverberating when a thick, boneless arm snaked out of an open doorway and wrapped around Zenga. A second such arm knocked Antor's blaster away and tightened around his neck.

Antor fought wildly. The appendage only got tighter, and it felt more like a tentacle than an arm. It kept strangling him, until he was sure his eyeballs were going to pop right out of their sockets. He clawed uselessly at his neck. The appendage was as strong as yulithium. Everything got hazy and Antor knew he would not be saving Holly after all, or becoming a better man. He would be dying instead.

18 Holly - Blast It

Blaster fire split the air. Holly jumped and whacked her head on the console she was hiding under. "Ouch."

"Shush." Teef peeked out.

"Is the coast clear?" Holly whispered.

"What coast? We're on a spaceship, not on a beach."

"It's an expression." Holly leaned out to have a look for herself. The coast and the bridge were clear. And Holly had had enough of hiding. She wasn't going to wait to be rescued, not while Antor and Zenga risked their lives against the pirates. "I'm going to find a blaster," she told Teef. "Wait here."

Teef said, "Okay," but she didn't look happy about it.

"Unless you want to come with me, even though you would be safer here."

"I want to come with you," Teef said immediately.

"Why didn't you say so?" Holly asked.

"Because I am supposed to obey. Obedience is important."

"You don't have to obey me! I'm your friend, not your mother. Come on, if you want, and stay down." Holly led the way, bent almost double, across the bridge which was three times bigger than the Comet Tail's.

Holly closed her eyes when she had to step over two bodies. Another one was sprawled just outside the bridge. It was still clutching a blaster, a big one. Holly freed the strap and draped the weapon from her shoulder. It was a lot heavier than she expected and she staggered.

"Do you know how to fire it?" Teef asked anxiously.

Holly had a look and made sure the safety was off, as she had seen Zenga do. "I think so, the trigger is here." Holly laid a finger over the button. She didn't mean to fire, she just wanted to be ready, but the weapon really did have a hair trigger. A light brush of her finger was all it took to blast a huge smoking hole in the wall of the corridor. Teef screamed.

"Oops. Sorry, Teef. We better get out of here, someone might have heard that." Finger nowhere near the trigger, Holly jogged down the corridor, heading away from the bridge. She skidded around a corner and came face-to-face with a big slimy alien who didn't look the least bit human. His arms were all bendy and very very long. One was wrapped around Zenga. The other was strangling Antor, and given the blue tinge of his skin, he was out of air and time.

Holly raised the blaster and targeted the alien's head. She didn't have a clear shot, because Antor was in the way. Her finger hovered over the button, hesitating. When Teef bumped into her from behind, she brushed the button. Again, she didn't mean to fire, but the weapon discharged. Holly slammed her eyes shut, terrified that she had just blasted Antor's head right off. She didn't want to open her eyes, yet she had to know. She peeked.

The alien was a mess on the ground, and Antor was down, too. Zenga was trying to free herself from under a heavy tentacle-arm.

"Did I kill Antor?" Holly wailed. "I did, didn't I?"

Zenga shoved the last loop of limb aside and shook his limp body. "Antor? Antor?"

He groaned, proving he wasn't dead. Zenga helped him up. He wobbled, clutching the side of his head. There was a lot of blood. It looked like part of his ear was missing, but he was alive! Holly put the blaster down very carefully and launched into his arms. "Antor, I'm so sorry I almost blasted you."

He held her close with one arm and staggered. "You did blast me, but only a little bit. I'll live, better than getting strangled. You saved my life, Holly. Please stop crying. There are still pirates aboard, they might hear you."

Holly tried really hard to pull herself together. She didn't want the murderous pirates to see her bawling like a baby, but she couldn't seem to stop. Antor held her tighter. "Are you okay? Are you hurt?"

She shook her head, to the second question.

"We have to get somewhere safer. We're kind of exposed here." More distant blasting proved his point. "Any pirates up ahead?"

"No." Holly sniffled hard. "Just the bridge."

"Let's head that way. We can access the ship's sensors and see what's going on."

Teef picked up the blaster and Holly said, "You should put the safety on."

Zenga leaned over and did it herself, before she retrieved her own blaster, and a second which could only be Antor's.

They made it to bridge without seeing another living soul, only the same bodies. Antor tripped when he stepped over one. He winced and said, "Pirates slaughtered everyone?"

"Unless they were hiding like we were. But there was a traitor aboard. The sensors were disabled and the pirate ship docked, without anyone knowing. Suddenly the pirates were running around, killing everyone. Space pirates! I've heard of ocean pirates, they attack boats, but I never imagined there was such a thing as space pirates. Who would have guessed?" Holly was babbling with nerves, saying more than she should in front of Teef. She clenched her teeth, trying to stop talking.

"Hiding was the smartest thing you could have done." Zenga scanned the main consol. "We need to hear what's happening on the rest of the ship. Antor, can you figure out how to do that?"

Antor dropped into the chair beside her and took a look. "This button here should open all communication channels, but it might be two-way, so everyone be quiet. Not a sound." He pressed the button.

Captain Hampelle's growly voice filled the room. "I think that was the last intruder. Now stand still, Willy." There were some faint clicks. "There, it's done. No memory of the battle or weapon used. Let's go find the rest of my motley crew."

Antor closed the channel. "We're not motley."

"What was that crazy weapon that made the pirate ships compress into solid metal?" Zenga asked.

"I've read about it. It's experimental technology, but I never thought the Comet Tail had such advanced weaponry. I bet the Captain had it installed when we were on Ja'Dorp. That's when those new buttons appeared."

"Why would he do that?" Zenga asked.

"I don't know, Zen. I think, like Willy, we should forget what we saw today, for all our sakes."

Holly hadn't seen the weapon in action, she was simply glad it had saved them. She took the seat beside Antor and tried to see what was left of his ear. Blood soaked hair was concealing the wound.

"Is there a first aid kit somewhere?" she asked, feeling awful.

"I'm fine," Antor insisted.

"There's one on the Comet Tail." Zenga exhaled loudly. "If there are no more survivors, we'll probably go back to our ship. I'm going to find Hampelle, you three wait here."

Antor made to rise. Zenga pushed him down. "Stop being silly. I'll be right back."

Zenga wasn't quick to return, and her face was grim when she did. "Let's go. Captain Hampelle and Willy are meeting us back on the Comet Tail."

"No survivors at all?" Holly asked.

Zenga shook her head. Holly swallowed hard, feeling sick. She hadn't gotten to know any of the crew very well, but they had been nice. It was hard to believe they were all dead, just like that, because of space pirates. The Universe was proving to be even more barbaric than she had first suspected.

"Did you see my chaperone anywhere?" Teef asked.

139

"No, I didn't see any downed Schwills. Maybe the pirates took her aboard their ship and she got compressed."

Teef cringed, then asked, "What about the traitor?" Holly had forgotten about that.

Zenga assisted Antor to stand and said, "Probably dead, killed with the rest of the crew, or on the squished pirate ship. Got what he or she deserved, if you ask me. Now, let's get out of here."

The ship did smell like death, and the reek was getting stronger by the minute.

"Do we just leave the Solar Wind floating in space?" Holly asked. It seemed wrong to abandon all the victims' remains.

"We'll call Zandee from our ship. She can arrange the retrieval. If we called anyone else, we'd be suspects—detained and interrogated." Zenga shuddered, as if Outer Space interrogation was akin to Earth's worst historical tortures. "Neither of you would make it to the Pac System in time to compete. So, let's go."

Stepping onto the Comet Tail felt like coming home to Holly. Zenga handed her the first-aid kit and went to contact Zandee.

"Come on, Antor. I'll clean you up in the galley. More elbow room," Holly said.

"I'm fine," he insisted, yet again. He was being such a guy.

"You're not fine. I'm going to bandage your ear whether you like it or not." Holly took his arm and turned them toward the galley.

Teef hovered while Holly did her best to patch up his poor ear. When she sponged off the blood with a mini sponge-tongue, a little piece of his ear was definitely gone, like a bite out of the side. And he'd had such beautiful ears, as beautiful as the rest of him. "Oh, Antor, I'm so sorry," she repeated, sponging more blood. Her ministration was making him bleed a lot more. "I don't think you should ever let me hold a blaster again."

"I didn't let you hold that one," he said, with a quirk of his lips.

"True, I kind of helped myself." Holly poked around in the first-aid kit. None of the products were familiar. "What do I use?"

Teef handed her a little spray can. "That will stop the bleeding."

Holly aimed it at Antor's ear and pressed. The spray hit him more in his face than on his ear.

"Ah! That stings."

Teef was quick to fetch a cup of water so he could rinse his eyes, which were turning red.

"Oh, I'm sorry, Antor." Holly bit her lip. "Maybe I should leave your ear, and the rest of you, alone."

He muttered something that sounded like, "I hope not."

Teef took over, spraying Antor's ear properly and applying a neat bandage that looked like real skin. She did a good job, much better than Holly.

By the time they joined Zenga on the bridge, the little shipper/transport was speeding along toward the Pac System. Captain Hampelle was nowhere to be seen. Holly assumed he was sleeping. The battle had probably tired him out.

"How's the wound, Antor?" Zenga asked.

"It's too small to be called a wound." He sat down heavily. "Did you reach Zandee?"

Zenga nodded. "She'll take care of it. I told her what she needed to know. She didn't ask too many questions and commended us for saving Holly and Teef. She's looking forward to hearing them sing again. I've promised we'll send her two personally autographed holographic files of them singing."

Antor closed his eyes and appeared to go to sleep right in the chair. He looked comfortable enough, so Holly didn't disturb him. She showed Teef to the cabin they would share.

Teef didn't comment on the smallness, bareness or noisiness. Holly apologized anyway. Teef smiled. "I'm simply glad, and lucky, to be alive, Holly. We both are. We survived the pirate attack together, now we're as bonded as sisters."

It was a heartwarming sentiment and Holly hugged Teef. "Sisters in adversity, I like that. I'm sorry about your chaperone getting killed."

"A lost life is always a tragedy," Teef said, dutifully. "It's odd. She was missing before the pirate attack, and she had instructed me to stay in my room with the door locked. That's why I went to get you, to keep me company in my room. It's lucky we were locked in together, and the pirates didn't search my room at all."

"We were really lucky," Holly agreed.

"Why do you think she told me to stay locked in my room?"

Holly shrugged and Teef said, "You don't know?" She remembered the gesture.

"I don't know."

"Me, either. I have no idea." Teef shrugged, as if practicing the move. It made her wings ripple.

Holly really needed to sit down. Her adrenaline rush was wearing off. "Do you want the top or bottom hammock?"

"Top," Teef said promptly. She climbed up and looked over the edge at Holly. "Perfectly comfortable."

"Good."

They ended up staying in the hammocks. It was officially night on the Comet Tail and they were exhausted. They went to sleep.

Over the next few days, Holly had no time alone with Antor. Teef was always around, and/or Zenga. Even Captain Hampelle was spending time out of his room. He liked to listen to Holly and Teef practice their singing. The little ship seemed crowded. It was frustrating, because Holly felt like there was a lot she wanted to say to Antor, even though she didn't know what it was.

When the Comet Tail had almost reached the Pac System, they passed each other in the narrow corridor. No-one else was in sight. Holly said, "How's your ear?"

Antor smiled down at her, his face very close. "It's fine."

"I didn't get to kiss it better," she blurted, inanely.

He looked puzzled. "Can you do that? Does your saliva have healing properties?"

Holly's cheeks felt hot, a sure sign they were turning red. "No, it's just an expression."

"It's not too late." His slow smile stole her breath.

"What?" Holly was having trouble following their conversation. It had something to do with Antor's eyes and lips, and close proximity.

"To kiss it better, it's not too late."

"Oh." She would rather have kissed his lips, but he didn't offer them. He turned his head. Holly leaned forward and kissed his ear lobe. She might have nibbled it a bit, and breathed warmly into it.

Antor made a hungry noise in his throat. "Holly … I never got to kiss you better."

"Hm?"

He stroked her cheek. "Your skin healed … beautifully, but I could still kiss it better, if you want me to."

"I do."

Antor kissed her cheek, lingeringly, warmly. And he didn't forget the other one. "Better?" he said. Holly didn't know quite how to answer that. In some ways, his kiss had made things worse, harder. Out of the blue, he said, "I'm sorry I lied to you about the Gorka."

Holly had spent a lot of time thinking about that, while on the Solar Wind. "I know you didn't let the Gorka out, Antor. And you saved my life, protecting me from them. The fact that they're on Earth isn't your fault, but please don't lie to me again. I want to be able to trust you. Trust is important, at least on Earth."

"In the rest of the Universe, too. I want you to be able to trust me. I won't lie to you again," he said solemnly.

"I'm glad."

"We'll get the Gorka off Earth as soon as it can be done. I'll do everything in my power to get them back on this ship, I promise." And then he kissed her forehead, which still had a small scar from hitting the wall on Ja'Dorp.

Holly leaned against his chest. As alien as he was, he felt just right. Perfect. She was hoping they might share a proper kiss, right on the lips, when approaching footsteps alerted them that someone was approaching along the curved corridor. They moved apart and went their separate ways.

19 Antor - Playara

Antor didn't want to reach the Pac System before he'd had a chance to share some quality time with Holly. Alas, he couldn't stop the ship or expand the galaxy. Much too soon, they reached their destination.

The Pac System was an intense little solar community with a ring of planets orbiting the single sun, at just the right distance to make them ideally suited for humanoid life. Universe Idol was filmed on one of the smallest—Playara. The whole planet was devoted to the entertainment industry. It had the tightest security possible, for a planet.

The Comet Tail had to prove it was carrying two of the Universe Idol finalists before it was permitted to drop into a low orbit. A luxurious shuttle craft arrived to carry Holly, Teef, Antor and Zenga down to the surface. They were met by a group of fussy types, who wouldn't stop fussing. They went on and on about the danger Holly and Teef had survived. A dozen armed and uniformed guards escorted them into the complex that would be their home for the next month.

Since Teef was without her chaperone, Holly invited her to bunk with them. She had listed both Zenga and Antor as her companions, so she had been assigned a suite with two bedrooms. The rooms were luxurious and designed for the human form. The soft beige tones were a nice change from the hard metal grays and rustiness of the Comet Tail.

Being the only male, Antor got one of the two bedrooms. The three girls shared the other. The sitting room that linked them was common ground. Holly and Teef were barely allowed time to settle in, before they were whisked away on Universe Idol business. With only two and a half days before the first show, there was a lot to do.

Antor and Zenga really were on vacation and went exploring. The Universe Idol complex was an odd combination of work and play, as befitted the entertainment industry. There were three theatres, and six grand hotels to hold all the visitors who came to watch the live filming. Tourist sites had sprung up outside the complex's security walls, to keep the audiences entertained between filming and shows.

Zenga got quite excited about one tourist trap that promised to make you the star of your favourite classic movie, for a reasonable cost. She insisted Antor act in it with her, as the villain, while she got to be the hero. Antor couldn't talk her out of it—and he did try.

He ended up paying the bill, and it wasn't nearly as reasonable as promised. They both had to be scanned, in motion and speaking, and then their holographic images were downloaded into the already existing movie sequence, in place of the actual stars. Some of the scenes they acted out, for the fun of it.

When they walked away, Zenga was smiling and wearing the ring disc of their movie on her finger. "I can't wait to show this to Holly," she said. "We can watch it tonight, and have our own movie night."

"Just what I want to see, evil me dying over and over again while you play the hero." Antor scowled, but he wasn't really displeased. He'd looked better in the movie than he did in real life, and his holographic, simulated self acted a lot tougher.

"Maybe Holly will be attracted to the rogue in you." Zenga flashed him a jaunty grin. Antor could hope.

They ate lunch in a high-priced restaurant and signed the bill to the room. Since it was only their first of many days, they roamed around, getting the lay of the land and eavesdropping on conversations. Almost everyone was talking about the Universe Idol contestants, who they wanted to win and who they wanted to lose. Holly and Teef's brush with death at the hands of space pirates was also making for juicy gossip.

Antor was back in their rooms, enjoying a nap on the couch, when Holly and Teef returned. Both girls looked worn out. "They had us running around doing photo shoots and getting fitted for costumes. We didn't even have a chance to practice singing," Holly said, sitting beside Antor's feet.

He yawned. "Sounds like hard work."

"Well, not really, not compared to real work. What did you do today?"

"I'll show you after dinner." He sat up. "Do you want to eat in or out?"

"Out. I can't wait to see more of another planet," Holly said promptly.

Teef sank carefully into the adjacent chair, draping her wings over the armrests. "You keep saying things like that, Holly. Did your parents keep you locked in a cage or something? To not know basic technology or … anything about the Universe?"

Antor was surprised that Holly hadn't confessed all to Teef, when they had been traveling together on the Solar Wind. The girls had almost died together, and still Holly had kept her secrets. Most would have spilled them. If Holly was typical of Earth humans, the race had more discretion than most.

When Zenga walked into the room, she distracted them all. "Antor and I made a movie today," she said. "Want to watch it?"

"After dinner. They barely fed us all day and I'm starving." Holly's stomach growled on cue.

"Let's order dinner here and watch the movie." Zenga sat on Antor's other side and flashed the ring disc.

Holly promptly sagged into the couch. "My feet are really tired. I guess we could eat here. Teef, what do you think?"

"Here is fine. I'm tired, too."

It was decided. Zenga ordered the meal, then placed the ring disc on the jutting nodule on the viewing screen. As soon as they were settled with their plates, Zenga started the movie. Holly watched the 3-D viewing screen with interest, until she began to look perplexed by what she was seeing.

"I'm not really bad, that's the part I'm playing. None of this is real," Antor explained. He didn't know what kind of movies she watched on Earth, or if she even watched movies, so he wasn't sure if she knew she was watching fiction.

"I know this isn't real," Holly said, "and I've seen this movie before."

"Well, of course you have," Teef interjected. "It's a classic. Everyone has seen this movie."

Antor glanced at Holly with a question in his eyes. Holly said, "I saw it last year. It was a big hit—last year, and I knew it by a different name."

Antor couldn't help but laugh. More than Universe Idol had been copied on Earth, it seemed.

Teef looked back and forth between them. "Maybe someday you'll tell me what's going on."

"I'd like to." Holly shot another glance at Antor. "But it's safer for you if you don't know." He nodded. It was safer for all of them.

Teef accepted that, and they all got back to watching the movie. When Antor, the bad guy, kissed Zenga, the hero, he thought it looked very forceful and passionate. Holly frowned fiercely, as if she didn't like it at all. Antor kind of hoped she was jealous, which meant she did care for him. He was jealous whenever he thought about Daniel, her mate. At least that Earthling was far far away, while Antor was close enough to touch Holly. His shoulder felt warm and electrified where it pressed against hers.

And in the end, when Antor the bad guy died, Holly looked very moved. They all clapped. Zenga stood up and took a bow. She pulled Antor to his feet to bow as well. "That was such fun," she said. "We should do another movie tomorrow. You could be the hero, Antor."

"I'd rather surf the air currents. You got to pick what we did today, tomorrow is my turn."

Zenga gave in with good grace. "Fair enough. Surfing the air currents sounds like a blast. I've never tried it."

146

"I wish I could go," Holly said. "I've never surfed air currents. I've never even surfed water." But she had to rehearse. There would be no vacationing for her.

Teef rose and stretched her arms and wings. "We have another busy day tomorrow, so I'm going to bed."

"I think I'll turn in, too." Zenga went with her.

Holly didn't rush away. Antor took that as a hopeful sign. He stayed beside her, unsure about what to do. She had a mate. He shouldn't be doing anything, or thinking anything. But he couldn't help thinking things. When Holly rested her head against the back of the couch, he angled toward her and said, "Tell me about this Earth movie."

"Oh, the title was different, and the setting, of course, but the storyline was the same, with the female adventurer and the search for the iconic artifact, and the death at the end. You and Zenga are good actors. Did you really have to kiss for that scene?" she blurted out.

"Yes, but we've kissed before, so it didn't feel strange," he said.

"You … you and Zenga? But I thought you were just friends."

"We are now."

"And before?" Holly looked deep into his eyes.

Antor waffled, but he wanted Holly to trust him and he had told her he wouldn't lie again, so he spoke the truth. "Before … we were more than friends."

"Oh. Oh. Really?" She looked very taken aback.

"Yes."

"You and Zenga were lovers?" Holly asked, pointblank.

"Yes," he said reluctantly.

"Huh. That's … unexpected. You and Zenga." Holly stood abruptly. "Well, I better get to bed too, busy day tomorrow."

Antor jumped up before she could make a run for it. He reached for her hand. "Holly, wait. Does it bother you that Zenga and me …?" He didn't know quite how to say it, and left the thought hanging in the air between them.

"Yes, of course it bothers me. And you were kissing her today, and that looked like one heck of a kiss." Holly jerked her hand free. "You should have mentioned this before, you know. You really should have." She ran into the bedroom.

Antor had blown it again, it seemed. And he'd been longing to kiss Holly properly for the first time. She hadn't been wearing a veil or anything. They'd been all alone and she had been looking so kissable. The moment had felt perfect, and then everything had gone wrong. Disheartened and feeling more alone that usual, Antor sought his own bed.

20 Holly - Ten Finalists

Holly tossed and turned until Zenga hit her with a pillow, or maybe it was Teef. It was hard to tell who was hitting her in the dark. She stayed still after that, yet sleep still wouldn't come. She kept thinking about Antor romancing Zenga, and other aliens. Maybe non-Earth humans thought nothing of hooking up with whoever crossed their path. They were awfully uncivilized in other ways, blasting each other at the drop of a hat, so maybe they weren't civilized about sex, either. Maybe they were like animals, rutting here and there and everywhere. Holly decided that she really needed to find out more about alien sexual practices before she considered getting up close and personal with Antor.

Holly must have fallen asleep eventually, because Teef woke her, saying, "We're going to be late. Hurry!" Holly was still half asleep when they left the suite. Zenga had stayed deeply asleep, and Antor was nowhere to be seen. He was probably sound asleep too, behind the closed door of his room.

All day long, Holly was kept busy preparing for her first performance as a top ten finalist. There was another photo session, and another costume fitting—at least she didn't have to try shopping again. All the contestants' clothing was supplied by Universe Idol, and they had a wider selection to choose from than any store, plus fashion consultants to offer the girls advice. After Holly selected her dress, there was a lengthy practice on the new, much bigger stage. As well as singing her own song, Holly would be performing a song and dance number with the whole group of ten, and a lot of them weren't very good dancers at all.

In addition to Holly the Humanoid, and Teef the Schwill, there was Ahah, the tall skinny orange Scarnivore that had beaten the Mannireplian. Choggle, the fourth finalist, was a short hairy male who looked like he shared some common genes with Captain Hampelle. The fifth was a Castorian, who looked like all the other Castorians that Holly had already met, and eerily like the pictures of Earth's stereotypical aliens. Mogg, the sixth, was another male. He physically resembled an Earth dwarf, except for his scaly lime-green skin and long waving antennae. He lacked rhythm and grace. He was the worst dancer of all of them.

The most disturbing alien in the top ten, as far as Holly was concerned, was the Banshom. She was named Vhergos and her body was kind of translucent, in a ghostly way. She could move really fast. She would be standing at one end of the stage and in the blink of an eye, she would be standing at the opposite end. Her hot gaze seemed to look right through Holly, as if Holly was the translucent one, not Vhergos the Banshom. If Holly had encountered her on Earth, she would have called the Ghostbusters.

Inx, the eighth of the finalists, crackled with electricity and occasionally gave off sparks. It seemed very peculiar, until Holly thought about electric eels on Earth. It also seemed dangerous, until Teef mentioned that Inx's tail acted as a ground, so he wasn't a risk to the other finalists. He was from a race called the Stinge, and Teef said that Stinges always kept their tails down and grounded, when they mingled with other species. They only raised their tails if they were alone with their own kind, or in a fight, although only a fool would fight with a Stinge, since one shocking touch was enough to knock them unconscious or kill them. Holly stayed far away from Inx after Teef told her that.

The ninth finalist, a close second in the disturbing category, was a Skoppire. Blyllygo, the quasi-humanoid, was shrunken in all ways, kind of like a shrunken head, except it had happened to every bit of her. She might have been mummified while still alive. Her skin was dark, tight and dehydrated, not to mention wrinkled. She even moved stiffly, as if she was as ancient as she looked, and not the same age as the rest of them. Teef said the Skoppire had evolved on an arid world with a near sun. Holly could certainly believe it, since Blyllygo looked half-cooked.

Last but not least, was the Emangster. She was darkly intense and reminded Holly of a teenage vampire. Her features were sharp and narrow, and her teeth were pointy fangs. Even her pale skin and black clothing favoured Earth Goth. If she had walked Earth's streets on any night other than Halloween, she would have sent people running. Holly had jokingly asked Teef if Dejanne drank blood. Teef had said, "Yes, that's part of an Emangster's diet."

Holly blinked. "Human blood?"

"Yes, and their own kind's blood. Most blood, I think."

"Do they avoid sunlight?"

Teef had looked thoughtful. "Their planet is always foggy with only one distant sun. It is a cold and forbidding world."

"Is it called Transylvania?" Holly said with a grin.

"No, it's called Drack." Teef had stopped being bewildered by Holly's ignorance of everything in the Universe. She simply accepted it now.

"Drack," Holly repeated. The name was too much like a famous vampire's to be a coincidence. She would have to tell Zenga and Antor that

149

she suspected the Emangsters of visiting her world, probably to feed. Vampire mythology dated back hundreds of Earth years, so the aliens must have been calling on Earth since it was a truly undeveloped world.

The group of ten was certainly an odd assortment of beings, when they stood together in a line. Holly was amazed by the diversity of life in the Universe, and she knew she was only seeing a tiny sampling.

After the group song and dance rehearsal, which was a very long and arduous practice, the contestants were given the evening off. They scattered, to eat dinner and practice their solo numbers on their own.

Teef and Holly performed for each other in their suite, offering constructive critiques. Antor and Zenga were still out, probably having fun together. The thought made Holly feel envious and hurt. She wanted to be the one having fun with Antor—the one with Antor.

When she and Teef took a break, they collapsed together on the couch and Holly sought her advice. "Teef, can I ask you about something kind of personal?"

"You can ask, and if it is too personal, I won't answer."

"Fair enough. Um … do most beings have sex with lots of partners, or only one, or do they wait until they're married?" Holly blurted.

"Holly, you must know … of course you don't. You don't know anything you should. The best answer to your question is that it is different with every race, and on every planet. Why are you asking?" Teef said.

Holly sighed. "I found out that Antor and Zenga were lovers, not anymore, but before."

Teef didn't look in the least surprised. "Antor and Zenga are both full humans, like you. They have no-one but each other on their ship. Are you surprised that they sought physical pleasure together?"

Holly slumped and scowled. "Not surprised I guess, when you put it like that, but hurt. Okay, I'm jealous. Anyway, I just wondered if … if maybe Antor had sex with anyone that caught his eye. I wondered if sex meant anything, emotionally, or is it simply a fun pastime in most of the cosmos."

Teef giggled. Holly was having trouble expressing herself.

"Do beings fall in love with each other? Does love exist?" she said.

Teef stopped laughing. "Poor Holly. How can you be eighteen and so naïve?" She didn't say it unkindly.

"I grew up … in a sheltered environment, that's all."

"You must have grown up in a box. Of course love exists. If there is one thing all humanoids, or half-humanoids, or part-humanoids, have in common, it is the need to love and be loved. We are incomplete without love." Teef looked very wise when she said, "Antor certainly doesn't seem the type to seek out meaningless sex. He seems the type to fall in love, and I don't think he is in love with Zenga."

"Oh. Do you love your betrothed?"

"I hope to, once I know him better," Teef said simply.

Before Holly could ask more questions, the door opened. Zenga came in, flushed and grinning. She had loved surfing the air currents and wouldn't stop talking about what great fun it was. Antor followed, quiet and looking kind of miserable, he was even hunching again. He hadn't done that since he had battled the pirates.

They all ate together in the sitting room. After dinner, Holly and Teef performed their songs for Zenga and Antor, who had nothing but praise for both girls.

Teef was again the first one to turn in. As soon as the door closed behind her, Holly leaned forward and said quietly, "I'm pretty sure the Emangsters have been visiting Earth for hundreds of years, to feed on human blood. I think some Emangsters have even settled on Earth, and are still living there."

"Why would you think that?" Zenga asked.

"We call them Vampires, but they look like Emangsters, all pale and pointy-toothed, and they can't tolerate direct sunlight, and they drink human blood. We've made movies about them, and people dress up like Vampires on Halloween. Earth's entertainment industry is rampant with tales about Vampires—Emangsters."

"Halloween?" Zenga said.

"A night for partying and wearing costumes, and pigging out on candy." Holly didn't go into more unnecessary detail.

Antor raised an eyebrow. "So Emangsters have been visiting Earth, too? I've never heard of a more popular restricted planet."

"It seems like Earth is almost the hub of the Universe, doesn't it?" Zenga flashed a grin. "Maybe it's the original Green World." She was joking, but Antor got a thoughtful look on his face.

"I wonder," he said.

"I'm kidding," Zenga stressed. "Enough about that. Holly, how are you feeling about tomorrow's big performance? Are you nervous?"

"Very. There is so much at stake." They all knew it. "I like Teef a lot, but I wish she wasn't such a good singer." Teef was Holly's greatest fear, greater even than the death threats that all contestants received. Security in the complex, and around the contestants, was so tight, Holly felt completely protected, except from Teef's talent.

"You're the best singer, Holly," Antor said loyally.

"You are," Zenga agreed. "Teef is really good, the best contestant in years, but you're better, Holly. No-one can sing like you, and I love your song choice for tomorrow. It's so lively. Girls do just want to have fun! I think every female can relate to that."

151

"I hope so." Holly leaned back and yawned. The long day, and the restless night that had preceded it, were catching up with her.

"You should get to bed, Holly. You look exhausted, and you need to be well rested for tomorrow," Zenga said. She was right, or maybe she wanted to be alone with Antor. Maybe she wanted him back. People, at least Earth people, tended to want what they couldn't have. Maybe Antor's interest in Holly had reignited Zenga's desire for him. She had liked him well enough to sleep with him in the past, so why not again?

Holly rose with a flounce. "I will need all my energy for tomorrow. Good-night, sleep well." She left them alone, wondering if they would end up sleeping well together in Antor's room. She couldn't relax until Zenga came to bed, which wasn't for two very long hours, while Holly imagined exactly what they were doing. She'd always had way too much imagination for her own good, all her friends said so.

21 Antor - Spiners

A ntor and Zenga spent the day on the Comet Tail, after Captain Hampelle summoned them to repair the engine. The ship had stalled over Playara and wouldn't restart. Luckily, it was in a stable orbit when it happened, since neither Hampelle nor Willy could get her going again.

Antor had to crawl into the coils to realign them. He laser welded a whole lot of weak spots, before he dared to try restarting the engine. As old and warn as the coils were, they restarted on the first try.

In Antor's opinion, the shipper/transport was on its last wings. It needed to be refitted with new coils, or junked. He told Hampelle that. The Captain wasn't concerned. He said, "I plan to replace her in the very near future, with something much bigger and faster." Holly's winnings would be more than enough to buy him a small fleet of super-sized, fully-outfitted, deluxe spaceships.

Zenga and Antor barely made it back to Playara's surface in time for Antor to rinse off a layer of oily grime. They dashed to the Universe Idol theatre. As Holly's companions, they had been given a free pass to all of the shows, and their seats were great, right near the front. Antor had really wanted to wish Holly good luck, but he had no chance to see her before the performance. The camera-mates started broadcasting as soon as he sat down.

Chrome Boreal strode energetically across the stage. He looked a lot smaller in person than he did on the viewing screen. He thanked the audience, he enthused about the exciting show to come, he introduced the judges—it was his usual spiel. Finally, the ten competitors paraded out to be introduced.

Antor breathed a sigh of relief to see Holly there, smiling and healthy. The behind-the-scenes staff of Universe Idol had worked their magic on all the varied contestants, but Holly shone like a star amongst them, at least to Antor's eyes.

Her dress was hot pink, tight on the top and draped in flounces below. The skirt stopped mid-thigh, exposing most of her legs. The corset top revealed a whole lot more. Antor's gaze seemed to get stuck in Holly's rounded cleavage for the longest time.

An orange sash was tied tight around her waist, with a theatrically oversized bow at the back. Her outfit looked like the kind of dress a girl would want to have fun in. Her hair was teased into a wild frizzy style, with a matching orange bow camouflaging the shorter middle patch, where her hair had been blasted off. Most of it had grown back, but it still wasn't as long as the rest. The style suited Holly, as did the exotic makeup that enhanced the rare blue colour of her eyes.

It was the first time the viewers had seen Holly properly attired and it could only help her performance. "She looks stunning," Antor said, leaning close so Zenga could hear him.

"Holly?"

"Of course, Holly."

"Teef looks good, too," Zenga said.

Antor checked out Teef. Her outfit wasn't playful. It was black, sophisticated and sleek, as befit the torch song she was going to perform. She did look attractive, but not as appealing as Holly. He surveyed the rest of the contestants. The Scarnivore's skinny, stick-like body made her gown hang like a curtain. The Castorian had opted for the traditional white robe of her race, but she had adorned it with elaborate metal jewelry, including a woven metallic war-vest overtop, and a jeweled headdress.

The shrunken Skoppire, the short scaly green Mogg, and the equally short, hairy, part-humanoid (who looked like a miniature Hampelle) couldn't really do justice to their outfits. Diminutive beings were at a disadvantage in the looks department.

The translucent Banshom wore veils in all the colours of refracted light, and her movements were so quick that the veils always seemed to be blowing in the wind, even though there wasn't a breeze. It was hard to focus on her. Antor was inclined to think the nonhuman portion of Vhergos originated in another dimension, making her not wholly tangible in his Universe.

The male Stinge was dressed rather plainly in a nonconductive material. The long blue robe completely hid his tail.

Beside the Stinge stood the Emangster, the race that Holly labeled Earth Vampire. The girl did look striking, all pale skin, black hair, blood red gown and lips. Aside from Holly and Teef, she was the most attractive contestant, in a darkly disturbing kind of way.

After the commercials, the ten finalists performed the group song and dance number that Holly and Teef had been practicing for two days. Each contestant took a turn at center stage, playing the part of lead singer for one verse, before dancing away again. Behind, the other nine contestants provided background vocals.

Holly sang her part flawlessly and sashayed away with flair. The finale of the song had all ten beings linking hands and turning together in a circle while singing in harmony, probably to signify unity or peace or something equally nebulous.

The audience was still clapping when there was a pause for the next commercial break. It seemed to drag on for ten minutes, not the normal three.

The individual performances began with the Emangster, Dejanne. She had a pure pitch and a hypnotic quality that made a person feel all woozy just listening to her. Antor thought she lacked life and verve. Cowbell Cumin said the same thing.

Dejanne was followed by the Castorian, who was boring and stiff. Mini-Hampelle and Mogg sang next. Both had deep powerful male voices. They were good, but audiences tended to prefer listening to female singers, as did Antor.

There was another commercial break and Antor looked for Holly. She was waiting at the edge of the stage. She kept twitching and shifting around, as if she was squirming with nerves. "I wonder if Holly is okay," Antor said in Zenga's ear.

Zenga studied her. "It looks like she has a bad case of the jitters, doesn't it. Probably just stage fright."

The show resumed with Teef's solo. She did a lovely job. Her rich voice was perfectly suited to the torch song. All four judges were extravagant with their praises.

Holly followed Teef. Antor had watched her practice this song a number of times and he knew that something was wrong as soon as she launched into the first verse. Her voice lacked the flowing smoothness that he had come to expect. Holly put so much frenetic energy into the performance that it was exhausting to watch. She gyrated from one end of the stage to the other, while she belted out the lyrics. She even tore off her sash and twirled it over her head, before she yanked open the lacings on her corset bodice, as if to prove that girls really did want to have fun—at least a certain type of fun.

When the song was over, she hopped from one foot to the other, while the judges gave their critiques. The Scarnivore was cool and critical. The Castorian said the performance was odd. X-Orgone loved it, all of it, the level of energy and Holly's ability to control her voice throughout the wild recital. Everyone held their breath, until Cowbell Cumin said, "Fantastic. Most entertaining performance of the night. And the most gutsy. I commend you for trying something so different. It is the sign of a true star. You are tonight's star, Holly Noel Tate."

"Thank you, thank you." Holly appeared to be grimacing instead of smiling, and from the way she was pressing her thighs together, she looked like a little kid that needed to pee. She hurried to the back of the stage and disappeared from sight.

Inx sang next. Zenga whispered that she thought he had the best voice of the three males who had made it into the finals.

Blyllygo was awful. The audience could barely hear her small voice. It was as shrunken as her body, and she was off key more than she was on key. When she approached the judges, her face was a picture of misery. Not one of them liked her rendition of a top ten hit. Cumin said the song was much too big for her. She was sobbing when she walked away.

Holly still hadn't reappeared.

The Scarnivore, Ahah, took the stage and gave a solid performance of a popular ballad. Vhergos the Banshom sang last. Her voice was as eerie as her appearance. It sent chills up and down Antor's spine. Three of the four judges thought she was unique and captivating.

The show ended with Chrome Boreal reminding the viewing audience to watch the results show the very next evening, when two of the ten finalists would be leaving Universe Idol. The contestants waved goodnight, and there were only nine. Holly was still mysteriously absent.

Antor nudged Zenga and they jumped up to avoid the exiting crowd. They flashed their identification passes to get backstage. They spotted Teef, before they found Holly. "Super performance, Teef. Do you know where Holly went?" Zenga asked.

"I don't know. She said there was something wrong and disappeared off the stage. She never came back." Teef seemed worried, too.

"We'll have to search for her," Antor said, trying not to panic. Holly didn't even have her personal guards anymore. The Manni's hadn't come to Playara. Only official Universe Idol security was permitted in the Universe Idol complex, and that security was tight. There were always at least two uniformed guards in sight. At the moment, there were six posted around the backstage area. It was a maze of small passages, going off in all directions. There were doors everywhere, and lots of moving bodies.

Zenga scowled all around. "Where do we start?"

"Go ask that big guard if he saw where Holly went," Antor said. The stern being was at least two heads taller than anyone else in the vicinity, and had the best view.

Zenga went and asked. He didn't know.

Accompanied by Teef, they began pacing along the corridors. When they passed Dejanne, Zenga asked, "Have you seen Holly?"

"I haven't seen her, but I can find her for you. Follow me." Dejanne led them behind the length of the stage, past a number of doorways and stopped. She sniffed and her nostrils flared. She turned right and kept moving away from the stage area.

Zenga and Antor exchanged a puzzled glance. "You can smell her?" Zenga asked.

"Oh, yes," Dejanne said with feeling.

"That's amazing. Can you scent everyone like that?"

"No. Her blood is exceptionally sweet. I can't say that I've ever smelled such nectar before, in any being. Her blood would taste like ambrosia." Dejanne looked kind of excited by the smell. Her white cheeks even had a tinge of colour. She turned left and led them up a staircase, then another staircase and down several corridors. They found themselves back at their own room, before they realized that's where they were headed.

Dejanne stroked a finger down the door and said, "You will find her inside here."

"Our suite." The door recognized Zenga and Antor as registered occupants and slid aside. Dejanne entered with them, as did Teef. The lights were on and water was running in the bathroom.

Antor banged on the door and said, "Holly, are you in there?"

"Yes."

"Are you okay?" he asked, so relieved she was there and alive.

"I don't know," she wailed.

"Can I open the door?"

"No!" she screamed.

Antor looked at Zenga and Teef for help. Maybe it was a girl thing.

Zenga took over. "Holly, can I come in?"

"No," she snapped.

Zenga motioned to Teef, who said, "Holly, it's Teef. Would it be okay if I entered?"

There was a moment of silence. "Okay, but only you."

Teef slipped inside. Antor strained his ears, but couldn't decipher a word of the whispered conversation. Dejanne must have had exceptional hearing. She smiled and said, "Holly's problem is not serious."

"Good. Uh, thanks for your help finding her. I'm Antor, and this is Zenga." The introductions were long overdue.

Dejanne nodded and introduced herself, even though they knew who she was. She stepped close to Antor and inhaled. "Your blood is tempting as well. Not as intoxicating as Holly's, but rich and potent. Very strong. Distinctive. I've only smelled such blood once before."

Antor might have asked where, if his head hadn't felt so dizzy. Looking into Dejanne's eyes and listening to her voice was having the strangest effect on him. She took one more step, closing in, and touched her nose to Antor's cheek. The tip was cold, her breath was colder. He stumbled back.

With a rather secretive smile, Dejanne said, "And now, I must be going. I look forward to our next meeting, Antor."

He couldn't say the same and was relieved when the door closed behind her. All her talk about blood was chilling his.

"I think she likes you," Zenga mentioned.

"She likes my blood, and I think she likes Holly's blood too much. She was almost drooling. It would explain why Emangsters visit Earth, and even live there."

Zenga nodded. "It would."

Antor pressed an ear against the bathroom door. Zenga slapped him. It was lucky he moved his head, because the door opened. Holly came out. She was wet and wrapped in a towel.

"What happened, Holly? Why did you leave the stage?" Zenga asked.

She shuddered. "I had bugs in my dress. It was full of creepy-crawlies."

"Bugs?" Antor and Zenga gasped.

"I thought I had fleas or something." Holly grimaced.

Teef came out of the bathroom, still drying her hands. "Spiners," she said.

She didn't have a chance to say more. Holly burst out, "They were crawling all over me when I was on the stage, inside my dress, and they were biting me. I was so itchy I wanted to rip my skin off." Her face crumpled up. "But I couldn't leave the stage and be disqualified, so I had to stay up there and sing, with my dress full of bugs. I made a fool of myself, didn't I? Dancing like a crazy person and almost stripping." Her eyes were tragic, and looked darker blue than usual. "There's no way I'll make it to the next round now."

Antor was just glad that she was okay. He smiled and couldn't resist hugging her close. She pressed her face into his shoulder. He stroked her wet hair and said, "Holly, Cowbell loved your performance, so did X-Orgone. You'll be moving on. Please don't be upset about it."

Holly sniffed weakly. "I don't know how my dress got full of bugs."

"More sabotage," Zenga said.

Teef nodded in agreement. "Yes, definitely."

Holly moved out of Antor's arms to look at them. "Sabotage?"

"Someone must have stashed the eggs inside your dress before you put it on. The heat of your body would have hatched them," Zenga said.

Holly shivered. "That's so gross."

"Antor noticed that you were squirming about halfway through the show, so that's probably how long it took for them to hatch. The question is, who put them there?"

"It could have been any of the other contestants, I suppose. We've all been in and out of the wardrobe area, getting fitted and dressed." Holly smiled at Teef. "But we can count Teef out, and me, so that leaves eight suspects and one is a Scarnivore."

"My coins are on Ahah," Zenga said.

Antor added, "It could have been one of the staff, too, if someone paid them off to put the eggs in your dress."

158

"That's true." Zenga moved toward the viewing screen. "I'm going to order some snacks. Antor and I haven't eaten yet."

"I better get dressed." Holly went into her bedroom.

Antor checked the bathroom, to make sure there were no bugs left. He didn't think he could have stood on stage with spiners crawling all over him, but Holly had—and she had performed her song from start to finish. She had gumption as well as talent.

There were a few drowned spiners in the bottom of the steamy shower cubicle. Holly's dress was there too, looking like a wet pink rag. Antor rinsed the last dead bugs down the drain with water wrung out of the dress. More soggy bugs rained out. He was quick to fling the dress over a hook to dry, before he joined the girls in the sitting room.

Holly looked comfy in a pair of yellow jumpsuit pajamas, provided by the Universe Idol complex. There was even a Universe Idol logo on the shoulder. Teef had changed into matching pajamas, as had Zenga. It was like a pajama party. The only male in leather trousers, Antor felt out of place, but he would have felt sillier dressed like the girls.

He let the floating trays of food into the room, before he claimed a place between Holly and Zenga. They discussed the sabotage while they ate. Everyone agreed with Zenga, that a Scarnivore was the most likely suspect to have planted the insect eggs. The Scarnivore finalist had certainly had plenty of opportunity.

After Teef went to bed first again, Antor told Holly how Dejanne had tracked her to the room. "She really liked your blood, she said it was very special. Maybe you are right about Emangster's living on Earth."

"She liked Antor's blood, too, or she liked Antor. I'm not sure which," Zenga said with a teasing grin.

Holly frowned and nibbled a veggie bar. "Do you think she'll drain our blood and kill us? Or maybe transform us into Vampires?"

"What?" Antor didn't know what Holly was talking about.

"Well, that's what they do. They bite your neck and drink all your blood, killing you. Or if they want to turn you into a Vampire—I mean an Emangster, they drink your blood then make you drink theirs. I think that's how a person is transformed into one of them."

Zenga burst out laughing. Antor chuckled, too, he couldn't help it. "Holly, Emangsters don't do that. They drink blood, yes, but only blood that is freely offered, and they never drink enough to harm anyone. They eat food, too, not just blood."

Holly shook her head stubbornly. "Not the Vampires on Earth. They only drink human blood and they do a lot of damage." She told them all about a Vampire called Dracula who supposedly lived five hundred years ago. It was an entertaining tale, but it sounded like pure fiction, not fact.

When Holly fell silent, Zenga rose and yawned. "I'm off to bed. I hope Hampelle doesn't call us to work again tomorrow. It spoils our vacation. Good night."

Antor said a silent thank-you to Zenga for leaving him alone with Holly. As soon as the bedroom door closed, he angled toward her on the couch. "Feeling better?"

She rubbed her arms as though chilled. "The bugs were awful. I'm sure I'll have nightmares."

"I'm sorry you had to go through that." He eased a little closer, trying to work up the courage to put an arm around her shoulders, to warm her. Her hair was still damp and smelled like flowers, as always. It was her own scent. Maybe Dejanne smelled flowers in Holly's blood, and that's why it was so delicious to her.

His rested an arm along the back of the couch. Holly closed her eyes and leaned her head back against the couch, and his arm. His hand moved to stroke her hair. His hand was being very brave.

Holly smiled and pressed her cheek into his hand. Suddenly, there was no air in the room at all. None. It was a vacuum, like space. "Holly -" He really had no idea what he was going to say, so he was glad when she cut him off.

"I'm sorry I got upset before, Antor. I was mad about you and Zenga, but I had no right. What happened between you two, that was before we met, and you and Zenga are only friends now, right?" Holly looked up at him with her beautiful blue eyes.

"Right." Antor's voice was so hoarse, he didn't recognize it.

Holly smiled and scooted a little closer. "I'm so glad you're not sleeping with Zenga anymore."

It felt like his heart stopped beating. At that moment in time, he wanted to keep his mouth shut more than he wanted to keep his limbs, but he'd promised Holly to be truthful with her. And surely the truth was nothing to get upset about. "Uh, actually, I did sleep with Zenga last night. We watched a movie and then we slept together."

Holly cursed and leapt to her feet. The Universal translator had a bit of trouble with the shocking phrase, yet it managed to bridge the gap. "Holly!" Antor was taken aback that she would speak to him like that.

"You slept with Zenga last night," Holly accused with such condemnation, he might have said he had murdered Zenga.

"It was no big deal, it was only for about twenty minutes," he said, defending himself.

"No big deal? Only for … for … twenty minutes? The time doesn't matter, it could have been two minutes—you took her to bed!" Holly screeched.

"No, it happened on the couch." Antor hoped that information would sooth her, since a couch wasn't nearly as intimate as a bed, but it didn't. She glared at the couch they had just been sitting on, as if she loathed the sight of it.

"Holly, calm down. Let's talk about this." Antor took a step toward her, wondering if they were having some sort of miscommunication. It did happen with Earth expressions, and Universal translators were not infallible.

"I don't want to talk to you, Antor. I don't even want to look at you right now! I thought you liked me—me, not Zenga."

Antor was at a complete loss, he didn't know what to say to fix the situation. "Of course I like Zenga, we're best friends, but that doesn't mean I can't … like you, too." Given the yearning in his heart, the word *like* felt sadly inadequate, when it was about Holly, but he couldn't say 'love', even though that's what he felt. It was simply too soon, and too risky.

Holly opened her mouth, no words came out. She spun around and ran into the bedroom, before he could tell her how much he liked her. Antor would have followed, except he didn't want to wake up the other girls. Plus, Holly seemed too upset to listen.

Clearly, sleeping together had a lot more significance on Earth than it did in the rest of the Universe. Antor slumped off to bed. He would clear things up with Holly in the morning. Or maybe he could get Zenga to talk to her, girl-to-girl. Females were usually better at communicating than males.

But in the morning, Holly was gone. She had left, taking Teef and all her things with her. The two girls had moved into Teef's assigned room. Zenga said that Holly had seemed really mad at her, too, and wasn't talking.

Antor was almost glad when Hampelle summoned them back to the ship to work. Banging dents out of metal helped him to vent some of his pent up frustration.

161

22 Holly - New Quarters

A long morning of signing autographs was followed by a social luncheon with VIP's and guest musicians, none of whom Holly had ever heard of, of course.

The afternoon was spent getting costumed and primped for the filming of a promo commercial to encourage viewers to watch the next exciting installment of Universe Idol, one week hence. The results show hadn't even taken place, and wouldn't until that evening, but they were already working on the next episode.

"No rest for the depressed," Holly muttered to Teef, as they smiled and posed for some sort of auto-mate camera person, whose head was as actual camera—but with real eyes. There were group shots, and individual shots, and action dancing/singing sequences. They moved from one location to another, being filmed both inside and outside.

Holly kept a close eye on Dejanne when they stepped into the sunlight, but the girl didn't sizzle up and turn into a pile of ash. She didn't even steam. All she did was squint against the bright light like the rest of them.

When the camera-mate closed its shutter eyelids, the filming was complete. Olliz told the contestants that they had an hour to rest in their rooms, before they had to regroup to learn the judges' decision, and find out which two contestants would be leaving. Universe Idol was different from the Earth Idol shows, in that the judges decided the winners, not a voting public.

Holly and Teef went to Teef's room. Holly didn't want to see Antor. It was too painful. She would still buy him back his limbs, and she would probably have to see him on the Comet Tail on the trip back to Earth, but she didn't have to speak to him. She told herself that her heart wasn't at all broken, or even bruised. Her feelings for Antor had been a misguided and short-lived crush, nothing more serious. Her heart didn't believe her for a second.

The door opened automatically for Teef and Holly followed her inside. The Schwill had only been given one room with two beds, and it seemed very small and empty. Holly dropped into a chair, avoiding the couch that was a twin to the one in her suite.

"Holly?" Teef sat down on the couch.

Holly stopped glaring daggers at the harmless piece of furniture. "Yes, Teef?"

"Do you want to tell me what's wrong now? And why you wanted to move into my room?"

Holly had been too upset to talk earlier, and the day had been so busy, there hadn't been another chance. But Holly was ready to spill her guts now. She needed to unload on someone, about what had happened, and Teef was a great listener. Teef was her best friend. Not Antor and not Zenga, but Teef.

Holly scowled and said, "Antor."

"Antor?"

"Antor and Zenga," Holly said, significantly.

"They are still romantically involved?"

Holly nodded.

Teef pursed her lips. "I wouldn't have expected that. Are you sure?"

"Positive," Holly huffed.

"How do you know?"

"Antor told me, last night," Holly fumed, "right in the middle of getting up close and personal with me!"

"I guess it must be true then. I'm sorry, Holly. You really liked him, didn't you?"

Holly pouted. "No."

Teef smiled gently. "Yes, you did."

"Okay, I did. But I don't now. I hate him." Holly sounded about four years old. She didn't care.

The viewing screen on the wall beeped and a little icon lit up in the corner.

"I have a message." Teef moved gracefully across the room and pressed the icon. The robotic voice said, "Teef Mosh, your chaperone has landed. She will arrive at your room shortly."

Teef frowned. "I guess the Roth family has made a choice. I hope it's someone nice. The last chaperone wasn't, although I shouldn't say that, since she's dead."

"Why don't you just tell them you don't need or want a chaperone? We would have more fun by ourselves. I could chaperone you. We're together most of the time anyway." Holly certainly didn't want to share Teef's room, or Teef, with another dour Schwill.

"I could never do that, Holly. It is my place to obey my betrothed, and his family, of course." Teef bowed her head submissively.

"Your place? Didn't your planet ever have a women's liberation movement?"

"No."

"Well, maybe it should have one now."

163

Teef didn't take offence. She asked, "What exactly is a women's liberation movement?"

Before Holly could go into details about burning bras and such, the door buzzed. Teef let in her new chaperone. This Schwill was shorter, wider and older than the last one, but had the same hard expression in her eyes. She looked familiar. Holly tried to remember where she had seen her before and couldn't. Considering the woman had just arrived on Playara, Holly was probably mistaken.

"Hello and welcome," Teef said politely.

The woman returned the greeting. She was followed by an auto-mate carrying a black plastic suitcase. It deposited the bag and left without a word. Auto-mates didn't expect tips.

The woman surveyed both girls and said, "Teef, I am Pala. The Roth family sends you their best wishes. They have entrusted me to be your new chaperone."

"Thank you for coming, especially after what happened to my last chaperone," Teef said frankly. "I have to be back at the stage in about half an hour. Holly, too, for the results show."

"I have been watching. You performed very well last night. I'm sure you will be the top winner," Pala said, almost warmly. She didn't mention Holly's efforts at all. It was rather rude, but Holly was getting used to aliens being rude. Most of them weren't nearly as polite as Canadians.

Holly stood there, feeling like an intruder. She might have left Teef and Pala alone, except she had nowhere else to go. Her own rooms weren't an option, not while Antor was there.

She retreated to the bathroom to freshen up. Teef took a turn after her. While the girl was gone, Pala ignored Holly. She unpacked her bag until Teef reappeared. There was no more easy conversation between the girls with the stone-faced woman there. When Teef said, "Time to go," it was a relief.

Pala followed them all the way to the backstage area, before she left to take her seat in the audience. Holly peeked through the shimmering curtains and spotted Antor and Zenga in their assigned seats. Pala settled only a few rows away from them. Holly's eyes returned to Antor and stayed there. She had lost control of them. He looked tired, and burdened. Holly missed his smile, she missed him, even though she didn't want to.

Teef tapped her on the shoulder. It was time to line up while Chrome Boreal did his thing. Again, an enormous screen replayed highlights from the previous night. Holly cringed when she saw herself almost ripping her top off, while gyrating and belting out her lyrics. At least she had stayed on key and in rhythm. In some ways, it was an impressive performance, not unlike Earth's old-school hard rockers. Smashing a guitar to pieces would have suited her performance.

164

The judges greeted the viewing audience and the contestants filed onto the stage. Holly smiled and waved to the ocean of faces that was little more than a blur, except for Antor's. His was the only one Holly could see clearly. He was smiling now, at her.

This time, the contestants who would be staying were identified one by one, in random order. Ahah, the Scarnivore, was the first to walk across the stage and sit in a safe seat. Vhergos the eerie Banshom was second, and Inx the electrical Stinge was third. Then there were commercials. Holly was starting to hate commercials more than she hated cabbage soup.

After the break, Teef was sent to the safe seats. Holly hugged her and said, "Congratulations. I knew you were going to stay." Mini-Hampelle was next. That was a surprise.

Holly was left standing with Dejanne and the two shortest contestants, shrunken Blyllygo and green scaly Mogg. Chrome Boreal strolled over and said, "Two of these four contestants will be leaving us tonight. We'll find out who, after this commercial break." Had everyone in the Universe forgotten that they'd just had commercials?

Holly groaned aloud and shifted restlessly from foot to foot. Dejanne stepped closer and inhaled deeply. It was unlikely the Emangster would try to drink her blood during Universe Idol, in front of zillions of viewers, but Holly edged away anyway, as nonchalantly as possible.

The lights brightened again and Chrome held up a golden ring disc. "Let's find out who is safe," he said and placed it in his mouth. Holly had time to count off eight seconds before he spilled the beans. "Holly Noel Tate, I am delighted to say that you will be staying to sing for us again."

She hurried across the stage to sit beside Teef and whispered, "Safe." Teef smiled her congratulations, and squeezed her hand.

It was almost anticlimactic when Mogg was the last contestant chosen. Blyllygo and Dejanne would be leaving the show. Holly hadn't expected Dejanne to be eliminated so early on, but she was kind of relieved. Keeping close company with a Vampire, as she thought of the girl, was unnerving.

Chrome Boreal wrapped things up quickly, reminding the viewers to watch again next week. The stage lights darkened and the show was over. Holly walked backstage with Teef. Antor and Zenga were waiting, as was Pala.

"Congratulations, Holly," Antor said, hunching. "And Teef, well done."

"You both made it into the top eight, that's great." Zenga smiled happily.

She should be happy. She must want Antor to keep his limbs, so he could keep sleeping with her. Holly recalled how quick Zenga had been to offer her limb in place of Antor's third. Maybe that should have been a clue as to how truly close the pair was.

"Thanks," Holly said shortly.

Teef acknowledged them more warmly, until Pala cut her off. "Time to go back to the room."

Teef's face fell. "Oh, but we usually celebrate after the show."

"There will be no celebrating until you have won all. Come along." Pala started walking and Teef followed, like a lamb.

"I'm leaving too. Bye." Holly went with Teef, even though she hadn't been invited.

"Holly, wait," Antor called. She kept going as if she hadn't heard him at all.

23 Antor - Emangster

"**W**ow, Holly is really mad at you," Zenga said. "What did you do last night?"

"I think she's mad at you, too," Antor pointed out.

"She did seem angry with both of us. So … how did you mess up last night?" Zenga linked their arms and started them walking. Antor peeked over his shoulder and caught a glimpse of Holly glaring after him. She looked even angrier than minutes ago. With a huff, she jerked her head around and marched away.

"Antor?"

He hadn't answered Zenga's question. "It's stupid, but Holly's mad because you and I slept together."

"Really? Are you sure? That seems silly."

"I know. I think 'sleeping together' must mean something different on her planet. I was going to ask Holly, but she won't talk to me." Antor turned sideways to edge around a slow moving Manni. The crowd exiting from the theatre was still thick.

As soon as they were clear of the throng, Zenga said, "I don't know what else sleeping together could mean." She must have been mulling it over. "Sleeping is sleeping, in any language. It's not something the Universal translator could mess up."

"That's what I thought." Antor was glad to have Zenga's support. He was feeling beaten. He'd spent his life more alone than most beings. Not belonging anywhere was all he had ever known, but when he'd met Holly, he had felt like he belonged with her. Now that she'd moved out of their rooms, his loneliness had returned with a vengeance, and it seemed to have grown all out of proportion. He didn't want that emotion back, he wanted Holly back.

When they reached their rooms, Zenga looked at his depressed face and ordered a bottle of red brandy from room service. Exported from the Ice Planet, it was potent stuff, and cost a fortune. Luckily, they weren't paying the bill.

"Do I look that morose?" Antor slumped on the couch, which felt too big and too empty.

"You do, Antor. I've never seen you like this. If you were a girl, you'd be bawling."

"Shut up," he growled. "Where's the brandy."

"On its way. I made a rush order."

He heaved a sigh. "You haven't gotten me drunk in months."

"How remiss of me," Zenga said with arched eyebrows.

When the door buzzed, Zenga went to answer it with a swagger. An auto-mate brought the beverage inside. Given its price tag, a floating tray would have been too risky. Only an empty tray would have arrived at the room.

Zenga opened the black bottle and handed it to Antor. They weren't going to bother with glasses, it seemed. He drank deeply and passed it back. Zenga imbibed freely, since she could drink Antor under the table any day of the week. She smacked her lips. "Tasty."

Antor extended a hand and wiggled his fingers. Zenga put the bottle exactly where it belonged. He drank more. Warmth filled him. "Better than dinner."

"We did forget dinner, didn't we? That's a first for me." Zenga sampled more, until Antor reclaimed the bottle. There was no more talk of dinner.

Much much later, when the door buzzed, Zenga was passed out in her bed. Antor was still nursing the bottle. His first thought was *Holly*.

He knew he was tanked when he tried to walk to the door. All he could do was lurch in a zigzag pattern, but he made it. He slid opened the door, really hoping Holly wouldn't be mad at him for being drunk.

It wasn't a pleasant surprise to find Dejanne instead of Holly, although it did explain why the door hadn't opened all by itself. Antor should have clued into that.

"Antor, may I come in?" Dejanne asked.

She didn't cross the threshold until he said, "Certainly." He waved an arm grandly, almost tipping over. Dejanne put an arm around his waist and guided him back to the couch. He collapsed there with her, no longer alone, but still alone because she wasn't Holly.

"Your blood smells quite intoxicating tonight, or maybe intoxicated," Dejanne said.

"I'm not s'prised." Anton was amazed that his numb tongue could actually form words.

"Drowning your sorrows, Antor?"

"How d'you know?" he asked, blinking owlishly.

"I don't smell Holly's blood."

Antor shook his head sadly. "No Holly, no Holly's blood, no Holly anything. She'sss gone."

"I wouldn't mind drowning my own sorrows tonight," Dejanne said. "I leave for home tomorrow. I really didn't think I would be voted off so soon. I can't believe that stupid Mogg got to stay. He really can't sing at all. And he certainly can't dance. Maybe he bribed the judges." She looked as depressed as Antor felt and added, "I thought I sang really well."

"You did." He was feeling empathetic toward anyone who could share his misery. "Here you go." Antor extended the almost empty bottle.

"That won't work for me. I can't drown my sorrows in the usual way," Dejanne said.

"Huh?" Antor didn't understand.

"I can only absorb alcohol through someone else's blood. I can't drink, someone else has to drink for me," she explained.

He thought she was hinting at something, but he wasn't sure.

"Why don't you have a little more?" She handed him the bottle. Antor could grasp it and lift it, so he could drink it. He drained the brandy until nothing but drops teased his tongue.

"S'all gone," he told Dejanne.

"My turn?" She looked ravenous and stared deep into his eyes. The room spun in circles and he had trouble thinking.

"Your turn?" he parroted.

"Can I have a little drink?" Even her hypnotic voice was making him woozier than the red brandy. Antor felt that he should say 'yes' so he did.

"Yesss." His voice sounded like it was coming from very far away, and from a hissing snake.

Dejanne leaned close and he felt a sharp pain in his neck. His reaction time was so slow it was nonexistent. He didn't even try to pull away and then the pain was gone, but Dejanne was attached to his neck. It felt very wet where her mouth was sucking. She was either giving him a monster hickey or she was drinking his blood—and the alcohol in his blood.

Antor strained his eyeballs to look down. His tunic had a big sticky red patch—his blood. She certainly wasn't neat about her bloodsucking. Antor thought he should protest, yet he just kept sitting there in a bit of a daze, letting Dejanne slurp. He seemed to have lost his will to think or move. Maybe Holly was right and Dejanne was going to drink all his blood and kill him, or feed him some of her blood to transform him into a Vampire Emangster. The room began to spin and still Dejanne drank. He groaned when he thought he was going to puke.

Dejanne jerked away. "Oh, Antor, sorry. I didn't mean to take so much. Your blood is just so delicious, as is the alcohol. Are you okay?" Dejanne's mouth was red and dripping.

Antor didn't think he was okay. His head lolled back; he couldn't hold it up. The room receded as if he was being pulled into a black hole. He tried to stand and fell off the couch, quite unable to feel his legs.

Dejanne crouched over him, a black shadowy figure. He was pretty darn sure she was going to drain the rest of his blood and finish him off. Before he could fight for his life, he passed out.

169

24 Holly - Dead Drunk

Holly stomped down the corridor, clutching a small bag that held all her Outer Space possessions—things she had collected since she had been abducted from Earth. She had her blue outfit, compliments of the Mannireplians, she had a pajama jumpsuit, compliments of the hotel. Ditto for the toothbrush. And that's all she had, aside from the borrowed clothes on her back, and the odds and ends in her pockets. She didn't even have a room anymore. She was homeless—kicked out by Pala, who didn't want her precious Teef associating with the likes of Holly.

It had been a little crowded in the single room, but Holly didn't think that factored into why Pala had sent her away. Pala just didn't seem to like Holly. And Teef hadn't made any protest, not even a token one. She had sat like a well-trained puppy, while Pala kicked Holly out!

Thoroughly disgruntled, and angry with Teef, Holly paced the corridors, trying to decide what to do. She didn't want to sleep in the lobby. It might not be safe, and too many beings would stare at her. And she didn't want to sleep in a public bathroom, that was just gross. And she certainly didn't want to go back to her own rooms and walk in on Antor and Zenga sleeping together. A bathroom floor was better than that.

When Holly passed a bench, she realized that her legs were exhausted from all the stomping. She plunked down and snuggled up to a big potted plant. It was blooming with crumply flowers and smelled fantastic. Better yet, it hid her almost completely. Holly considered sleeping right there, even though the bench seat was as hard as pavement.

She leaned back and sighed, more homesick than she had felt since she had left Earth behind. She wanted her own bed, and her own room, and her own clothes. She missed her Mom, and even her sister. She wasn't missing Daniel so much, but she missed Fiona regardless of her friend's betrayal. And maybe she even missed school. She wasn't sure about that.

When Dejanne staggered by, she didn't notice Holly behind the potted plant. Dejanne's eyes were glazed. She had blood all over her chin and splattered on her white top. She was also bouncing off of the walls, and coming from the direction of Holly's suite.

Holly dared not breathe until Dejanne reached the end of the corridor and disappeared from sight. Terrified of what she would find, Holly leapt up and raced in the opposite direction. Her room door opened automatically at her appearance, and she fell inside. She didn't see anything alarming, not until she stepped around the couch.

Antor's body was sprawled on the floor, unmoving. Blood red stained the front of his tunic. Two deep puncture wounds in his neck proved that Dejanne had murdered him. He was so deathly pale and bonelessly slack. Holly had never seen anyone look deader, not even on CSI. She screamed.

When Zenga rushed out of the bedroom, Holly tried to block her view of the body. She stepped toward Zenga and gripped her arms saying, "Don't look."

Zenga rubbed her sleepy eyes. "Don't look at what?"

"Antor is … Antor is …" Holly couldn't say the words and began to sob.

"Is what? Drunk?" Zenga guessed. She smelled like booze herself, and her eyes were bloodshot.

"No, not drunk. Dead." Holly tried to say it gently. It came blurting out on a ragged sob.

Zenga gasped and stepped around Holly. When she saw Antor's body, her whole face crumpled. "What happened?"

"Dejanne drained his blood," Holly said, unable to look away. Even in tragic death, Antor was a beautiful sculpture of a man.

"What? No, I don't think so." Zenga stooped beside Antor. She laid a hand over his heart and said, "He's not dead, Holly."

"He's not?" Holly didn't believe it until she crouched beside Zenga and felt his wrist for a pulse. It was there, but slow and weak.

An empty bottle lay on the floor beside him. Up close, Antor smelled like alcohol, not death. Still, there was a lot of blood and the punctures looked brutal. Holly pointed to them and said, "See, Dejanne was drinking his blood. Oh! Do you think she transformed him into a Vampire? And that's why he's not dead?"

Zenga actually smiled. "No, Holly, I don't. I think Antor will be fine."

In Holly's opinion, Zenga should have been upset, not cracking smiles. She said, "Antor is your lover. Don't you even care that he's hurt?"

Zenga looked at Holly as if she was nuts. "What did you say?"

"That you and Antor are lovers. He told me." Holly sniffed and touched his skin. It felt too cold.

"No, we're not. We were a long time ago, briefly, but we aren't now. We're just friends. That's why you're mad at him? Because you think we're still lovers?"

Holly nodded. "He said you were sleeping together."

"Ah." That meant something to Zenga. "Let me guess, on Earth, sleeping together means mating—not sleeping, but sex?" she said clearly, as if she didn't want there to be any misunderstanding.

171

"Uh, right. On Earth, sleeping together means having sex," Holly parroted, just as clearly.

"In that case, Antor and I are not sleeping together, although we did have an accidental nap on the couch after the movie the other night." Zenga took Holly's hand and pressed it, palm down, on Antor's heart. "He really likes you. He's never liked anyone the way he likes you, Holly. He almost died for you, didn't he? Have more faith in him. He has earned it."

Holly felt ashamed of herself when Zenga said that. She felt like a silly girl. She'd hurt Antor, she knew she had, and he didn't deserve that. "I think I was freaked out by all the differences between Earth humans and Outer Space humans. I have a lot to learn about your customs, but you're right. I should trust Antor. I think I have to trust myself, too. Can we move him to his bed? He feels so cold."

Together, they half-dragged and half-carried Antor to his room. He groaned a few times, but didn't rouse, not even when they pulled off his stained top and tucked him under a warm blanket. He looked so much less dead in bed under a blanket, but Holly was still worried. "Should we call a doctor?"

Zenga checked Antor over again and said, "He seems okay. The punctures will heal by themselves. I don't think Dejanne drank enough blood to harm him, Emangsters really don't do that. He's probably going to have one heck of a hangover, but that's no reason to call a physician."

"Okay. I might sleep here, and keep him warm. Make sure he's okay," Holly said, unable to control the blush that heated her cheeks.

"Good idea. Good-night, Holly."

"Good-night, Zenga. And thanks."

Zenga waved and closed the door on her way out. Holly cuddled up to Antor in her clothes. She held him close and it was wonderfully cozy. Sleep came quickly.

Holly was still holding Antor when she awoke. He hadn't moved, but his eyes were opened, watching her.

"How are you feeling?" she whispered. His skin was so pale, he looked like a Vampire.

He blinked. "Holly?"

"You were hoping for someone else?" she quipped.

"Never. I thought I was imagining you. My head doesn't seem clear. I don't remember how I got here—how we got here."

Holly cuddled closer and told the story of finding him dead. She made sure to mention Zenga's helpful revelations about their miscommunication.

Antor chuckled at that point, then clutched his head. "Sounds like I had quite a night, getting drunk, Dejanne draining my blood, you pronouncing me dead at the scene, and sleeping with you ... sleeping," he stressed and pulled Holly intimately close. "I wish it wasn't just sleeping." Antor nuzzled her neck, sending hot tingles down to her toes.

"I'm just glad you're alive, Antor. We'll have other nights." At least she hoped so, if he could forgive her for acting so childish.

"But what about Daniel?" he asked.

"Oh, we broke up. He's dating someone else, my best friend, Fiona."

Antor studied her face. "Does that make you sad?"

"I'm sadder about Fiona than Daniel." It was the absolute truth.

"Good … I don't mean good that you're sad, but -"

"I know what you mean, Antor."

"Uh, bad timing, but I have to go … freshen up." Antor stood and almost fell over. He found his balance and walked gingerly from the room. Holly edged over into the warm spot left by his body and waited for him to return. He took so long, she got up and made sure he was okay. He was in the steamy shower cubicle, probably rinsing off blood.

Holly had a drink of water and went back to bed. Antor returned, damp and much fresher. He was wearing pajama bottoms, his beautiful chest was still bare. She lifted the blanket and he rolled in. They smiled at each other like idiots for the longest time. Luckily, no-one could see them but each other.

Under the covers, Holly ran her hands down Antor's back, marveling at the velvet texture of his skin. He slipped his hands under her shirt and stroked her back. "You're so warm. Do you know I've never even kissed you, not really?"

"Yes, Antor, I am aware of that. Very aware. I certainly wouldn't have forgotten my first alien kiss -"

Antor stopped her nervous babbling with his mouth. His lips were even softer than his skin, and so gentle in spite of the passion that made his hands shake when he pressed their bodies together. His kiss put to shame every Earth kiss she had ever known.

Before Holly burst into flames or had a heart attack, they both came up for air.

"Wow," Holly gasped, and, "wow." Once hadn't been enough.

Antor looked endearingly worried. "Is wow good? The translator is unsure of that word in this context. And maybe you don't kiss like that on Earth. Am I supposed to be using my tongue? Because if you don't want me to use my tongue, I won't."

"*Wow* means never stop kissing me, Antor, and please use your tongue."

He did, until they were rudely interrupted by banging on the bedroom door.

"Send them away," Holly groaned. All they had done was kiss. She wanted to do more than that with Antor. She'd never lived in paradise before, and she didn't want to leave.

"Go away," Antor bellowed at the door, sounding more menacing than she'd ever heard him.

"Holly, you have to go to work," Zenga shouted through the door. "Teef sent a message for you to meet her backstage. You have to learn the choreography today, for the new group song and dance."

Holly squeezed her eyes closed and pressed her forehead against Antor's. "I do have to go. I'm singing for you."

"I know." The orange flecks in Antor's eyes flared hot. "And I want to keep my hands to touch you, feel you. Do you know I still haven't touched most of you?"

Holly couldn't stop the smile that took over her face. "I do know that, Antor. And now I have to go. I expect to find you right here when I come home for dinner."

"Here? In bed?" His smile robbed her breath.

"Don't you dare move." She kissed him lingeringly and left quickly. It was the only way she could wrench herself from Antor, and still it hurt. It felt like an amputation, but it was love. She had gone and fallen head over heels in love with an alien.

25 Antor - Pariah

After Holly left, Antor went back to sleep in the warmth her body had left behind. Her flowery scent was on the pillow and on his skin. He might have stayed there all day, recovering from his hangover and bloodletting, if Zenga hadn't invaded his private space. At least she brought breakfast on a floating tray.

He sat up, realizing he was quite starved. "Thanks, Zen."

She nudged the tray lower, until it was at the perfect height for him. "You need to eat, Antor. You really did look like death last night." She perched on the edge of the bed and checked his puncture wounds. "Ouch. Dejanne really bit you good. At least she's left the planet. I verified her departure."

"You think of everything, Zen."

Zenga entertained him with her version of what had transpired the night before. The facts were as Holly had related them, but the point of view was quite different. Antor simply listened, too busy enjoying his food to talk. Zenga had ordered all his favourites— potcakes with meat grinds, and scrambled weggies, and two kinds of fruit juice.

Only when his platter was clean did she share the bad news. "Hampelle called a little while ago. He wants us back on the ship."

"But the engine is fixed, and I banged out all the dents yesterday, and quick-metalled all the erosion made by the Gorka. Why does he want us on the Comet Tail?"

"He claims he's accepted a small delivery contract in this sector, and he's satisfied that Holly is well-guarded in the entertainment complex, so we've been called back to work. I don't think he has the patience to sit on the ship and wait."

Antor's heart sank all the way down to his toes. "But I told Holly I would be waiting for her, right here." He blushed. "Uh ... how long will we be away?"

"He says we'll be back before next week's show. He wasn't more specific than that."

"Next week?" Antor's heart sank lower still, until it must have reached the planet's core. His plans to spend as much time as he could with Holly had been the most wonderful plans he'd ever had.

175

"Sorry, Antor. The shuttle is picking us up in half an hour. You better get ready." Zenga rose and nudged the tray ahead of her, toward the door.

"Are you sure he wants both of us?" Antor was grasping at straws.

"Yes, Antor. Get a move on." Zenga shut the door behind her.

An hour later, they were stepping onto the Comet Tail's bridge. It was a bit of a shock to find that Captain Hampelle wasn't alone, and Antor didn't like the look of the hard-faced trio that was keeping him company. The most eye-catching of the three was a Demigorgon. The part human species was reputed to be cruel, untrustworthy and best avoided, if at all possible. Antor didn't usually believe hearsay, but he'd heard that opinion enough times to know it held some truth.

"Red Belial," the Demigorgon introduced himself with slimy smoothness. His sienna orange skin was almost steaming. Pointy black horns sprouted from the vicinity of his ears, snaked along his head, and jutted out from his scalp at a 90 degree angle. If he head-butted anyone without an exoskeleton, they would be dead meat.

Antor and Zenga introduced themselves, without getting too close.

The remaining two were former prison inmates, although Antor didn't think their burned brands were from Gehenna. Red had probably bought the pair at another prison's slave auction.

It was hard to tell one from the other. Or impossible. They were Binares with no trace of human in their DNA. Binares were spawned into the world as conjoined twins, and they guarded each other's backs on their predatory planet. Binares only separated cellularly from their double at physical maturity, when they had the full strength to survive as individuals.

Compared to humans, they were massive above the waist. Their combined shoulders took up most of the extra bridge space, especially when they stood back to back, as they were inclined to do, probably an ingrained habit since they had grown up that way. Their jaws rivaled their shoulders for jutting out and occupying far too much space.

Antor swallowed and tried not to stare. He had never been so close to a set of Binares. Their jaws were as big as his whole face. Their mouths were gigantic enough to bite his head right off. Red referred to them as Bo, not even Bo One and Bo Two, so they even shared the same name.

"You took your bloody time getting here," Hampelle snapped. "We've been ready to leave orbit for an hour."

"Sorry … uh, we?" Antor asked. It sounded like the threesome would be traveling with them.

"We." Hampelle shoved to his feet. "Course is already set. Start flying, top speeds. We'll be in the galley. Don't interrupt us."

Antor pressed himself against the wall when the Binares lumbered by, one then the other. It felt like the metal flooring bent inward, but there were no dents after the pair left. Antor checked.

"I wonder if those three are our cargo. What do you think Hampelle is scheming now?" Zenga hissed as soon as they were alone.

"Wish I knew, Zen. First the Gorka, then that crazy weapon, now these characters—a Demigorgan and Binares." Antor had a bad feeling in his gut, and he didn't think it was only because he was leaving Holly behind. He sat down and boosted the ship out of orbit. When he checked the course and destination that Hampelle had input, he borrowed one of Holly's curses.

"What now?" Zenga asked.

"I think I know who our passengers are—or maybe I should say 'what' they are."

"What?"

"Smugglers—or something akin." Antor pressed buttons and their plotted course was illuminated on a galactic map on the big viewing screen.

Zenga scowled. "We're going to Pariah? Even the UGS won't go within a light year of that dump. Why would Hampelle be so foolish?"

"Maybe he feels invincible with that new weapon of his, and Binares aboard. I wonder if A-1 knows about this little jaunt."

Zenga snorted. "Not a chance. And I bet they don't know that Hampelle is expanding on his private contracts. Why doesn't he just wait for Holly to make him wealthy?"

Antor had no answer except a guess. "Some beings crave thrills. Hampelle sure enjoyed that battle with the pirates. He acted like it was a party. Maybe he's bored with orbiting in space, and there's still almost a month of waiting to go."

"So he's thrill-seeking?" Zenga shifted sideways in her chair and draped her legs over the armrest. "He could do that without me and you. Why bring us along?"

"Probably so he can sleep, Zen. I'm going to send Holly a message while we're still in short-range." Antor called her room and said, "Uh, hi Holly. It's Antor. I'm not there, I hope you noticed." Zenga smirked at him. He felt self-conscious with her listening, but he couldn't ask her to leave. He continued, "Captain Hampelle called us back to work. We've left orbit and we won't be back for a few days. I miss you already, I hope you miss me." He shot Zenga a dark glance when she giggled. "We'll be back before the filming of the next Universe Idol and I'll see you then. Stay safe, Holly. I miss you. I already said that, didn't I? Uh, bye."

After he closed the channel, Zenga said, "You are so smooth, Antor." It was sarcasm.

He told her to zip her lips and went to check if he still had a cabin. He didn't. Someone had taken over the little room. Antor suspected it was one or both of the Binares, because his hammock had collapsed to the ground.

177

He watered his plants, packed his belongings in his duffle bag, found Holly's scarf, and took everything to her former cabin. It didn't look like anyone had claimed that noisy cramped space, so he did. Using the scarf as a pillow, he had a nap. He was still recovering from his hangover, not to mention all the blood loss.

When he awoke, Zenga was snoozing in the overhead berth. She must have lost her cabin to Red. Antor hoped Holly wouldn't be mad that he was sleeping with Zenga again, since it was only sleeping and they each had their own hammock.

The next day, they reached the planet Pariah, and learned exactly why Hampelle had brought them along. He stomped onto the bridge with a blaster dangling from his shoulder and said, "I'm going down to the surface with Red and his mates, to meet some potential clients and inspect some product, before it's brought aboard the Comet Tail. I shouldn't be gone more than a couple of days. You two guard the ship." He approached the main console and pointed to the cluster of new buttons. "Those control the Compactor, the weapon that will keep the Comet Tail safe."

Antor gulped. "But ... I don't know how to use it." And he didn't think he wanted to.

"Instructions are here." Hampelle pressed a couple more buttons, bringing the information up in the data-stream. "Both of you read them, memorize them, and keep this ship in one piece until I get back. Willy is recharging." With a growl, he shoved Antor out of his chair and blew into the console vent, activating his Captain's security override with his breath, before he keyed in more commands.

"What are you doing?" Zenga demanded.

"Disabling long-range communications until I get back. Don't want you making any calls that you shouldn't. I've also activated the proximity kill-switch. You can defend the ship if need be, but you can't leave orbit. If you do, the engines will shut down, and they won't restart without my breath."

"But ... we'll be trapped here until you return?" Antor didn't like that at all. "What if you don't make it back? Pariah isn't the safest planet."

"Then you better hope I do come back, still breathing." Hampelle snarled once and left the bridge.

"He doesn't trust us, not any more than we trust him," Zenga muttered.

A shuttle picked up Hampelle and his three passengers, and then Antor and Zenga were alone. Zenga was quick to activate the viewing screen, allowing them to see the shuttle zooming toward the mud-brown planet.

"Should I blast them now?" Zenga's finger hovered over the button that fired the Compactor.

178

"Don't! We need Hampelle to get us the Gehenna out of here."

"I'm joking, Antor. Have you lost your sense of humour? I only want to see where they land," she said more seriously.

"Oh, of course. I don't think there are many places to go down there." Pariah was a sparsely populated planet for many reasons, including the arid climate, the rocky landscape, and the violent inhabitants.

The shuttle landed outside a town called Blackfist. Zenga accessed information on the site. She read the highlights aloud to Antor, in her own words. "Sounds like a lawless hole. Small population of crooks, pirates, smugglers, slavers and the like. They run a thriving traders' outpost for ill-gotten and illegal goods. Hampelle and Red Belial will feel right at home down there. No landing passes needed to visit, but you visit at your own risk." She scrolled down the data-stream. "Here's an interesting fact. The town is named after a legendary smuggler by the name of Black. His ship, The Fist, crash-landed there a millennium ago, when the planet was completely uninhabited. It went down loaded with all his accumulated wealth, booty, bizoux. What survived the impact was strewn across the rock and buried by the blowing sands. Treasure hunters came a'calling, some stayed and founded the town of Blackfist in his honour. That's its claim to fame, such as it is, unless you're looking for something you can't get anywhere else."

"I wonder if the merchandise Hampelle is inspecting, is something he can't get anywhere else," Antor said.

"Of course it is. Why else would he come here? Watch the bridge, I'm going to search Red's things, see if he's left any clues about what they're up to."

"If you want to search the Binares' stuff, they're staying in my cabin," Antor called after her.

When she returned an hour later, she hadn't learned a thing and said, "I even tried to break into Hampelle's cabin, but he's locked the door with his stinky breath."

There was nothing else to do, so they watched some entertainment broadcasts. Time dragged in the worst way. After two days of pacing, choking down space rations, and waiting for Hampelle's return, Antor better understood the Captain's latest actions—seeking a profitable distraction, instead of orbiting Playara and waiting for Holly to win Universe Idol.

Restless and concerned about his and Zenga's safety, Antor spent a few hours tinkering with the ship's systems, to reconfigure both the door and the communication panels in the cabin where they were sleeping. It was a complex task, to link them to the rest of the ship's systems in ways they weren't meant to be linked, and to crosswire functions in unexpected ways. In the end, he felt a little more secure. To test his modifications, he

179

eavesdropped on the bridge. Zenga was still watching broadcasts. He joined her.

On the third day, Antor acted as impulsively as his Captain, and more like the man he aimed to be. He knew that Zenga wasn't going to like his plan, so he didn't reveal it, not until he was ready to leave. At that point, he called her to the bridge and said, "Your turn to watch the ship. I'm going down to the planet to scout around."

Zenga gaped at him. "Are you insane? You can't go down there, especially alone. And why would you want to?"

"Hampelle is overdue. I'm just going to sniff around, see if I can track him down. Maybe I can find out what he's doing down there, and I'd like to buy Holly a present from the smuggler's market, a souvenir of her trip to Outer Space."

"Antor, stop acting stupid, and wait for Hampelle to return. I'm sure he'll be back anytime."

"I'm not acting stupid. I'm fed up with being trapped on this ship. Hampelle never gets up before noon, so we won't see him for hours if he does come back today. I have plenty of time. Willy can keep you company, he's fully recharged." Antor patted the blaster he carried, to give himself courage, for what he was about to do. "My shuttle is waiting, I promise I won't be more than four or five hours. I'll be fine, Zen." She shook her head in mute protest. "I'll bring you back something, too. How about some real food?"

Zenga kept shaking her head, looking at Antor as if it was the very last time she would see him. It made him angry. "I'm not a child, Zen. I'm capable of looking after myself. I've done it all my life, haven't I? I'll see you soon."

He left the bridge and boarded a decrepit little shuttle. It reeked of old sweat and dirty feet, but it got him safely to the planet's surface. He disembarked outside the market proper and joined the foot traffic entering the streets of stalls. There were no crowds, but enough bodies for Antor to feel inconspicuous. Growing up amid rough types, he knew how to be invisible better than most. He stuck his hands in his pockets, kept his eyes down and slouched when he walked. He'd worn his oldest brown tunic over threadbare pants, and he blended right in with the dirt that coated every surface.

Pariah was a desolate world, and that was the best thing you could say about it. It was as dusty and windy as it was dry and flat. There wasn't a plant to be seen. Breathing the air made Antor cough, until he wrapped a kerchief around his lower face to block the dust, as most beings had done. Feeling safely disguised, he strolled through the aisles, keeping watch for Hampelle or his cohorts.

It took a couple of hours to scout all the market lanes. Most of the booths were nothing more than slab-tables under flimsy canopies that blocked the sun. Antor shopped a bit, asking the nicer beings, usually the females, if they had seen anyone blue-black and furry, horned and red, or really, really big in duplicate. No-one had—or they weren't saying.

If Antor had had bribe money, he probably could have found out a lot more, but he didn't. One pretty humanoid invited him into a canteen for a drink. He went, hoping she would have some information for him. She didn't, but she made a proposition that he might have found tempting, before Holly. He wasn't tempted now, and he was on a mission. Antor gulped his drink and ran.

He spent the few coins he had on a takeout meal, and a gift for Holly. It was a pretty piece of jewelry. He hoped she would like it, since it was all he could afford at the moment.

His self-imposed time limit almost up, Antor skirted the market, peering into dilapidated bars and eateries on the way to the shuttles. He didn't catch a glimpse of anyone who resembled his quarry, not until he reached the parking lot.

Antor didn't want to believe his eyes, yet he couldn't deny that Hampelle and Red were standing right there, as big as life. The pair was talking furtively with two robed humanoids, while the Binares loaded crates into the biggest shuttle in the parking lot.

Clearly, Antor had lingered a few minutes too long in Blackfist. He ducked behind the nearest parked vehicle and made sure his kerchief was covering most of his face. He knew if Hampelle caught him on Pariah, he would probably be abandoned there. Antor had to get back to the Comet Tail before the Captain, but he didn't see how that was possible now. He slunk from shuttle to shuttle, moving closer. He snuck as close as he dared and tried to eavesdrop on what was being said. He couldn't hear a thing over the steady wind and idling ships' coils.

The clones finished loading the shuttle and approached Hampelle. Their backs were to Antor and the shuttle doors were still ajar. It gave Antor an inspired idea about how he could make it back to the Comet Tail without being seen, if he was lucky. He usually wasn't, so maybe he was due. His plan was highly risky, yet it was the only one he had.

While the Binares' shoulders were blocking everyone's view of the shuttle, Antor darted toward it, staying low. He dove through the side door and between two boxes. There was just enough space. He shifted a couple of the cartons and was hidden completely, crouched in an uncomfortable little ball, his blaster sticking into his side. By the time the doors closed and the passengers piled in, Antor's legs were already cramping, but it was too late to move them, or the blaster. He just hoped the safety was on.

The shuttle's takeoff was rough. The vehicle had probably exceeded its maximum recommended load weight, and Antor didn't think it had a thing to do with his extra pounds. The Binares and the cargo alone probably weighed too much for any basic shuttle craft.

Red expressed alarm over the bumpy launch. Hampelle just laughed it off. Antor strained his ears, listening to the conversation in the cab. The Binares were the strong silent types, and kept their mouths clamped all the way to the Comet Tail, while Hampelle and Red never shut theirs. And what they were scheming was so immoral, Antor felt sick in his gut to hear it. Hampelle was evil. Antor simply hadn't realized how truly evil, until that moment. And Red was just as bad, maybe worse.

Antor learned all kinds of valuable information on that half hour shuttle ride, including the fact that Hampelle and Red had a long history of nefarious activities together. The Gorka belonged to Red. He had invested several years of his life plotting to get his hands on a female, and then carrying out that complex plot. He wasn't at all pleased that Hampelle had temporarily released his mating pair of Gorka on a restricted planet. In fact, he was pissed.

When the shuttle docked against the Comet Tail, Antor knew he would need a whole lot more luck to get aboard unseen. And if Hampelle found him stowed away now, after what Antor had overheard, he would be dead before his feet touched the ship's deck. Zenga was probably having ten fits on the bridge, believing Antor still on the planet.

The four passengers piled out. The Binares started sliding boxes across the shuttle, to the side docked against the Comet Tail.

Antor crouched smaller as his camouflage disappeared around him. He strained his ears and couldn't hear Hampelle's or Red's voices anymore. They had probably left Bo and Bo to do all the heavy lifting, which would definitely work in Antor's favour. Still, the Binares weren't blind. They might even be brighter than they appeared.

When two crates were taken away at the same time, Antor grabbed a third and carried it out of the shuttle. He staggered under its weight and his knees almost buckled. The Binares had their backs to him as they lumbered away.

"Don't look back," Antor muttered under his breath. They didn't. He had enough time to stow his blaster and shopping inside the door of C-2 before he followed them into smaller C-8.

"Thought you could use a hand," he said, as if he had been on the Comet Tail all along. The pair didn't suspect a thing.

"Thanks," said one.

The other nodded.

Antor helped them unload the rest of the crates and asked, "What's inside?"

182

"Don't know," said one.

The other stared blankly ahead.

As soon as the pair disappeared up the slide to the bridge deck, Antor cracked the lid on the nearest carton. He found bottles of red brandy nestled inside. The smuggled goods were illegal, there was no doubt, but Antor had expected to find much worse. Being caught with smuggled alcohol wouldn't even get a ship and crew impounded. It was a slap on the wrist transgression. So why had Hampelle gone all the way to Pariah to get a few dozen crates of brandy? It didn't add up. He must have visited Pariah for another reason entirely. Frustrated, Antor helped himself to one bottle, figuring it wouldn't be missed. After the stressful morning, he felt like he'd earned it.

He retrieved his shopping and blaster. He stashed everything in Holly's cabin, before he switched into his regular clothes and rushed to the bridge. He was rather terrified that Zenga would confess that he had abandoned ship, before he could show her he was back.

Zenga was on the bridge with Hampelle and Red when Antor walked in. Her eyes almost popped out of their sockets at his miraculous reappearance.

"Captain Hampelle," Antor said with a tight nod. "How was Pariah?"

"None of your damn business," Hampelle ground out. "Get the ship moving."

"Back to Playara?" Antor sat down beside Zenga, even though she was glowering at him as if she wanted to hurt him in a serious way.

"Back to Playara, via Aldage. We have some cargo to drop off there."

"But … Aldage is away from Playara." And Antor needed to get back to Holly. Aside from the fact that he missed her terribly, he had to talk to her about the truly appalling scheme that Hampelle and Red had been discussing in the shuttle.

"Aldage, then Playara." Hampelle didn't linger. He puffed into the console vent to remove his security lock, and shuffled away with Red.

Zenga waited, as still as a stalking mimanthos, until Hampelle was well away from the bridge, and probably tucked in bed, before she rounded on Antor, her tone as sharp as claws. "What the Gehenna were you playing at, Antor? You almost gave me a heart attack! I was about to tell Hampelle not to leave orbit, because you were down there! And how in Gehenna did you get back on the ship?"

"Sorry, Zen. I know I gave you some bad moments. I came back on the same shuttle as Hampelle, hidden behind some crates of red brandy he's smuggling. I have a lot to tell you, but not here. Later, in Holly's cabin, I mean, in our cabin." He glanced toward the outer hallway to make sure they were still alone.

"What happened on Pariah?" Zenga demanded.

He shook his head. "Later. Do you want to set the course, Zen?"

She glowered wordlessly.

"Or I can do it. What are the coordinates for the nearest wormhole? Or do we have to make our own?"

Zenga crossed her arms and stewed, too mad to be helpful.

Antor checked the data-stream, input the course and piloted the ship away from the disreputable planet. As soon as they were in open space, Zenga called Willy to the bridge and told him to take over. "We'll talk now," she growled at Antor and stormed away. He followed. He didn't dare not cooperate, after what he had put Zenga through.

Alone in Holly's cabin, Zenga punched him on the arm, hard, and said, "I hate you right now. You really scared me, Antor."

"Sorry, Zen." Antor rubbed his arm. "Do you want to hear what I discovered?"

"No," she snapped.

"I think you do. You need to know this."

"Oh, tell me then," she huffed.

Antor began with the most alarming of what he had overheard on the shuttle. "Our Captain is planning to become an illegal slaver. He's going to use Holly's winnings to buy himself a ship that can outrun and outfight the UGS, and even the pirates. And that's not the worst of it. When he returns to the Earth, Red's Gorka aren't the only thing our Captain intends to take from the planet."

"Red's Gorka?" Zenga gasped.

Antor nodded. "They're his. Hampelle and Red are partners in crime. And Zen, the Gorka aren't all they are going to take from Earth," he stressed.

"What else?" she asked.

"Earth's singers."

"Oh no!" Zenga sank onto the lowest hammock.

"Holly probably gave him the idea when she said that her planet was overflowing with great singers. Remember she said that there are even long lines of singers, whenever they hold auditions for the Earth Idol shows. Imagine all the singers Hampelle could abduct from those lines. Thousands. And if they can sing even half as well as Holly, he'll make a fortune selling each one into slavery."

"And Red Belial and his Binares are working with Hampelle?" Zenga assumed.

"Yes. This is too big for Hampelle to manage alone, and he knows we won't help him. In the shuttle, Red talked about his network of contacts. He's going to orchestrate the selling and distribution of the singers, as slaves."

Zenga exhaled loudly. "Could it get any worse?"

"It can always get worse. At least Hampelle hasn't told Red where he deposited the Gorka and picked up Holly, not even what galaxy. I think he's holding that secret as an insurance policy, to keep himself safe. Even though they're partners, it's obvious they don't trust each other. Red was trying awfully hard to get Earth's location out of Hampelle in the shuttle. I think I trust Red even less than our Captain, if that's possible."

Zenga exhaled. "So Hampelle, me and you are the only ones who know where Holly hails from?"

"Yes. Holly doesn't even know where her planet lies, in the Universal sense, so it's our secret. Just the three of us." And Antor wished it could stay so.

"Earth will be a world in trouble if that secret got out." Zenga began rocking the hammock back and forth.

Antor sank into the swing seat that dangled from the ceiling. "Holly is going to be really upset when I tell her."

Zenga frowned at him. "You can't tell her."

"But ... why not?"

"Think about it, Antor." Zenga didn't give him a chance, before she continued, "She can't do anything to stop Hampelle, so why torment her. She has to concentrate on winning Universe Idol, for you, so you won't lose your limbs."

"My limbs aren't as important as a whole planet." Facts were facts.

"Regardless, it would be cruel to tell Holly how much trouble her planet is in, when she can't do a thing to help it, and she's smart enough to figure out that it's her fault."

"It is not her fault. It's Hampelle's fault." Antor felt compelled to defend Holly.

"You know what I mean! It's not her fault, but she'll feel like it is."

Antor waved her to silence. "We have to report Hampelle to A-1, or the UGS."

Zenga considered that briefly, then shook her head. "If we do that, Holly will never see her home again. They won't let her return, knowing what she knows about the Universe. All of us will be carted off to Gehenna for Hampelle's crimes, Holly included." Zenga leaned closer and gripped his hands tight. "Let Holly sing, undistracted by all this for now. If she wins ... well, money has a way of solving a whole host of problems, doesn't it?"

"It also has a way of creating them. Holly's winnings will put her planet at risk, by financing Hampelle's scheme. She should at least be allowed to choose whether she wants to win or lose, whether she wants to endanger her planet or not," Antor said.

Zenga sighed and looked at him sadly. "Antor, if she loses on purpose, you lose your limbs and she'll never get home again. Don't put Holly in the position of having to choose. That would be cruel. Now that we know what he's planning, we can find a way to stop Hampelle. He doesn't know that we know what he's plotting, does he?"

"No."

"So we have lots of time to figure out a way to stop him. Just let Holly sing for now. We'll stop Hampelle," she stressed. "We're in the perfect position to do that."

"Why can't Hampelle just be satisfied with Holly's winnings?" Antor was disgusted with his Captain.

"A steady harvest of amazing singers would make Hampelle one of the richest beings in the Universe. No way will he be satisfied with Holly's winnings now that he's hatched this plan."

Antor slumped down on the swing seat. "I don't want to keep things from Holly."

"I know, Antor, but I really think it would be best, at least for the time being," Zenga stressed.

"Maybe you're right." Antor needed to think. He reached for the sack of dinner he'd brought back, even though his stomach was churning. He took out the fruit and sticks of spicy meat. "We better eat this before Hampelle finds it, or he'll know I visited the planet."

"True."

They would have enjoyed the meal a lot more if they hadn't lost their appetites, still, it tasted so much better than space rations that they devoured every bite of the evidence. While they ate, they discussed possible ways to stop Hampelle. They didn't come up with any surefire ideas and had to return to the bridge, before Willy was discovered in charge. The Captain was the only one allowed to break the rules.

26 Holly - Electro Shock

The lights brightened and the intro music cued. Universe Idol had begun. Holly peeked out at the audience, hoping to see two familiar faces. Antor and Zenga's seats were still glaringly empty.

Holly sighed and Teef said, "I'm sure your friends are fine. The delivery probably just took longer than expected."

"I guess." Still, Antor could have called to say he would be back late. Holly missed him, she was worried about him, and he was acting just like an Earth guy by not calling!

Teef nudged her. "Antor will be watching the show on the Comet Tail, even if he can't be here." Holly hoped Teef was right.

Olliz motioned the eight contestants closer. "Good luck everyone. I know you will all sing your very best." Of course they would, but regardless, two more would be eliminated. "Remember, after the group number, there will be a commercial break, and then the solos. First up will be Holly. Holly, make sure you've caught your breath after all that dancing. Next up will be Vhergos, then Inx."

Holly nodded. They had already been told the singing order.

Applause drowned out Olliz's voice. Chrome Boreal had taken center stage. He welcomed the viewers, promised a spectacular show, introduced the judges, and then there were commercials. As soon as those were over, the Universe Idol finalists paraded onto the stage. It was time to perform.

The song and dance number was very different from the previous week. The contestants had been paired up to sing a compilation of duets. Mini-Hampelle had been teamed with the dwarf-sized Mogg. They were the same height and their deep male voices harmonized naturally. They sounded better as a duet than either did as a solo performer.

The Castorian had been paired with Vhergos. Both had reedy voices; neither drowned out the other. Teef got to sing with the Scarnivore, Ahah, and she wasn't pleased. She had wanted to sing with Holly, and Holly had wanted to sing with her, but they hadn't gotten to pick their own partners. The judges had decided that.

Holly was left to sing with Inx. She knew his grounding tail ensured he wasn't dangerous, but she couldn't help feeling skittish when they had to link hands. In a way, it was like she was holding a live wire.

Mogg and Mini-Hampelle got the audience clapping with their rhythmic stomping feet and lively lyrics. In contrast, Vhergos and the Castorian sang a slow haunting ballad, while floating and gliding around on the stage as if they were lost on a foggy sea. Special effects mist hazed the ground, emphasizing the ethereal atmosphere.

Teef and Ahah's song was more energetic. Teef had trouble keeping up with the fast pace. Holly had heard Teef sing enough times to know that she did much better with slower rhythms. As soon as the pair retreated to the background, Inx gripped Holly's hand and they headed for center stage, with dance moves similar to Earth's basic waltz.

Holly had gotten to know Inx a little bit during their practices. He seemed like a nice enough being, if reserved, and he was always a considerate dance partner. He guided Holly through their moves rather than tugging. Physically, she didn't find him at all attractive. He was narrower than an Earth human, as if he had been stretched, and his complexion was yellowish, like he had a serious case of jaundice. Even the whites of his eyes were yellowish.

Their duet was a love song about a young couple who were saying goodbye, never to see each other again. There was lots of staring deeply into each other's eyes. Holly pretended she was singing to Antor and made the words ring true. She felt Inx's emotional performance was lackluster, but maybe he didn't have anyone to imagine as a love-interest in Holly's place.

At the climax of their song, it began to rain on the stage. The bright spotlights glinted off the water, making it sparkle like a shower of diamonds. It was a beautiful special effect, but it had never rained on them in practice, so it was a surprise.

Inx forgot his lines and his eyes darted toward the back of the platform. Holly continued singing her part, trying to keep Inx dancing. His feet stopped moving entirely. She followed his wide-eyed gaze and spotted Olliz motioning urgently to them. She wanted them to get off the stage! Holly skidded in a puddle and the tip of Inx's tail hummed and sparked.

In a flash, she knew she was in grave danger. It wasn't supposed to be raining! The waterworks must be a malfunction, and the liquid would disrupt Inx's grounding tail. His electricity would be conducted to anyone nearby. Holly was very near him. She was touching him! "Lift you tail!" she gasped.

He shook his head. "Then I'm not grounded at all. Back up."

They backed away from each other, but they were still sharing the same conductive puddle of water. The air began to crackle. Holly felt the hair on her head stand straight up. She opened her mouth to scream—she didn't have a chance.

Holly had never been electrocuted before, and everything seemed to happen in slow motion. A sizzling lightning bolt jagged outward from Inx's body. It zagged toward her and Holly felt the charge rip through her, from her toes up to her head. She went flying through the air in a cascade of blinding sparks that must have looked spectacular on camera. She landed hard and all the brilliant lights burst, or it was her brain short-circuiting. The world shrank to one pinprick of light, like a distant sun, before even that blinked out.

***

Holly tried to open her eyes. She knew there was something really important she had to do, she just couldn't remember what it was. She heard someone singing through the buzzing in her ears. She was supposed to be singing. She had to sing for Antor.

Holly forced her eyelids up. It might have been the hardest thing she'd ever done. Each lid felt like it weighed about a hundred pounds. Her eyeballs hurt so bad, they might have been simmering in vinegar. Her brain felt charcoal crisped and it hurt to think. Holly whimpered. Two shadowy figures leaned over her. One was a Castorian. She screamed.

Olliz put a firm hand on her shoulder. "Holly, stay still, stay calm. Everything is fine. You're going to be fine. The physician got your heart started again."

"I was dead?" she mumbled.

"Only for a short while," Olliz said soothingly.

"I got 'lectrocuted," Holly remembered in the part of her brain that wasn't completely fried. Even her tongue felt foreign, as if a fat slug had crawled into her mouth to replace it, while she had been temporarily dead.

"Yes, you did get electrocuted. The doctor is here, he's going to take you to the medical center to make sure there's been no permanent damage."

Holly didn't trust Castorian doctors as far as she could kick them. They would be the ones inflicting permanent damage by cutting off her arms and legs. "No doctor. Is the show still on?"

"Yes, but no-one expects you to sing, not after what happened. You're lucky to be alive, Holly!"

Holly shoved herself into a sitting position and discovered her elbows were broken, or at least it felt that way. She must have landed on them when she hit the rock-hard stage.

"Holly, lie down. You can't get up!" Olliz was starting to sound distraught.

"Can so get up," Holly muttered and swung her legs over the side of the stretcher she was on. It was floating in mid-air, like one of the food

189

trays. She groaned in severe pain. She must have landed on her butt as well as her elbows, because if felt just as broken—it actually felt more broken, because it was bigger.

Before she lost her nerve or someone wrestled her back onto the stretcher, Holly stood up. She would have fallen if Olliz hadn't caught her. The skinny Castorian didn't even try, Holly outweighed the doctor twice over.

"Is it my turn to sing?" Holly rasped. She took steps in the direction of the lights, weaving from side-to-side. She was punch drunk, there was no doubt, but she had to sing.

Olliz stayed by her side, talking to someone on her headset. They reached the back edge of the stage and Holly peeked out, trying to focus her eyes, which kept vibrating. It looked like Teef was exiting, stage left.

"My turn?" Holly asked.

Olliz turned to face Holly directly and patted her hair as if trying to force it down. Holly wondered what she looked like after being soaked and electrocuted. There was no handy mirror, so she stopped wondering. Olliz said, "Yes, you can sing. The producers think it will be great for the ratings, for you to go back on stage after your near death experience, or death experience. Your music is cued. Can you stand upright?"

Holly really didn't think she could, without Olliz. She clutched the woman's arm tighter. "Walk me out?"

"I'll walk you out, then you're on your own. Okay?"

Holly nodded and instantly regretted it. It seemed she had whiplash as well as broken elbows and a broken butt and a fried brain.

Olliz didn't seem to like being in the spotlight. She set a brisk pace to cross the stage. Holly stumbled along at her side, simply trying to stay on her feet, and she realized that she had lost one of her shoes. No wonder it was so hard to walk. She kicked its partner off. Both her feet stung on the bottom. Definitely burnt.

The floor had been mopped up. It was as dry as it should be. Under the bright lights, Holly's dress looked scorched black in spots. At least it was too wet to be smoking. She tried to pluck clingy material off her breasts. She certainly didn't want to look like she was participating in an Outer Space wet T-shirt/singing contest.

They reached the front of the stage and the audience cheered. Olliz fled. Holly planted her feet and swayed like a thin tree in a hurricane. She closed her eyes and concentrated on the music, her music. This week, she had chosen a laidback jazzy song about yearning for a lost love. It had been inspired by Antor's absence.

Holly didn't even think of dancing. It took all her inner fortitude to simply remember the words and stay upright. She did fall down once, but it was during a musical interlude so she didn't mess up her lyrics. The audience even applauded when she managed to rise to her feet again.

The last note of the ballad was quivery and she couldn't hold it half as long as it should have been held, but the audience didn't care. They celebrated her efforts so loudly, Holly thought her throbbing head was going to crack apart like an eggshell.

When the judges could finally make themselves heard, Chrome offered an arm to help Holly limp across the stage to hear her critique. "I'm just going to sit down for this," she murmured and lowered herself carefully onto the very edge of the stage, legs dangling over the platform.

The Scarnivore critiqued her first and said her performance was blatant grandstanding. The Schwill said her vocals weren't as strong as they needed to be. X-Orgone scolded both of them, before she said, "For sheer bravado, you have my vote Holly. Only a true idol could and would perform after such an ordeal, and still, you sang beautifully. Kudos, Holly."

Before he spoke, Cumin leaned back in his chair and smiled. He really had the most charming smile on the rare occasions that he shared it. "Holly, Holly, Holly. What are we to do with you?"

"What?" she asked, her brain working a lot slower than usual.

"Each week, you manage to entertain our viewers in the most dramatic way. We've never had a contestant quite like you, Holly Noel Tate. On a more serious note, I do wish you weren't so jinxed tonight, because I wanted to hear your voice at its very best, now I will have to wait for next week, and that is just one of many reasons that I will see you back on this stage. You have my vote."

"Thank you, thank you," Holly said, over more head-splitting applause. Audiences tended to root for the underdog, and given Holly's streak of bad luck, she certainly filled that role.

It was time for her to leave the stage. She couldn't remember which way to go, or stand up by herself. Chrome helped her up and steered her left. "This way, Holly."

"This way?"

"Yes, this way." He guided her through the holographic curtains.

Olliz was waiting on the darker side of the barrier. "Well done, Holly."

Holly blinked, trying to bring the familiar face into focus. She said, "I think you should lie down, I mean, I think I should lie down." She needed to be horizontal rather badly, and the floating stretcher was nowhere in sight. "I don't have to go back on stage, do I?"

"No, you are excused from the final line-up. The guards will help you to your room, or perhaps you should visit the medical center." Two big Universe Idol guards stepped forward.

"No. My room. Can I get carried?"

"If you like."

"I think I would like," Holly said, leaning against her. "Thanks, Olliz."

"Just doing my job," she said with an amused smile.

One of the guards scooped Holly up. He carried her like a swooning heroine, all the way to her door.

As soon as she stumbled inside, Holly yanked off her wet clothes and pulled on the warm jumpsuit pajamas. She was covered in goose bumps, and shivering hard for some reason. "You've had a bad shock," she told herself and giggled rather hysterically at the awful pun.

It felt heavenly to crawl into Antor's bed. She had been keeping it warm for him since he left. Wishing with all her heart that he was there with her, she succumbed to sleep, or she fainted.

27 Antor - Results Show

Antor switched off the viewing screen with a shaking hand.

"Told you they would be able to revive her," Zenga said, looking distinctly rattled by what they had seen on the live broadcast. Holly's spectacular electrocution had been replayed in slow motion, more than once, highlighting her flying through the air on the end of a lightning bolt, and smashing into the stage. And the aftermath, Holly lying in the sparking puddle, looking extremely dead, before the camera cut to commercials.

"Ya, but I didn't believe you. I don't think you believed you." Antor sank into the adjacent seat, glad they had the bridge to themselves. "Someone is trying to kill Holly. It's not just performance sabotage anymore."

"No, it's not. I can't believe she sang after that. She could barely stand up."

"That's our Holly." Antor smiled, in spite of everything. "She sang, and she sang well." Proving she was still very much alive and in contention. Antor checked the consol. "We'll be over Playara in less than an hour." The ship had never felt so slow. Antor had already booked a shuttle. It would dock against the Comet Tail as soon as the ship powered down in orbit over Playara.

To pass the time, Antor packed a few belongings that he wanted to take down to the surface, including Holly's gift, and the outfit they had bought on Ja'Dorp, and the red brandy. He freshened up as best he could and returned to the bridge to pace. Zenga ordered him to stop pacing. He sat down and drummed his fingers until she told him to stop that, too.

The shuttle was waiting as soon as the ship's coils stopped spinning. Antor and Zenga were descending toward Playara, before Captain Hampelle had even rubbed the sleep out of his beady eyes. He wasn't pleased about taking the night shift, but he did want them to make sure that Holly really was okay.

When they finally reached Holly's suite, Antor thought she wasn't there. She wasn't in her bed or on the couch or in the bathroom. The last place he looked was in his bedroom, and there she was, dead to the world, but not really dead.

"Found her, Zen," Antor called softly, sagging against the doorjamb.

"Thank goodness. I'm going to bed, then. I'm exhausted. See you in the morning."

"Sleep well." Antor shut his door and slipped into bed with Holly. He wanted to wake her up, to tell her he was there. He restrained himself admirably. She had been through enough and needed her rest to recover. He eased closer and tucked an arm around her. Holly felt smaller and more breakable than the last time he had held her. It made Antor feel stronger, and protective. Holly seemed to sense he was there. She sighed and snuggled into his shoulder. He kissed her cheek softly and realized that he had drained all his energy worrying. He wanted to stay awake to know he was holding Holly. He fell asleep instead.

Holly woke him up. She was groaning as if she was being tortured.

"Holly? What's wrong?"

"Antor! Ouch. You're back. I'm so glad you're back. Ouch."

"Me too. I missed you." His arm was still around her and he hugged her.

"Ah! Please don't. I mean, I like it, but it hurts. It really hurts. I hurt, everywhere. Ouch. When did you get back? Where were you?"

Antor smiled and almost hugged her again, because she looked so adorable. "We got back last night. Hampelle's pickup and delivery took a little longer than we expected. We watched Universe Idol on the viewing screen on the ship. You must have flown twenty feet through the air. I thought you were dead, I'm so glad you're not." Antor was the one babbling now. "Uh, is there anything I can do? To help you feel better?"

"You can kiss me. My lips don't hurt, I don't think—unless I have morning breath. If I have morning breath, you don't have to kiss me."

Antor smiled and kissed her. Her lips must have been undamaged. She kissed him back with such passion, he almost melted. When he had to come up for air, he said, "No morning breath, but you do taste a bit burnt."

"I got fried on stage," Holly said, as if he needed reminding.

"I know. How about I kiss you where you hurt, kiss you better?" Antor nuzzled her neck.

Holly blushed. "I don't think so. I landed on my butt. It's probably black and blue, so you're not allowed to see it, or kiss it."

"There must be somewhere else I can kiss." Antor smiled into her eyes, unbelievably content to be exactly where he was, intimately alone with Holly.

In spite of her aches and pains, her eyes sparked rather wickedly. "Oh, the possibilities, Antor. You're lucky I'm too sore to move or I would jump your bones."

"Jump my bones?" The Universal translator drew a complete blank. It didn't even attempt a translation.

"I shouldn't have said that. Never mind what it means." Holly leaned in and kissed him for a very long time. He was so happy her lips weren't injured. They were still at it when someone knocked on the door.

"Pretend we're not home," Holly whispered.

He groaned from deep in his chest. "I think they know we're in here."

"I know, Antor. Who is it?" she called.

"Zenga, and Teef is here. We're wondering if you're okay."

Holly looked at Antor with regret. He kissed her nose and said, "We'll be right out, Zen."

Getting Holly to stand wasn't easy. She limped slowly to the door on burnt feet, wincing with every step. Antor offered to carry her, but she thought that would hurt more, because of her butt. She made it to the couch and eased down as slowly and carefully as if the furniture was made of glass shards.

Teef tried to help. Holly waved her back. "Best not to touch me anywhere. I hurt everywhere, well, almost everywhere. I think my tailbone is broken."

"I've never noticed a tail on you," Teef said. Neither had Antor, and he had been closer to Holly than anyone.

"I don't have a tail, just a tailbone, and mine is broken I think, or cracked, or bruised. It hurts to sit down."

"Do you want to stand up again?" Antor asked, hovering.

"No, I'm not moving again, ever." Holly patted the seat beside her. Antor settled as close as he could without touching her.

Over the generous breakfast Zenga had ordered, they caught up on each other's news after the week apart. Teef reported that the Universe Idol staff had already investigated the unplanned waterworks. They had concluded that a simple valve malfunction had generated the rain. Antor didn't believe it for a second, but he didn't say so in front of Teef.

A message came in while they were lounging around. Holly had been granted a day off, if she wasn't up to practicing. "I'm really not," Holly said. "Can you tell Olliz, Teef?"

She nodded and rose. "I will, and if you like, I'll come get you before the results show tonight, and tell you what you missed today."

"Thanks so much, Teef. You're such a good friend. I don't know what I would do without you."

"I'm glad we're friends, Holly. See you later." Teef was smiling until she opened the door to join her chaperone.

Holly leaned back against the couch and yawned. The dark circles under her eyes looked like bruises on her pale skin. "Maybe you should have a nap, Holly," Antor said, "since you have the day off."

"A nap sounds fantastic. Unfortunately, I have to use the bathroom first. That means I have to move, doesn't it." She whimpered.

195

Antor stood and extended his hands. "Get it over with, then you can nap."

She took his hands and rose with care. He walked her to the bathroom and shut the door. He opened it again when she screamed. "What's wrong, Holly? What happened?"

She simply pointed at the mirror as if it was a monster. "Why didn't anyone tell me—I can't believe I went on TV looking like *that*? And you kissed me, while I look like that! You really should have told me, Antor."

Antor thought he should offer comfort, because she was so distraught. "You didn't look that bad on TV, Holly. Considering you'd been electrocuted, you really didn't look bad at all. I mean, your hair was kind of sticking straight up and singed, and your eyes looked a bit bug-eyed and staring, I think because your eyebrows were gone. And your ears were a lot redder and more swollen last night. Those metal decorations you wear must have burnt them. And the water had smeared your makeup all over your face, most of that has rubbed off by now ... but you still looked fine." He noticed Holly glaring at him as if she wanted to kick him instead of kiss him. He didn't seem to be doing a very good job of comforting her. He decided he should stop talking, and maybe leave quickly. Antor backed toward the door.

After she slammed the door in his face, he said, "Call me if you need any help."

Holly didn't call him. It sounded like she had a very long bath. She didn't come out of the bathroom for an hour, and then she hobbled straight into Antor's room and slammed that door, too.

He was sharing the couch with Zenga and sought her guidance, since she was a female. "Should I go talk to Holly? Or do you think she wants to be alone?"

"Go see her, but don't say another word about how bad she looked."

Antor did do a better job of kissing than talking. He could try that. At his bedroom door, he knocked. Holly didn't tell him he couldn't come in, so he entered. She was curled up in the bed. Antor joined her. Holly sighed and said, "I'm going to be voted off, Antor, and you'll never get to keep your limbs." She burst into tears.

He couldn't kiss her when she was crying, so he had no choice but to try to offer comfort again. "There's no way the judges will get rid of you, Holly. Universe Idol is seeing the highest ratings in ten years, the highest ratings since the show started, and that's because of you. And you're by far the best singer." There was more serious stuff that Antor needed to talk to her about, but even he knew it wasn't the right time. Holly didn't need to hear that someone was now trying to kill her. She had likely figured it out for herself. And Zenga was probably right, he should hold his silence about

Hampelle's evil plans, as least for the time being. Holly had more than enough to contend with, merely trying to stay alive and win the contest.

Antor held her while she cried, until she fell asleep. He tucked her closer still and they napped until Teef returned, before the results show.

She had brought along a soft, tunic dress that shouldn't hurt Holly's singed and bruised skin. Antor checked it thoroughly for spiner eggs, before he passed it to Holly and left the bedroom. Teef helped her dress and they all escorted Holly to the backstage area, where a beautician took charge.

Antor guarded the door with Zenga, until Holly reappeared. Her pale face had colour and her singed hair had been tamed into some sort of sleek up-do that made her look older and more sophisticated. The beautician had even penciled in eyebrows. They didn't look real from close up, but they looked a whole lot better than no eyebrows at all.

Holly smiled when she greeted Antor and waggled them saying, "They put more of the hair-growing cream on and I should have my real eyebrows back in a couple of days, or at least by next week's show, if I'm still here."

"You'll still be here." Antor knew she would. They strolled at Holly's slow pace to where the other contestants were waiting. Inx stepped forward and Holly froze. Antor moved between them, it was instinctive.

Inx peered around him. "Holly, I just wanted to say how sorry I am about what happened. I didn't mean to electrocute you. I tried not to, but I was trapped by the water and I couldn't stop it happening … anyway, I'm glad you're okay." His thin face was pinched with distress until Holly smiled at him.

"I know it wasn't your fault, Inx, so please don't feel bad. There was nothing either of us could do once it started raining, and I am fine, or I will be soon." She didn't step closer or reach out to touch Inx, yet her words were sincere.

When Olliz directed her charges onto the stage, Antor and Zenga hurried to their seats. Antor was looking forward to the show. He really enjoyed watching Holly on stage, and nothing bad had ever happened at the results shows. At least he could relax during those.

197

28 Holly - Evil Auto-mate

T he filming lasted no longer than usual, yet Holly found the time on her feet a lot harder than she had anticipated. When Chrome finally broadcast that they would reveal which of the contestants were staying, her head was spinning.

Holly's name was called at once, without the usual long and drawn out pauses. Chrome made a joke of it by saying, "Holly Noel Tate, you look like you need to sit down, and you can, over in the safe seats." He crooked his elbow and offered to escort her.

"Am I staying?" Holly said, still not sure.

"You are staying!" The audience confirmed it, loudly. Chrome guided her across the stage. She sank onto the safe seat with shaking legs. She had made it through another week, and another sabotage attempt—the most dangerous one yet. She had actually died, if only for a little while. In the back of her mind, she couldn't help but wonder if she would survive the next show, and the next attempt to stop her from winning, or living.

It was not the time to have dark thoughts, she should be rejoicing. She did, when Teef joined her. Ahah was next, then Inx. Holly might have felt less endangered if he had left the show, but the electrical accident hadn't been his fault, and she applauded his success along with everyone else. Vhergos and the Castorian were the last two to be declared safe, which meant that Mini-Hampelle and Mogg would be leaving. They were the two shortest contestants, and two of the three males. Before they left the stage for the last time, the pair thanked the judges, said that the Universe hadn't seen the last of them, and announced that they were going to continue singing together—as a duet. It was not a sad departure.

The show concluded with a special guest performance by one of the Universe's biggest musical stars. The idol contestants stayed exactly where they were, on stage, and had the very best seats to watch the true idol.

On Earth, Circe's voice never would have gotten her a recording contract. Holly was much better, so was Teef, but Circe was the star. The crowd loved her. They applauded wildly when her rousing song was over. As far as Holly could tell, it was a dramatic recounting of a famous warrior's last battle. The hero's death at the end had brought tears to many eyes. Circe bowed and waved until the lights dimmed and the camera-mates stopped broadcasting.

"It's a wrap," Holly murmured to Teef, almost too tired to move. Sitting had stiffened up her abused muscles in the worst way.

In passing, Circe shared a few encouraging words with each of the wannabe idols. Teef was thrilled to meet the star. She was still talking about her when they walked backstage to find Antor and Zenga waiting, and Pala. The latest chaperone was always lurking backstage when Teef performed.

Antor enfolded Holly in a hug and said, "Congratulations."

"Ouch, gently."

He released her as if she was on fire. "Sorry."

She tucked an arm around him. "I didn't mean let me go."

They shared a smile and turned toward the exit. Teef wasn't allowed to join them, she was forced away by Pala. Zenga offered to keep Teef company and went off with her.

"She's granting us time alone," Antor murmured in Holly's ear, sending tingles down her spine.

"How thoughtful of her. Too bad I'm one big aching bruise."

"Except for your lips," Antor reminded her, with one of his slow sexy smiles.

"Except for my lips." They smiled into each other's eyes and Holly knew afresh that she had fallen dangerously, Romeo and Juliet in love with Antor. And their love would be as doomed as that ill-fated pair's. An alien and an Earthling didn't stand a chance of living happily ever after. But she had the now, and if that's all she had with Antor, she wanted special memories to cherish after he disappeared into the wild black yonder of space.

She was destined to have more than memories. Antor had bought her a keepsake on a planet he called Pariah. He presented it to her when they were alone in his room. He seemed so pleased to have a gift to give her that Holly tried hard not to flinch when he fastened the bracelet around her arm.

"It's pretty. Um, is it a real dead thing?" It resembled a snake, except that the long body was hard and segmented, to resemble strung beads.

"Dead and mummified, and one of the most decorative vypedes I've ever seen. Do you like it?"

"I do, Antor. Thank you." Some lies were okay, and this was one of those kinds. "The coloured spots are so bright, and such pretty colours." Holly hoped she wasn't overdoing it.

"The brighter the vypede, the more poisonous. This one's venom will kill most beings, no matter how big they are."

"Really?" Holly swallowed hard and tried not to move her arm. "It's not still poisonous, is it?"

"No, of course not. They remove the sack of poison in the mummification process, before they turn it into jewelry. At least they're supposed to." A frown creased Antor's forehead. "Maybe I should check, since I got the bracelet on Pariah. It might be an assassin's weapon instead of jewelry."

"Please do." Holly extended her arm.

Antor removed the bracelet slowly and carefully, avoiding the head and fangs. When it was off, he fetched a skewer left behind by one of the floating food trays. He wedged it inside the snake-like mouth. A drop of dew appeared on the end of one tooth. Antor cleared his throat. "I'll have to get you another present," he said, pokerfaced.

"That's okay, I don't need presents." Holly stayed well back when Antor carried the deadly bracelet away, dangling on the skewer. He didn't come back. Holly had to go find him, and she really didn't want to move her body. He was standing by the window as still as a statue, staring at the stars. Holly leaned against him from behind and could feel every tense muscle.

"I almost killed you, Holly. If the fang had scraped your skin, you'd be dead."

"But it didn't. It was sweet of you to get me a present and it's the thought that counts, as they say on Earth." Holly rested her cheek on his back. "Stop beating yourself up and come back to bed. I'm too sore to stand here and I've missed you."

"I missed you more." He pressed her arms tighter against him.

"Not a chance. Come on." She tugged his hand. Antor came back to bed, where they tired out their lips before they fell asleep.

The next morning, over breakfast, Holly found out that she wasn't going to get a second day off, and she didn't feel any healthier than the previous day. In truth, she might have been feeling worse.

Holly scowled at the door when both Olliz and Teef came to pick her up, together. Maybe they were expecting a protest. Before they dragged her kicking and screaming from the suite, Antor said, "Stay safe, Holly. Do you want me to walk you to the stage?"

"No, I'll be okay with Olliz and Teef, and I spotted a couple of guards skulking outside. I'll see you tonight?"

"I'll be waiting." He smiled and kissed her gently.

Missing him already, Holly went to work. It was a long day of practices and fittings and photo sessions. Holly barely survived the day, and when she got back to the room, Antor wasn't waiting. He was gone again.

With a sense of foreboding, she touched the flashing icon on the corner of the viewing screen, and heard his voice as clearly as if he was standing beside her, except he wasn't. He was far far away. "Holly, it's

Antor. I'm not there again. Rotten luck, but Hampelle has changed his mind, he does that a lot. He accepted another delivery contract, so Zenga and I are back on the ship." His voice dropped to a whisper. "We had to go with him, to keep tabs on this latest scheme he's hatching. Anyway ... I miss you, and Hampelle promised we'd be back to Playara in a few days, not that his word means anything, but ..." His sigh was audible. "I can hope, can't I. Be really careful, Holly. Stay near your friends. I miss you. See you soon. Bye."

Holly replayed the message more than once, just to hear his voice. Exhausted, sore and sad, she went straight to bed. The whole week dragged. She had no opportunity to create cherished memories with Antor. All she did was work her butt off, and when she wasn't doing that, she was missing Antor, which was exactly what she would be doing once she was home again.

On the day of the next Universe Idol broadcast, the Comet Tail still hadn't returned. Holly's body wasn't hurting anymore, most of her bruises had faded, and she had eyebrows again. She was grumpy regardless.

Antor hadn't even called, not once. Holly was so worried that she tried to call him. The Comet Tail wasn't answering, which made Holly feel a hundred times worse, thinking that maybe the ship had been blasted by space pirates or disintegrated by UGS or vaporized by some other evil force that lurked out in space.

Holly was glad she had chosen an emotional ballad about being married to a ghost. It was a heartbreaking story in a song—the kind of song that could make a person cry. It suited Holly's mood.

To avoid any attempts on her life, she stayed safely locked in her room for the whole day. She waited for the Universe Idol guards to pick her up, as Olliz had arranged. When the buzzer sounded a bit early, she couldn't wait to escape her four walls. She was suffering from severe cabin fever. Holly peeped through the security imager in her door and couldn't believe her eyes when she saw Antor and Zenga standing outside. For some reason, the door hadn't recognized them and had failed to open automatically.

Smiling uncontrollably, she released the double security locks and slid the door wide. When she tried to hug Antor, her arms closed around nothing but air. She stepped right through his body. He wasn't there! She thought *hologram* and tried to fall back into the safety of her room. A metallic figure gave chase. It was the only thing outside her door, and it was no hologram, as Holly found out when it grabbed her with cold fingers and tossed her over the threshold. It locked the door, sealing them in her room together.

Fright was the rational response to such an attack, but that's not what Holly felt. Her temper flared out of control before fear could take root. She

201

was too damned mad to feel anything but seriously pissed off. Just once, she wanted to sing her best without interference. Holly didn't think that was too much to ask, not after all she had endured.

She backed away from her attacker, who looked unnervingly like Willy, except he wasn't. There was no dent in this auto-mate's head and his eyes were more pinkish, like a white rabbit's. Holly scanned for anything to throw at the auto-mate, or hit it with. It kept pace, moving forward with her.

"Stay back," Holly shouted.

The intruder answered by misting the air with orange spray from its mouth. It was probably poisonous gas, or sleeping gas so she could be abducted—again. Holly held her breath and leapt over the couch. The auto-mate wasn't agile enough to do that. It had to take the long way around. Holly tossed whatever she could across its path, including small chairs and a not so spindly table. The auto-mate shoved them aside or smashed them apart, barely slowing down.

Holly grabbed a long floor lamp and swung it like a bat at the metal head, making contact and actually denting the metal. The blow knocked the auto-mate to the ground. It crawled closer, spraying another cloud of orange gas.

Fighting not to draw air into her starved lungs, Holly lunged for the wall panel and pressed the button that activated the cleaning wind in the room. All the gas was sucked away in one big whoosh and she panted hard while the air was fresh. It helped to clear her head. She dove for the door and banged the button to unlock it. She shoved it wildly aside, almost off its track.

Antor and Zenga were standing right outside again. Holly wasn't dumb enough to fall for the same trick twice. She hurtled out of the room, intending to go through Antor. She hit what felt like a wall and went down. The Antor hologram fell with her and groaned. Warm hands clasped her around the waist.

"Antor?" Holly gasped. "Is it really you?"

"It's me. Uh … what's going on?"

Zenga screamed and dropped where she stood. She had breathed some of the vapours coming out of the room. The auto-mate followed the vapours.

Antor took one look and reacted. He shoved Holly backwards and dove around the auto-mate. It kept coming for Holly, eyes focused on her. There was nothing to throw at it in the hallway. She was sure she was doomed until Antor ripped something out of its metallic back. The auto-mate froze as if turned to stone.

"Is it disabled?" Holly cried.

202

"Yes. No power cell." Antor shoved the cell in his pocket and bent over Zenga.

Holly edged around the awful auto-mate. "Is she ...?"

"She's alive. Stay with her, I'm going to summon help."

Holly was cradling Zenga's head in her lap when Antor returned. He crouched close and said, "Physician is on the way. Are you okay?" She shook her head, not sure she was. If Zenga died because of her, Holly would never be okay. "Holly, what happened before we got here?" Antor asked, putting a reassuring arm around her shoulders.

"That auto-mate was at the door, except it projected a holographic image of you and Zenga, only I didn't know it was a hologram. I thought it was you, I mean, it looked just like you, didn't it?" Holly was so upset she was babbling. "So I opened the door and it attacked me, and kept spraying gas out of its mouth. I was trying to escape when you arrived. I thought you were the hologram again." She leaned her head against his shoulder. "I'm so glad you're back, but sorry Zenga got hurt. Do you think she'll be okay?"

"She's still alive and I don't think she breathed more than a trace of the gas. I hope she'll be fine," Antor said.

"You saved us, Antor, by disabling the evil robot."

"You were doing okay before I arrived," he said, modest as always.

The Universe Idol guards and the Castorian physician arrived at the same time. The guards wanted Holly to leave immediately. She told them to hold their horses, which simply confused them.

The Castorian doctor was the same one who had treated Holly for electrocution. He gave Zenga a cursory examination, after the guards lifted her onto his floating stretcher. He said that she did not appear to be in immediate danger, and that he would perform some tests. At least the medical bill would be covered by Universe Idol.

Antor shoved the disabled auto-mate inside Holly's room and sealed the door, saying he would check out the auto-mate's memories later.

"Antor, I have to go and sing, otherwise I would stay with you and Zenga." Holly felt awful for leaving them.

"I know you have to go. I'll see you after the show, okay?" He kissed her sweetly.

"Okay."

Antor brushed tears off her cheek with his thumb. Holly had been unaware that she was crying. She cried way too much in Outer Space.

29 Antor - Broom Closet

It felt like a lifetime passed before the Castorian physician returned with news. Antor was holding Zenga's limp hand when the skinny being strode into her private room, saying, "All should be well. It does not appear that she inhaled enough of the gas to harm her."

"Are you sure?" he asked.

"As sure as I can be."

It was the best guarantee Antor was going to get. "What did she breathe? What was the gas?" he asked.

"A powerful paralytic. In higher concentration, it would have stopped the breathing entirely. The low dose merely reduced her air intake to the point that she could not remain conscious. It should wear off within a few hours. And for now, nothing but sound sleep for your friend."

Antor sagged into his chair. "Thank Celeste."

"Will you be remaining by her side?" the physician asked.

"Well, I'm sure not leaving it." If he did, Zenga might be missing a few limbs when he got back. "Can I turn that on?" He motioned to the viewing screen in the wall.

The Castorian clicked it onto Universe Idol before he left. Antor settled in, wishing he could be in two places at once. At least this week's attack had already taken place, and failed, so Holly should be safe on the stage.

The show followed the usual format of too many commercials and a slow buildup of suspense. Holly was the first contestant to perform their solo, as she had been scheduled to do the previous week, before she was electrocuted.

She walked gracefully across the stage, safe and undamaged, wearing the outfit from Ja'dorp. She smiled into the camera with confidence, before she began to sing with such emotional longing, her voice brought tears to Antor's eyes. No being could sing like Holly, and she was proving it to the whole Universe. Her song choice demanded a full range of vocals, from clear high notes to throaty low tones. It demanded control and rhythm and emotion, the skills a singer needed to be truly outstanding. And Holly was. She didn't falter once. She didn't hit one wrong note. Her song was perfect and so was she.

204

When her voice trailed into silence, there was not a peep of noise from the audience, not for five heartbeats. The profound stillness was shattered by such an explosion of cheering, Antor thought the noise might even rouse Zenga from her state of unconscious.

Holly bowed and waved and approached the judges for her critique. It was long in coming, the crowd wouldn't settle down. Finally Cowbell Cumin started talking and they fell silent to listen. He didn't have much to say, except, "Finally, we have seen the true Holly Noel Tate, and the next Universe Idol." It was extravagant praise. The sentiment was echoed by the other judges, except the Scarnivore, who merely said, "Well done," in a grudging tone. Ruce probably didn't dare to malign Holly's performance for fear of losing all credibility as a supposedly impartial judge.

Five contestants sang after Holly and each performance seemed anticlimactic. Even Teef lacked her usual spark and struggled through the lyrics. Antor felt bad for her—for anyone competing against Holly. They must have known they didn't stand a chance, hence the sabotage and attempts on Holly's life. It made Antor wonder if perhaps it wasn't only the Scarnivores who were trying to stop her.

The show was barely over before Holly rushed into the room. She had wasted no time locating the medical sector. "How is Zenga? Is she going to be okay?"

Antor rose and nodded. "She's going to be fine. If she had breathed more of that gas, she would be dead. Luckily she didn't."

"Because you stopped the killer robot and saved her." Holly squeezed him tight and didn't let him go. She was stronger than he'd realized.

"How did you avoid breathing the gas?" Antor asked.

In more detail than the earlier rushed account, she described battling the auto-mate and turning on the cleaning wind in the room. The quick thinking had saved her life. Antor held her as tight as she was holding him and she didn't wince at all, proving she was feeling a lot better than when he'd last held her.

"You sang so beautifully tonight," Antor murmured. "No-one could touch you."

"It did go well, didn't it? Finally, I got to sing properly."

They sat down together on the small couch and talked quietly, guarding Zenga. When Holly's eyelids started to droop, Antor said, "Do you want to go back to our room?"

"Will you come?"

He wanted to go with her, more than anything, but he shook his head. "I better stay with Zenga, make sure she's okay. We can call the guards to walk you back there, if you want. You must be tired." He tucked an escaping lock of hair behind her ear.

Holly curled up against his side. "I'm tired, but I'd rather stay with you." Antor had been hoping she would say that.

Somehow, they slept together on the little couch, all night long. Teef woke them up, coming to check on Zenga. She woke Zenga up, too, by accident. The girl didn't have a clue where she was and blinked owlishly around at the unfamiliar room, and her visitors.

"How are you feeling?" everyone asked her.

"Sort of heavy and slow. What happened? The last thing I remember was Holly tackling Antor, and there was an auto-mate that wasn't Willy, and now I'm here ..." She trailed off, brow furrowed, straining to remember.

After they explained about the poison spewing auto-mate, Antor said, "I need to check and see if the auto-mate has any memory record of who sent it to attack Holly."

"The Scarnivores," Zenga interjected.

"Maybe, but I still want to check. Do you feel healthy enough to get up, Zen? And go back to our room?"

"Yes, I want to get up." Zenga stood, proving the point. "I feel fine, let's go."

First she had to get the all clear from her physician. He agreed that Zenga was well enough to leave and said, "I am pleased it was not more serious. If you need me again, I am called Tetong."

"Thanks for helping Zenga, Tetong," Antor said.

"My pleasure." He bowed and went into a little office.

On the way back to their suite, Holly asked Teef, "Where's Pala? I thought she didn't let you out of her sight?"

"I snuck away. She was in a particularly foul mood about something this morning and said she had to make a call to the Nastos family. She'll find me soon enough, I expect."

"Maybe she won't find you until after breakfast, or we can hide you," Holly said, grinning.

When they arrived at the door, it recognized them and slid open. Antor entered first and activated the cleansing wind, to be on the safe side. The auto-mate was as he had left it. The power-cell was still in his pocket, but he wasn't about to reinstall it and have the auto-mate kill them all. Holly shivered and gave it a wide berth. Antor said, "It can't hurt you now."

"It's still creepy."

The girls settled Zenga on the couch with a pillow and blanket, and ordered breakfast. They cleared up the wreckage of furniture, while Antor tinkered with the auto-mate, trying to figure out how to access its memories, without replacing the power-cell. He ended up taking its chest apart and removing the auto-mate's artificial brain. Once that was separate

206

from the body and the poisonous gas, he rigged up a direct link to the power cell. He hooked the assembly to the viewing screen.

"Antor is a whiz with that kind of stuff," Zenga said, from the couch.

Antor suddenly realized that he had a small audience, and flushed. "Not a whiz, but I can usually figure things out."

"A whiz," Zenga translated.

Antor began pressing keys on the remote unit and, as he'd hoped, an auto-mate's unemotional voice came out of the screen. Antor was really glad his piecemeal assembly was successful, given the audience. He wanted Holly to think highly of him. He wanted to impress her as much as she impressed him, or half as much.

"Okay, here goes," Antor said, and asked the detached brain unit, "Who sent you to harm Holly Noel Tate?"

"I don't know," the monotone voice answered, via the broadcast screen.

"Who programmed you to spray gas?" he tried.

"I don't know."

"Who installed the canister of gas?"

"I don't know."

"Who sent you to Holly's room?"

"I don't know."

Holly moved to his side. "Antor, can it tell lies?"

"Not really, unless it has been programmed to give false information to specific questions, which seems unlikely. It can refuse to answer, if it's been programmed to keep silent. And of course, it can't answer a question if the information has been erased. I think that's the case here. The trick is to ask it a question that it can answer, information that hasn't been erased, which might give us a clue as to who sent it. Since the culprit wasn't expecting their assassin to get caught, they may not have been as careful as they should."

"So you'll try to go through the backdoor," Holly murmured.

Antor thought he understood the Earth expression well enough, without needing an explanation. "Who owns you?" Antor asked the auto-mate next.

"I am owned by the Universe Idol complex," it said.

"What is your job?"

"I make deliveries to guestrooms."

Antor flashed Holly a smile. "What is the last delivery you made, before coming to Holly Noel Tate's room?"

"I made a delivery to a storage closet."

"Not a guest room," Antor murmured. "What did you deliver?"

"Cleaning supplies," it said.

"Well, that's not very helpful," Holly said.

207

Antor scratched his chin. "Did anyone receive the supplies?"

"No."

"You just left them in the closet?"

"Yes."

Antor thought for a moment, before he asked, "Where exactly is this closet?"

The auto-mate told them. Antor glanced at Holly. "Worth a look, I think."

"Nothing to lose," she agreed.

The floating trays of breakfast arrived before they could investigate for clues. Antor certainly wasn't about to go anywhere yet. After another week of gross space rations, he was starved for some real, delicious food.

After breakfast was eaten, Antor and Holly went to check out the closet. Zenga and Teef elected to stay behind, and Antor didn't mind the chance to be alone with Holly. They had been apart a long time.

The closet was exactly where it was supposed to be. Inside were cleaning supplies, not much else. Certainly no Scarnivores waiting to confess their guilt. A search didn't turn up anything significant.

"I guess this was a waste of time," Holly said.

"Oh, I don't know." Antor shoved the door shut behind them. In the darkness of the little closet, he turned her into his arms, hungrier for her than he had been for breakfast. "Broom closets have a certain ... ambience."

"Do they?" Holly was trying not to laugh.

"Do you know I haven't had a chance to kiss you properly since I returned?" Antor was feeling welcomed and secure enough to flirt, and he wasn't the flirty type.

Holly nuzzled his neck. "I'm pretty sure you've had a chance."

Antor groaned and gathered her so close, everything was shared: their breath, their warmth, the fitted shape of their bodies, their desire. Holly in a broom closet was as close to paradise as Antor had ever been.

Holly met his kiss halfway, and his passion. Her fingers wandered as many unexplored paths as his did. Things got so hot, it might have been a steam closet they were in, at least until Antor began knocking cleaning products off the shelves with his elbows.

All the loud banging and clanging cooled the mood rather rapidly, especially when a heavy can landed on his toe. "Ouch." He hopped onto his other foot, and stepped on something that rolled. Antor flipped backwards and landed on his ass, which was simply embarrassing. Someone was muffling their giggles. Since Holly was the only other occupant in the closet, it had to be her.

"It's not funny," he growled.

"It kind of is," Holly laughed.

They were both distracted when an auto-mate opened the door, probably to investigate all the noise. Broom closets were usually quiet places. At least it wasn't as intrusive as if a truly alive being had walked in on them. The auto-mate showed no trace of emotion. It merely activated a bright light and began picking up bottles and cans.

Since he was on the floor anyway, Antor retrieved a few that had rolled under the shelf. His fingers found something else, a silver ring disc that was deep in the shadows. He palmed it and rose. "Ready to go, Holly?" She was straightening her clothes and trying to control her giggles.

"Yes, ready to go. Two's company and three's a crowd, isn't it." She blinked one eye as if she had gotten dust in it. The auto-mate shooed them out. They were getting in its way.

"Is your eye okay?" Antor asked.

"I guess you don't wink, like you don't shrug or blow kisses."

"Wink?"

Holly did the eye thing again and explained what it meant. She also explained how three beings could be a crowd. Three had certainly been a crowd in the intimate little closet, whereas two had been heavenly, before he had gotten clumsy and spoiled the moment.

They were approaching their room when Teef appeared with Pala behind her. The woman had tracked Teef down, and Teef didn't look at all happy about it. "I have to return to my room," she said, without being asked.

"At least I'll see you at the results show. Maybe we can celebrate together afterwards." Holly glanced at Pala, questioningly.

"No," the woman said implacably.

"If I will be celebrating." Teef sighed. "I didn't sing my best last night, while you sang with Celeste's own voice. I've never enjoyed a song more." She smiled warmly at Holly.

"Oh, thanks, Teef. But you'll be celebrating, too. You have a fantastic voice, you beat everyone else."

"Except you. Any other year I would have been guaranteed to win, except this year." Teef was completely accepting of the circumstances, yet Holly seemed uncomfortable. She glanced kind of helplessly at Antor, as if she wanted him to say something, probably something complimentary.

He gave it a try. "Uh, you didn't sing that badly last night, Teef. There will still be four contestants remaining after two are eliminated tonight, so I'm sure you won't be eliminated this week."

Holly scowled at him. As if it was a confession, Teef said, "I don't want to go home yet. I like being here."

Pala snapped, "We are blocking the hallway. Move." The broom closet auto-mate was heading their way. Holly hugged Teef before she let the girl leave.

"Sorry," Antor muttered as soon as the pair was out of earshot. "I didn't know what to say. I couldn't say she was better than you. That would have been a lie."

"Well, some lies are okay, especially if they're to protect someone's feelings." Holly wasn't mad at him, she looked kind of exasperated. She hugged him, too, before they started moving again. Antor was simply relieved to hear that she thought some lies were justified, since he hadn't been completely forthright with her about Hampelle's plans. And that was to protect her, so maybe it was okay.

Zenga was reclining on the couch, questioning the murderous auto-mate, when they walked in. "Learn anything worthwhile?" Antor asked.

"No. This auto-mate is so stupid, it doesn't even know its own name, or maybe it doesn't have one. Find anything interesting in the broom closet?"

Antor tried not to turn red. Holly did the eye thing and winked at him. He winked back, not sure he was doing it right. He might have blinked both eyes. "Uh, I found this." He displayed the ring disc. It didn't look dusty, so maybe it was a clue.

"What's on it?" Zenga asked.

"Only one way to find out." He put the thing in his mouth and absorbed the data, which did prove to be directly related to the latest attempt on Holly's life.

"What's on the disc?" Zenga repeated impatiently.

"A clue. Someone visited the tourist place where we made that movie together, Zen. They got their hands on a copy of our digital images and loaded them into the auto-mate in that broom closet, so it could project us."

"Tricking me into opening the door," Holly murmured.

Zenga frowned. "But no-one knew about that movie except us."

"And Teef," Antor said, even though he didn't want to.

"Teef wouldn't hurt me," Holly said, without taking even a second to consider the possibility.

Zenga shot Antor a look that said *shut up* as clearly as words. Antor shut up.

"Of course Teef wouldn't hurt you," Zenga said. "There must be another explanation. Antor and I will visit the movie place tomorrow, and find out who made a copy of our holograms."

Antor took the disc out of his mouth and tucked it in his pocket. It was important evidence, and he didn't want to lose it. They all took turns in the steam shower and even went out for dinner. From there, they went directly to the results show. When Holly was safely with Olliz and the Universe Idol guards, Antor and Zenga took their seats in the audience, happy to be there since they kept missing shows.

210

"Do you think Teef is our culprit?" Zenga whispered in his ear, while Holly was nowhere near.

"It makes a lot of sense. She would probably win if Holly was eliminated."

"Except she's never seemed that desperate to win, and she really is nice. She's helped Holly throughout the competition."

Antor had been mulling things over all afternoon. "Maybe she was simply smart enough to pretend friendship, to get close enough to Holly so she could disrupt her chances. And when that didn't work, to try and get rid of her permanently."

"It's possible, I suppose. We'll have to keep a close eye on Teef." Zenga didn't seem happy about it, though.

"A very close eye. They shouldn't be alone together," Antor added.

Zenga shifted deeper into her cushiony seat. "I'd rather it was the Scarnivores than Teef."

"Me too, Zen." Antor didn't want Holly betrayed by a friend. That kind of hurt went deep and took a long time to heal.

The stage lights brightened. The Universe Idol show began with the usual projection of fireworks and shooting stars. After too many commercials and a guest performance by last year's winner, the six remaining contestants moved to center stage to learn their fate.

Holly and Teef stood together in the middle, flanked by the Scarnivore and Inx on one side, and the Castorian and Vhergos on the other—six very different beings united by music, which was considered the Universal language.

Inx, the only remaining male, was the first to be sent to the safe seats. He looked surprised and pleased. Holly was named the second contestant to be moving on. The audience approved the choice.

Vhergos was the third safe contestant. She was a blur of indistinct movement when she crossed the stage to sit, translucent and exultant, in the second last chair. Three contestants remained standing and only one would be staying. Chrome announced a commercial break and the lights dimmed.

"Who's going to stay, Zen?" Antor whispered.

"It will be Teef." She sounded certain.

Antor held the same opinion, and as soon as the lights brightened again, Teef was named the fourth. Ahah the Scarnivore, and the skinny pale Castorian would be leaving.

"You know what this means," Zenga murmured.

"What?" Antor asked.

She motioned toward the judges. "No more Scarnivore or Castorian in the competition. Those two judges won't be able to vote for their own kind now, so the judging will be more impartial, which means Holly is the sure winner."

It was good news in another way. "And if the Scarnivores are the ones trying to get rid of Holly, they've lost their motivation, haven't they?"

"That they have."

Holly only had to survive two more shows and two more weeks. And Captain Hampelle after that. Antor and Zenga hurried backstage to make sure Holly stayed safe.

30 Holly - Red Brandy

Holly tried her best to free Teef from Pala, she even invited Pala to join in a little post-show celebrating. Pala was having none of it. Poor Teef was escorted away to be locked in her little room for the night, and she went as meekly as a lamb to the slaughter.

A flashing icon message greeted Holly when she stepped into her suite. "I don't want to know what it is," Zenga declared straight off, dropping into a chair.

"Still, we better check it." Antor's anxious expression made Holly feel worried, too.

"Do you think Hampelle scheduled another delivery?" she guessed.

"It wouldn't surprise me." He glanced at Zenga.

"Oh, fine." Zenga rose with a huff and ordered snacks from room service, before she played the message. It was Hampelle. He growled that Holly was perfectly safe now that the Scarnivore was out of the running, and that he expected Antor and Zenga to report for duty the next morning. He didn't say how long they would be away.

Holly intercepted a particularly grim look shared between Antor and Zenga. "What?" she asked. Neither wanted to say. "Antor, tell me." He frowned and avoided eye-contact. He even hunched.

Zenga said carefully, "Holly, we're not absolutely positive that Teef is a true friend. We think she may want to stop you from winning, so she can win. We don't feel safe leaving you alone with her."

"But ... of course she's my friend. She wouldn't hurt me. She's never cared about winning, not like I do, and I only care so much because Antor's health depends on it, and me getting home. You're wrong about Teef."

"I hope so, Holly," Antor said. "But if we're not wrong, you should just be extra careful around Teef, around everyone."

"I don't think you're any safer with Hampelle than I am here. I'm always worried that you're not going to come back, and you never call, so I think you've been blasted by pirates or UGS or -"

Antor shook his head. "Holly, Hampelle doesn't let us make long-range calls when we're away. He disables the communication system, otherwise I would call."

"Oh." The news made Holly feel so much better. "What about the communicator you invented for me to call Earth? Could you use that?"

"No, it only communicates with Earth now that it's linked to your cell phone and I don't want to mess with it, in case you need to call home." Antor was as considerate as always.

"I should call home again." Holly had been meaning to ask Antor about that.

"Now?"

"No time like the present," she quipped.

He fetched the communication device from his room. He was halfway through the sequence of numbers when the cell phone died.

"Oh, it's out of power," Holly said. "And my charger is in Daniel's truck, not that I could plug it in here."

Antor studied the mechanism. "I should be able to rig up a separate power source, but I'll need some things from the ship. I can do it tomorrow, since I'll be back on the Comet Tail."

"That would be great, Antor. I can call home when you come back, if you've managed to get the phone powered." And Holly had no doubt that he would.

Zenga tucked her legs under her and said, "I can't believe we're going to be trapped with Hampelle, probably for the whole damn week. Some vacation this is turning out to be."

"Don't forget Red and the Binares. They might still be cluttering up the ship."

"Red and the Binares?" It sounded like the name of a band to Holly.

"Red is Hampelle's new business partner. He has two sidekicks. They're all shifty characters." Zenga frowned all the deeper. "I should have ordered a few drinks from room service, along with the snacks, to celebrate Holly's win, and drown my sorrows."

Antor grinned mischievously and went into his room again. This time, he came out with a black bottle. "Red brandy from the Ninth Ice Planet," he said, holding it up.

"Where did you get that?" Zenga asked.

"I stole it from Hampelle's smuggled crates."

She grimaced. "You better hope he doesn't find out, or that bottle might cost you your life."

"One bottle won't be missed." He opened the brandy while Zenga fetched three glasses. When Antor tipped the bottle to pour, the liquid didn't flow out right away. He looked baffled until a thick drop crept over the rim and hung there. It glowed like molten gold, shot with silver mercury and peppered with acid green. It looked hard to swallow, and it certainly didn't look like Earth alcohol. In fact, it didn't look like anything Holly wanted to put in her stomach.

214

Antor froze and his eyes got so big, he might have been part Schwill. "Zen," he breathed.

She glanced over and gasped out, "Don't move." Her expression mirrored Antor's.

"What?" Holly asked, clueless.

Zenga hissed, "Holly, don't move, don't breathe, and don't talk."

"But -"

Zenga glared daggers and Holly shut up. Antor darted his eyes at the door, significantly. Zenga shook her head, the minutest amount.

"Go," Antor whispered. He gradually tilted the bottle level. The thick drop balanced on the rim crept backwards.

Holly opened her mouth to ask questions, then thought better of it. Danger was so thick in the air, she could have paddled through it. Zenga moved in slow motion, easing up and backwards. With a tiny tilt of her head, she signaled for Holly to do the same. Holly didn't want to leave Antor, but since she couldn't ask questions, she copied Zenga's manner of super slow locomotion.

All the way to the door, Zenga didn't move any faster, so neither did Holly. It took them five minutes to cross the room and in all that time, Antor sat like a mannequin. Sweat began to run down his face. The muscles in the arm holding the bottle tightened visibly and the veins stood out like cord.

At the door, Zenga hesitated to press the button that would activate it. She looked back at Antor, questioningly, tragically. He nodded a fraction of an inch. She bit her lip and pressed. The door slid opened and she murmured, "Out, slowly."

Holly glanced back at Antor. He was watching her as if she was leaving forever, except she suspected he might be the doomed one, because of what was in that black bottle. She hesitated and he winked. Tears filled her eyes and she whispered, "I love you," because it might be her last chance to tell him. Zenga nudged her and she eased into the hallway. The door closed automatically. Zenga put an icy hand on Holly's arm to tug her away.

When they were about twenty feet from the door, Holly whispered, "Can we talk now?"

"Quietly. Damn, damn, damn." Zenga's eyes were red and wet.

Holly rationed her words. "What's in the bottle?"

"Fuel. Highly explosive fuel from Gehenna, harvested from blast beetles by the prisoners. Most of them blow themselves up in the tunnels. That fuel is worth its weight in bizoux a thousand times over. Unfortunately, it's no longer stable once it touches the air."

"It touched the air," Holly gasped. She stopped when Zenga would have kept them moving. "And Antor?"

215

"Don't ask."

"I already asked," Holly pointed out.

"He'll try to put the bottle down, I imagine, once he knows we're safely away. We've got a long way to go before we're safe." Zenga tugged Holly to get a move on.

Holly balked. "There must be some way to help him."

Zenga shook her head. "It will be a miracle if he can right that bottle and set it down, without getting blown up. We have to get out of here. He wants us safe and we can't help him except by not getting blown up."

Holly looked down the hallway to where Antor was trapped by a bottle that had become an unstable bomb. A floating tray of food approached their door from the other end of the corridor. It couldn't touch the buzzer!

Holly spun around and raced toward the tray. It was a lot closer to the door than she was. She didn't think she was going to make it, not until the tray slowed as it approached the doorway. Holly lunged in front of it before it could nudge the buzzer button. The tray bumped her breast instead. Holly's heart was beating so wildly, she thought it might set off the fuel-bomb. She stood as still as she could and panted, with one hand on the tray to stop it from detouring around her body. It was holding so steady, the bowl of sauce wasn't even rippling, not at all.

Zenga beckoned to her from the end of the corridor. The smell of food off the tray was making Holly feel queasy. She didn't know what to do. She wanted to help Antor, except Zenga didn't think there was any way to do that. The tray nudged her again, as if to get a move on. The sauce didn't so much as twitch. Holly hadn't realized, until that moment, how balanced and steady the portable carriers were. It gave her a gigantic light bulb kind of idea, if there was still time to enact it.

Before she could second-guess her plan, Holly removed all the food from the tray and placed the bowls on the floor. Zenga was making frantic motions for Holly to return to her. Holly pretended not to notice. When the tray was empty, she turned and faced the door. It opened as soon as it recognized her.

Antor was sitting as she had left him, except his tunic was now drenched with sweat. He had moved the bottle almost upright while still in the air, but it didn't look like he was going to be able to place it on the table. His shoulder and bicep were shaking. It was a miracle that he was still managing to keep a steady hand on the other end of that arm.

When his eyes met Holly's, he flinched as if he'd been stabbed, but still he held his hand steady. Holly tiptoed closer, guiding the tray. Antor begged her to leave, with his eyes. She pointed at the tray. Antor was smart enough to catch on to her idea. He didn't seem to like it though. He shook his head once.

Holly kept inching forward. When she reached Antor, she guided the tray under the bottle, raised it up until it was almost touching the base, and released. It floated exactly at the level she had determined. All Antor had to do was lower the bottle half an inch, then the tray could cart it far far away.

He didn't. "Go," he breathed, shaking everywhere except his hand.

If he tried to hold the bottle level, until she was safely away, he wouldn't survive. Antor was displaying superhuman control, but he wasn't Superman like in the movies. Holly reached out, her hand steady with resolution, to do it for him, or with him. Together, they lowered the bottle until it touched the tray. He fought to release stiffly clenched fingers and Holly helped. Only when the bottle was free-floating did he go limp.

Holly began to back away from the bomb. Antor rose from the couch and swayed. A couple of deep breaths seemed to steady him. Holly crept toward the door, expecting Antor to follow. Instead, he went the opposite way. Even worse, he floated the tray along with him, toward the window.

Holly wanted to scream or throw something at him, rather badly. She wasn't quite that stupid and simply growled. He didn't acknowledge the feral sound and eased the window wide enough for the tray to pass through. Before he released it to the air outside, he deftly pressed buttons on the server's mini-control panel. The tray rose smoothly toward the sky.

Antor closed the window and stepped back. Holly stumbled to his side and watched as the tray kept floating up, up, up, until it disappeared. When the heavens exploded with deafening booms and cascading streamers of fiery light, she screamed. The blast was bigger than an entire violent thunderstorm compressed into a moment of time. If it had happened in the Universe Idol hotel complex, nothing but a crater would have been left.

Before Holly could do more than gape, Zenga dashed in and scanned the room wildly. "Antor! Holly! Thank Celeste you're alive!" She stumbled over and hugged them both. "Holly, that was quick thinking with the tray. Antor, I can't believe you survived!"

"Me either, Zen." The three of them laughed together, giddy and a little out of control until a beep warned of an incoming call. "You don't think Hampelle ...?"

Zenga shook her head fearfully, eyes on the viewing screen, which had been left on from earlier, from before the bomb. Hampelle's dark visage appeared, glowering at them. A ruddy sienna-skinned figure was lounging in the background. Holly gasped aloud. If she wasn't mistaken, a devil was on the ship with Hampelle, and the devil had hot eyes on her. He must be the business partner, or she was having hallucinations. Or maybe she had exploded and ended up in hell with Hampelle and the devil. And Antor. Except Antor shouldn't be in hell, and Holly had never done any truly evil deeds, so maybe she shouldn't either. Holly hugged Antor tighter, to make sure they were both still solid.

"Zenga and Antor, I have need of your services," Hampelle growled through clenched teeth.

"Uh, now?" Antor hunched. He seemed to catch himself and he straightened.

"Yes, now. Right this bloody instant."

"It's kind of late, and we shouldn't leave Holly alone. There are still dangers to her, even in the complex," Zenga stressed.

The red devil stepped closer on the screen. "Then by all means, bring her along. I would love to meet the best singer in the cosmos."

Hampelle elbowed him aside. "I am more concerned about another little matter. Be here in half an hour or you will both be fired and by fired, I mean jettisoned—in pieces, lots and lots of little pieces." The viewing screen turned black.

"Do you think that's worse than just being jettisoned whole?" Zenga muttered.

"I'm guessing the devil on the ship is Red?" Holly said.

"Devil? That was Red, Red Belial. He's a Demigorgon, a part-human species."

It must have been a very small part. "I guess that's who I mean," Holly hadn't seen anyone else on the little bridge.

"Hampelle's partner," Zenga confirmed. "We don't like him, and we trust him less than Hampelle."

"No wonder. He looks evil." Holly didn't mention the being's resemblance to Earth's concept of a demon. Antor and Zenga had enough to think about, and they had to leave again.

"Holly, you'll be safer down here and …" Antor touched her cheek.

"I know. You have to go. Why does Hampelle want you to return to the ship so urgently?" she asked, even though she could make one good guess.

"The missing bottle of blast beetle fuel couldn't have gone unnoticed, and now that he's seen that display in the sky -" Antor pulled a face.

"He's put two and two together," Holly finished for him.

"Two and two?"

"He's figured it out," she translated.

"Ya, he's probably figured it out." Antor smiled badly. "Hopefully we'll be back soon."

"Hopefully we'll be back at all," Zenga added. "Antor, go change your shirt. I have to ride in the shuttle with you."

"I'm going to do more than change my shirt," he said and headed into the bathroom for a steam shower. After he'd had a few minutes in his room to dress, Holly followed him to share a proper farewell.

Antor closed the door for privacy and pulled her back into his arms. Held tight against him, she could feel his heart pounding much too hard. He looked into her eyes and said, "Did you mean what you said before, when you were leaving? Or was that just a nice way of saying goodbye?"

"I meant it."

"I love you, too, Holly." He kissed her with such heat, she thought she would melt right into his skin.

"I wish you didn't have to leave," she said, lips touching his, her eyes stinging with tears.

"Me too, but I have to go. Hampelle is scheming something big and nasty, and we have to find a way to stop him, otherwise there's no way I would risk returning to the ship." Antor looked like he was about to say more. Zenga banged on the door and shouted that she was leaving, with or without Antor.

"We'll talk about it when I get back," he promised.

"Just make sure you come back, Antor." They kissed farewell until Zenga started banging on the door and shouting at them again.

31 Antor - Red Belial

The shuttle ride to the Comet Tail didn't take nearly long enough. Antor knew exactly how big a risk it was to return to the ship, yet felt he and Zenga had no choice. They needed to retain relations with their Captain for so many reasons. They had to find a way to stop his scheme, and Holly needed a ride home, not that Antor wanted her to go home, but he did want her to be happy. He didn't think she would be, if she never saw her family again.

They had also lost their chance to investigate who had taken their holographic images from the tourist site, where they had made their movie.

Hampelle was prowling on the bridge, waiting for them. Red and Willy were keeping him company. "You didn't bring Holly, and I was so looking forward to meeting her." Red's pointy black tongue flicked out to lick his lips.

"She's needed on the planet, if she's going to win Universe Idol," Antor stressed, so the fellow wouldn't get ideas.

"Enough," Hampelle roared. "Explain that explosion in the sky."

Zenga played innocent. "We saw that. It was huge. Did a spaceship blow up?"

"It was caused by blast beetle fuel, and I am missing a bottle from a shipment I delivered recently, to Aldage."

"Quite a coincidence," Red drawled.

Hampelle told him to butt out. The two didn't appear to be getting along as well as earlier. "Antor, Bo said you helped carry the crates aboard. You had every opportunity to steal from me, before I locked that cargo door with my breath. The bottle is -"

"Of no consequence," Red interjected. "It matters not in the grand scheme. Drop the matter, Hampelle."

Hampelle rounded on Red. "I'm starting to think you're more trouble than you're worth, so stop sticking your nose where it doesn't belong."

Red's eyes narrowed to black slits. "My nose belongs right here. You need me to succeed in our venture, and you owe me!"

"What I needed was the profit from shipping the blast fuel, and I have lost a chunk of it, thanks to Antor." Hampelle's gaze shifted and he stepped threateningly close. His breath was foul enough to make Antor's eyes water. "You're the only one who could have taken it and exploded it below. You stole from me, didn't you?"

It was an accusation more than a question. Antor couldn't think of a plausible lie, so he gambled on the truth. "I did, but I didn't know what I was taking. I thought it was a bottle of red brandy, one stupid bottle to drink. I opened it tonight and almost blew up Holly, Zenga and myself, before we managed to get it on a floating tray and send it up to the sky. No-one down there knows where it came from, and they won't be able to find out. All the evidence is gone, but so is the fuel. I'll never steal again, not after that experience. I'm sorry, Captain Hampelle."

Antor stood firm when he made his confession. He didn't stay upright for long. Hampelle's first blow rocked him. The second knocked him off his feet and felt like it broke his face. A vicious kick almost made him pass out. Antor had no doubt he would have been kicked to death, if Zenga hadn't leapt into the fray, screaming for Hampelle to stop. Surprisingly, Red backed her up, stepping between Antor and Hampelle.

"Get the Gehenna out of my way," Hampelle raged at both of them. "I'm going to kill him, then I'll kill you." The Captain was incensed enough to do it. He might have, too, if the Bos hadn't come to investigate all the noise. The Bos loyalty belonged to Red and Hampelle knew it. He stepped back, growling low in his throat like a wild beast. It was lucky he didn't have a blaster handy. He was mad enough to use it on all of them.

With a deadly calm that was in direct contrast to Hampelle's tantrum, Red said, "We need Antor, so you will keep your hands off him. Go calm yourself in your cabin. I'll watch the bridge."

Hampelle cursed a vile protest, yet wasn't in a position to do more than that. The Binares flanked him and escorted him away as if he was a prisoner. The authority on the ship seemed to be shifting. Antor didn't think Red was an improvement, despite the fact that he had just saved Antor's life. Why he cared enough to intervene was something of a mystery, as well as disturbing.

Zenga helped Antor to stand and assisted him to a chair. His face was bleeding rather profusely. "Oh, Antor. Don't move." She squeezed his shoulder and disappeared.

Red got the ship moving with a rough grind and some severe tilting. Clearly, he wasn't a pilot. That done, he approached Antor and looked down. Antor tried not to flinch when Red gripped his chin and tilted his head for a better look at his battered cheek. He whistled and said, "It was foolish of you to steal from your Captain."

"No kidding. One bottle shouldn't have mattered."

"If it was one of the bottles of brandy, it would have mattered little. You just had the misfortune to take one of the bottles of blast fuel, concealed amongst them." Red released Antor's chin and smirked. "Lucky you didn't drink any. It is a hazardous product to transport. Hampelle didn't mind the risk. Seemed to enjoy it. His words: one bottle will blow you into as many atoms as a dozen. He does have a point. He was paid a fortune to ship the stuff. He has lost a large portion of his profit for that venture, because of your sticky fingers."

Antor mopped blood with his sleeve. "Am I supposed to feel bad?"

"We didn't sign on to be smugglers," Zenga said, returning with the first aid kit.

"And yet you are smugglers." Red moved aside so Zenga could play healer.

"I'm okay, Zen," Antor said. It was a token protest. He was far from okay.

Zenga tucked his hair aside and tended his left cheekbone. It was split open and already swelling. She stopped the bleeding with clotting spray and bandaged it closed with a skin-dressing that would prevent scarring. "There, does that feel better."

"Much. Thanks, Zen."

"What about the rest of you?" she asked.

"Not quite broken." He wasn't foolish enough to try smiling, nor did he feel the urge.

Red said, "He'll live. I need a little help here."

Zenga took a look at the consol. "The Magi Starway, is it." She adjusted their course and got the coils running a lot more smoothly. "There. Don't touch anything. I'm going to get Antor to his cabin, then I'll be back," she told Red.

"I can get to my cabin alone." Antor rose, to prove to Red that he wasn't completely useless, and maybe tougher than he looked. Zenga trailed him out, spoiling his point entirely.

"I don't need mollycoddling," he growled.

"Stop being grumpy. We need to talk," she added, quietly.

Antor was too grumpy to stop being grumpy. "About?"

"The Magi Starway. Why do you think we're going there?"

Antor recalled what he could about the galaxy. "It has a couple of hundred inhabited planets. They're all pretty ordinary, technologically advanced. Maybe this is a legitimate pickup or delivery."

"I doubt it."

"I doubt it, too, especially after the blast beetle fuel. At least it's no longer on the ship," he said.

When Zenga left him at the door of the cabin, he said, "Keep an eye on Red, Zen."

"Don't worry. I will. You just rest and call me if you need anything."

Changing his bloody shirt for a dry one almost made him pass out. He thought a couple of his ribs were cracked. He eased into the lower hammock and slept like the dead for a good six hours. He limped onto the bridge as soon as he woke up. Red was still keeping Zenga company.

"I'll take over, if you like," Antor offered, sitting carefully. In spite of his best efforts to contain it, a groan escaped.

Red didn't take the hint to leave. "Too bad your lover isn't here to comfort you, to distract you with pleasure to make you forget the pain," he insinuated, rather nastily.

Antor didn't dignify his words with a response.

"Holly must miss you when you are apart, when she is alone and so far from her home, an unlisted planet with an unknown location. The Universe must seem a very big place to a girl from a restricted planet. One small planet amid a myriad."

"You don't need to concern yourself with Holly and me, or her planet." Antor didn't even like hearing Holly's name on Red's tongue.

Red kept rambling. "You two looked very sweet together after the explosion. Two young lovers comforting each other. Ah, love, nothing like it to rip your heart out. Will Holly keep your heart when you return her to Earth? Earth, unimaginative name for a planet. Might as well name it Dirt or Ground or Soil or Mud. I think that's my favourite. Mud." He imposed a star map on the viewing screen. "Where is Holly's Earth, Antor?"

Antor breathed a silent sigh of relief. At least Hampelle still hadn't told Red where Earth orbited. He kept his eyes fixed straight ahead, not daring to even glance in the direction of Earth's galaxy. "I'm sure Hampelle can tell you," he said.

"Oh, he will. So many galaxies, so many star systems, I wonder if one is called Mud." Belial turned the map off and padded to the door. "Time for bed, I think, even though it is empty." He leered over his shoulder at Zenga. "If you wish to return to your cabin, we could share it."

"In your dreams," Zenga snapped. As soon as Red was out of sight, she shivered. "And in my nightmares. He is so sinister."

"Don't want to warm his hammock, Zen?"

"It's my hammock! He's in my hammock, and I'd rather share it with a nest of vypedes. How are you feeling?" She focused on his cheek.

"Like both Bos used me for a trampoline." As if Antor had summoned one by name, a Bo appeared. He stood sentry, watching their every move. Antor would have bet all his remaining coins that the other Bo was still stationed outside Hampelle's door.

Once Zenga had assured herself that Antor was healthy enough to pilot, she went to have a nap. Antor steered the ship through a couple of wormholes and moved his body as little as possible.

It took another day and a half to reach the Magi Starway. Hampelle reappeared at that point, with Red by his side. The two were again amicable with each other, as if they had called a truce. Both did have a lot to gain if they could successfully maintain their partnership, and they knew it.

Hampelle coldly ignored Antor, and aimed the Comet Tail's nose at Lynus, an industrial and technologically superior planet. As soon as they were in orbit, Hampelle ordered a shuttle, and pointed both Zenga and Antor into their cabin—Holly's former cabin. He even escorted them to the door and shoved them inside.

Zenga asked, "Why did you bring us along? If you're just going to restrict us to quarters?"

"I wasn't planning on bringing you along at all. I was planning to leave you guarding Holly—until Antor almost blew her, and the whole bloody complex, to smithereens," he snapped.

"Oh." Put like that, it was no wonder Hampelle wanted to keep tabs on them.

"I'll let you out when we're finished our transaction, or maybe I won't. Maybe I'll leave you to starve and rot in there forever." With that taunt, Hampelle locked them in with his breath.

"I can't believe he jailed us!" Zenga banged on the metal. "We're prisoners on our own ship. He didn't even give me a chance to use the facilities, or grab some space rations. We could be locked in here for days!" She kicked the door.

Antor grinned, he couldn't help it. He might have even chuckled if his ribs weren't torturing him. Zenga glared daggers. "What the Gehenna is so funny?"

He winked. "We're not as locked in as Hampelle thinks."

"Do you have something in your eye?"

Antor explained winking, and then he told Zenga that he had rewired the control panel. "Hampelle hasn't locked us in at all, but he has blocked my ability to eavesdrop on the rest of the ship."

"Tough. I'd rather be able to get out." Zenga hugged him, until he reminded her about his ribs.

When the Comet Tail rocked, they knew the shuttle had docked with their ship. Antor tried to listen through the door. He couldn't hear a thing. The shuttle was quick to detach with a second lurch.

"Let's hope they all left," Antor said. He opened the door cautiously. He and Zenga strained their ears, but couldn't hear a sound. They scouted out the whole vessel, proving they were alone, except for Willy. The auto-mate was watching the bridge and paid them no attention, since they didn't speak to him. Zenga used the facilities and Antor fetched space rations. Their basic needs taken care of, they set out to investigate for clues.

Hampelle hadn't bothered to security lock his door. He had caged his crew instead. His untidy quarters smelled like him, rather strongly, and the air inside was chilly compared to the rest of the ship. When Antor opened his closet, there was a party-bot staring right at him. It gave him quite a fright. He slammed the door on it.

They combed through the Captain's possessions, trying to discover any evidence of his scheming. All they found were some miniature models of racy, top-of-the-line spaceships.

"Maybe he's here shopping for a new ship," Zenga said.

"Maybe." Antor placed one in his palm. It launched off his hand and flew a spiral pattern before it coasted in for a perfect landing. "This is my favourite," he said. It was long, sleek and black, with flared red fins and an arched curve to the dynamic body.

Zenga surveyed the choices and selected a fat silver saucer with a hat-like top. "Sure you wouldn't prefer this one?" she said with a smirk. It soared straight up and twirled in high-speed revolutions, before it stalled and she caught it.

"A Scarnivore Disc, Zen? I don't think so."

She tossed it down and they kept searching.

Under normal circumstances, Antor would have felt uncomfortable invading Hampelle's private space. These weren't normal circumstances. He was trying to save Holly's planet. Their search didn't uncover more clues, so maybe Hampelle was on Lynus to look at ships, or to pick up legitimate cargo.

"Nothing here. Let's check Red's room," Antor said.

Red's berth—Zenga's former cabin, wasn't locked either. In contrast to the Captain, Red was obsessively neat. He had brought a square trunk aboard. Everything he owned must have been stored inside it, because there was nothing in the room that was his, except the trunk.

"He even tidied my stuff," Zenga cried, outraged. "He folded my underwear. He pawed through my panties! Yuck!"

Antor was less concerned about her undies and more interested in the chest. He examined the mechanism that sealed the lid. It wasn't electronic or a breath-lock. It was an old-fashioned puzzle lock. A challenge.

Zenga leaned over his shoulder. "Can you open it?"

"Maybe." Antor traced the intertwined metal links that framed the deadbolt seal. "I have one chance to find the link-pin that will open the chain. If I pick the wrong one, I have a feeling I'll end up either dead, or chained to the trunk until Red returns."

Zenga straightened. "Don't do it, Antor. We don't need to know what's in there."

"It wouldn't hurt to know." Antor stared at the puzzle, trying to see the pattern woven within. He unfocused his eyes, seeking the flaw in the design of undulating spirals. He blocked out the sounds of Zenga poking around and kept concentrating, and suddenly, there it was, the link-pin stood out like an exploding sun. "Got it," he murmured.

Zenga stepped close. "Are you certain?"

He smiled and twisted the link, releasing the chain that secured the bolt. It slid free by itself. Zenga cheered, before she raised the lid. "He even folds his own underwear," she said, as soon as the contents were displayed.

"Red Belial is a neat fellow." Antor carefully lifted out piles of clothes, searching for an arsenal of banned weapons, or something equally damning. He didn't find anything except a spare pair of boots, slippers, gloves, a woven fur vest, and half a dozen standard weapons. One was a dartgun, with ten unmarked darts. They were probably the lethal type.

Zenga shoved some socks aside and Antor said, "Be careful to put everything back exactly as it was. Red is the type to notice if his underwear has been disturbed."

Zenga flashed a grin. "He's disturbed."

Antor stuck his hand into a boot, wishing he didn't have to. There was something in the toe. He pulled out a small pouch.

"What is it?" Zenga squatted, to get a better look.

"Don't know yet." Antor opened the drawstring. He dumped the contents on the floor, rather than into his hand, just in case it was dangerous. A black medallion clinked against the metal deck. It was strung on a chain along with a ring disc.

Zenga picked it up. "The medallion is Castorian. It's a contract, like the one Holly signed to save your limbs.

"Ya." A shiver of foreboding ran up Antor's spine. He took the chain out of her hand and removed the ring disc from it. Trying not to think about whose mouth it had been in last, Antor slipped it onto his tooth. The data he absorbed wasn't totally unexpected, and at the same time, it was.

"What's on it?" Zenga prompted.

"My contract, my limbs. Red has bought my contract from the Castorians." He tried to sound unconcerned, and didn't succeed.

"Can he do that?" she gasped.

"Yes, it's in the fine print. The Castorians have the right to sell contracts, and they will if they can make a profit." He spat the ring onto his palm.

Zenga gripped his shoulder. "But … why would Red want your contract?"

"I can think of too many reasons, Zen, and not one of them is good." He sighed heavily.

Zenga dropped cross-legged to the floor, beside him. "Such as?"

"If Red owns my limbs, he owns my life, really. Maybe he thinks he can force me to tell him where Earth lies, if Hampelle won't." He wiped his spit off the ring disc.

226

"But if Holly pays the Castorians the money owed, or Red now, as she has the legal right to do, Red gains nothing."

"True. He actually loses, since he must have paid the Castorians more than the face value of the contract." Antor threaded the ring back onto the chain.

"So, what does he hope to gain?"

"I don't know. Maybe Earth. It's obvious that he has some twisted plot in place, and I'm an integral part of it." Antor stuck the chain back in the pouch, and then the boot. Stealing the documentation from Red wouldn't negate the registered contract, so he returned it to the trunk, as he had found it.

The ship rocked and Zenga gasped. "They're back already! We have to get out of here."

Together, they rushed to replace everything in the chest, exactly as they had found it. There wasn't time and Antor could only hope that Red wouldn't notice. He closed the lid and the puzzle lock snapped into place.

They raced for the door and skidded down the hall. Hampelle's booming voice echoed from the direction of the bridge. They barely made it back into their cabin before feet thumped by their door. Bo and Bo could never be accused of having a light step.

Antor flung himself into the lower hammock and rocked, trying to catch his breath. Zenga took the swing seat and chewed on a fingernail.

The opening door made them both jump. Hampelle gazed inside and said, "There you are, right where I left you. Pilot the ship, I'm going to have a nap."

Antor rolled to his feet. "Uh, is the course set?"

"It is. Don't deviate." Hampelle lumbered away.

Antor and Zenga barely had time to warm the bridge chairs before Red turned up. He settled in as if he was planning to stay for the long haul.

"Everything went well on Lynus?" Antor asked, hoping Red would be more informative than usual.

"We saw what we needed to see," Red drawled.

"So, what were you doing on the planet?" Zenga tried for nonchalance. She didn't manage it.

Red chuckled. "Aren't you the curious one, when there is nothing to be curious about. You do crave to know all things, don't you? Even those you should not know." Dark undertones stained Red's banter.

"I just wondered what you were doing down there," Zenga said.

"Zenga, Zenga, Zenga." Red arched one thin winged eyebrow. "You will know all things in good time."

Zenga glanced at Antor, as if for help.

"Uh, where are we going now?" Antor was more than ready to return to Playara.

"A few light years off the beaten track. Relax, we'll be back to your precious Holly in a week or two." Red leaned back and closed his eyes.

Relaxing was the last thing Antor was about to do. He checked the ship's destination himself. It was another unsavory planet, populated by blackguards and lowlifes. Just the type of hole to sell pirated ships, if Hampelle opted to go that route. Given his lawless streak, he probably would.

32 Holly - The Wrath of Fog

The week leading up to the second last show was even busier than the ones that had come before. With only four contestants remaining, each one would be performing two solo songs. Holly almost didn't have time to miss Antor. She did anyway. She missed him when she fell into bed at night and when she awoke alone. Her heart knew he was gone and kept her painfully aware of its pining. And she worried about him. Hampelle must have been furious about the exploding fuel. Antor would have taken the brunt of his anger. Holly couldn't help but agonize that Antor was never coming back, because he couldn't. The longer he was gone, the bigger her fear grew.

Teef tried her best to cheer Holly up. Holly knew that Teef was not the one trying to harm her, and had no reservations about being alone with the girl, who was her best Outer Space friend. Holly wished she could confess all, about coming from a restricted planet and Antor's almost blowing up the complex, but she couldn't. They weren't her secrets alone. They were also Antor and Zenga's, so Holly had to hold her silence.

The day before the filming of the show, Teef had an unexpected visitor. Nastos Roth arrived to support her. Teef wasn't expecting her betrothed for another week, so it was a complete surprise.

Holly was introduced to him that evening, when Teef brought him to her room. She seemed excited for Nastos to meet Holly, and for Holly to meet Nastos.

He was shorter than Teef, and his exoskeleton was a lot darker, as were his eyes. He was scrawny and overly intense with small wings. It wasn't often that Holly disliked someone for no reason, but something about Nastos rubbed her the wrong way. She didn't like how he hovered too close to Teef with a possessive grip on her arm that shouted, 'She's mine!' Or maybe Holly was simply jealous at having to share her friend.

Nastos was perfectly polite when introduced. "Pleased to meet you," he said and bowed his head. Schwill did not shake hands. Holly had yet to meet an alien who did. Only Earth humans seemed to embrace that unsanitary practice.

"Likewise." Holly bowed her head in response. "So, you're here until the finale?"

229

"I am here until Teef wins the title of Universe Idol, as she deserves." His tone was civil, the undertone was not.

Keeping things light, Holly said, "How nice. I'm hoping to win that title, too."

Nastos laughed as if she'd told a joke. "Are you?" If he'd been from Earth, he probably would have added something like, 'Dream on'.

"Yes, I am, but Teef and I are okay with that. One of us may win, and one of us will lose, or we both may lose, but we both can't win. We haven't let that interfere with our friendship," Holly said, maybe a little too sweetly.

"Teef will win and then we will wed, after which I will be the one to decide who is a suitable friend for Teef," Nastos stated, no longer masking the sharp edge to his voice. Clearly, Holly wouldn't pass muster as Teef's friend.

"Teef might have something to say about that." Holly wasn't trying to cause trouble between the pair. She simply couldn't hold her tongue. And since she could have said something much more confrontational, she figured she was behaving.

And Teef didn't say a word. She stood beside Nastos with a small fixed smile on her face. He gloated unpleasantly, before he moved Teef toward the door, even though they had just arrived. "And now, we wish to be alone after so long apart."

The girl allowed herself to be steered out the door without protest, as if Nastos was the boss of her. Now that her betrothed had arrived, it looked like she was all set to obey him as if he was her master. No chaperone waited outside, so apparently the chaperoning didn't apply to Nastos.

After making sure the door was double security locked, Holly had a long steam cleansing. She pulled on the soft jumpsuit pajamas and snuggled into Antor's bed, wishing for him with every beat of her heart. She awoke alone, and there was still no message icon flashing on the viewing screen. It was the day of the second last show and Antor still wasn't back.

After all their hard work, the contestants had been given the day off to recharge their energy. Holly holed up in her room, to stay safe. By midday, she was crawling the walls.

When the door buzzed, Holly was still in her pajamas. She checked the security imager and wasn't thrilled to see Nastos outside. She wasn't going to open the door, until she spotted Teef behind him. Holly unlocked the door and slid it aside.

"Hi Teef. Nastos." Holly motioned them in.

"Hi Holly. Nastos has a wonderful idea," Teef said.

"Does he?"

"He offered to take us both out, since we have the day off. There are so many fun things to do on this planet, and we haven't had a chance to do any of them. So, what do you think?"

Holly didn't want to spend the day with Nastos, but she couldn't say that to Teef, not without hurting her friend's feelings. "I don't know. What do you think? What would we do?"

Nastos answered. "Teef would like to visit the replicated movie sets from the greatest movies ever filmed."

Holly didn't know what the greatest Outer Space movies were and couldn't admit her ignorance. "Is that what you want to do, Teef?"

"Nastos suggested it, and yes, I would like to visit the movie sets." Her voice had a dutiful ring to it, not true enthusiasm.

"Okay, if you want me to go with you, I'll go. But are you sure you two don't want to be alone? Alone together—you know what I mean, because I would understand if you didn't want me tagging along as a third wheel."

"Third wheel?" Nastos said, not understanding the expression.

Teef gave her a shove toward the bedroom. It had unexpected force. "Go get dressed, Holly. I want you to come, and Nastos is the one who suggested inviting you, so we both want you to come. A day out will do us good. And I want my best friend to get to know my betrothed."

If Holly wasn't mistaken, Teef really did want Holly to accompany her. Did that mean she didn't want to be alone with Nastos? If that was the case, Holly wasn't going to abandon her. Teef had helped Holly out of more than one tight jam. It was time for Holly to return the favour. "Okay, Teef. Give me a minute to get ready."

Holly tossed on clothes and brushed her hair, which was back to normal now, as were her eyebrows. She smiled at her reflection, looking forward to the day out, in spite of Nastos. It was better than being trapped alone in her room, and maybe they could ditch Teef's intended.

When they exited the complex's main front entrance, Holly paused. "Should we take a few Universe Idol guards with us?"

"No," Nastos replied instantly.

"It might be a good idea. The show is tonight and that's when bad things tend to happen, especially to me."

"I am perfectly able to keep you both safe if there are any threats," Nastos declared with offended arrogance, as if Holly had insulted his manliness or Schwillness or something. "And we aren't going anywhere dangerous or isolated. The movie sets are a popular tourist destination."

Teef said, "We'll be fine, Holly." Her big eyes begged Holly to not make a fuss, to be as subservient as Teef. Against her better judgment, and out of consideration for her friend's feelings, Holly agreed.

231

Nastos led the way, a possessive arm around Teef's waist, under her wings. He could have been groping Teef and no-one would have been the wiser. He knew exactly where to go to catch a chartered shuttle. He bought three tickets and paid for them with his own coin. Holly didn't protest, since she didn't have a dime on her, or a bizoux.

The shuttle was different from the ones that soared into space. This one kind of hopped, and it held as many passengers as a bus. It was about half-full.

One gigantic sproing and they had arrived at their destination, outside the walled Universe Idol complex. The sproing hadn't taken more than five minutes, yet Holly couldn't even see her home away from home on the horizon, and she could see the whole horizon if she turned in a circle. Only one domed structure jutted up from a flat sandy landscape, as far as the eye could see. It was enormous, easily as big as fifty football stadiums.

Under sunny skies, they joined a moving line of tourists. The girls ended up signing a whole bunch of autographs, as soon as they were recognized. When they reached the entrance gate. Nastos bought three passes. He was handed a ring disc along with the tickets.

The world inside the dome was flat, barren and boring. There was nothing to see yet. Nastos popped the ring in his mouth. "This way." He turned left without consulting either girl. The ground was a sort of hard gray-blue clay with marked trails in different colours. There were so many trails to choose from, that the crowd thinned immediately. Nastos followed the orange path.

"What movie set are we visiting first?" Teef asked.

"Jaw Wars, one of my favourites." Nastos strutted along until the path bisected a paper-thin, yet solid wall. As soon as they stepped through an archway, the world was transformed. Holly found herself standing on the shore of an ocean. Gray-purple water disappeared into the far distance. There was even a watery horizon line, which was impossible, so it had to be some sort of illusion. The orange path led straight into the sea.

There was no-one in sight, not on the shore or swimming in the water. "Are we supposed to go in the ocean?" Holly asked.

"Of course." Nastos waded in, taking Teef with him, right up to their necks.

Holly stayed put. "But ... how can we breathe, and won't we get wet? Not that I mind getting wet, I'm not scared of water or anything."

Teef started to say something. Nastos cut her off. "Follow us." He ducked under. Teef disappeared with him, as if she had been tugged. Holly kept watching for them to reappear. They didn't. Were they drowning?

Holly had to make sure her friend was okay. She dashed in with a great deal of splashing. The sea didn't feel cold and as soon as she reached hip level, Holly dove in head first. The water wasn't as buoyant as she

232

expected. Holly hit bottom as hard as if she was on land. Luckily, it was her arms and chest that took the brunt of the impact, rather than her head. All the air whooshed out of her. Holding her breath, she tried to swim up for air and discovered she couldn't swim at all. The Outer Space water was not like Earth water. Nor could she spot Teef or Nastos, even though the water was crystal clear and populated by all kinds of alien sea creatures.

Before she could stand up, a long shape darted toward Holly. A tentacle wrapped around her ankle. She was tugged deeper into the ocean and desperately tried to kick free. It wouldn't let go and Holly's lungs were about to burst. She wrestled madly and everything got fuzzy. Holly knew she was about to die by drowning. It was completely unexpected. She wasn't at all prepared. She started to pass out and must have breathed by accident, because suddenly, there was air in her lungs. Holly gasped again and her vision cleared. She was still underwater, yet she could breathe, so she did. If it was a hallucination, it felt as real as life, or maybe that was normal for a hallucination. Since she'd never had one, she really didn't know what to expect.

The tentacle released her leg and Holly stumbled to her feet. She staggered forward, until she spotted an orange stripe on the seabed. She followed it, wanting to get the heck out of the ocean of breathable water that was like a bad drug trip.

It only got worse. Two shark-sized fish, that resembled beetles with fins and fangs, began to rip each other apart, right beside Holly. The water turned blood red and foamy. Chunks of flesh that looked like raw chicken polluted the water. Holly tried to flee. It wasn't easy to run through the water, even though it wasn't like real Earth water. It took a lot of effort to leave the monsters behind.

As soon as she was clear of them, she spotted something even worse. Humanoids with webbed feet and hands were being torn apart by a school of the shark-beetles. It was bloody mayhem everywhere. Holly expected to be next and panicked when one of the shark-beetles surged straight at her, mouth gaping wide and bloody teeth exposed. She dove out of the way and she still wasn't buoyant. She crashed into the seabed for a second time, almost dislocating her shoulder. The monster surged by overhead.

Sobbing without sound, since sound was muffled in the odd water, Holly stumbled up and ran again, following the orange path and trying to avoid the mutilated body parts that floated around her. She bumped into one severed leg and screamed. She was still screaming when her head broke through the waves, and her hysteria was so much louder above the waterline.

There were people on the shore, including Teef and Nastos. Everyone turned to stare at her. She tried to quash her panic and stumbled out of the awful sea. Holly collapsed to the ground when her shaking legs wouldn't hold her up. She was trembling all over and couldn't seem to stop.

Teef hurried over and crouched beside her. "Holly, what's wrong?"

"Monsters! There … there are monsters in there, and blood. I almost drowned, and got eaten. It was awful. People are getting eaten." Holly wiped away tears and noticed that her face was the only part of her that was wet. She was dry, as were Teef and Nastos, and everyone else on the shore.

Nastos looked down at her and laughed. He didn't have a nice laugh. It was both superior and sniveling, all at the same time.

"None of it was real?" she whispered, finally cluing in and feeling like the Universe's biggest fool.

"It's a sensory holographic experience, not real at all. I thought you knew." Teef bit her lip and rubbed Holly's back. "I guess I should have realized you might not. I'm sorry, Holly. You must have been terrified."

"Yes." Terrified was putting it mildly. Holly closed her eyes and took a deep shuddering breath. "Some of the things felt so real, like the tentacle that grabbed me, and the floating leg."

"Those are actual props to make the experience truly authentic, but they can't hurt you," Teef said.

"Oh."

"Ready for the next movie set?" Nastos asked, proving he had the sensitivity of a chunk of moonrock. The more time Holly spent in his company, the less she liked him, not that she had ever liked him, but now she was more inclined to hate him.

Even Teef frowned at her betrothed. "Perhaps Holly needs a moment to recover, Nastos," she said timidly.

"Of course, take all the time you need, Holly. The movie sets can be scary." His tone couldn't have been more patronizing.

Anger gave her legs strength. Holly stood up, so she could look down at him. He started walking, taking Teef with him. Holly followed, hands clenched into fists so she wouldn't punch him.

Nastos's second choice was an Outer Space horror movie. A desire to be frightened must have been another thing all humanoids had in common, but even on Earth, Holly hadn't liked horror movies. She liked them even less in space, where they were so real, they might have actually been happening.

At least this time, Holly knew it was all an illusion. She didn't enjoy the set of Bloodbath at all, but she didn't freak out when a gang of auto-mates with chainsaws for hands charged her. They were running amok, hacking apart every living thing in their path. It was a lot louder than Jaw Wars and Holly felt half-deaf by the time she left the holographic set of Bloodbath.

As soon as they could hear each other speak, Teef said, "Perhaps we should go back to the complex now. Holly and I have to prepare for the show."

Nastos shook his head. "Lots of time for one more movie set. It's my personal favourite."

"Of course, Nastos. Is that okay, Holly?" Teef shot an anxious glance at Holly, who had reached the point where she wanted to shake some sense into the girl.

Holding her tongue as she had all afternoon, Holly said, "It's okay, Teef. I can handle one more movie set, then we'll get the heck out of here."

"Good. I've saved the best for last." There was something alluded in the way Nastos said that. He strode off down the white path with a brisk step, pulling Teef with him. Holly followed at a slower pace, sorely wishing she had never left her room.

The white path led into a bank of thick fog, and it was impossible to tell if they had crossed through another wall. "What movie is this?" Holly asked Teef, who was barely visible except as a ghostly shadow.

"It must be The Wrath of Fog. Have you heard of it?"

"Maybe." It sounded like a compilation of several Earth movies, but if the Outer Space version was like 'The Fog', Holly was about to endure yet another horror. "Doesn't this place have romances or comedies? Nice movies?" she asked.

"It does, but I guess we won't get to see those." Teef sounded wistful.

Nastos loomed up beside Holly. "Be ready to be scared," he said with a chilling smile. Maybe it was the eerie mist that made him look diabolical. Holly gripped Teef's free hand and stuck close, following the white path.

Blood curdling sound effects echoed out of the mist all around them. There was howling and chewing and what sounded like tearing flesh and breaking bones. When shadowy shapes began to close in, Holly had a hard time controlling her overactive imagination.

Nastos shouted, "Fly!" He took Teef up into the air with him and Holly lost her grip on her friend's hand. Being wingless, Holly was left behind. She didn't even get to see Teef fly, which she would have liked.

In a heartbeat, she was alone in the fog with the monsters. Something dark rushed by her. She flinched away, even though she knew none of it was real.

Staying on the white line, Holly moved forward, simply wanting to escape the movie set. When a dark, hooded figure blocked her path, Holly stopped and scowled at it. Her temper was ripe for the picking. "Get out of my way," she ground out.

It stepped closer and the holographic quasi-humanoid looked plenty murderous, with a jutting brow, snarling lipless mouth and thick, super hairy arms. He carried a weapon, of course, since he was probably supposed to be the twisted serial killing star of the show. The blade was a cross between a sword and a corkscrew. The tip looked as sharp as a diamond drill bit, but neither it nor he had a drop of gore on them anywhere.

"You're not very bloody. Shouldn't you be covered in guts and gore?" Holly demanded. "I mean, you want to look authentic, right? Not pristine."

The serial killer blinked rapidly, as if he didn't understand. Maybe he wasn't programmed to chat with tourists, only chase them. "Okay, you're very scary. I am scared. You've done your job, now move along or dissipate, or whatever."

She went to step through him and bounced off his rock-hard shoulder. He was as solid as she was. He was actually a lot more solid, so he must have been one of the props, or a hired actor.

"You're not waiting for a tip, are you?" she guessed.

He pointed the blade at her. It began spinning and whining, not unlike a high-speed dental drill. Holly leapt back. "Hey, stop that. I don't want to play, so just get out of my way. Believe me when I tell you I'm not in the mood for this, not after the day I've had. I can't believe people pay to experience this place. Maybe a romance would be worth it, or a comedy like the one with all those funny plants -"

The serial killer lunged with the spinning blade, probably to shut her up. Holly jumped back and it missed by a hair. Since she knew he wouldn't really hurt her, she grabbed his wrist before he thrust again. He didn't seem to be expecting retaliation. Holly had taken a basic self-defense class at school, and she'd seen a few kung-fu movies with Daniel, so she tried yanking his fingers backwards, assuming the prop wouldn't feel pain. He howled as if it really did hurt. She jerked the weapon out of his hand. When he tried to grab it back, she stabbed at him. The spinning tip bit deep into his arm and blood spurted out. The special effect was very realistic.

"That's better. Now you have some blood on you. Are you going to get out of my way now?" Holly pointed the blade at the serial killer, imagining it was Nastos. The villain backed up, dripping blood. She thought he was leaving and lowered the weapon. When he lunged forward with no forewarning, Holly flicked the weapon up again, getting it between them.

He impaled himself on the spinning tip and knocked Holly backwards with force, crushing her under his heavy body, and bleeding all over her. The liquid felt warm, and it was wet in a sticky way. It felt a lot more real than the holographic water.

"Get off!" Holly cried and fought to shift his dead weight. She rolled and squirmed and shoved, finally managing to dislodge the serial killer. In the process, her arm caught on the blade and it stung. "Ouch!" Holly shoved the rest of him off her and staggered up. She was soaked in blood that even smelled coppery real. Her arm was truly bleeding from a deep slice that definitely wasn't fake.

None of the scene made sense. There was no way the holographic world could have gotten inside her mind to that degree.

She might have stood there and scratched her head, if she hadn't heard something else moving toward her. No longer sure what was real and what was illusion, Holly fled blindly into the fog. She lost sight of the white path and kept running.

The sounds of a torture chamber followed everywhere she went, as did the flashes of movement. Holly avoided everything, until she was so out of breath, she had to stop. She stood, bent double, and her wheezing sounded like part of the soundtrack. Blood kept dripping down her arm, proving she really had been endangered by the hooded figure. It must have been this week's attempt to silence her, and she hadn't even realized. And she had killed her attacker! It had been an accident, but he was still just as dead. Holly felt like puking.

Something solid brushed by on her right. It didn't see her or hear her, yet it reminded her that she had to get back to the real world, ASAP. Holly started moving, trying to retrace her steps, scanning for the white path. She didn't dare call out to Teef. It would have pinpointed her location if there were more serial killers on her trail. And Teef was probably long gone. Unless Teef was responsible for the attack. Maybe Teef and Nastos were working together to eliminate Holly from the competition. The prize would be one heck of a nest egg for them to start their married life. And no-one else could have known Holly would end up in the fog, since Holly hadn't known it herself. She hated to even suspect Teef, but circumstances didn't lie. Maybe Antor and Zenga weren't wrong after all.

The fog didn't seem to have an end. Holly zigzagged blindly, wasting precious time. She had to get to the Universe Idol complex for the show, before it was too late. She tried moving steadily in what she hoped was one direction. She bumped into a wall before she found the path. She followed the length of the wall to the exit, or maybe it was the entrance. Holly didn't care, except about being able to see again.

She stepped into the visible world and she truly was drenched in very real blood. The sky was almost dark. The complex appeared deserted. It was even later than she had realized.

Holly took off running, tracing the white path to where it intersected with the other coloured paths. She didn't see another soul and raced toward the entranceway. It was closed and unattended. The tourist site must have shut down for the night, or for the taping of the Universe Idol show. She was trapped, and maybe still being stalked. As terrified as if she was back in the fog, Holly hammered on the metal door. Her arms went right through, followed by the rest of her. It was another illusion.

237

Outside the dome was as deserted as inside the dome. The flat landscape couldn't have hidden anyone, unless they were as small as a squirrel. Teef and Nastos certainly weren't waiting, and there were no shuttles. Holly had been abandoned. "But maybe there's still someone inside," she murmured and tried to step back through the metal door. She hit a solid surface. "Ouch. One way illusion door," she guessed. "Now what?"

She turned around, feeling as crushed as an ant that had been stomped under a boot. She had failed Antor. She should never have left the shelter of her room.

Overcome by grief, more grief than she could handle, and guilt for being stupid enough to leave her room, Holly sank to the ground, sobbing like a baby. Under normal circumstances, she was not one to cry at the drop of a hat. Outer Space and repeated attempts on her life were not normal circumstances, not by any stretch of the imagination.

When a light arced across the sky in her direction, she wiped tears from her eyes, wondering if she was seeing a shooting star. The light kept getting closer, until she recognized a small ship. One of the hopping shuttles descended fast. It landed right in front of her. The ground vibrated beneath her feet, proving it was no mirage. The door opened and the compartment was empty. Holly hesitated to hop aboard, wondering if it was a trick, maybe to abduct her yet again.

The driver opened his window and said, "Holly Noel Tate?" He looked human enough except for the purple tinge to his skin and the stringy nodules dangling from his chin like a weird beard.

"Yes." Her voice shook.

"Thought that was you. I'm a huge fan," he said, grinning to show purple teeth.

"Uh, thanks."

"That's a lot of blood on you. Are you okay?" he asked.

"Yes. Most of it belongs to a serial killer from the movie set."

"You don't say." He didn't ask questions. "I'm supposed to take you back to the Universe Idol complex, as quick as I can."

"But ... how did you know I was here?" she asked.

"The other singer, the Schwill, she sent me back to get you, bribed me with a nice little chain of coins. She said there should be just enough time for you to make the show, so you better get in now." He tilted his head at the door.

Holly leapt aboard. The vehicle took off as soon as the door sealed. Teef had sent the shuttle for her, to save her! "Thank you, Teef," she breathed. "I'll never doubt you again."

"What?" the driver called back.

"Oh, you can hear me?" Holly hadn't realized.

238

"Loud and clear." The partition between them disappeared into thin air.

Holly moved to the seat nearest the driver, now that she could see him. She asked, "The other Schwill, the guy, did he see Teef bribe you?"

"No, she waited until he'd stepped out of the cab. Told me I would find the coins on the seat and there they were. He forced her to go with him when they left here. He looked an unpleasant sort. Bossy. Bossed the girl around as if he owned her."

"Yes, I've seen him in action." Holly vented about what a domineering jerk Nastos was for the rest of the ride. The chauffeur was a good listener. When the shuttle bumped down and didn't hop again, Holly knew she had arrived. "Thank you so much," she said.

"Go through that pink door. It will lead straight to backstage, and good luck," he called.

"I'll need it, as usual." Holly took off running and hurtled through the pink door. The guards looked startled by her sudden and bloody appearance, but waved her through when they recognized her. Holly slipped into the costume department. It was empty. She grabbed a dress at random and switched it for her gory shirt and pants. It only took a minute and she was off and running again. Olliz spotted her as soon as she appeared behind the stage. Vhergos was singing.

Olliz spoke into her headset, then whispered, "Thank goodness you're here. You'll sing after the commercials, and after Teef. Get on stage."

Holly slipped quietly through the shimmering curtain to stand beside her loyal friend. She linked their hands and whispered, "Thank you, Teef, so much."

Teef returned the pressure. "I'm so glad you made it, Holly. I've been worried sick. I didn't want to leave you ... Nastos insisted. He can be very forceful." She bit her lip and her eyes looked damp.

"It's okay, Teef. I'm here now. You need to get ready to sing." Holly squeezed her hand warmly.

"At least I feel like singing, now that you are here," Teef said, and they shared a smile.

33 Antor - Terribly Tardy

Sighs of relief echoed around the crowded bridge of the Comet Tail when Holly stepped onto the stage, after being absent when the show began. Two finalists had already performed one song each. Holly had arrived in the nick of time, but she wasn't properly primped at all. Her windblown hair and bleeding arm shouted of yet another attempt on her life.

"Well, well, well, look who has come late to the party," Cumin drawled as soon as Vhergos had been critiqued.

"Yes, sorry, so sorry. It was unavoidable. There was an accident of sorts." Holly waved to the audience and the camera. "Sorry everyone!"

Cumin said, "Holly Noel Tate, you are the most accident-prone contestant we've ever had on this show." He consulted X-Orgone. "Should we let her sing? Or has she forfeited the right by being so tardy?"

"Oh, I would forgive her and hear her voice, but I suppose we must vote on it," X-Orgone said with regret.

"I don't think we are the ones to decide." Cumin swiveled on his throne chair to face the live audience. "If you would like to hear Holly Noel Tate sing, make some noise."

The audience made so much noise, it sounded more like a riot than a singing competition. When Cumin could finally make himself heard again, he said, "Those of you who do not believe Holly should be allowed to continue in the competition, let's hear from you." There were a few weak voices, probably loyal supporters of the other contestants. They were quickly silenced.

"Well, that decides it. Holly, you will sing," Cumin decreed.

"After the commercial break," Chrome cut in, before an advertisement for a trendy brand of hovering shoes came on.

Zenga exhaled loudly. "I have to admit, I was pretty worried."

"Me too, Zen."

Hampelle growled, "I am the one deeply in hawk now. I have already signed a promissory note for payment on my new ship. If Holly had not appeared on the show, more than one debt collector would have been hunting the Comet Tail as compensation." So the Captain had chosen his new ship, unbeknownst to Antor or Zenga.

The commercials ended and Antor focused on the viewing screen. Teef was up first. She started shaky, but gained confidence. Her voice was

240

lovely, as always, but she lacked variety in her song choice. She had opted for yet another sultry torch song.

The judges were not as complimentary as usual. All of them had the same complaint, they wanted to see something different from Teef. X-Orgone said the song was too old-fashioned for someone Teef's age. Cumin requested a lively song, if she was still there next week. She nodded and retired to the back of the stage.

After yet another commercial break, Holly's music filled the bridge. She was resilient, there was no doubt. Someone had run a comb through her hair, and wrapped a hasty bandage around her arm. Blood was still seeping through, but she moved around on the stage as if she was completely undamaged. She had chosen a playful and lively song for her first solo, all about being caught red-handed while cheating. She gave it her all, both in voice and dance. Antor found himself smiling and tapping his toes in tune with the throbbing drum beat. Holly's hips undulated to the rhythm. Antor had never seen her move quite like that, and the bridge suddenly felt steamy and airless.

Red flicked his black tongue and purred. "I wouldn't mind a private performance from that one."

Antor's ire flashed hot and caustic. "Keep your eyes and hands off Holly," he said, even though he was normally the last being in the Universe to confront anyone about anything.

Red laughed at him, it was insulting.

Before the situation could escalate, Zenga said, "Quiet, I want to hear the judges!"

The audience was cheering as Holly wrapped up her performance. The judges all had something enthusiastic to say. The Castorian liked Holly's versatility. X-Orgone said that while the song was not vocally demanding, it had made her want to dance. Cumin leered and said her hips had made the act hot and sexy. Holly blushed pink and looked so endearing, Antor ached to be with her.

The Comet Tail was still about a day away from Playara. If Antor was lucky, they would arrive before the results show, and Hampelle would let him off the ship. After almost blowing Holly up, the Captain might not trust him to be within a thousand light years of her. And Hampelle didn't even know about the close call with the venomous bracelet.

Inx and Vhergos sang their second songs. Both did a solid job, but neither was in the same league as Holly, or even Teef.

Teef's second song was a lot like her first, and she looked embarrassed to be singing it. The judges' comments were a replay of their earlier critique. Holly was the last to sing before the show ended. In contrast to the cheerful first song, she had chosen a dark moody song that was incredibly complex in its ever changing beat and pitch. There was fast

241

singing and slow singing, high notes and low notes, shouty parts and soft whispers.

Antor had never heard Holly practice the song, and he'd never heard a harder song to sing. Her performance was dynamic and her voice was so versatile that the audience gave her a standing ovation. Even Cowbell Cumin rose to his feet and applauded. That was the extent of his critique.

The show had run overtime, probably because one of the contestants had been late. There was barely time for the other three judges to congratulate Holly on her vocals, before Chrome reminded the audience to watch the results show the very next evening.

When Hampelle turned off the viewing screen, he was smirking with satisfaction. "One more week and I'll have my fortune," he said. After the way Holly had performed, only a catastrophe could stop her from winning.

Red fingered the pointy end of his horn. "One more week. Not a lot of time to finish preparing for our new … project. We need to make one more trip to Pariah."

"A week is plenty of time for that," Hampelle countered. "Antor, Zenga, since Holly is still endangered, I'm going to have to leave you to guard her, while we make the run to Pariah. Keep her safe this time or you'll pay with your lives. And don't forget, I'm the only one who can take her home, so I expect your full cooperation. Zenga, watch the bridge. Antor, you can take the next shift."

Antor didn't question the wonderful news that he would get to spend a week with Holly, after all. He went to get half a night's sleep.

From his cabin, he did a bit of eavesdropping on the galley. He didn't hear anything vital. Hampelle and Red were simply bickering again, sniping at each other as they did most of the time now. It sounded like both wanted to be the boss on Hampelle's ship.

He turned off their argumentative voices and, too restless to sleep, packed what he wanted to take to Playara. He placed the cell phone/communicator carefully on top in his bag. He had attached a power source and the device was functioning again, but it had been a long time since Holly had called home. Antor picked up the charged cell phone again, wondering if he should give Holly's mother a call and tell her that Holly would be calling very soon. Holly would probably want him to do that, so her mother wouldn't worry.

It seemed like a good idea. Antor pressed the redial button he had installed. There was only one ring before a woman said, "Hello."

"Uh, is this Holly's mother?" Antor suddenly wished he had planned ahead and rehearsed what he was going to say.

"Yes. Who is this?"

"Antor, Antormand Falling Star. I'm a friend of Holly's, a good friend. A very good friend," he stressed, so the woman would know he

242

could speak for Holly. "I'm traveling with her in the singing contest, in Europe." He remembered that's what Holly had told her mother.

"Are you? And why are you calling instead of Holly? Is she okay?"

"More or less. I mean, she's had a few accidents, but she isn't hurt, not badly anyway."

"A few accidents?" The woman's voice had risen in pitch.

"Uh, yes."

"And why isn't she calling me herself?"

At least that was an easy question to answer. "Because I have the cell phone."

Holly's mother wasn't reassured. "I'm sure there is more than one phone in Europe. Where exactly is Holly? What city?"

That was an impossible question to answer, since Antor didn't know the name of even one European city on Earth. He was starting to think that calling Holly's mother had been a very bad idea. In fact, he was sure of it. He wanted to hang up, but felt that would only make matters worse. He was distracted when Zenga walked in.

His phone silence had lasted too long. "Is she in a hospital? She is, isn't she? Or is she dead and that's why she can't call?" Holly's mother's voice verged on hysterical.

Zenga gaped at him and he whispered, "Holly's mother. I called her to tell her Holly would phone her soon." More loudly, he said, "No, Holly isn't in the hospital. She's not dead, either. She's fine, she really is. She was singing tonight."

Holly's mother started crying. Maybe Holly took after her mother, or maybe all Earth females were prone to tears.

When Zenga took the phone out of his hand, he was eternally grateful. "Hello? Mrs. Tate?" Zenga sounded efficient and controlled.

It settled the woman down. She was marginally calmer when she said, "Yes, this is Mrs. Tate. What has happened to my daughter?"

"Nothing has happened to Holly. She truly is fine and she will call you tomorrow. I must apologize for Antor. I'm sure he had the best of intentions when he phoned to say Holly would phone soon, but he doesn't always think things through." Zenga glared at him. "He didn't realize how his call might worry, rather than reassure you."

The woman said something and Zenga frowned. "No, you can't call us. This cell phone only makes outgoing calls. Holly will phone you tomorrow, I promise."

After polite goodbyes, Zenga ended the call and handed Antor the phone.

"I don't want to talk about it, Zen," Antor said, before she could speak a word. "I'll go watch the bridge." He left quickly and got no sleep that night at all, although he managed a nap the next morning.

In the afternoon, Antor and Zenga piloted the ship while Hampelle slept. Even Red made himself scarce and left one of the Bos in his place. Antor ignored the silent fellow and talked more or less freely with Zenga. He kept smiling, thinking about the coming week. Zenga told him he looked ridiculous.

"A week with Holly, Zen! I'm allowed to smile. I just wish we could make it to Playara before the results show, but I don't think that's going to happen." Antor was pushing the Comet Tail hard, and the little ship was balking.

They were still in space when the results show began. It was no surprise to anyone in the Universe that Holly and Teef were the two winning finalists. The true competition had always been between the two girls, and that's what it had come down to in the end—Holly versus Teef. Now, one of them would win and one of them would lose.

If Teef was the one trying to sabotage Holly, she would only have one more chance. The week before the finale might very well be the most dangerous week so far for Holly. At least she wouldn't be alone. Antor would be there to watch her back, and her front, and every inch of her. He was also going to nip over to the tourist site and find out who had gotten their hands on the holograms.

There was one last chore that he was not looking forward to, at all. He had privately made a difficult decision. Now that the end of the competition was looming, he was going to tell Holly about Hampelle's plans for Earth. She deserved to know, and he didn't feel right not telling her the truth, even though he was keeping silent to save her pain. When she knew all the facts, she could make her own decision about what she should do. It wasn't up to Antor to make Holly's choices. She was the one to decide if the safety of her planet was worth more than Antor's limbs, and her getting home again.

34 Holly - Red's Summons

Holly was dozing on the couch when Antor and Zenga arrived. She forgot all about being exhausted, hopped up like an Energizer bunny, and hugged them tight. She was so profoundly happy they were there. "You're both alive! And you're here! Oh Antor, your poor face. What happened?"

He touched his cheek as if he'd forgotten it was injured. "Hampelle. It's nothing. You're more injured than I am. What happened to your arm? And why were you late for the show?"

They had a lot of catching up to do. Holly settled close beside Antor on the couch and, as usual, Zenga ordered food. While they snacked, Holly told them about being attacked in the fog, and accidentally killing someone or something (she just wasn't sure what) while touring with Teef and Nastos.

Antor and Zenga shared a glance that Holly had no trouble interpreting. She shook her head. "Teef wasn't involved. She sent a shuttle back for me, so stop thinking that she's plotting against me. And Nastos just arrived on the planet, so even if he arranged this attack, he couldn't have been responsible for all the ones that came before. Right?"

"Right." Antor smiled his slow smile and delivered some great news. He and Zenga would be staying on Playara for the whole week. And he had more good news. Looking embarrassed about it, he produced her cell phone from inside his packsack and said, "It has power now. Uh, I called your mother to tell her you would be phoning. Today."

"Thank you, Antor. I'm sure she appreciated it."

Zenga giggled and Antor pressed one button. "I'm not sure she did. I don't think I made a very good impression over the phone. Anyway, you can talk to her now, so she'll know you're not dead or hospitalized."

"Why would she think that?" Holly asked.

The phone started ringing and Antor tossed it over, as if it was a hot potato.

"Holly, is that you?" her mother cried, before she could speak a word.

"Yes, Mom. It's me. Sorry I didn't call earlier. The phone's battery was dead and I had misplaced the charger."

She held the phone away from her ear when her mother started yelling, loudly, about the fact that there was more than one damn phone in the whole of Europe. She went on for awhile. Antor grimaced apologetically.

When Holly could get a word in edgewise, she tried to explain that she was doing really well in the singing contest, and might even win. Clearly, her mother was not in a listening mood. Holly got another earful about her irresponsible behavior, followed by a series of questions, starting with what city Holly was in.

"London, England," she said.

And when she would be home.

"About two weeks."

And was there a phone number where Holly could be reached.

"No, we move around a lot."

And why was Holly travelling with a young man who claimed to be very good friends with her, emphasis on the very.

"Antor? He's been looking out for me, he knows the territory. He's from Europe."

Holly got another lecture, about men, especially European men.

Finally Holly said, rather desperately, that she really had to go. "I love you, Mom. See you soon. Yes, I'll call again. I promise. Bye." She tossed the phone back to Antor. He turned it off. They both sagged into the couch. Antor put his arm around Holly's shoulders and held her tight.

Zenga must have taken that as her cue to leave. She rose and said, "I'm beat. I'm sure I'll sleep like one of those Earth logs. Goodnight."

She wasn't as subtle as she thought she was. As soon as her bedroom door closed, Antor kissed Holly with such longing, it made her feel weepy. He asked, "Tired?"

"Not anymore."

Antor took her hand and they relocated to the bedroom, and the bed. Antor rolled her on top of him and groaned. It was such a deep hungry sound, Holly lost her breath. He cupped her face and kissed her so thoroughly, she could feel it all the way down to her toes, routed through her heart.

"Holly, can we ... do Earth humans ... uh ...." He was floundering.

Holly giggled. "I missed you, Antor, so much. Are you asking me if I want to make love with you, or have sex with you, or sleep with you without the sleeping part?" She didn't want there to be any misunderstanding.

"Yes, because I want to with you, if you want to with me, if Earth humans do that, I mean, every species of human has different practices and ... and we've never talked about Earth's customs, but physically, we are compatible since we're both pure humanoids."

246

He was talking way too much and he felt very compatible pressed against Holly. She kissed him and said, "As long as you have protection."

"Protection? A weapon? Like a blaster?" Antor looked so worried that Holly started giggling.

When she managed to stop, she said, "No, not a weapon. Protection so I don't get pregnant. What do aliens use for protection? I mean, it must be the same as on Earth, right? Since you're physically the same as an Earth guy? Do you have a condom?"

"Pregnant? Fertilized? With child?" Antor seemed slow to understand.

"Yes. I don't want to have a baby, I'm too young and I'll be single. Being a young single mother sucks." She didn't mention the fact that it would be an alien baby. That was another issue entirely. Antor might be a human, but he was also an alien. She had seen enough horror movies to know that Earthlings should never, under any circumstances, have an alien's baby, unless they wanted to be gutted from the inside out, or bring about the apocalyptic end of the world, maybe both.

"Holly, are you saying you could have a baby, our baby, after only one time together?"

"Well, it only takes once, hence the need for protection—birth control. A condom." Holly wasn't convinced that the universal translator was successfully doing its job.

"What is a condom, exactly?"

That wasn't easy to describe. "Sort of like a balloon, but not inflated. Thin latex, like the finger of a rubber glove, but bigger. You wear it, the guy wears it on his … you know, to stop the little swimmers from going anywhere they shouldn't."

"Little swimmers? Fish? Do Earth humans include fish in their mating rituals?" Antor looked aghast.

"No! That's not what I meant at all." Holly's half-baked explanation had only confused Antor.

"Holly, I don't have a balloon, a condom, a rubber glove, or a fish. And I'm astounded that Earth humans can be impregnated so easily, although it does explain your planet's extreme overpopulation problem. One time? Most humanoid females can only conceive once a year."

"Oh, well, that's not true for Earth females. So you don't have any protection?" Holly said sadly.

Antor sighed and shook his head as if the decision had been made.

"So, we can't?" Her words sounded more like a question than a statement.

Antor tightened his arm around her. "Holly, I grew up with no father and mother, with no-one. It's not an easy way to live. It's … hard. I would never risk bringing a child into the Universe, not if I couldn't be there for it." He was being noble and considerate, which made Holly care for him all

247

the more, if that was possible. And there was no arguing with the facts. Lack of birth control was an insurmountable problem, especially with an alien lover.

She counted days in her head. It wasn't even a safe enough time to gamble, yet. Holly rolled off him and rested her head in the hollow of his shoulder. "This really sucks. I want to be with you in every possible way, before we can't be together anymore. After I go home, I'm going to need a whole lot of memories of you, Antor, to keep me company when you're gone. And I want one of those memories to be making love with you." She slipped a hand under his top and stroked his chest.

Antor took a shuddering breath. "I want to be with you, too, Holly, more than I've ever wanted anything … let's go for a walk."

"What? A walk?"

"I don't think it's a good idea for us to stay here. Come on, I'll show you something you've never seen before."

"I was trying to get a look at something I've never seen before," Holly tossed back.

Antor rolled to his feet. He held out a hand and pulled her up. Holly went with him, down to the ground floor and out the backdoor of the complex.

It was a beautiful night. The planet was only slightly cooler than during the day. They strolled down a long path that ended in a secluded flower garden, except it was nothing like an Earthly garden. The carpet of flowers glowed as if each one had a tiny light inside. It was a bit like Christmas lights, but a million times better. The garden smelled like nature's perfume, and the multi-coloured lights spread out as far as the eye could see. Antor led her over to a swinging bench and they cuddled together, rocking back and forth.

"This is so beautiful, Antor. How did you know it was here?"

"I overheard one of the guests talking about it, sounded nice."

"It's more than nice. Nothing quite like this exists on Earth." Holly relaxed with her head on Antor's shoulder and tried to imprint the spectacular scene on her brain. She never wanted to forget the garden, or how it felt to be with Antor in the romantic place. And at least they would have a whole week together.

It was very late when they returned to the room, or very early. Holly was tired enough to sleep with Antor, and only sleep. If she'd known what the morning would bring, she wouldn't have slept a wink.

A message icon was lit up on the viewing screen when Holly and Antor emerged from their room. Holly pressed the little button, expecting to hear some update about the day's rehearsal schedule.

248

A gravelly male voice said, "Antor and Zenga, small change of plans. You are needed on the Comet Tail. Report at once." The message ended with no more information than that.

Holly gasped, "No, it's not fair!"

Zenga appeared from her room. "What's not fair?"

"We've been summoned back to the ship, Zen," Antor said, sounding simply depressed.

Her face fell. "Hampelle called?"

"No, Red. He wants us now, right now."

"Well, he can wait. I'm going to eat properly, before I'm stuck with rations again. And I'm going to order enough to take a … a giant doggie bag to the ship." Zenga went ahead and ordered a massive breakfast. Antor slipped away to made use of the facilities, and have a steam shower, before he was back to rationed water.

Holly sat on the couch, every bit as depress as Antor. He was about to leave, again, and she was going to miss him, again. Their time together was fast running out. After anticipating a wonderful week, his impending departure made her heart ache.

When the food arrived, Holly had no appetite. Nor did Antor. They watched Zenga eat until Antor said, "We better go."

He slung his pack over his shoulder and kissed Holly lingeringly at the door. It felt like they were saying goodbye forever. "Be safe, Holly. Don't trust anyone," he said, holding her too tight.

She dredged up a smile. "Not even you?"

"Well, yes, of course me, and Zenga, but no-one else."

"I can also trust Teef, so you should, too." Holly kissed his cheekbone carefully. It looked so sore. "Come back to me."

"Always," he vowed. "I would have to be dead to not come back to you."

Holly gasped. "Don't say that!"

"Sorry." They kissed again.

Zenga was getting fed up. "Enough! We'll be back next week, not next year. See you then, Holly." She dragged Antor away. When they were out of sight, Holly security locked the door and had a good cry. She was allowed. She was still in Outer Space.

35 Antor - The Underbelly of Pariah

Knowing they were late, Antor and Zenga jogged all the way to the shuttle pickup. There was no time to find out about their holograms. Antor realized, that with the unexpected change in plans, he had also missed his chance to discuss Hampelle's evil scheme with Holly.

Sitting in the shuttle, Zenga brought up the subject of the latest attack against Holly. "I think a Schwill is behind it," she declared.

Antor wasn't so sure. "I don't know, Zen. It can't be Teef, she rescued Holly. If not for her, Holly would have been eliminated. She has proven that she's a true friend, and I'm glad she is."

"It still could have been Nastos," Zenga said stubbornly.

"Yes, he could have orchestrated the attack in the fog, but what about the previous attempts? He wasn't here."

Zenga thought that over. "But those Schwill chaperones were, hired by Nastos's family. They had plenty of time to arrange the attacks on Holly, and they're always hanging around. Teef might have even mentioned the movie to Pala. With a bit of bribery, she could have gotten her hands on a copy of our holograms."

"It's certainly a possibility," Antor agreed.

"It's a good possibility, except ..." Zenga trailed off.

"Except what?"

"Teef didn't have a chaperone when Holly's dress was laced with the spiner eggs."

"True. Well, maybe that was the Scarnivores."

"Maybe." Without hard evidence, it was all guesswork.

When they docked against the Comet Tail, neither Antor nor Zenga wanted to face the Captain. They went together to the bridge, to support each other. Hampelle wasn't there. Red Belial was squatting in his chair. At least the Binares weren't crowding up the small space.

"You're late," Red told them, as if he was their boss. He thrust the lever fully forward. The Comet Tail spun shakily out of orbit.

"Sorry, we didn't get your message right away. Where is Captain Hampelle?" Zenga reached over to correct the ship's alignment.

"Sleeping." That was nothing new. "I'll keep charge of the bridge. Zenga, you can assist me. Antor, you'll take the next shift, so go get some sleep."

"Uh, is Pariah our destination?" Antor said, hanging around in spite of being dismissed.

"As a matter of fact, we are going back to Pariah." Red didn't say why, he stalked the bridge on flat silent feet, loose hips rolling. Something about his demeanor made Antor's skin crawl more than usual in his presence.

Antor left the bridge and stowed his pack in Holly's berth. He spent a minute listening in on Hampelle's snoring. It didn't sound like the Captain was going to stir anytime soon. He eavesdropped on the bridge to make sure Zenga was okay. Red was quizzing her in a chatty manner, about everything Holly and everything Earth. Zenga was being uncooperative, obtuse even, but not hostile. She was too smart to show her hand.

Too restless to nap, Antor returned to the bridge and said, "Want me to take over? I'm not tired enough to sleep yet." He hunched so as to appear generally subservient, a culled member of the pack. Hampelle would have told Red that was his character, yet since he'd met Holly, it wasn't completely true anymore.

Red absently touched the sharp tip of his right horn before he rose. Antor didn't think there was anything absent about it. "Watch the bridge, Antor. One of my men will keep you company."

"I don't need company, Zenga is here. Or Willy could keep me company if you're tired, Zen. Willy and me, we're used to working together," Antor said. "Uh, where is Willy?"

"Temporarily deactivated, since I don't need his services." Red was sounding more and more like he was the boss of the Comet Tail. Perhaps he had won the power struggle with Hampelle, while they had been away from the ship, when it was three against one.

"Zenga, you will retire to a cabin or share a meal with me," Red added, giving her two choices, neither of which was to stay with Antor. Was Red deliberately keeping them apart, so they couldn't plot or compare notes? Antor suspected that was the case. And one of the Binares would monitor everything Antor did on the bridge.

"I'm not really hungry for space rations, but I am tired." Zenga left quickly, probably to get as far away from Red as she could.

Red frowned after her and said to Antor, "Bo will be with you momentarily."

"Which Bo?"

"The quiet one," Red said so dryly, Antor suspected him of actually having a sense of humour—something Hampelle lacked.

Antor sat down in the Captain's chair and Red padded away. "Good riddance," Antor growled. He figured he might have three minutes of privacy on the bridge. Three minutes wasn't enough time to do anything but send a message to Holly, so he tried. The message wouldn't transmit.

251

All outgoing communications were completely blocked, and unblocking them would have taken more time than Antor had.

Bo lumbered onto the bridge in under four minutes. He rubbed his eyes and dropped into a chair, almost collapsing the metal.

"How's it going?" Antor asked in a friendly tone.

Bo simply looked at him balefully. It was going to be a very long shift.

Twelve hours later, Red finally showed his face again. Antor was more than ready to sleep by then. He hadn't even been able to nap on the bridge. Every time he nodded off, Bo leaned over and poked him in the back, almost knocking him out of his chair. Antor was feeling distinctly out of sorts after twelve hours of being prodded and said, "What about Hampelle? Isn't he going to take a shift?"

"No, he is not," Red drawled.

"Uh, why not?"

"None of your business."

There wasn't much Antor could say to that. He rose and stretched. "Do you want me to get Zenga?"

"No, and you will wait for her to arrive before you leave." Red stepped close and shoved Antor back into his chair.

"But you've got Bo there to keep you company until Zenga gets here." Antor really wanted a few private words with Zenga.

There was no chance. She walked onto the bridge saying, "Hey, Antor. Have you been here all night?"

"All night, just me and Bo. Anyway, gotta use the facilities." After twelve hours on the bridge, with Bo refusing to let him step off it, Antor had another need to take care of rather urgently.

He slept until they reached Pariah. Antor had really hoped that he and Zenga would be left alone on the ship, while everyone else visited the planet, but it didn't turn out that way.

Red opted to take Antor with him, leaving Zenga in charge of the Comet Tail. Hampelle didn't show his face, and hadn't yet. It was beginning to seem odd. Antor might have thought the Captain had been jettisoned, if it wasn't for the periodic snoring coming from his cabin. And it was the Captain's snoring, Antor knew the distinctive sound, since he'd heard it so many times.

Red armed himself with a big blaster. Antor didn't get so much as a dagger. One of the Bos accompanied them, while the other stayed with Zenga. She must have gotten the one who talked, because the Bo that travelled to Blackfist didn't open his mouth once.

Red more than made up for the Binare's reticence. He proved himself a gregarious being with a knack for telling stories. Antor actually enjoyed the wild tales, while reminding himself that Red was the enemy,

252

Hampelle's partner-in-crime, who planned to abduct and enslave Earthlings.

As soon as the shuttle landed, Red led the way through the market to a hole in the nearby towering rock face. Bo was posted outside. Antor followed Red down a steep dark passage that led into an underground cavern.

Antor certainly hadn't spotted the hideaway when he'd explored Pariah alone. Inside the cave, a being could buy all kinds of seriously illegal goods directly from crates. Antor spotted vials of drugs, probably Cloud Nines and Seventh Heavens. Beside those, there were blasters and dartguns, including a wide selection of lethal darts for those guns. There were familiar crates of red brandy that Antor hoped were truly red brandy. There was even technology for sale that Antor didn't recognize, and a dozen or so slaves chained to the wall, both male and female, with their prices scrawled across their foreheads. It was the rotten underbelly of the seedy settlement of Blackfist.

A scrawny, badly scarred humanoid greeted Red as if he knew him well, and led them to the darkest recesses of the cavern. Antor trailed behind, wishing he was just about anywhere else in the Universe.

"Did you acquire it?" Red asked, when the being stopped beside a black crack in the rear rock wall.

"I said I would. Wasn't easy, but I did. I expected Hampelle would come for a look-see himself." The being kept twitching.

"He sent me to inspect it first, make sure it wasn't damaged. You got a problem with that, Ephine?"

"No problem. I don't care whose hand pays me, as long as I am paid," Ephine simpered.

"You will be paid next week, as arranged, including a bonus for your additional assistance. Let me get Antor settled, before I inspect the new ship."

"Uh, I wouldn't mind seeing the new ship," Antor said. "I like ships, a lot."

"You will see it in good time, or perhaps you won't." Red laid a hand on his blaster. "Did you find that other little item I requested?" he asked Ephine.

"I did. They're getting harder and harder to locate, but I managed, so I will expect that bonus." He removed a tarnished ring disc from a dirty finger and handed it to Red. "Seems like a lot of fuss over one paltry human."

Antor thought he should leave, forthwith. Before he could take one step, Red had the blaster sticking him in the ribs. Ephine wrenched Antor's arms behind his back and clapped slave bracelets around his wrists. The links retracted to weld Antor's arms so tightly together, it felt like bone was grinding against bone.

"What the Gehenna is going on?" Antor tugged wildly.

Red hit him in the face with the butt end of the dartgun, almost knocking him off his feet. He must have aimed, because he reopened Antor's cheek. Antor was dragged through the crack in the wall and it fused closed behind them. Clearly, it wasn't just a simple split in the rock, but a quick-rock fissure. No-one would find the deep, secondary passage, not unless they knew it was there.

The only light came from ahead. Barely able to stay on his feet, Antor was forced down a steep rock staircase. It ended in a descending passage that didn't seem to have an end, at least not one Antor could see. They travelled along it, passing branching tunnels, until Ephine turned into a sizable pocket of a cave. The floor was as crooked as the tunnel. The walls glowed with naturally occurring luminescence.

Antor spat out a mouthful of blood so he could talk. "Why have you brought me here?"

Red didn't answer. He said, "Ephine, I'll need some time alone with Antor, before I inspect the hijacked ship. Don't disturb us."

Ephine bobbed his head and backed out of the cavern. Red waited for the sound of his cohort's footsteps to fade, before he padded toward Antor, who backed up until the rock stopped him.

In the soft light, Red looked more rosy pink than reddish-orange, yet no less menacing. "Why have you taken me prisoner?" Antor said.

"You are quite a valuable being, Antor. You know the location of Holly's Earth."

"So does Hampelle. Why don't you ask him?"

"I did, rather forcefully. A little too forcefully as it turned out, which means I've had to amend my plans." Red's tongue flicked with irritation. "Bo doesn't know his own strength and your Captain ended up inconveniently dead, before I had convinced him to talk, or transfer full control of the Comet Tail over to me."

Antor leaned against the rough rock for support. "I heard Hampelle snoring."

Red's eyes narrowed. "I programmed Willy to mimic his snoring. Alas, Willy has no recorded memory of Earth's location either. I went through every particle of the Comet Tail's data-stream. There's no reference to an unscheduled stop on a restricted planet. In fact, Hampelle had wiped out every trace of your ship's route before Playara. I didn't think he was that smart, but there you have it. Now, only you and Zenga and Holly know the location of that treasure trove of a planet."

"Holly doesn't know, not in terms of the Universe," Antor said, hoping to protect her still.

"That makes sense. She wouldn't have a clue, would she? You are speaking the truth." Red tilted his head a bit, and even that small movement seemed menacing. "So it falls to you or Zenga to pinpoint Earth for me," he drawled.

"Why do you want to find Earth so badly?" Antor asked, since he wasn't supposed to know the truth.

Red wasn't fooled. "There are few secrets on small ships and I have no doubt you already know the reason." Red paced once around the cave, before he stopped in front of Antor. "I want my Gorka back, and Earth's singers will make me wealthy beyond even my wildest dreams, so I need to know Earth's location." His eyes narrowed. "Holly cares what happens to you, Antor. She wants you to keep your limbs and your life, both of which are in my hands now." Red took the Castorian medallion from his pocket and dangled it in front of Antor's nose. "But you already knew I had this, too, didn't you? How did you escape your locked cabin? And break into my trunk?"

"I know the Comet Tail inside and out, and the puzzle lock wasn't even challenging." It wasn't smart to taunt Red and Antor expected to get belted again, or worse.

Instead, Red chuckled. "I do wish you were more interested in profit than integrity, Antor. You could be a big help to me on Earth, with your abilities and looking as human as you do. You could walk on the planet as one of my talent scouts."

"Make me an offer. I might be interested."

"I'm not a fool or easily fooled," Red said, and made no offer. "Holly has influence with both you and Zenga. If she is willing to barter some of her world's inhabitants for the life of her lover, why should you play the part of martyr? Love, it makes fools of us all, does it not?"

"Holly won't betray her planet for one life, not even mine. Her family lives on that planet," Antor said. "And I'll never tell you the location of Earth."

"Oh, I think you will, after we've spent some quality time together." Red rubbed his hands together for warmth. The cave was dank and chilly. The cold of the rock was seeping through Antor's thin tunic, into his back. "So, where might I find the Earth, Antor?" Red asked with deceptive friendliness.

As much as he wanted to keep Zenga safe from Red's interrogation, and save himself a whole lot of excruciating pain, Antor couldn't reveal Earth's location. He couldn't betray a whole world. And Holly would hate him if he sold Earth for his own life. He would hate himself.

"I really can't tell you," he said, sealing his fate and making a stand as the man he wished to be, a man worthy of Holly. It would probably be his last stand, but he could live with that, or die with that, which was much more likely.

"How sad—for you. I wonder what it will take to break you. Hampelle saw you as weak and spineless. I'm not so sure he was right." Red stroked his blaster. "And I can't damage you beyond repair quite yet, since Zenga isn't a stupid girl. She will certainly demand proof of your health, before she will reveal Earth's location to save you, if you don't break first. One of you will tell me, it is simply a matter of time."

"She won't tell you, either," Antor said. "Why don't you just take Holly's fortune and leave us alone. It's more than enough for any one man."

Red snorted. "For an unambitious man, perhaps." Apparently, Red wasn't that type of man. He displayed the tarnished ring disc.

"What is that?" Antor asked.

"Besides being banned in every galaxy in our dimension?" Red chuckled. "Ever heard of a hellring, Antor?"

As a matter of fact, he had. His heart almost stopped beating then and there.

Red smiled. "I see that you have. Pain felt by the mind is as real as if it is happening to the skin and bones, whether it is burning, flaying, amputating, crushing, drilling, and there is no damage to the physical body." Red's eyes glowed. "I believe that is the first series of tortures, although I've never experienced the disc myself."

He lunged with the speed of a striking vypede, grabbed Antor by the chin and twisted hard. His fingers were unbelievably powerful. Antor's teeth unclenched before his jaw shattered. The ring disc was thrust in place and locked tight, before Antor could bite down hard on those fingers, and then he couldn't think at all. His feet were burning. He was standing in a puddle of molten lava. It bubbled slowly higher, creeping up his legs, igniting new nerve endings.

Red's voice penetrated the fiery hell, asking for the location of Earth's solar system. Antor screamed, "Never," and the lava continued to rise with excruciating slowness. Some parts are more sensitive than others and when the fire reached his groin, Antor fell, unaware of hitting rock. The lava spread across the ground, igniting every inch of his skin, which cracked and blistered and melted. Antor could see the mutilation and smell his searing flesh. Red kept asking his question, over and over. Antor was mad with pain, but he didn't break. When the fire blistered his eyes, he must have fainted.

Antor was shaking hard and drenched in sweat, when he regained consciousness, sprawled face down on rock. The ring disc had been removed and he was no longer being burnt alive. Antor groaned and rolled onto his back. Red appeared in his line of vision, sitting cross-legged on a smooth boulder and looking bored. "Ready to talk?" he inquired.

Hatred as hot as the imaginary lava bath he'd just endured, seared through Antor. "No," he rasped, his throat so raw from screaming, he couldn't swallow.

The ring disc was locked back in place, before Antor could roll away. A very different brand of pain overwhelmed him. It made thinking impossible.

The cycle of torture repeated twice more, with different torments and the same question, over and over, until Antor blessedly passed out again.

The next time he revived, he was alone, with no idea how much time had passed. Alone was better than waking to find Red hovering over him like a vulture, ready to shove the cursed ring back into his mouth. He might have been driven to the edge of insanity, because he laughed rather uncontrollably when he felt his skin and it was still there, not flayed off.

Antor tried to stand. It took three attempts, since his hands were still cuffed and he had no strength in any part of him. He stumbled toward the wall, searching for a way out. The doorway proved elusive, so it must have been sealed with quick-rock, like the outer one. Antor circled the perimeter of the cave slowly, but could find no cracks or hidden panels.

Completely drained, he curled up and shivered, tormented by the possibility that Red was interrogating Zenga now, instead of him. He drifted off without meaning to and awoke still alone. It felt like he was dying of thirst and he might have been, after sweating a bucketful.

Hours or days passed, before a patch of rock disappeared and Red stepped into the cave, looking very vibrant in a gray world. Antor lacked the energy to stand, or even raise his head. Red looked down and said, "Awake again? Do you have an answer to my question yet?"

Antor eyed the bottle of water Red held. He might have sold his soul for a sip, but he wouldn't sell Earth. He told Red what he could do with his question. Red fingered the chain around his neck. The tarnished disc was strung on the chain with Antor's contract, they were rubbing together. "There are about fifty different tortures on this ring disc, but I don't think even that number would be enough to break you, not without killing you. The heart has a limit to how much stress it can endure, unfortunately."

Antor didn't contribute anything to the conversation. He imagined breaking his shackles to kill Red with his bare hands, slowly and painfully, after he forced Red to eat the disc.

"I have inspected my lovely new vessel and she's a beauty. I'm still trying to decide on a name for her. I'm thinking of Inferno. Like it?"

Antor had heard worse names. He didn't tell Red that. Red opened the lid on the bottle and Antor licked cracked lips. Even his tongue was as dry as Gehenna sand. "Some refitting will be done, while I return to Playara for

257

Holly. I will also have the compacting weapon that Hampelle managed to get his paws on, moved to the new ship when I return. It will certainly come in handy." Red crouched beside Antor and poured a stream of water over his face. Antor desperately tried to swallow some. Red laughed nastily. "Thirsty, Antor? Want a drink?"

Antor nodded. Red stopped tormenting him and positioned the bottle at his mouth. It might have been pure poison, but Antor drank every drop and wished for more.

Red said, "Zenga sends her regards."

"Did she tell you ...?"

"Not yet, but she will, to save you. I played her a little sample of how I was encouraging you to talk. You made a lot of lovely noise, Antor, begging for me to stop burning you alive. Music to my ears, although Zenga didn't appreciate it, nor did I tell her the fire wasn't real, except in your mind."

No, Zenga wouldn't appreciate hearing Antor scream himself unconscious. Antor only hoped she would continue to hold her silence. If he had to listen to her being tortured, he doubted that he could keep even one minor secret. "If you hurt her -"

"Relax, I'm not all bad. I rarely torture females. Doesn't sit right with me, and I have every confidence that Zenga will reveal Earth's location to save you. Once we've picked up Holly, and I've collected her winnings, we will move onto the Inferno, and then we'll all be taking a little trip to Earth, together."

Red had it all worked out in his evil brain. He had disposed of Hampelle. He was about to become the Captain of a powerful new ship financed by Holly's winnings. He had all the collateral he believed he needed, to force Earth's location out of either Antor or Zenga. With Bo and Bo's super strong arms to enforce his will, everything seemed to be falling nicely into place for Red. Antor didn't see a way out—not for him and Zenga, or Holly and Earth.

"Why did you buy my limbs?" he asked, when the thought struck him. Owning Antor's contract seemed rather redundant.

"I wasn't sure I could steal you away from Hampelle. His death changed everything. And there was always the possibility that Holly would lose the singing competition. It doesn't hurt to have extra insurance, since a person never knows exactly how events will unfold, until they do. I like to be prepared for all possibilities." Red recapped the empty bottle. "Even now, there is no guarantee that Holly will win, so I must be prepared for that, too, and I am." Red's voice was laced with threat. He rose to tower over Antor. The cave seemed to be fading to gray, and getting smaller.

"You're leaving me here, until you come back for the ship?" Antor guessed.

"That would be the logical thing to do, except I don't want to let you out of my reach, nor do I trust Ephine. He's slime."

"And you're not?" Antor fought to speak, feeling weaker rather than stronger, despite the water. "You're taking me with you?"

"Of course, but don't worry, Zenga won't suspect you're on the Comet Tail, and you'll be in no condition to tell her. She'll believe you're still on Pariah, out of her reach."

So the water had been dosed, after all. Still, it had been worth it. The cave kept shrinking, as if it was compacting. Antor might have thought he was dying, except Red needed him alive.

Antor had no idea how much time passed, before he revived. He was immobilized in one of the cargo bays on the Comet Tail. The lingering stench gave the location away, even though the room was as dark as Red's heart.

Red visited several times, to give him more water to keep him knocked out. It always sent him into the dead zone, as Antor came to think of the place. He was vaguely aware that his mouth was kept gagged, his wrists and ankles shackled, and chained to the wall. Red was taking no chances.

Antor didn't see another soul. Given how Red trusted no-one, maybe the Bos didn't even know he was aboard. Antor had probably been brought back onto the Comet Tail stuffed in a crate or something. Zenga certainly didn't know he was there. She would have found a way to save him, or at least visit him.

He learned what day it was when Red brought him a recording of the final Universe Idol broadcast saying, "I thought you might like to watch Holly's last performance."

Antor wasn't sure why Red had stirred himself to show Antor any kindness, not until he saw a replay of the show on the portable viewing screen. Red's act wasn't benevolent after all, but cruel and conniving. As soon as Cowbell Cumin declared Holly disqualified from the competition, Red turned off the screen.

He removed Antor's gag and said, "Now I'm glad I have the Comet Tail. As limping a ship as she is, she will still get me to Earth at least once. The Gorka will finance my new ship. The only way you will continue to be a whole man is by telling me Earth's location. Do you know, I could release you now and still own your life, legally, since Holly has no winnings to buy back your limbs? Or to get herself home, unless I take her. You're both mine." Red leaned close and pressed the tip of his horn against Antor's forehead. "But I'm not going to release you. It's much more fun to do it this way. Tell me what I want to know, before I leave for Playara, and I won't have any need to torment your girlfriend, or cut your limbs off when I get back." Red pressed harder with his horn, drawing blood.

"Do you know, Antor, there's nothing in the Castorian contract that cites how I cut your limbs off? As long as I don't kill you, the method of amputation is left entirely up to me. Do you think the girls would like to watch the show, as I remove your limbs slowly? While you are awake?" He left that awful threat hanging in the air.

Antor might have shaken his head in protest, except it was somewhat impaled on Red's horn. He suggested a different location where Red could stick his horn. It involved Red's own anatomy, although it wasn't physically possible.

Red's black eyes flashed with searing fury. He removed his horn with a painful upward jerk and rose to tower over his prisoner. "You are being surprisingly stupid for a clever man. Holly has lost. You've lost. Point me to Earth and neither of you will need to suffer further."

Antor shook his head, now that he could.

"Is that your final answer?"

He nodded once, blinded by the blood flowing into his eyes.

Red crouched again, directly in front of Antor, who fully expected to get stabbed one more time. Instead, Red rubbed the blood from Antor's eyes with a rough thumb, almost poking his eyes out in the process. "Look at me," he growled.

Antor glared into Red's soulless eyes. "I'm going down to Playara now, and I'm going to get very cozy with Holly. I'm going to make her sing like she's never sung before. You think about that while I'm gone." Red flapped his black tongue suggestively. It was revolting.

"You stay away from her," Antor ground out and fought his bonds.

"I will, if you tell me where Earth is."

"No. I can't. I won't. No."

"Then I'll be sure to give Holly a big wet kiss for you." Red went on to say much worse. It wasn't normally something Antor would do, but since his options were so limited, he spat in Red's face.

Red retaliated swiftly and ruthlessly. He could hit as hard as Hampelle, maybe harder. He'd forgotten all about keeping Antor undamaged, it seemed. Antor was barely conscious when Red held the bottle of water to his bloody swollen mouth. Most of the liquid poured down his neck. Regardless, he was still out cold before Red replaced the gag and left the cargo bay.

36 Holly - Unwelcome Visitors

As per usual, Holly had no word from Antor or Zenga all week. She barely saw Teef, since there were no more group practices, and Nastos was proving as unwilling to let Teef out of his sight as the most rabid chaperone. Teef was bowing to his authority, still bound by her parents' betrothal arrangement, and her own submissive nature, or maybe she really was attracted to Nastos, although Holly couldn't see how that was possible.

Holly wished they could talk about it, girl to girl, but Nastos was always within one wingspan of Teef. All they could manage were a few snatched words, before he would interrupt them, as if his was the only voice worth hearing.

When Holly wasn't fulfilling her Universe Idol obligations, she stayed securely locked in her room. With the climax of the show so close, Olliz had posted two guards outside her door. They carried blasters and followed Holly everywhere, when she was out and about. Holly felt safe, but crowded. Teef had her own two guards, who followed her and Nastos.

The night before the filming of the last show, Holly locked herself in her lonely rooms and practiced her song all by herself, unsettled with the end of the contest in sight, and Antor so far away from her. And her family and friends much further away than that.

Before she strained her voice, she went to bed. Sleep passed the time so much faster than being awake. Holly had nightmares, probably because of the high level of stress she was under, and she ended up sleeping in. By the time she had enjoyed a long steamy bath, the day was half over.

Olliz picked her up for an official luncheon with the show's producers. Teef was there, shadowed by Nastos. The affair lasted for hours, and then it was time to prepare for their very last performance.

Holly stopped at her room for messages. There were none. Antor and Zenga weren't back yet. "Where are you?" she sighed, gazing out the window and up at the sky, as if she might see the Comet Tail with her naked eye. Of course she couldn't.

The guards escorted her to the stage area to be primped. Holly kept her eyes alert. Since no-one had attacked her yet, she figured it could happen at any time. Or maybe it wouldn't happen. All week, she had been super careful to avoid potentially dangerous situations, and she had her two big guards.

After her clothing, makeup and hair products had been examined for booby traps, Holly dressed and got the beauty treatment. She had chosen a two-piece crimson outfit that was beautifully bouncy and sparkly, and showed her midriff. Teef had opted for white. It made her look pale, or she was pale from hanging around with Nastos. In Holly's opinion, his company was enough to suck the life out of anyone.

Together, the two girls left the dressing room. Nastos was lurking outside. He walked them backstage. Before Holly could escape his clutches, he hugged her stiffly, saying, "Best of luck, Holly." It was unexpected, because Nastos wasn't a hugging sort, and he didn't like Holly any more than she liked him. His cologne was cloyingly strong. She jerked away as soon as she could. Nastos left with a jaunty wave. He didn't hug Teef at all, which seemed odd.

As soon as the lights brightened and the music cued, Chrome introduced the final show—the highlight of the whole contest. The audience was even rowdier than usual. He had to shout to be heard. Teef and Holly stood alone in the wings, hands linked. Teef leaned close and said, "Holly, I don't want to win."

"What?" Holly choked. Her throat felt too tight.

"I have gotten to know Nastos and I have no desire to spend my future with him. He isn't nice or kind. He is selfish and self-absorbed, and cruel and shallow. If I win, there is no way out of the betrothal. I must unite with him. If I lose, I might have a chance to be free, if both sets of parents agree …" Teef squeezed Holly's hands hard. "You must win. We both want the same thing, and your voice is the winning voice."

Holly tried to clear her throat to speak. It was starting to feel numb as well as tight. Before she could reply, it was time to take the stage. Holly and Teef paraded into the bright lights.

Chrome introduced the last two idol contenders and Holly waved. Teef did her wing thing. Holly was scheduled to perform first, so she moved to the center of the stage, alone. Her music cued. She took a deep breath, opened her mouth and tried to sing. No words came out. Not even a mouse-sized squeak of sound emerged from her strangled throat. Holly covered her mouth and coughed, hoping to clear whatever was blocking her vocal cords. She tried to sing again, with the second line. Still, not a peep came out of her mouth.

The audience started to murmur. Cumin signaled for the music to stop. Holly crossed the stage toward the judges and pointed at her throat. She tried to say she had laryngitis. She could barely whisper.

"Holly, what is the matter?" Cumin asked.

She pointed at her throat again and shook her head.

"Oh dear me," X-Orgone said in distress.

Cumin looked grave when he said, "You have no voice to sing?"

Holly shook her head. And she didn't have to strain her brain to know that Nastos was responsible for robbing it.

The four judges put their heads together for a brief consultation. Cumin stood up to deliver the verdict. "Holly Noel Tate, it pains me to say, unless you can sing, you are disqualified from the show. Those are the rules and they must be abided by."

Holly shook her head in mute protest. Surely she hadn't survived every attack to be bested by Nastos on the very last night. It was beyond unfair.

She was still shaking her head when Chrome announced that Holly Noel Tate was disqualified from the competition. She stood frozen in shock, until he said, "Holly, you must leave the stage so Teef can perform."

She went, her feet so heavy they felt like two twenty pound sacks of potatoes.

When she passed Teef, Teef stopped beside her. "Holly, what happened?" she whispered.

"Nastos," Holly croaked like a bullfrog, pointing at her throat. It just had to be his poisonous cologne that had frozen her voice, since it had been perfectly fine before he had hugged her—for luck. Ha! He'd hugged her to ruin her chances.

Teef's mouth rounded in an 'O', then she winked. Holly had taught her winking, but she didn't know why Teef would be winking now. There was certainly nothing to wink about that Holly could see.

She only clued in when she watched Teef's performance from backstage. It wasn't a singing performance—it was an acting one. Teef opened her mouth to sing, but no words came out. It appeared that she had laryngitis, too, except Holly knew she didn't. She was clever, there was no doubt, and the best friend Holly had ever had.

The judges had another consultation, before they delivered good news. "Since both contestants are unable to sing, neither will be disqualified. The show must go on!"

The Castorian physician was summoned and Teef joined Holly backstage. The girls grinned at each other. Teef couldn't talk, since Olliz was hovering, and Holly couldn't speak a word, so she pantomimed, 'I love you', touching her eye, heart and pointing at Teef, who merely looked baffled. She hadn't understood the message.

Tetong was quick to arrive. He greeted the girls and examined Holly first, sticking a wire in her mouth. The wire had little legs. It crawled down her throat and the sensation was revolting. Holly gagged and almost puked, before the wire crawled back out.

Cumin came backstage for the very first time ever. "Have you discovered why the girls are unable to sing?" he asked, crouching beside them.

The physician hummed and hawed a bit, before he said, "Holly's vocal cords are unresponsive to stimulation, as if they have been paralyzed. I would speculate the same for the second contestant, although I have not yet examined her."

"Is it a permanent condition?" Cumin asked.

"No. The muscles and nerves have been numbed, not destroyed. The affliction is temporary." It was great news.

"How long until it wears off?" Cumin demanded.

"Hours at least, unless I can undo what has been done."

"Try it. We'll put the guest artists on right after this batch of commercials, and hopefully by the time they've finished singing, our two finalists will be healthy enough to perform," Cumin said.

"I will do my best," Tetong promised.

While a male/female duo performed three numbers, Holly drank a hot steamy potion and had her throat sprayed with something tingly, both inside and out. After that, another wire crept down her throat and shocked it with mild electrical impulses. Holly could feel that.

Teef received the same treatment. She waited for Holly to try singing first, so she could follow her lead. Holly crossed her fingers and her toes, took a deep breath and attempted the first stanza of her song. At first, she could only whisper. That improved to rasping. The longer she sang, the more her voice cleared, until she sounded like herself again. Teef sang next, and—no surprise, she had back the voice she had never lost.

Olliz clapped her hands happily and spoke into her headset, sharing the good news with the show's producers. "Okay, girls, you are back on, right after this commercial message. Holly first! Get ready."

They stood and thanked the Castorian doctor most profusely. Tetong did seem pleased and confided, "I was so looking forward to hearing you both sing tonight. And now I will."

"Thanks to you," Holly said and hugged him. She was fully prepared to tell him she loved him, her hero. He scuttled away with a flush to his white face, before she could.

When the girls returned to the stage, they were cheered all over again. Holly sang first, deeply happy to have the chance. After the ordeal that had come before, the actual singing was almost anticlimactic. Her voice held strong and true throughout the angelic Celtic ballad she had reserved for the very last show. And the final verse, she sang without music, A capella, relying on her voice alone. Holly finished her performance on a powerful note that sounded bigger than life in a dead quiet auditorium. Her voice

264

faded to silence and Holly bowed to the appreciative crowd, well pleased with herself.

Teef sang next and she sang beautifully, as if she couldn't help herself, even though she didn't want to win. The show had to end in a rush, given all the delays that had come before. The judges thanked both girls for their magnificent efforts and their commitment to the show. Chrome reminded the audience to watch the very next night, to find out who would wear the Universe Idol crown. The lights dimmed and it was over.

After the camera-mates stopped broadcasting, there were congratulations all around. The judges, the show's producers, and their assistants, all converged on the stage. Auto-mates brought out trays of drinks and finger foods. Holly and Teef were both congratulated and toasted warmly.

An informal celebration followed. Holly enjoyed the gathering and managed to catch Teef alone. "Thank you so much for helping me," she said, and glanced around to make sure they couldn't be overheard. "Is Nastos going to be angry with you?"

"Why? I must have caught whatever caused you to lose your voice," Teef said innocently, with a wink. She seemed to really like winking.

Holly grinned back. "Do you want to come to my room after this party, and avoid Nastos? He isn't going to be happy about how things turned out." Nastos and the chaperone were nowhere in sight, which was odd.

"I shouldn't. I can't, Holly."

"But you don't want to marry Nastos, and he's dangerous. Come with me, we have to celebrate our last show, together. It might even be our last night together," Holly cajoled.

She could see Teef was tempted, but not tempted enough. "I am still betrothed to him, Holly. I must abide by his wishes."

"But he poisoned me! You shouldn't have anything to do with him," Holly cried.

"My family signed the contract. I cannot shame them, Holly. I hope to earn my freedom by losing to you."

"Do you really think your parents would want you to marry a jerk like him?" Holly said frankly.

"I shouldn't have to marry him when I don't win, but today I am still betrothed." Teef looked over Holly's shoulder and her eyes darkened. "He's here."

They had missed their window of opportunity. Nastos and Pala closed in. Holly backed up. "You stay away from me, far far away." She pointed an accusing finger at Nastos. His face was the picture of innocence, surprise and puzzlement, all rolled together. Before she strangled him in front of hundreds of witnesses, Holly stormed off. She went back to her room, trailed by only one guard. He didn't even hang around after he saw her to her door. Now that the singing was over, the tight security had eased, or he wanted to go back to the party on the stage.

The door recognized her and rolled aside. For a lovely moment in time, Holly thought Antor and Zenga were back. Her heart flip-flopped in alarm when she saw who was with Zenga. It certainly wasn't Antor. It wasn't even human. It was the devil, Red.

"Where is Antor?" she asked, as soon as she found her voice, which had been briefly lost to shock. Coming face-to-face with the devil was enough to stun anyone.

Zenga's answer was to hug Holly, hard. It was uncharacteristic. She was even trembling, which was deeply alarming in itself. Red strolled over, as if it was his suite, not Holly's. "What a pleasure to finally meet you in person, Holly Noel Tate. A real treat." He smiled with warm charm, but it sent a cold shiver down Holly's spine. "Red Belial, at your service." He bowed with grace. If he had a tail, it was hidden in his black leather trousers.

She couldn't manage any pleasantries in return and repeated, "Where is Antor?" The question was directed at Zenga, whose face crumpled. "Oh no, did something bad happen to him?"

Red motioned to the couch with a long-fingered hand. "Sit and I will explain."

"Explain?" Holly sat, because her legs failed her. Zenga joined her, nice and close. Holly gripped her hand and held on tight, like a lifeline. "Is he ... dead?"

"Antor is alive, for the moment." Red padded back and forth with catlike stealth. "He will be retrieved, once I know the location of Earth."

"What?" Holly was sure she'd heard wrong.

"Antor is a hostage, Holly," Zenga said, no beating about the bush. "Red has killed Hampelle and taken over the Comet Tail. He wants your winnings, and has plans to use them to finance -"

Red cut her off with a sharp hiss that sounded like escaping steam. "Say more than you should and Antor will pay the price."

It was enough of a threat for Zenga to hold her tongue.

"But what does any of this have to do with Earth?" Holly didn't understand.

Red toyed with a chain that dangled from his neck, drawing her attention to the medallion that looked exactly like the Castorian one she had pressed her thumb against. "I hold Antor's limbs, and his life, in my hands, yet no matter how I have tried to persuade him to talk, he stubbornly refuses to tell me where in the Universe your Earth spins."

"Persuade him to talk?" Holly didn't like how Red said that, not one little bit.

266

"Tortured," Zenga said.

Red arched an eyebrow. "Call it what you will."

"I'm calling it what it is," she cried with a flash of defiance.

Red ignored her and kept addressing Holly. "I've discussed the matter with Zenga, hoping that she would be more forthcoming than Antor, in revealing Earth's location, to save her friend's life. Alas, she hasn't been as helpful as I had anticipated." Red stopped in front of Holly and gazed down. His black eyes looked like pits. "I'm sure you can set her straight, Holly. Advise her to reveal Earth's location, and Antor will be restored to you, still breathing. You will be taken home, safe and sound." He sank into the adjacent chair and leaned forward. "I can't take you home if I don't know where your home is, now can I?" He sounded so reasonable, and beguiling, but Holly wasn't fooled. Any deal with the devil was for his own benefit. Anyone foolish enough to make a pact with the devil was selling their soul. "If, however, you refuse, Antor will die slowly and painfully, and you will never see your home or your family again. Clear?"

"Crystal," Holly ground out, "except for why you want to find Earth so badly."

"I merely want to retrieve my Gorka. They don't belong on your planet. I'm sure you want them off Earth as much as I want them back," he replied smoothly.

Zenga glared daggers at him. Clearly, he wanted more than his Gorka. Given the great lengths he was going to, this wasn't just about a couple of furry purple monsters. Why was Red so desperate to know her planet's location?

Holly narrowed her eyes on him. "You want more than the Gorka, don't you?"

"You're not as gullible as you look," Red snapped, abandoning his attempt to charm her. "So what if I want to offer a chosen few of your planet's singers a chance to travel the cosmos, to broaden their horizons. Is that a crime?"

"Singers?" Holly blurted out. Hampelle had gotten a scheming look in his eye when she mentioned Earth's abundance of singers, and Red was his partner. The Universe was captivated by singers, and Holly knew she was one of the best singers they had ever heard, as were so many on her planet. "You can't abduct people from my planet and sell them! On Earth, we call that slavery and it's outlawed," she cried.

"How pedestrian," Red drawled with a curled lip. His gums were as black as charcoal, making his pointy teeth gleam all the whiter.

"I suppose Hampelle had the idea first." She glanced at Zenga, who nodded.

Red drawled, "Yes, once he found out that Earth is overpopulated by great singers, he did plan to harvest them from your primitive little dying world."

"Because I told him?" Holly realized in dismay.

Red inclined his head, as if in gratitude. "And your winnings will buy a ship that no UGS can catch or track, a ship that will destroy anything that crosses its path. The Comet Tail is on her last coils and a superior vessel will be necessary to transport Earth's singers all across the Universe. The price I will demand for each will make me wealthy beyond even my wildest dreams. A thousand bizoux will be spare coins, once I've established a reputation as the purveyor of the Universe's best singers."

Holly honestly couldn't believe her ears. Thanks to her, Earth was about to be invaded by aliens, its musical population decimated. Or Antor would die and she would never see her home again. Both her options were unacceptable. She couldn't choose either. "You're evil! You're disgusting and vile and … and cruel. You really are the devil!" Holly shouted at Red, hating him with every fiber of her being.

Red simply strolled over to the viewing screen and removed a ring disc from the chain around his neck. "This will help you to make an informed decision." He placed it on the little node on the control panel and pressed buttons. An inhuman sound filled the room. The being was screaming in such anguish, their torment was beyond imagining. Holly knew it was Antor's voice, but at the same time, it wasn't.

She couldn't listen and covered her ears. "Turn it off! Please turn it off."

At least Red silenced the agonized sounds.

"Is Antor on the Comet Tail? Is that happening on the ship?" Holly asked Zenga.

Zenga shook her head. "I think he's still being held on Pariah."

"He is," Red admitted, as if that bit of information was no matter. "An associate of mine is taking special care of him while I'm here. Antor will continue to suffer, until you reveal Earth's location. And if you tell anyone about this, you will never see him again and you certainly won't find him, not where I've stashed him. Oh, and if anything happens to me, if I don't return for Antor, he will be tortured until his heart gives out. That can take a very long time if done properly. My associate is an expert."

Holly's eyes burned and she swallowed sickly. "I have to think." But she couldn't, except about poor Antor. Inside her head, she could still hear him crying out.

"Of course you must think about this, as long as you do your thinking here," Red said magnanimously, his façade of civility a farce. "The three of us will be keeping very close company, until you are crowned as the next

Universe Idol, and claim your fortune—my fortune—tomorrow night. We won't be leaving Playara until then."

"Can you stop hurting Antor until tomorrow?" Holly said. "Please?"

Red inclined his head in a deceptively courtly manner. "Agreed. I will arrange it. Consider it a gesture of good faith."

Holly fled to the bedroom to escape Red. Zenga followed. Before she could shut the door, Red trespassed on their space. "Separate rooms," he said. He mustn't want them plotting together. Holly glanced at Zenga, who gazed hopelessly back.

"I'll take the other room," Holly said. The room she had shared with Antor.

"Now," Red said, not moving.

Holly stomped around him and into Antor's room. She slammed the door as hard as she could, and curled up on Antor's bed, arms clasped tight around her chest, as if she could somehow hold the fractured pieces of her heart together. She pressed her face into the pillow, trying to think or trying not to think. She had to figure out what to do. She couldn't be responsible for thousands of people being abducted as slaves, but she couldn't leave Antor to be tortured. She couldn't do either thing. How could Red expect her to choose? And then she realized something crucial—Antor had already chosen. Even though Red was torturing him beyond endurance, Antor had protected her planet with his silence, and he wasn't even from Earth. He didn't have family or friends or a home on Earth. He didn't even know what it was like to have those things, and still, he hadn't broken.

Holly knew what she should do, what Antor wanted her to do, she just didn't know if she had the strength. She started to cry, shaking with the force of it, quite unable to stop. She couldn't betray Earth and she couldn't abandon Antor to be tortured to death on Pariah. It felt like her heart was ripping right down the middle. She wanted the nightmare to end. She wanted Antor safely beside her, to hold him and kiss him better. If only they knew where on Pariah he was hidden, maybe they could rescue him from Red's clutches, and Red would lose all his leverage. Both Earth and Antor would be saved. But how could they find him on a planet, which was not a small thing? Holly only had twenty-four hours to figure out what to do, and Pariah was more than a day away, she knew that much.

After hours of straining her brain, in-between bouts of tears, Holly must have drifted into an exhausted sleep. She awoke from a nightmare, damp with sweat and sprawled on top of the bed in her clothes. The awful dream was still in her head. She had been with Antor on Earth, being chased by the Gorka through deep snow. Holly's legs had been as heavy as anchors when she tried to run. Antor reached back to save her, backlit by a beautiful golden kaleidoscope light. Salvation! Until it revealed Castorians dead ahead, holding big corkscrew swords, waiting to cut Antor to pieces.

269

Holly sat up with a start, bringing the dream world and the real world colliding together. "Oh, oh, oh!" she gasped. Her sleeping brain had had a huge revelation. Antor had a tracking chip inside him, like the Gorka. He said the Castorians put it there, so they could find his limbs. Holly could find him, with that chip, if the Castorians would cooperate. And they might—for profit. Holly could give them one heck of a profit, as long as she won Universe Idol, but tonight might be too late. She needed to talk to a Castorian now. Holly only knew one Castorian personally. He was even close and seemed a decent sort. But how to speak to him privately? She didn't even know if aliens respected doctor/patient confidentiality.

There was only one way to find out.

Prepared to be an actor, Holly left the bedroom. Red was snoozing on the couch, probably in case they tried to sneak away. He was a very light sleeper. Even Holly's soft tread roused him.

"Holly, how kind of you to wake me. I didn't mean to sleep so late." He sat up and stretched. He had slept in his clothes, too.

She opened her mouth, but no sound came out. Holly clutched her throat and tried to speak again, or so she hoped it appeared.

"Problems?" Red asked.

Holly widened her eyes and pointed at her throat.

"Lost your voice? Again? Oh well, no matter. You've finished singing."

Her ruse was not playing out as she had planned. Holly stomped her foot and glared daggers at Red, who said, "As a matter of fact, I prefer you speechless. Less chance you'll blab about Antor. No talking to anyone."

Holly wanted to shout at him in the worst way, but she couldn't. Clearly, she had miscalculated about Red calling the Castorian doctor to heal her voice. When the door buzzed, Holly moved to answer it, since she was standing the closest.

Red grabbed her arm. His hand was almost hot enough to sear her skin, and as rough as sand paper. "No, I'll get it." He checked the security imager and didn't seem alarmed. He opened the door.

Holly was hoping to see someone who could help. She was simply happy to see Teef. She felt in need of a friend's comfort.

"Hi Holly." Teef hovered just inside the door, keeping her distance from Red, as if he made her nervous. Teef was alone for once.

Holly waved.

Red said, "Holly seems to have lost her voice again."

Teef's face fell. "Oh no!"

Holly faced her and winked. Teef blinked back, in confusion.

"Holly is going to rest now. You will see her at the show tonight." Red was keeping his polite façade in place.

"Oh." Teef glanced at Holly, for confirmation.

Taking a chance, Holly stepped forward and hugged her goodbye. As soft as a breeze, right in Teef's ear, she whispered, "Get me the doctor."

Teef stepped back and said, "See you tonight, Holly. I hope you're feeling better." Holly wasn't sure that Teef had heard her, not until the girl winked again.

As soon as he sealed the door behind Teef, Red said, "Get back in your room and stay there." He seemed grumpy. Maybe he wasn't a morning alien.

Holly couldn't argue, so she went. She stayed in there for what felt like hours, until the door buzzed. Ignoring Red's instructions, she emerged, hoping against hope that it was the doctor.

Red was getting off the couch. There was no sign of Zenga. Holly was growing worried about the girl. Maybe Red had decided to torture Zenga, too. She knew Earth's location as well as Antor.

With a scowl in her direction, Red peered through the security imager. This time, he hesitated to open the door. It buzzed again, long and loud. Zenga emerged from her room and Holly was deeply relieved to see her unharmed.

"Back in your room and stay there," Red growled. He waited for Zenga to disappear, before he opened the door. Holly was thrilled to see the Castorian doctor. She hid the emotion. Tetong walked in without an invitation and made a beeline for Holly. "You've lost your voice again?" he asked.

She nodded.

"How do you know about that?" Red demanded.

"Teef came to see me, concerned that she would lose her voice again as well. I gave her an examination and she is fine. Holly, however, is not fine. I should have been summoned at once to examine her. She has a show tonight, she will need her voice to speak." He rounded on Red. "Why was I not called?"

Red stepped back from the small, irate being, rather like a Doberman pincer avoiding a poodle. "She's finished singing, it didn't seem serious."

"Are you a doctor?" He didn't give Red a chance to answer. "No, you are not! You are no judge as to whether her condition is serious or not. I will examine my patient now, in private."

Holly pointed at her bedroom and walked that way, daring Red to stop them. He didn't. Holly knew she might only have a minute alone with Tetong and didn't squander it. As soon as they reached her room, she whispered, "I'm only pretending to have laryngitis so I could talk to you." He nodded as if he knew that much. "Red has abducted my friend Antor. You met him, the really sweet guy, the cute one." She was wasting time. The Castorian nodded. "Anyway, Red is trying to torture information out

271

of him, somewhere on Pariah. We need to find him to save him, and that's why we need your help."

"How can I help?" the doctor said.

"Antor has a Castorian tracer chip inside him. He owes three limbs if I can't pay the bizoux owed for his medical treatment, if I don't win Universe Idol. I'll pay you ten bizoux, or whatever you want, if you can locate Antor for me, so we can save him."

"If we own his contract, I should be able to arrange it," Tetong whispered back.

"Red bought Antor's contract."

"Ah, I thought I spotted a Castorian medallion around his neck. That might be a problem." He paused and Holly listened for Red. They were running out of time.

"But can you do it?" she hissed.

"I will need the medallion to access Antor's tracer chip."

"Okay, I'll try and get it off his neck." Holly shut up when the Castorian motioned her to silence.

Red appeared in the doorway and leaned against the jamb. "What is the prognosis?"

The little doctor sounded perfectly calm and collected when he said, "It is not serious. Her voice will return, with help. Holly needs to gargle with a special stimulant. If she could accompany me, I will provide it."

"Bring the medicine here," Red countered.

Tetong nodded. "As you wish."

Red saw him out the door, without delay. Holly didn't know what was going to happen next. She and Tetong hadn't had time to finish planning. She sat down on the couch and stared blankly at nothing.

Zenga came out of her room as soon as the outer door closed. She joined Holly on the couch. Seeking comfort, Holly leaned against her, powerless to say a word with Red's ears so close. Even his eyes were narrowed on them. Holly realized she was wringing her hands like some overwrought historical heroine, and made a conscious effort to relax them.

Zenga said, "Is your voice going to be okay?"

Holly nodded.

"That's good. Can we order lunch, Red? You haven't fed us all day." It was an accusation.

Red waved a hand. "You do seem to crave food more than the rest of us, so go ahead. Order for me, as well."

Zenga ordered for three and they waited. The silence was oppressive until the Castorian doctor returned. He had brought the fake gargling medicine himself. Red accepted the little purple bottle and Tetong said, "Remember Holly, gargle with this as soon as possible, and then I would recommend a little nap." He stressed the word nap.

Holly nodded, suppressing the hundred or so questions that begged asking. Red tossed her the bottle when the food trays appeared behind the doctor. The Castorian said, "Enjoy your meal," and departed.

The smell of food made Holly feel sick when her stomach was in such a knot of worry over Antor. She could barely stop herself from leaping across the table and skewering Red with her pointy eating stick, right through his eye. He'd scream like Antor if she did that, and it wouldn't bother her at all. Holly had never realized she had a violent streak, but she did. Outer Space was bringing out the worst in her.

Before she indulged in carnage, Holly retreated to the haven of her bedroom to examine the purple bottle. She closed the door and held it up to the light. A small dark object floated inside. Curious, Holly opened the lid.

The liquid smelled like fruity water. She poured it into an empty glass and a medallion on a chain fell out. It was a twin to the one that Red wore around his neck, complete with one ring disc and a medallion. Holly wasn't sure what to do with it. Was she supposed to press her thumb to it and return it to the Castorian to sign the new deal? No, more likely, it was a decoy to substitute for the one around Red's neck.

Holly licked it off, since it was so sticky. She pressed her thumb to it, just in case, before she concealed it in her pocket, handy to switch for Red's. With both possibilities covered, she turned her attention back to the liquid. Was it merely camouflage for the medallion? Holly yawned and poured it back in the bottle, until she figured out what to do with it.

"One step at a time," she reminded herself, trying not to worry about how they would get Antor off of Pariah, once they knew his location. The bottle went into her pocket along with the medallion. Holly yawned again and rested her head on the pillow for just a moment.

The next thing she knew, she was opening her eyes in a dark room. Holly shoved her hair off her face and sat up. She couldn't believe she had fallen so soundly asleep for hours, especially under the circumstances— unless there was a reason. She did feel unusually dopey. She touched the bottle in her pocket. She had tasted a bit, and Tetong had emphasized falling asleep. Was the liquid to sedate Red, so she could switch the medallions? She thought that was it, which meant she had to get him to drink it, without delay.

Still dazed, Holly stumbled from the bedroom. Zenga was perched on the couch, tense and pale. Red was talking on the communicator. It sounded like there was some problem with the ship's mechanics.

"How is the voice?" Zenga asked.

Holly shook her head and checked the time. There was little more than an hour to spare, before she had to report to the stage area for the final results show.

Red kept talking and turned his back to them. While he was distracted, Holly leaned close to Zenga's ear and whispered, "Drinks."

Zenga gaped at her. She opened her mouth to speak. Holly shook her head, eyes wide. "Drinks," she mouthed, not daring to talk more than that.

As soon as Red ended his call, Zenga said, "I could really use a drink. How about a bottle of red brandy?" It sounded like a challenge, and it wasn't at all the kind of drinking Holly had meant.

Red chuckled. "Sounds good to me. If I can get you drunk, maybe you'll rock my hammock." Holly thought for sure that Zenga would punch Red into the next galaxy for that comment.

"You'd have to kill me first," she said lightly.

"We'll see about that." Red was quick to order the bottle. An automate brought it, with glasses. Zenga poured three servings, and Holly remembered the last time she had seen such a bottle. It had almost killed them and destroyed the Universe Idol complex. The brandy that came out of this black bottle looked normal enough, except for the bright pinky-red hue.

Red downed the first cup and declared, "Ah, delicious." Zenga downed hers. Holly merely tasted a small sip. She had rarely drank booze on Earth, and the space alcohol was so strong, she choked.

"Not much of a drinker, are you, Holly Noel Tate?" Red motioned for Zenga to refill his cup. She did, and poured herself another. Holly sipped again, and choked again. If she wasn't mistaken, Outer Space alcohol packed way more of a punch than Earth's. Or she wasn't much of a drinker.

The way Red was belting them back, maybe he would get drunk. If he passed out, the medallion could be switched and delivered to the Castorian doctor, with Red none the wiser.

Since that was unlikely to happen, Holly watched for any opportunity to dose his drink.

Zenga was pouring them a third round when the communicator signaled an incoming call. Red left his glass on the table and went to answer it. Quick as a pickpocket, Holly had the purple bottle in hand. She removed the lid while Zenga watched, wide-eyed. Holly poured a dash into Red's glass, and then a second dash for good measure.

They could only hear Red's side of the conversation, which was short and curt. He said, "Don't touch it. No, don't try to fix it, you'll only make it worse. I'll have a look when I get back." He hung up and said, "That damn ship is going to fall apart, before it makes it back to Pariah."

"The Comet Tail?" Zenga said.

"Do we have another ship?" Red snapped. He reached for his glass. He finished the contents in one swallow. As if he'd been hit on the head with a mallet, his eyes glazed over and he crumpled to the floor. Holly had been hoping for something a little less dramatic, like Red sitting down and drifting off.

Zenga gasped, "Holly, what did you put in his drink?"

Finally, she could talk freely. "A sleeping draught. I've made an arrangement with the Castorian doctor to find Antor, using that tracking chip they put in him. But once they find him, I don't know what we'll do. Pariah is so far away." Holly pulled the decoy chain from her pocket and displayed it. "They need Antor's contract to access his tracer chip."

Zenga crouched beside Red. She removed the all-important medallion and replaced it with the fake one, transferring a tarnished ring disc from one chain to the other. Once it was back around Red's neck, she said, "Okay, what now?"

"Uh," Holly hesitated. "I'm not sure. I've kind of been figuring this out on the fly."

"You're not flying, Holly. You can't fly."

"I know. It's an expression." Holly peered closely at Red's face. It was as slack as wet cotton. He was even drooling. "I have to get the medallion to the Castorian doctor, and then … I don't know. He'll tell us where Antor is on Pariah, I hope, but I don't know how to save him, or what to do about Red." Her unformed plan needed Zenga's input.

"We'll figure something out, but first, let's get the medallion into the right hands. We'll go from there, on the fly, is that right?" Zenga asked.

"Right. Okay, I'll be quick." Holly stuck the chain in her pocket. She hurtled from the room and ran through the corridors. She found Tetong at the medical center, alone in his office. She put the contract in his hands, panting hard. "What now?"

"Now you will sit down and take a deep breath, Holly Noel Tate." He tilted his head at the nearest chair.

"Is that medical advice?"

"Of a sorts."

Holly sat and tried to calm herself, while Tetong activated a small viewing screen on his table. It looked just like a laptop computer on Earth. He angled it so they could both see. "I can tap into the Castorian communication network to find your Antor from here," he said.

Her Antor. Holly liked the sound of that. "Do I have to sign a contract?"

"No, Holly. Let us keep this between us."

"You're helping me?" It was unexpected and very sweet.

"I am helping you, and Antor. You have faced more than your share of adversity throughout this competition. It is time someone aided your cause."

"Thank you, Tetong." Not all Castorians were motivated solely by profit, it seemed. Like humans, there were probably good and bad Castorians, and everything in-between.

A map with a lot of crisscrossed lines appeared on the viewing screen. Holly pulled her chair closer. "What is that?"

"An array that exists between our ships in this sector." The Castorian put Antor's ring disc contract on the little node on the control panel.

"That's a lot of ships," Holly said. There were hundreds.

"Yes." Buttons were pressed and the screen zoomed in on one dirty brown planet.

"Is that Pariah?"

"It is." The Castorian frowned and pressed different buttons, zooming in closer and from different angles. He shook his head and said gently, "Holly, I have bad news."

"I don't want more bad news," she said.

He patted her hand. "And I don't want to deliver it, but Antor's tracking chip is not displaying his location."

"What does that mean? Is he …" Holly couldn't say dead, she just couldn't.

The Castorian sat down beside her. "There are a number of possible explanations. The chip could be malfunctioning, or it could have been damaged if Antor was … damaged, or he might be in an insulated chamber that blocks the signal, or very deep underground."

"Oh, like in a dungeon," Holly whispered. Dungeons were where they tortured people, at least on Earth. She shook her head in denial. Antor was still missing and possibly dead. She had been so optimistic that he would be found by the Castorians, and now they couldn't locate him. It came back to Red. Holly gathered her resolve and stood up. "Thanks so much for trying."

The Castorian nodded heavily. It looked like his big head might break his skinny neck. Before he turned off the screen, he zoomed out. Holly turned to leave.

"Wait!" Tetong said.

She spun around and saw an orange blip on the screen. "What is that?"

The Castorian smiled widely. "That is your Antor. He is not on Pariah."

"Oh! Where is he?" Holly leaned closer to the screen.

"Much, much closer." Tetong zoomed in on the blip.

"Where?" Holly wanted to shake the answer out of him.

The doctor pointed up. "In orbit above us."

"Oh! On the Comet Tail. Red lied!" she cried.

"Are you surprised?"

276

"No, I guess not." Holly smiled rather mistily. Antor was alive, and so very close. "I used that sleeping potion on Red to get the medallion. That was a great idea, by the way. When will he wake up?" Holly needed to know.

"How much did you give him?"

"Two pours, maybe an eighth of the bottle."

The Castorian grimaced.

"Too much?" Holly had suspected so, given how Red had fallen like a chopped tree.

"Yes. It is unlikely he will revive before tomorrow."

"Maybe that's good. I think that is good, so we can get aboard the ship without him and save Antor." Holly was thinking aloud. Zenga would know a lot more about how to do that than Holly. She couldn't wait to tell her the good news about Antor.

"I wish you luck, Holly. Let me know if I can be of further assistance." The Castorian stood up and gave a little bow.

"I will, and thank you so much! I better get back to Zenga, and then there's the results show tonight." In all ways, it was the thing Holly was the least concerned about.

She hurried back to her suite, dreaming about seeing Antor. She wasn't paying a whole lot of attention to her surroundings and reached her room before she was expecting to. As the door opened automatically for her, there was a rush of movement behind her. An arm clamped around her neck and something pointy pressed into her back. She might have thought Red had revived, except she could see him on the floor, still dead to the world and all tied up, Zenga was calmly sipping brandy and guarding him—until she noticed that Holly wasn't alone that is.

Holly was shoved roughly into the room. She spun around to see who was tormenting her, now that Red couldn't. Nastos didn't come as a surprise, at all. He sealed the door and kept what looked like a miniature plastic harpoon gun aimed at Holly. It was smaller than a child's toy.

Nastos did a double-take when he spotted Red on the floor, but the weapon stayed firmly trained on Holly's heart. "Who is that?" he asked. "And why is he all tied up?"

"Bad guy, like you," Holly snapped, without elaborating. "What are you doing here, Nastos?"

He rolled his eyes. "Can't you figure it out?"

"Probably. Where's Teef?"

"Preparing for tonight's show. Preparing to lose," he snarled.

"Nobody knows who will win or lose, until the results are announced," Holly said, biding her time, wondering if he held a real weapon. It looked fake, but looks could be deceiving, especially in Outer Space.

"It is obvious who will win, unless something is done to change that result." Nastos moved deeper into the room. "Who is that?" he asked again, of Red.

"Someone else who is ruining this competition for me, or was." Holly backed toward Zenga, who hadn't budged. She did seem to be taking the weapon seriously. "And what do you mean, change the result?"

"One of the two finalists should withdraw."

Holly snorted. "Me."

"If you make a call right now and officially withdraw, I will leave you alive. Given a choice, isn't your life more valuable than winning the competition?"

"It's not just my life," Holly said, or she might have withdrawn.

"So you will not make that call?" Nastos tilted his head at the viewing screen.

Holly shook her head firmly. "No, I can't."

"You can."

"Okay, I won't," she said clearly.

Nastos touched the trigger, but didn't press it. Holly stared down the barrel of yet another space gun and kept talking. "Have you been behind all the attempts to stop me from competing?"

Nastos smirked. "I'm not the only one who wants you to lose, but I have been behind the more creative attempts—not me personally, of course. I've hired some help. My family needs those winnings."

"The new chaperone? She wasn't really a chaperone, was she?"

"She served more than one purpose," Nastos said.

Holly's temper grew like a weed inside her. "You don't even care about Teef, do you? All you want is her prize money. You've been manipulating her and using her! She deserves so much better than the likes of you." Holly looked down her nose at the short swarthy Schwill, who was actually looking kind of pale and pasty at the moment.

"Teef is lucky I lowered my standards and agreed to the betrothal. She is pretty enough and will make an obedient wife, but she isn't of my caste and never will be."

"Maybe she's not as obedient as you think," Holly said. "If you get rid of me, maybe she'll keep her winnings and dump you!"

"Dump me?" The expression confused Nastos.

"Ditch you, break up, end the betrothal," Holly said.

He pursed his lips in annoyance. "You are ignorant of Schwill culture and customs, aren't you? A betrothal is as binding as a marriage. It takes both parties to dissolve the contract, and Teef would never shame her family's honour by breaking the oath they made in her name. And all property is owned by the male. Married females own nothing, they are owned by their husbands. Teef's winnings are my winnings and Teef will

278

obey me in all things, absolutely," he said with petulant haughtiness. Clearly, he believed his own words and liked hearing his own voice.

"That's too archaic to believe, and they call my planet primitive," Holly muttered in disgust.

The door buzzed. Nastos lost his smug smile. Holly's hopes flared that rescue was at hand. They sank again when Nastos backed out of sight of the door and aimed the gun at Zenga, saying to Holly, "Get rid of whoever it is, or I'll kill them."

Holly had no doubt he meant it. But could the funny little gun he was holding do the job? "Is that a real gun?" Holly asked Zenga, not Nastos. Zenga nodded, emphatically.

The buzzer repeated, more urgently. Holly went to answer it. As soon as the door slid away, Teef tumbled in as if she was being chased. Holly had no chance to refuse her entrance. She grabbed Holly and gasped, "I only have a minute. Nastos left me alone -" And then she spotted him. Her eyes widened, first on her betrothed holding a gun, then on Red littering up the floor. "What's going on?" she said.

"Nastos is crazy, and that's the nicest thing I can say about him," Holly burst out. "He wants me to withdraw from the competition so you'll win by default, so he can take all your bizoux and force you into a loveless marriage, and he'll expect you to obey his every sick, twisted whim. He's going to shoot me if I don't cooperate." Holly's mouth was running away with her.

"Silence!" Nastos waved his weapon. "Teef is my betrothed, she will obey me. As a matter of fact, I'm glad she's here. I want her here to prove her devotion to me, not you! You are nothing to her, except a rival to be bested—one way or another."

"Nastos, what's in the dartgun?" Teef asked, taking the weapon very seriously.

"Vulture nanos," he boasted with unpleasant smugness.

"Is that bad?" Holly glanced at Teef, trusting her word.

"Very bad. The worst."

Nastos took over. "Once they're injected, the nanos eat you alive from the inside out. Death is excruciatingly slow and painful." It did sound gruesome. "Now that you understand, go and make that call."

"I can't, I mean I won't." It amounted to the same thing. She backed away from him when he stalked toward her, too close.

"Then you'll die." Nastos aimed the gun at the middle of her chest with a shaky hand, yet he still didn't pull the trigger. Holly wasn't sure why he was delaying. Teef stood wide-eyed and immobile behind him, like a deer in the headlights.

"We all have to die sometime," Holly said, keeping her attention on Nastos. It was a standoff. The gun shook harder, and in spite of the fact that he was the one holding it, he looked trapped. He'd probably never had to murder anyone before, even though he'd hired others to do the deed. He had probably expected Holly to simply withdraw, and now he had to look in her eyes and end her life. Even though he was an ass, that couldn't be easy.

"Just make the call," he ground out, whining a touch. "My family is counting on me to save them from financial ruin. I have to do this. Teef has to win and marry me. It's all arranged."

"Oh, now I feel so much better about dying." Holly's sarcasm was overdone. Her temper was creeping out from behind her terror. "As long as you and your family can roll around in bizoux, Antor and I will have died for a worthy cause. Teef will be miserable and unsatisfied for the rest of her life, but as long as you're happy, she won't mind. You won't mind a life of subservient misery, will you, Teef?"

Teef opened her mouth, no sound came out.

"She will be a dutiful and submissive wife. Schwill females know their place." Nastos clenched his jaw and got a tighter grip on the weapon. Holly stopped talking. By antagonizing him, she was strengthening his resolve.

Nastos's trigger finger moved. He was going to kill her. Holly closed her eyes, picturing Antor. She hoped someone else could save him, since she wouldn't be around to do it. She hadn't even had a chance to tell Zenga that he was orbiting overhead.

A hollow thud coincided with a popping twang that was surely the dartgun discharging. Nothing hit Holly, although something that sounded like a mosquito whizzed by her neck. Her eyelids flew opened. Teef was clutching the bottle of brandy and Nastos was on the ground. Teef must have thumped him on the head, but not hard enough—or his head was uncommonly hard. He was already rising.

Holly lunged forward and scooped up the weapon. She pointed it at Nastos and cocked it, as if it was a paintball gun. Another dart dropped into position, needle nose aimed at his chest.

"Look what I've got," she said. Nastos did, and froze. Zenga was quick to leap over the couch and yank his arms behind his back. He squirmed until Holly said, "Is this the trigger? Here? Is it a hair-trigger? That might go off by accident?"

Nastos took a look at her hovering finger and stopped struggling. He turned as limp as an overcooked spaghetti noodle.

Holly grinned at Teef, proudly. She couldn't help it. "Well done, Teef. Nastos, on the couch. Hands up and keep them up, unless you want to be eaten alive from the inside out. A slow painful death, I think you said. Or was it excruciating?"

Zenga tossed him onto the seat and he stuck his arms way up in the air. His face was so pale and tight, it looked almost shrunken. "Teef, you can't do this," he said. "Your parents signed a betrothal agreement. You belong to me, you have to listen to me. If you don't, I'll make your life with me worse than time on Gehenna."

"I would prefer a life sentence on Gehenna to one with you." Teef glanced at Zenga. "Can you gag him?"

"My pleasure." Zenga borrowed some of Red's restraints, since he really didn't need them. She tied a swatch of cloth around Nastos's mouth, almost strangling his face, before she tied his wrists just as tight. "Is that better?" she asked Teef.

"Much better."

Holly hugged Teef. "Thank you for saving my life." And then she hugged Zenga. "I'm so glad you're not hurt. Now what?"

The three girls stood close together and surveyed their captives. Nastos was glaring and Red was dead to the world, lying at his feet.

"I don't know what to do about that one." Zenga kicked Nastos in the shin.

"Are you going to be in trouble, Teef? Will you have to marry him anyway?" Holly asked. Nastos nodded and growled through the gag.

"I might, if he wants revenge for this."

Zenga lifted the dartgun out of Holly's hands. "Or I could shoot him now, and then you won't have to marry him, Teef."

Holly thought Zenga was serious, until she winked. The winking was coming in very handy, like a secret code. "I like how you think, Zenga," Holly said, straight-faced.

Nastos whimpered and shook his head wildly.

"Might as well shoot Red, too, get rid of both of them," Zenga added. She liked scaring Nastos, there was no doubt. "We don't need Red anymore, right, now that we know where Antor is stashed."

"Antor isn't where we thought he was," Holly said. "He's much, much closer." She was as bad as Chrome, building up the suspense.

"Holly! Where?" Zenga gasped.

Holly pointed up. "On the Comet Tail."

Zenga kicked Red with force. "He was lying! He had Antor hidden the whole time, and I didn't suspect a thing."

"So, do we need Red to get on the ship? Bo and Bo must be guarding Antor."

Zenga sat down, looked at Nastos beside her, and hopped up again. "I have to think."

The viewing screen buzzed and they all jumped. A message was coming in. Holly pressed the icon. Olliz wanted her to report backstage, without delay.

Holly hesitated. "It's time to get ready for the show, unless I don't go, unless we save Antor now and head directly for Earth. What do you think?" she asked Zenga, hoping the girl had an opinion or an idea or a plan. Anything.

Zenga considered the possibility briefly, then shook her head. "You have to go. If the Universe Idol guards come to search for you, I don't want them to find these two, like this. We'll be the ones in trouble then. And I don't know how we're going to rescue Antor with both Bos on the ship. I need some time to figure that out. You should go," she said firmly.

"But will you be okay? Alone with these two lowlifes?"

Zenga aimed the gun at Nastos's face. "I'll be fine. I don't know about him though."

"Shoot if you must." Teef headed for the door. Nastos didn't even get a farewell. Holly was impressed. Teef was taking to her newfound independence like a duck to water.

"We'll be back in a couple of hours," Holly said.

Zenga walked her to the door. "And when you get back, I'll have a plan worked out for how we can save Antor."

"It has to be tonight." Holly couldn't wait any longer. She needed to know that he was alive, she needed to hold him.

"Tonight," Zenga agreed.

37 Antor - Plans and Plots

Antor was regaining his senses when the Comet Tail rocked. If he wasn't mistaken, a shuttle had docked. Red must be back. Antor had slept the entire time he had been away.

Two sets of heavy feet lumbered past his door and Antor strained to hear what was happening. The feet creaked all the way to the side hatch and fell silent. The ship rocked again. The shuttle had detached without dropping anyone off. Instead, it had picked up two large passengers. Everything was still and dead quiet for a very long time.

Antor shook his head, trying to wake up his brain. It certainly sounded like the Binares had left the Comet Tail, which might mean that things were not going smoothly for Red down on Playara. It wasn't really surprising, since he was up against Zenga and Holly. They weren't going to make things easy for Belial. Antor hoped they were giving him hell. He stopped smiling inside, when he thought about Bo and Bo crashing that party.

Antor had to help, he had to contribute something to the cause. He'd been useless so far, simply a victim who had been beaten and chained, and now he was alone on the Comet Tail ... or almost alone. The Binares had to have left someone on the bridge. There was only one other someone, or something, that could be.

He edged around on his back and began kicking the wall, as hard as he could, over and over. He didn't hear the footsteps approach and blinked when the door opened. The light went on. Willy stood in the doorway, scanning for the source of the noise. Antor struggled to his knees and tried to talk through the gag.

Willy focused on him and approached. Antor kept trying to speak and Willy said, "I cannot understand you, Antor."

Antor rolled his eyes.

"Do you have instructions, Antor?" Willy asked. Antor nodded. Luckily, Willy understood that gesture. "What are your instructions, Antor?" Antor tried to talk again. "Would you like me to remove the cloth from your mouth so that I might hear your instructions, Antor?" Willy asked. Antor nodded vigorously. Willy yanked the gag down and out. He wasn't gentle.

"Thanks, Willy. Are we alone on the ship?" Antor gasped.

"Yes, Antor."

"Do you know where the Binares went?"

"Yes, Antor."

He sighed. "Where did they go, Willy?"

"Red did not check in with them as prearranged, nor is he answering their hail. They have descended to Playara to verify his wellbeing."

"Then please unchain me. Get these damn shackles off."

Willy efficiently unlocked metal links until Antor was blessedly free. With no time to waste, he said, "To the bridge, Willy!" He stumbled when he tried to walk on stiffened limbs and Willy assisted him.

"Willy, I don't know what I would do without you." Antor dropped an arm around metal shoulders and grinned. "I've missed you."

"I have missed you, Antor."

"I think we better make a little detour," Antor realized. Willy was lucky he didn't have a nose. Antor changed his repugnant clothes for fresh ones, but only after a quick cleansing to wash a whole lot of blood of his face and chest.

He used the facilities and, faint with thirst and hunger, stopped at the galley to drink about a gallon of pure water. He carried a bowl of space rations with him to the bridge, devouring some on the way. Antor had never before realized that space rations were absolutely delicious, at least to a starving man. It was a revelation.

Antor was surprised to discover that he had lost only one day instead of the usual two, probably because he hadn't swallowed the full quantity of dosed water. The first thing he did when he reached the bridge was click on the viewing screen, since it was time for the Universe Idol results show. He simply wanted to see Holly, even if she had lost. He hoped she wasn't too upset about not being able to save his limbs. Even more, he hoped that Red wasn't hurting or abusing her.

Antor smiled when the viewing screen showed her, healthy and safe, on the Universe Idol stage. "I'll be right down, Holly," Antor told her, even though she couldn't hear him. A commercial break came on.

The second thing Antor did was try to call a shuttle. The communication system was completely disabled. Not just long range calls—all calls. The Bos must have been told to do that before they left the ship, as a precaution.

"You're not going to stop me that easily," Antor said to an imaginary Red Belial. Antor didn't need a shuttle to get to Playara. The Comet Tail was a small ship. It could just as easily fly on down there and land on the surface.

Antor tried to break orbit and coast down to the planet. The ship was unresponsive. The controls were as disabled as the communication system. Trust Red to make sure that safeguard was in place, before he left the ship.

Not ready to give up, Antor tried to override the disablement. While Chrome droned on, Antor wasted time proving to himself that it couldn't be done, at least not quickly, and quickly was all Antor had.

"Well, I guess I'll have to wait for you to come to me," he murmured. He couldn't wait to defeat the man who had tortured him, and threatened Holly and her planet. After he defeated Red, Antor would get Holly safely home and retrieve the Gorka. He would need a ship to accomplish all that. The Comet Tail would have to do. At least Antor knew how to keep her flying, most of the time.

Being alone on the Comet Tail was a boon he hadn't expected and he was going to make the most of it. Antor calculated how much time he might have to act as saboteur. The final results show was about a quarter over, and that special program normally lasted two hours. That probably wouldn't change, even though Holly had officially been disqualified. If Red rushed everyone directly back to the Comet Tail after the show, Antor still probably had an extra hour.

"Okay, Willy, we have about two and a half hours to make the Comet Tail our friend and Red's enemy. It will have to be done manually, with the wiring. Fetch the tool array for me," Antor said.

The viewing screen replayed the highlights of the previous night's show and Antor was completely distracted. Holly had been disqualified, but the replay showed her singing a familiar ballad, the one that had kept him alive when he had been dying. And she sang it so brilliantly, Antor couldn't move until it was over. Clearly, the devious Red had not shown him the whole show, and Holly had recovered her voice to sing, and compete. She could win tonight.

"We're going to survive, Holly," he promised her. He lifted the top panel off the primary console without removing his gaze from her face. His hands knew what to do.

Willy plunked the tool array on the adjacent seat. "Thanks, Willy." Antor reached for a Scarnivore splicer and focused on the innards of the panel, thinking hard. He would need to be able to control the Comet Tail from a location other than the bridge. He eyed the buttons that controlled the magnetic compactor and glanced at Willy. "Any ideas, Willy?"

"I don't have ideas, Antor."

"I know. Well, let's start by messing things up on the bridge, while I think." Antor demonstrated what he wanted Willy to do.

Willy cross-wired console components as shown, and Antor nipped around the ship, fiddling with door panels and communication systems. As soon as Red returned, Antor should have no trouble trapping him in some cabin or other, or on the bridge. The bridge would be best, because it had a blaster-proof door. Red wouldn't be able to shoot his way out. It was a simple plan, but sometimes that was the best kind.

He watched as much of Universe Idol as he could, in-between his tampering. Holly was less animated than usual, and tense. He didn't think that was because of the show. Red would have been with Holly for about twenty-four hours, tormenting and threatening her, maybe even hurting her. Antor intended to put an end to that, with flare.

He checked on Willy's project. It was perfectly done. "That's great, Willy. Red won't be in control much longer." Antor eyed the buttons that powered the compacting weapon again. Surely there was a way to make that technology work in his favour, without killing everyone in the vicinity.

The data-stream hadn't been disabled and Antor accessed detailed specs about the compactor. He inserted his core-text wire to absorb everything he could about how the magnetic chain reaction functioned. He had to soak up massive amounts of information much faster than was advisable, and his nose started bleeding, but what he learned was worth it. The information inspired an idea that was maybe a little crazy, or a lot crazy. "But it just might work," he murmured. "Willy, I'll need your help for this."

"Yes, Antor."

"Actually, I could use your help with something else. I've just thought of it." Antor wished he'd had the brainstorm earlier. He checked the clock. There might still be enough time to pull it off, maybe.

"Willy, sit in the Captain's chair, in front of the primary console and open your recharge panel."

"Yes, Antor." Willy sat and popped open the panel.

While Universe Idol dragged on with replays from every single show, Antor reconfigured and exchanged vital hardware in both Willy and the consol. He rerouted bounced signals and even crawled into the engine coils to reverse magnetic currents in the compactor's hardware.

In the end, Antor wasn't quite sure what type of monster he had turned the little Comet Tail into, and he wasn't about to test it. Most of what he'd done would only be activated as a last resort, if everything else went horribly wrong. If he could do nothing else, Antor could at least save Earth.

When Chrome Boreal announced that he would reveal the winner of Universe Idol after a commercial break, Antor sat down beside Willy and took his first deep breath in ages. "This is it, Willy," he said, leaning forward.

"What is it, Antor?"

"The big moment! The winner of Universe Idol is going to be announced."

"Should I watch the viewing screen, Antor?"

Antor smiled. "Yes, watch with me. Keep me company, Willy."

"Yes, Antor."

After almost seven minutes of commercials, Chrome returned. Cumin and the other judges joined him on the stage. X-Orgone was holding the Universe Idol crown. It was a jeweled work of art that the winner got to keep forever. Each year's crown was a little different. As if this one had been tailor-made for Holly, it had blue gems that were as glowing as her eyes.

Cumin began his speech by thanking the audience and repeating what an interesting season it had been, with two of the most talented contestants ever heard on the show, and a string of intriguing mishaps to spice things up. He beckoned Holly and Teef forward to stand with him, front and center.

They came, hands clasped together. Cumin didn't need a ring disc, he knew exactly who was about to win. "Holly Noel Tate and Teef Moss, you are both winners in the eyes of the Universe, but only one can wear the crown."

X-Orgone stepped closer and placed it on Holly's head, saying, "Congratulations, Holly Noel Tate, you are this year's Universe Idol."

She looked surprised. "I won? I really won?"

Cumin confirmed it. "Holly Noel Tate, you are the new Universe Idol." He began to applaud and everyone joined in, until the sound was thunderous. The stage lit up with holographic fireworks that were every bit as loud and blinding as real ones.

Antor cheered and Willy kept watching the viewing screen. "You can cheer if you want, Willy," he said with a grin that made his split lip start bleeding afresh.

"I do not, Antor." Willy wasn't given to emotional displays, unless he was under orders.

"That's okay." Antor could celebrate enough for both of them. The first time he had heard Holly sing, he had known she could win Universe Idol, and she had!

Teef didn't seem upset. She hugged Holly and looked so joyful, she might have been the winner. Holly hugged her back and the camera-mate zoomed in on Holly's face.

"I wish I could be there with you," Antor said. "But I'll see you soon, and get you home. Red won't have a chance to hurt anyone on Earth." It was a solemn vow, even though she couldn't hear him. Commercials replaced Holly, and Antor began packing up tools. He borrowed a couple of the smallest and handiest. He would need them for an integral part of his plan.

When the bridge had been put to rights and every sign of Antor's tampering erased, he returned to his quarters and picked up his blood encrusted shirt. It stank. He didn't want to put it back on, but he had to look exactly as Red had left him. No-one could suspect he'd been roaming the ship. The tools went up his sleeve, tucked securely in the cuff.

"Willy, walk me back to the cargo bay. We need to talk," Antor said.

"Yes, Antor."

"I really don't want to go back there, you know." He sighed.

"I did not know, Antor," Willy said.

Antor returned to his prison, only because it was vital to his ruse. Before he replaced the gruesome gag and had Willy chain him back to the wall, he erased all Willy's memories of what they had done. Lastly, he input one verbal trigger, a word that would activate a simple series of encoded instructions for Willy to follow.

Willy snapped the slave bracelets and anklets back on Antor's raw skin, then chained him to the wall. The auto-mate walked away without a backward glance. He had already forgotten what he had just done.

Lastly, Antor banged his forehead with his chained wrist, making the puncture wound from Red's horn bleed. Since he'd washed his face, he had no choice but to replace that blood.

The ship was as silent as a tomb for hours. Antor soon regretted how quickly he'd had himself re-incarcerated. He was dozing when he heard lighter feet moving about the ship. It must be Zenga … or Holly, or it could be Red, who had a light step in spite of his muscular frame. Antor's heart beat faster.

He squinted when the door opened and the light went on.

"Aren't you a sight," Red drawled. "Get up. Someone would like proof that you're alive. You would think that my word would be enough, but it isn't."

The shackles around his ankles were released and he was unchained from the wall. The gag and slave bracelets stayed in place. Antor shuffled stiffly ahead of Red to the bridge.

It was crowded. Both Holly and Zenga were there, which wasn't unexpected. What was a surprise was that Teef and her betrothed, Nastos, were there as well. The whole group was being guarded by the Binares, holding blasters. Willy stood against the wall and paid no attention to Antor.

The girls looked undamaged. Holly cried out and leapt to her feet when she saw him. Antor wanted to tell her to keep her distance, given his lack of personal hygiene, except he couldn't talk.

She embraced him gently and didn't seem to care. He couldn't hug her back with his wrists fused together. He could only absorb the feel of her. It was enough. Zenga looked at him tragically. He grunted, wishing to speak.

Holly reached up to remove his gag. Red didn't like that. "Leave it on," he growled.

She sighed and touched Antor's forehead. "At least get me the first aid kit."

"No need," Red replied, coldly. "He's fine, aren't you, Antor?"

Antor nodded and gazed deep into Holly's eyes.

"You're not … you're not fine. You're hurt, and thin and -" Tears welled up in her beautiful eyes.

Without warning, Red gripped her arm and almost tossed her into a chair. "Antor will be perfectly fine, if one of you will tell me where in the bloody Universe Earth spins! Tell me now and you can give Antor all the tender loving care you want," he shouted in Holly's face. She cringed back into her seat. "If you don't, all of you will suffer more than you can imagine. So, who's it going to be? Who will tell me the location of Earth, before I take Antor back down to the cargo bay for a little more of my persuasion? Zenga? No? Holly, how about you? Why don't you tell Antor that it's okay to spill his guts, before I do it for him?"

Silence filled the bridge. Holly started to sob. Red turned even redder than he was naturally. He was trying everything he knew to make them talk, and no-one was cooperating. Spitting a string of curses, he grabbed Antor and dragged him back to the cargo bay. He didn't shut the door before he removed the gag and stuck the cursed hellring in Antor's mouth. Antor tried not to scream, but he did.

Again, Antor lost touch with reality. He had no idea how much time had elapsed before he awoke. One of the Binares was dragging him. In a daze, Antor stumbled to his feet. He banged into a metal wall when he couldn't walk straight. Bo gave him a helping hand. He ended up back on the bridge. It was where Bo wanted him to go, and there was no refusing someone that big, especially when you didn't have usable arms or any strength in your body.

Everyone was there, more or less as he had left them. The girls looked deeply shaken, and they'd been crying.

Red circled the room, surveying his collection of captives. He stopped in front of the viewing screen as if it was a stage. "Who's ready to talk?"

Antor hated the part he was about to play, but given how events were unfolding, it seemed the best way to defeat Red. At least Antor had suffered enough to make it appear real. Although, given how long he had held his silence, would Red believe he had finally broken Antor now?

Before he could open his mouth, Red lunged toward Holly. He leaned over and pointed his horn directly at her right eye. She shrank back as far as she could against the hard back of the chair. Red leaned in until the point pressed against her eyelid. "Should I poke out one eye, or both?" he snarled in her face. "I could take both and still keep you to sing for me, forever." He leaned in and Holly cried out in pain and terror.

It was time for Antor to act. And Red would believe him now.

He cried out, "No! Stop. Don't hurt Holly. I'll tell you where to find Earth, if you take Holly home, unharmed, and if you promise to leave her and her family alone." He ducked his head and hunched, as if ashamed of yielding to Red.

Red lifted his head, taking his dangerous horn with him, away from Holly. He narrowed his black eyes. "I'll stay leagues away from her city, if it gains me the rest of the planet."

Antor nodded heavily. "And you have to let Zenga go, too."

"Don't!" Zenga shouted. "Don't you dare sell Earth for my freedom! I'm not worth a whole planet, and neither are you. Even Holly isn't worth her whole planet. She doesn't want you to do this."

It was hard to tell what Holly wanted at that point. She had sagged into the chair and looked about to faint or be sick.

"Stand up for what's right, Antor. Remember what's at stake," Zenga added.

"I don't have a choice, Zen." Antor slumped lower in defeat. "He's got us all trapped on the ship. He has Holly's winnings. All we can do is save ourselves. There's no other way out of this mess."

"There's always a way out." Zenga looked so disappointed in him, Antor dropped his eyes and stared at his boots. They were as bloodstained as his shirt.

Holly still didn't say a word. She might have been in shock. Teef stepped up and gripped her hand, trying to comfort her. Nastos stood closer to one of the Binares, a little apart from the rest of the hostages.

"I'm not sure if I believe you, Antor." Red studied him keenly. "I would like proof of your good faith."

"And what show of good faith will I get in return?" Antor couldn't appear too cowed.

"I won't kill or torture anyone. How's that?" Red smiled coldly.

"Not bad."

Red ordered the Binares to take Teef and Nastos away, before he turned on the viewing screen and accessed a star map of the whole Universe. Zenga shoved out of her seat and approached Antor.

Red didn't stop her. He watched avidly, waiting to be entertained.

"Antor, think. You know this is wrong. Don't tell him anything."

Antor stepped around her to approach the map. He touched a spot in the lower left corner with his shackled hands. Red zoomed in on the area and Antor said, "Earth, Holly's planet, is in this quadrant." It was the truth. Antor figured Red must have deduced that much, so he didn't risk a lie.

And knowing the quadrant wouldn't help Red find Earth, he would need much more information to do that.

Zenga started toward Antor. Red caught her wrist. "Show me the solar system, Antor."

"Not yet. Once we reach that quadrant, I'll tell you where Earth lies, if you keep your promise to not kill or torture anyone, including me. That's the deal."

"Fair enough." Red freed Zenga, who looked at Antor with such loathing, he half-expected to shrivel up and die. She slapped him across the face hard enough to start fresh blood flowing down his cheek. Antor made no move to defend himself and hunched as if he was ashamed. Before she turned away in disgust, Zenga winked. It caught Antor off-guard. Surely if Zenga had realized he was acting, and she was playing along, she could have slapped him with less vigor.

Red turned off the screen and summoned one of the Bos back to the bridge. He said, "Allow Antor to tidy up and eat something, before he returns to his quarters." Antor figured quarters meant cargo bay. He glanced at Holly. She seemed to have withdrawn into herself, as if she was in a stupor.

"Look after Holly, Zen," he muttered, before he went with Bo.

After he used the facilities, Antor located clean clothes, slipped his concealed tools into his pants pocket, and washed up thoroughly. He ate more space rations and gulped water. When Bo chained him back to the wall, some strength was returning to his limbs. He wasn't even gagged, which was a tremendous relief.

Antor reclined, listening to the humming coils as the Comet Tail zipped along. Red would be heading for Pariah to pick up his new ship. Antor's scheme should stop him. Red wasn't going to be too happy about how things unfolded, but Antor was prepared for the toxic fallout. With all the tampering he had done, he could only hope that he'd covered every possible contingency.

It wasn't long before he had company. Nastos was dragged into the bay and chained up across from Antor, by Red himself. "Running out of room for captives?" Antor said.

"Something like that." Red wasn't as gregarious as usual and didn't linger.

Nastos yanked at his chains until Antor said, "You might as well save your energy. Chains are stronger than flesh and bone. Where are the girls?"

Nastos settled down against the wall. "Red has them each locked in a different cabin. He's not letting them talk to each other."

"What happened on Playara?"

Nastos pursed thin lips. "I managed to knock Red out, he was threatening the girls. I had everything under control until those oversized

Binares turned up and captured us. I told Holly and Zenga that I would help you, if I could. I don't suppose you have a plan to get us out of this mess? To get Holly back to Earth?"

There was something about the Schwill that unsettled Antor, perhaps because he had suspected Nastos of trying to make sure Holly lost Universe Idol. But he was Teef's betrothed. He had been captured along with the rest of them, and because of them. And Antor could really use some help defeating Red. He decided to reveal something of his plot to Nastos, but not all.

38 Holly - The Traitor

Holly was sound asleep in her little cabin when a tremendous thump made her hammock rock wildly, shaking her awake. She had been trapped in her room for a day and a half, so the timing seemed about right to have arrived at Pariah. She pressed an ear to the door and heard running feet. Her door slid open without warning and Antor tumbled inside, almost knocking her down. He wrapped both arms tight around her middle and held her as if she was falling, even though she wasn't.

"Antor!" She clung just as tight. She never wanted to let him go. "Are we at Pariah? What was that big bump? How did you get free?"

He closed her door and kissed her tenderly, before he answered her questions, in order. "We are in orbit over Pariah. The thump was Red docking his new ship against the Comet Tail. He's not a very skilled pilot. And I escaped while he was doing that. I wasn't really going to tell Red where to find Earth—I have a plan," he added in a rush.

"I figured you did."

"Really?" Antor looked baffled by that.

"Of course. I know you, Antor. I knew you'd have a plan. And look at what you've already endured to protect me and my world." She stroked his bruised face and leaned in to kiss his cheek tenderly, trying not to hurt him. Her faith in Antor hadn't wavered, not for a second.

He gripped her hands. "Holly, if I hadn't had a plan, I couldn't have watched Red blind you. I could never -"

She kissed his mouth, stopping his confession. "It didn't happen, Antor. I don't want to think about that ever again. I'm just so glad you're here, and free." She couldn't stop smiling, even though her eyes kept tearing up. She was so happy to see him, and hold him. "So, what's your plan?"

"It's already underway. I rewired a lot of the ship's control panels, while Red and his Binares were on Playara. I need your panel to eavesdrop on the rest of the ship." Antor pressed buttons on her door panel, listening to different locations. Most of the ship was silent, until Red returned to the Comet Tail. They could hear him talking to the Binares about moving everything of value from the Comet Tail onto his new ship.

"Okay, he's on the bridge now with both his pets. I'm going to lock them all in there." Antor pressed more buttons. "Done, now the three of them are trapped."

"But Antor, he can control the ship from there," Holly pointed out.

"Not anymore, he can't."

"The rewiring?" Holly guessed.

"Yes. The whole ship in now completely controlled from one panel and Red can't access it. Only I can." Antor smiled just a bit. His face was clearly too sore to do more.

"So we're saved, just like that?" Holly leaned against the wall. It felt like the stuffing had gone out of her.

"Just like that," Antor confirmed.

It seemed anticlimactic, but Holly wasn't about to look a gift-rescue in the mouth, so to speak. She cupped Antor's battered face and said, "Thank you, Antor."

"My pleasure." His eyes glowed into hers. "Now to free Zenga and Teef." He pressed more buttons, opening the other cabin doors from Holly's room somehow.

Zenga and Teef peeked out, like turtles from their shells. Antor motioned them closer and said, "Follow me." He led them to the cargo deck. Willy was there, standing against the wall. Antor gazed around happily. "This is going exactly as planned. Red and the Bos are locked up and I have control of the ship from here."

Zenga glanced all around, as if she didn't believe they were safe. "What next, Antor?"

"If we can, fly the new ship to Earth, and leave Red and the Binares floating in orbit, trapped on the Comet Tail. They won't be able to call for help. After a week or so, we can send Zandee to arrest them. By that time, we'll be long gone and untraceable. I'll pick up the Gorka, and you'll be safe, Holly, back with your family." Antor faltered for a moment. "You and your planet will be safe."

"Yes." Holly should have felt overjoyed. She was deeply relieved that the Earth would not experience a mass alien invasion, and that she would see her family again. Saying farewell to Antor forever was another matter entirely. There was nothing joyous about that.

Antor glanced toward the slide. "I wonder what happened to Nastos. He was supposed to meet us here," he said, with no clue of the verbal bomb he dropped.

"Nastos?" Zenga gasped.

"Teef's betrothed, the winged fellow."

Holly gripped his arm. "Antor, Nastos is one of the bad guys. He allied with Red down on Playara. He tried to kill me with a dartgun! Nastos is the one behind the worst of the attacks against me, including hiring those pirates. And now he's helping Red."

"He wants bizoux and he doesn't care how he gets them," Teef said resentfully.

Antor closed his eyes as if he was in severe pain. Given how beaten he was, that shouldn't have been a surprise, but Holly knew it was more than that. "What, Antor? Tell me."

"I had this rescue all worked out." Antor's fists were clenched tight as if he wanted to punch the walls. "And they locked Nastos up with me in the cargo bay, as if he was another prisoner."

Holly clapped a hand over her mouth. "Oh no. You told him your plan?"

"I told him too much, that's for sure. I expect he's freeing Red right about now," Antor said.

"Already done." Red strolled into view with a blaster. Nastos was on his heels, holding a second smaller blaster. He did like his weapons. "I can't tell you how disappointed I am in you, Antor." Red's finger hovered too close to the trigger.

"Am I supposed to care?" Antor bit out.

"I'm finished playing nice. You are going to tell me exactly where Earth is, now, as you promised."

"I never promised." Clearly, Antor was done with cooperating and Holly was afraid for him, for all of them.

"You will tell me anyway."

"I don't think I will."

Red smiled with such evil intent, Holly shivered. When he grabbed her by the hair and jerked her against him, she screamed. Antor started forward until Nastos fired at him. A smoking hole appeared in the wall beside Antor and he clapped a hand over his ear. Blood leaked out between his fingers. It was the same ear Holly had shot.

Through clenched teeth, Red said, "Nastos, I need Antor alive. If you can't be more careful with that blaster, you will not be permitted to carry it."

"I was careful. He still has his head, doesn't he?" Nastos shifted his weapon. "I could shoot off his other ear." With Red on his side and by his side, Nastos was much bolder than he had been on Playara.

"Lower the bloody blaster. There are better ways to ensure Antor's cooperation, as I have learned through experience. He has one lovely weak spot." Red yanked hard on Holly's hair and she cried out.

"But I like this way." Nastos's whiney tone must have grated on Red as much as it did on Holly, and probably everyone in hearing range, because Red said to him, "I'll shoot more than your ear off if you don't lower that blaster."

Nastos took the threat as seriously as it was delivered. He aimed the gun at Antor's toes instead.

Dragging Holly with him, Red started moving toward the end of the curved corridor. There was nothing there except the rear hatch. The new ship was docked against the side hatch, so she wasn't sure why Red wanted to go the wrong way. When they reach the dead end, Red opened the inner seal of the hatch and said, "Step inside, Holly."

"Inside there? But it doesn't go anywhere."

"Of course it does. It leads directly to the stars."

"Huh?" Holly wasn't usually dense, but she didn't understand what was happening, or maybe she didn't want to. It seemed she was the only one in denial. Everyone else was looking staggered.

"Antor, tell me where I can find Earth," Red said. The *or else* was more than implied.

"Don't put Holly in there," Antor gasped and took a step forward.

Nastos's blaster rose again.

"Now you can shoot off his other ear," Red said to Nastos. Holly screamed and bit Red's hand. It tightened and she was lifted off her feet. She kicked him. He laughed and tossed her into the sandwiched space as if she weighed no more than a doll. The door sealed behind her. Holly was pressed inside the claustrophobic double hatch, and she had seen the mechanism in action when waste had been jettisoned. If the outer door opened, Holly would be jettisoned. She would swoosh away never to return. Hampelle had threatened to get rid of her this way, but Red was the one who was actually going to do it.

Holly screamed and hammered on the inner door. She cried and begged, terrified enough to have a heart attack or faint or wet herself. Maybe all three. She could see everyone through the thick bubble window and it looked like they were making a lot of noise, too. Antor and Red were debating something, hotly. They were both shouting at the same time, neither listening to the other. Red raised a hand toward the eject button. Antor shut his mouth. Nastos kept Antor, and everyone, at bay with the blaster. Antor began talking again, he might have been begging. Red shook his head and toyed with the tip of his horn.

In the end, Antor gave in. He hunched and said something that made Red very happy indeed. Holly didn't need the soundtrack to know Antor had revealed Earth's true location, to save her, and she wasn't angry with him for the choice he had made. If their positions had been reversed, Holly would have done the same thing. Principles got lost in the face of violent death. And maybe, just maybe, Antor had a reserve plan up his sleeve, and he was buying time. She could hope.

She waited for the inner seal to open, freeing her. It didn't happen. Red left the cargo deck after stationing Nastos beside the eject button.

296

Nastos liked that, he raised his weapon and gloated. He spoke to the silent trio who faced him and smacked the panel with his hand. Holly expected to die by jettisoning then and there, but nothing happened. Nastos was simply taunting them all. He smacked the panel again. He was such a jerk.

Holly scanned for something to hold onto, in case Nastos stopped playing around and decided to get rid of her. He'd never liked her and she had spoiled his plans by winning Universe Idol. He wouldn't even have to look her in the eye to kill her, all he had to do was press a little button. What could be easier?

A metal handle caught Holly's eye, beside the inner door. She gripped it so hard, her fingers felt welded to the thing. She held on for dear life and bided her time along with the rest of them.

Clearly, the others were all waiting for something, probably Red's return. Willy walked by, further down the corridor, carrying a storage chest. Antor said something to him. Willy immediately put the chest down and headed up the slide.

Nastos was still banging at the panel and laughing like a lunatic. Teef shouted something at him, Antor and Zenga joined in. The three of them faced Nastos down.

He must have felt threatened, because he raised his blaster. The butt end banged the panel and Holly heard a disturbing click.

She tightened her grip further, just in case.

It was lucky she did, because the door behind her began grinding upward, ever so slowly. Even through the small crack, the vacuum was enough to suck Holly backwards with force.

She held her breath as if she was underwater, trying to stop her lungs from being sucked out of her chest. Air that was frigid enough to freeze time, groped her ankles. Her skin turned so cold, it felt like it was burning, and the portal to her own personal hell just kept getting wider and wider.

39 Antor - Willy's Secret

Nastos had a trapped look in his eye, even though he was the one holding the blaster. "Stay back or I'll shoot," he said and jerked his blaster higher, aiming at Antor's head. The butt of the blaster banged the panel. As if in slow motion, Antor saw the eject button depress. Nastos's face fell. "I didn't mean to do that," he said, whining like a spoilt little boy.

The outer door started cranking upward. It moved in true slow motion. Since the Gorka had dented it all out of shape, it was one sluggish door—thank Celeste.

In the glass window, Holly's face was ghostly white and petrified with terror. She didn't have long. Space was so frigid, it flash froze the moisture in an exposed body. Praying Willy was just around the corner and ready to play his part, Antor lunged for the button that closed the hatch. Nastos got in the way, perhaps inadvertently, since he had nothing to gain by seeing Holly jettisoned at that point.

"Move," Antor roared. He punched the button that reversed the door's direction and the grinding stopped briefly. When it started moving again, the door was closing, not opening. Antor held position, guarding the panel. Nastos didn't challenge him and hung back, clutching his blaster like a lifeline.

The millisecond the outer hatch sealed, Antor hit the button that opened the inner door. It probably didn't ascend at a speed comparable to evaporating water, yet it seemed that way to him. He was peripherally aware of Nastos waving the nose of the deadly gun indiscriminately in his direction. He was beyond caring about his own hide.

When Holly fell into the ship, Antor caught her. After the brief brush with Outer Space, her flesh was colder than snow. He held her tight. "I'm sorry, Holly. It will be okay. It will all be okay." He rubbed her arms, trying to generate warmth.

She couldn't reply. Her teeth were chattering too hard and fast. It was actually a good sign. It meant she hadn't gotten fatally cold. Antor wiped a frozen tear from the corner of her eye. "I have to put you down for a minute, okay. Plan B is underway, and there is no Plan C."

And Antor had lost track of all the moving parts of his plan. He lowered Holly against the wall and spun to face the room. Nastos still had the upper hand. Willy had impeccable timing. He was approaching at his usual steady pace, carrying a blaster.

Nastos wasn't sure about the new arrival. "Did Red send you to back me up?" he asked.

Willy replied by reaching out and yanking Nastos's blaster right out of his hands. No-one was expecting the action, except Antor, who had encoded Willy to take weapons away from anyone holding them, except himself and Zenga. Simple but effective.

"Lock him in the hatch, Willy," Antor ordered. He grabbed one of the two blasters and took off running. He didn't have much time to corral Red, if it wasn't too late already.

At the top of the slide, Antor hugged the wall and kept moving. He paused in the doorway to the bridge. Red had his back to Antor. His full concentration was on the star map. He had pinpointed Earth's solar system and zoomed in on it. He was staring hungrily at the third rock from an unimpressive sun, his coveted prize.

With a steady hand, Antor pressed the buttons that would lock Red inside the room, for a second time. Red heard the door start moving. He turned around, more curious than alarmed, until he spotted Antor, blaster raised and legs planted. The closing door concealed Red's reaction, which was probably disbelief, or fury, or some combination of the two.

Adrenaline still pumping, Antor spun around and raced back to the cargo deck. Everything there was lovely and calm—all under control. Nastos had replaced Holly in the jettisoning chamber. He was screaming his head off, without sound.

Antor's eyes skipped over to Holly, who was now wrapped in a heated membrane from the first aid kit, while Teef and Zenga rubbed warmth into her limbs. Antor crouched in front of her. "Holly, are you okay?"

She nodded and did seem to be. Her eyes were focused on him and they'd never looked more beautiful or more alive. He pulled off her shoes and socks, and checked her toes. All ten were turning pink. She wouldn't lose any.

"This little piggy," Holly whispered through chattering teeth.

"What?"

She shook her head and attempted a smile. Antor smiled back and replaced her socks, giving her feet a squeeze.

"Where's Red?" Zenga asked.

"Locked up on the bridge, again."

"Thank Celeste. And we've got Nastos where he belongs, and Willy on our side. And the Binares?"

"Not on this ship." Antor kept holding Holly's icy feet and glanced at Zenga, questioningly.

"Good," Zenga murmured.

"Good and bad. The other ship is faster and in better repair than the Comet Tail." Facts were facts.

"We would have more chance on the other ship," Zenga said.

"Ya, that's what I was thinking." While Zenga considered their options, Antor moved his attention to Holly's hands. He breathed warmly on her fingers. She touched his face. He was overwhelmed with emotion. She was still alive, and he was going to keep her that way. "Zen, we have to act fast."

"I know, I know."

"Two choices," Antor said.

"Fight the Bos for the new ship, or take off in this bucket of collapsing coils," she voiced.

"Willy, you were on the other ship. Where were the Bos?" Antor asked.

"On the cargo deck, Antor."

"Anyone else on the ship?" he asked, as an afterthought.

"Yes, Antor."

"Damn. How many?"

"I saw eleven, Antor."

Zenga's eyes widened. "Red's already moved his new crew onto the ship!"

"Probably plucked from the finest criminals that Pariah has to offer, and I bet they all look pure humanoid, able to walk around on Earth." Antor shook his head. Eleven were far too many to battle, and there could be many more that Willy had not seen.

"I don't want to fight anymore," Holly whispered. "I want to go home. I'm not being a baby or anything, but I want to go home." Almost dying in space had robbed her of her usual brave spirit.

Zenga frowned. "But we'll be at such a disadvantage on the Comet Tail."

"Maybe not." Antor had a few more tricks up his sleeve that would work to their advantage, if they remained aboard the Comet Tail. "And we can't fight that many, Zen. We wouldn't have a chance."

"I guess not, but I'd like to." Zenga worried her lip.

With no time to waste, Antor rose and approached the side hatch that connected them to Inferno. Knowing it sealed their fate, one way or another, Antor closed the doors and cut the magnetic current. The ships did a little bump and grind as they floated apart.

"Farewell, Bo and Bo," Antor said with a salute. He motioned for Zenga to squeeze over. He sat down on the deck beside Holly, with an arm around her shoulders, holding her close. The last of his adrenalin ebbed away. They weren't near any safe port, but he needed a moment.

It was a short one. Willy said, "There is a message coming in."

The trapped Red had reactivated the communication system, probably to call for backup, as Antor had expected, except Red wouldn't be able to send any messages. Now that the communication channel was functioning again, Antor had control of it, and he had been expecting a communiqué. "What is it, Willy?"

"The Inferno would like to know why the Comet Tail has separated. Should I reply, Antor?"

"Not yet, Willy." Antor had to think. "Don't answer them until I tell you, no matter how many times they hail us."

"Yes, Antor."

"How is Willy doing that? How can he receive the hails?" Zenga said.

"Our friend Willy is now the Comet Tail's main control panel, main everything, really," Antor admitted.

Zenga chuckled. "Well played, Antor. Red forgot to disable Willy's obedience protocol to us?"

"He did." It was about the only thing that Red had forgotten, and it had been a key omission. "Now we have to move Red into the cargo bay, before he does any major damage from or to the bridge. Holly, do you want to lie down in your cabin."

She nodded. "Unless ... unless you need my ... my help." She was in no condition to do battle or hold a blaster, not that Antor ever wanted her to hold a blaster again.

"No, we'll manage." Antor helped Holly to her feet. She shuffled more than she walked to her cabin. He tucked her in her hammock under a pile of blankets and even her coat.

She smiled sleepily up at him. She was definitely in mild shock. "Be careful of Red, Antor. Don't take any chances when you move him. Shoot him if you have to."

"I might shoot him just for the sheer pleasure." And for what Red had done to Holly. "You just get warm. I'll be back as soon as the ship is put to rights."

"Hurry. I don't want to be alone. I was alone in that ... that chamber." She started trembling harder. "Could Teef sit with me? Until you come back?"

"I'll get her, Holly. Sleep, and I'll be back before you wake up." Antor tucked her in tighter, kissed her lingeringly, and returned to the waiting girls.

"Teef, Holly was asking for you. Do you want to stay with her?"

"I would like to, if you don't need me to guard Nastos." She gave her betrothed a glare that would have made even a better man shrivel up and die.

"No, he's not going to get out of there on his own."

Teef smiled. "Good." She was still smiling when she waved to Nastos and left.

"Should we shift Nastos into one of the cargo bays?" Zenga asked, while they were on the topic.

Antor didn't even have to think about that. "You know, I like him where he is for now."

"Me, too." Nastos wasn't screaming anymore, he was glaring, his face distorted by the thick window.

"Time to relocate Red, then." They each took one of the blasters. They slid up to the bridge and peeked through the small window in that door. Red had the console off the main panel and he was poking around.

"Fire if he tries anything, Zen," Antor said. "Anything."

"Don't worry, I won't hesitate." Zenga hoisted her blaster tighter into her arms. Antor unlocked the door and it slid aside.

Red didn't even look their way. He said, "You really messed up this ship, Antor. Nothing works as it should."

"That was the point. Get up and walk slowly to the cargo deck." Antor had no desire to share words.

Red turned to face them. He didn't even blink at the weapons. "You're making a stupid mistake. We could have been rich together, we still can."

"You have no idea how badly I want to shut you up, permanently," Zenga bit out. "So zip it and start walking."

Red didn't zip it. "You won't get away with this. The Bos and my new crew are loyal to me. They know I'll make them a fortune. They're at the helm of a ship that can fly circles around this hunk of junk. You can't outrun my Inferno and you can't outfight her. I've already moved the compacting weapon over to my new ship, so you don't even have that. It's all hooked up on the Inferno, ready to crush the Comet Tail. You can't win."

"Should I shoot him now, Antor?" Zenga's finger stroked the trigger button.

"I'm not going to stop you." Antor aimed at Red's head. "I think I can take off one of his ears, or maybe a horn, without killing him."

Red started walking. He glided down the slide and entered Antor's former bay, as directed. He didn't put up a fight. He was depending on his new crew to do that for him.

Zenga surveyed cargo 6. Chains dangled from a metal loop, blood spattered the wall and floor. "You were kept here, Antor," she murmured.

"Only for a week." He changed the subject. "You want to do the honours?"

"Very badly."

While Antor stood back with his blaster aimed at Red's head, Zenga chained Belial to the wall, wrists and ankles shackled. "Don't forget to check his pockets, make sure he doesn't have any tools or mini-laser cutters." Antor had used two such items to escape his bonds. He certainly didn't want Red to do the same.

Zenga scowled. "I don't want to grope around in his pockets."

"Pat him down, then."

"I don't want to do that either." But she did. Very thoroughly, she checked Red from shoulder to ankle. He smirked as if he was enjoying it and made lewd suggestions. All she found was a dagger in his boot. She tossed it to Antor.

It was old, with a bone carved handle. The blade was sheathed inside a tight skin. Antor removed it carefully. Pure white metal gleamed even in the low light. The blade was so sharp, you could cut your eyes looking at it.

"Very nice." Antor slid it back into the sheath and tucked it in his own boot.

"Family heirloom," Red drawled. "Guard it well, until I reclaim it and use it to gut you."

"That's not going to happen." Antor took Red's boots away, too. With great satisfaction, he security locked the door with Red inside, and heaved a sigh of relief. "Glad that's done. We have to get flying, Zen, without delay."

"Do you think the Inferno will try to stop us?"

"They might. We better have a chat with whoever has taken charge of Red's ship."

They detoured to pick up Willy. On the bridge, Antor showed Zenga which button now activated the viewing screen. It was the button that formerly fired the compactor. She brought up a live feed of space. "Oh Antor, look at that!"

He paused in repairing the panel that Red had disassembled, and had his first look at the Inferno. "Wow." He might have started drooling. "Isn't she a beauty, Zen?"

Zenga sighed with longing. "I wish we'd seen her, before we opted to stay on the shoddy little Comet Tail."

"Likewise." If Antor had laid eyes on Inferno's sleek, sexy black hull and sculpted red fins, curved nose and long arced body, he probably would have fought a dozen men for such a ship. "Hampelle had good taste in ships," he murmured. Hampelle had selected Antor's favourite, and the former Captain would have piloted her with the skill she deserved.

Antor sat down and wondered if there was a way to bargain, to trade one ship for another. No, that was a fantasy. He knew he couldn't risk all their lives to acquire the ship of his dreams. If things worked out in Antor's favour, the Inferno would soon be nothing but a block of compacted metal anyway, which was a crying shame. He tried not to think about that and said, "Ready to talk to the Inferno?"

"Tell them Red is still alive. Hopefully they won't destroy the Comet Tail with him aboard. He is their ticket to finding Earth, or so they believe."

Antor sat down and tried to feel commanding in the Captain's chair. "Okay, Willy, time to reply. Audio only."

"Yes, Antor. The Inferno has hailed us nine times. I will open an audio communication channel now." And Willy did.

A familiar voice said, "Red, finally. What the Gehenna is going on over there? We were about to ram that little shit bucket, and break open the hatch to find out for ourselves."

"Ephine, it's not Red."

There was a long pause. "Antor? Still alive, imagine that. Where is Red?"

"Tied up at the moment, or maybe I should say chained up. The Comet Tail is about to leave orbit. We don't want to be followed. Red is our hostage and he doesn't want you to interfere with our departure. Let us leave and we won't kill him."

Ephine didn't even take a minute to consider what Antor had said. He replied, "I have an alternate proposition. Lead us to Earth and we won't obliterate you. You can hand Red over to us when we get there, and go merrily on your way."

"I'll think about it," Antor said, to buy them time. He closed the channel and glanced at Zenga. "Time to go, I think."

"Top speed," Zenga said, tongue-in-cheek.

"The Comet Tail's top speed," Antor corrected, which wasn't the same thing at all. He accessed the data-stream and plotted a course toward Ja'Dorp. It was in Earth's basic direction and wouldn't reveal too much. He transferred the information to Willy and the ship kicked free of orbit. It made for the nearest wormhole. Inferno followed, staying uncomfortably close. Antor felt like he was about to get rammed.

"I'm going to check on Holly. Can you watch the bridge, Zen? And keep an eye on the Inferno?"

"If you show me how to control the ship through Willy," Zenga said, very dryly.

"Oh, right." Antor was kind of distracted by wanting to get to Holly. He explained as briefly as possible and Zenga said, "I'll call you if I need help."

Antor really had cross-wired all the ship's functions. "Call me," he agreed, "but only if you have to."

Zenga rolled her eyes and said, "Go."

He tended to his own wounds with the first aid kit, before he sought out Holly. She was sound asleep. Teef was in the upper hammock, quiet as well. It was peaceful in the little cabin. Antor slipped under the blankets with Holly, almost tipping them both out of the swinging bed. Holly didn't even stir.

Antor meant to rest for just a minute, holding her tight. He must have been more exhausted than he'd realized. He fell deeply asleep, cuddled up with Holly. Given all that had come before, and what was going to come after, it was a lovely respite.

40 Holly - Jettisoned

Holly awoke disoriented, shaking from a vivid nightmare that was a replay of her near-death experience. She was delighted to find Antor cuddled up with her. She clung to him, and she wasn't the clingy type. He was so sound asleep, he didn't even know she was clinging, but she wanted him to wake up.

Before she roused him, she had a good look at his latest ear wound, since the ear was face up, so to speak. It had been cleaned, but left un-bandaged. The injury wasn't as bad as when she'd shot him. It was actually more of a nick than a missing chunk.

In comparison, his face was in worse shape. Some Outer Space bandages had been applied, to eliminate scarring, but the bruising still showed, and there was a lot of it. They had both been through hell, yet Antor's skin wore the evidence.

Holly's damage was more on the inside. She had experienced enough trauma to last a lifetime. After Outer Space, she was clingy and scared of her own shadow, and she wanted to go home to her Mommy. Problem was, going home meant saying farewell to Antor, forever and ever. In some ways, that was scarier than almost being jettisoned. Holly didn't want to live without him. She wasn't sure she could. It would be like living without her heart.

To wake him up, Holly kissed his ear better, and his cheek. His lips needed kissing better, too, so they got kissed.

A smile grew on his face and he opened his eyes. "Holly, my sweet."

"I'm sweet?"

"Sweeter than sweet."

Teef snored softly overhead, reminding them they weren't alone. It was lucky she did, Holly had been about to do a whole lot more than kiss Antor. "What happened after I fell asleep?" she whispered.

Antor gasped and leapt to his feet, almost spilling her out of her hammock. "I've been asleep for hours. Damn. I have to check the bridge." He leaned in and kissed her, before he ran, almost in a panic.

Holly figured it was time to get up anyway. Her feet and legs stung and they looked all sunburned, even though they were ice-burned. She pulled socks on, very carefully, and freshened up before she went to find Antor and Zenga.

They were on the bridge. Antor had tools out and seemed to be rewiring control panels. Zenga was watching the viewing screen, keeping an eye on another ship, a red and black racy one. "Nice," Holly said. It looked a bit like an old-school corvette, if a corvette had been transformed into a gigantic spaceship.

"Ya, very nice." Antor shook his head with regret.

Holly said, "What have I missed. Catch me up, and before you do, I have to be clear that I don't remember some parts of yesterday, at least not very well." She sat down beside Zenga.

While Antor kept working, Zenga brought her up to speed and ended with, "The Inferno, piloted by Red's less than upstanding new crew, is tailing us as closely as if they really were a tail. They call every once in a while to threaten us, but so far they haven't fired any weapons. The Comet Tail hasn't broken down, yet. All in all, it was a quiet night. Peaceful. And now it's my turn to sleep. Antor, you have the bridge."

Antor grinned and saluted over his head. "Most of the ship is back to normal. I'm going to leave Willy linked to the main control panel though. It's convenient."

Zenga nodded her approval. "I'll check on Red and Nastos on my way to bed. We have to do something about moving Nastos, I suppose," she was saying, as she left the bridge.

Antor claimed the Captain's chair beside Holly. The bridge seemed emptier than it should, and it took her a minute to figure out why. "Where's Willy?"

"He had to recharge. He uses a lot more power now that he's linked to the ship." Antor reached across the gearshift thing and took her hand in his, holding it tight.

"What happens next, Antor?" Holly knew they couldn't head for Earth with the Inferno shadowing them all the way. That would be like leading a fox to the hen house, and opening the door for it to trot on inside and rip out every feathery little throat.

Antor shifted to face her. "I'm trying to figure that out, Holly. It sort of depends on how the Inferno reacts, what they do. If an opportunity to escape presents itself, we'll take it. Hopefully one will."

"So you don't have another scheme up your sleeve?"

"Well, one, sort of, but it relies completely on chance, and it will destroy the Inferno." They were both distracted when Zenga trotted back onto the bridge with a wild look in her eye.

"I can't find Nastos," she blurted.

Antor leapt up. "What about Red? Has he freed Red?"

"No, Red is where he should be." Zenga grimaced. "I think Nastos might be missing in a different way." She was definitely alluding to something.

307

"You mean gone rather than missing?" Antor guessed.

"Yes, Willy did some tidying up. He jettisoned some waste."

Holly clapped a hand over her mouth. "Willy jettisoned Nastos?"

"I think so. I'm pretty sure. Yes." Zenga finally said it.

There was shocked silence on the bridge. "Does Willy know what he did?" Holly asked.

"He won't know," Zenga said. "If Nastos was slumped and sleeping, Willy would have thought he was clearing the hatch of stuck waste, before he refilled it."

"Which doesn't change a thing. Nastos is still gone." Antor glanced toward the door. "I wonder how Teef will feel about it."

As Teef's closest friend on the ship, it would be Holly's job to deliver the news. But Holly wasn't about to wake her up to do it. There was no rush. Knowing wouldn't change the fact that Nastos was gone, as Holly had almost been gone. She felt sick to her stomach thinking about the reality of Nastos's grisly end.

Zenga didn't go to bed after all.

The three of them were sitting in rather stunned silence, when Teef appeared. Holly stood right up and said, "Let's go get something to eat. Or how about a warm drink—a hot drink. I wish Outer Space had coffee. I never drank coffee on Earth, but I really feel the need for it now. Hot chocolate is really good, too, I could go for a hot chocolate, except Outer Space doesn't have chocolate. If Red knew about chocolate, he might forget all about kidnapping singers and start exporting chocolate, and coffee. I wouldn't recommend tea, it's not nearly as good." Holly talked them all the way to the galley.

They heated water in the stanislizer. When they were each seated with a hot tasteless drink, Teef said, "What's making you so nervous?"

"Besides … everything?" Holly flapped a hand around in the air, to emphasize the everything.

"Yes."

Teef knew her too well. Holly exhaled and gripped her hands. "I do have bad news, Teef. It's about Nastos -"

Her eyes widened with fear. "He's escaped?"

"Well, that's what we thought at first, but it turns out that he didn't escape. He is, however, gone." Holly hoped she was leading into the news delicately.

"Gone … from the ship?"

"Yes." Before Holly could find the right words, Teef figured it out.

"He was jettisoned?" Her eyes had widened.

"Accidentally," Holly stressed. "Willy was cleaning up and, well, Nastos got cleaned up … and cleaned out of the ship."

Teef sat there with dropped jaw, absorbing the news. When she closed her mouth, she said, "So he's really gone. I don't have to marry him? It is a tragic thing to happen, of course. I'm trying to feel a little sad, Holly, but I don't. I am simply relieved that I will not be joined to him for the rest of my life, which is a very long time."

"A lifetime, yes. So, you're okay?" Holly sipped her drink, enjoying the warmth, if not the lack of flavour.

"I'm fine." Teef sipped, too. "I'm relieved, and happy, but don't tell anyone."

"I won't."

They continued to sip their hot water and Holly relaxed. She had delivered the disturbing news, and Teef had received it well.

Changing the subject, Teef said, "At least I've found out why you're so clueless about space."

"Sorry I didn't tell you where I came from, Teef. I wanted to." Holly still felt guilty about keeping so much from her Outer Space best friend. "But it wasn't just my secret, it was Antor and Zenga's secret, too. And they would have gotten in a lot of trouble if anyone found out they had visited a restricted planet and abducted one of the natives—me. I wanted to tell you so many times."

"It's okay, Holly. I do understand," Teef said, perfectly accepting.

"So, you forgive me?"

"There is nothing to forgive."

Holly hugged her. They took space rations back to the bridge. Holly had poured hot water over one bowl, to see if that would improve the flavour and texture. Antor was alone, staring fixedly at the star map. She handed him the steaming bowl and a spoon she had found. He sniffed and frowned at the mush.

"I made you dinner," Holly said.

"Oh, thanks." He tasted a spoonful.

"Do you like it?"

"It's … interesting, uh, different." He took another spoonful and gagged, before he managed to choke, rather than swallow, it down.

"It can't be that bad." Holly borrowed the spoon and tried the invented recipe for herself. It was so awful, she couldn't even swallow. She grabbed the bowl from Antor and stepped off the bridge to spit the food back into the bowl. She called, "I'm going to jettison this, I mean, get rid of it."

She came back with dried rations and said, "I should have tasted it first. I've never been much of a cook. Even on Earth, I couldn't make good food, but I never made anything that bad. Why did you eat it?"

"Because you made it." Antor said simply.

"Well, you still didn't have to eat it. You could have said it was awful. Maybe space rations can't be improved upon, maybe they're already as good as they can get." Holly sat down. "Zenga went to have her nap?"

"She did. Zen and I will have to take turns on the bridge, until we get wherever we're going, or wherever we end up. There can be no leaving the bridge unattended, not while we have our shadow." He darted a glance at Teef, who was sitting nearby.

"I told Teef about Nastos, Antor," Holly said. "She's okay."

"Oh. Good. I don't mean good about Nastos. I mean good that you know, Teef." Antor stopped talking, rather abruptly.

"It's okay, Antor." Teef touched his shoulder as if to reassure.

They crunched the dry rations and stared at the star map with Antor. He kept zooming in, closer and closer, on one patch of space. Every time he magnified the view, more stars revealed themselves. He didn't speak and it was like he was in a trance. He kept referring back to the data-stream, and finally connected his core-text wire, so he could absorb all the information he accessed.

"Are you searching for something?" Holly finally asked.

"I was trying to plot the fastest route to Earth, when I discovered something odd. There's a series of wormhole shortcuts that lead directly to your solar system. It's not easy to trace the convoluted chain, but it exists." He frowned as if that was bad.

"And we didn't take that route when we left Earth?" Holly guessed.

"No, because we were skipping around, making deliveries. And the route is almost impossible to spot." He scratched his temple. "It's unnatural the way the wormholes line up so conveniently. Once you know they're there. It's almost like a path. Of course, you would never find the path, unless you knew exactly where Earth was located."

"Why not?" Holly asked.

"Because there are billions of wormholes."

"So it's like an Outer Space maze?" Holly studied the corner of space that Antor had zoomed in on, trying to spot the path.

"Sort of like a camouflaged maze. What's weirder still is that there are similar paths connecting to Earth from all corners of the Universe, almost as if someone constructed them." Antor approached the viewing screen and said, "We're here, see, and this is the path to Earth. That's Earth's solar system." He traced the wormhole route to a pinpoint dot that was indistinguishable from the plethora of identical dots. It wasn't a direct path, but a zigzagging convoluted line that even crossed itself.

"Are you sure that's a shortcut to Earth?" Holly asked, more than skeptical.

"Yes, the ends of the wormholes, the black holes that suck ships in and the white holes that spit ships out, are so conveniently lined up, it

310

would take no time to reach your home. See, black hole, white hole, black hole, white hole, on and on, all the way to Earth."

"I can understand why no-one would find the path." Holly couldn't see it and Antor had traced it for her. She couldn't even find Earth again, without Antor's finger pointing it out.

"And there are similar paths to and from Earth, from all over the Universe. It's like the Earth is the hub of the Universe. Could someone have constructed them?" Antor wasn't asking anyone but himself. He paced back and forth, studying the star map.

"Can wormholes be artificially created?" Holly asked. There was so much she didn't know about the Universe. Everything, really. She hadn't even known what white holes were, until Antor told her, and explained that wormholes bent space, which is why they worked as shortcuts.

Antor mulled over her question. "Black holes form when a massive star collapses to the point of infinite density. Space-time gets all jumbled up at the singularity, the center of the wormhole, and ceases to exist as we know it. Both space and time stop following the rules of physics, so to speak. That's the simple explanation." It didn't sound simple to Holly. "If these paths were 'built' for want of a better word, it had to have happened billions of years ago. I checked the age of your solar system and it's more than four and a half billion years old. Your planets began to form at the same time. I wonder if all the black holes were formed after that."

He dropped back into his chair and reconnected his wire to the data-stream. After about half an hour, he detached. "I haven't checked them all, not even close, but every one I checked is less than a billion years old, so they formed after your planet and solar system did. Even odder, they all formed around the same time. That can't be a coincidence. This makes no sense, Holly. None."

"Will knowing when and why the paths to Earth were created help us escape the Inferno?" Holly asked, before Antor went off on a complete tangent.

"Well, no, but it's fascinating." He flashed her a quirky, apologetic smile.

Holly returned it. He was so appealing when he looked like that. "What was the scheme you mentioned before? The one that depends on chance?"

"I guess we should discuss it, with Zen. Maybe we should wake her up, because by following the chain of wormholes, we could reach Earth in less than a day."

Holly wasn't expecting that news. "Less than a day? And I could be home?" Her heart both rose and sank. If they could escape the Inferno, she could see her family, and say farewell to Antor, tomorrow. It was so much sooner than she had expected. She sat dumbfounded while Antor summoned Zenga.

Zenga turned up, heavy-eyed and tousled. "What's up, Antor?"

"We need to talk," he said.

Zenga plunked down and yawned. "So talk. I'm all ears."

"I've discovered a fast track to Earth."

Zenga sat up straighter. "A what?"

Antor explained about the conveniently located chain of wormholes. She didn't believe him, until he showed her the route on the star map.

"That's astounding, Antor. How did you even spot that? I mean, it's invisible. Where is it again?"

Antor retraced the route. "Right there, Zen."

"Okay. I believe you. I don't know how you found it, but it's there." She shook her head. "It's like that puzzle lock, isn't it? You can spot such things."

"The Inferno won't find it," Antor concurred. "Even if we took it part way to Earth, they wouldn't figure out our final destination."

"The Inferno is the problem." Zenga stated the obvious.

"Yes, that's what we need to discuss. I, uh," Antor cleared his throat, "made some adjustments to the magnetic compacting weapon, before it was moved over to the new ship." It sounded like he was about to confess something.

"Antor! What did you do?" Zenga gasped, a gleam in her eye.

"Reversed the current," he said, sheepishly.

Zenga's eyes widened. "Does that mean what I think it means?"

"What does it mean?" both Holly and Teef asked.

"It means if they fire the weapon at us, they compact themselves." Antor switched the viewing screen to a live feed of the Inferno. "If they try to destroy us, they'll destroy that beautiful ship and everyone inside."

Zenga snorted. "Inside are cruel, murderous slavers. If they try to kill us and kill themselves, it's not on our heads, or your head, Antor. Don't go getting all righteous. We have to save Earth and our own skins. If the Inferno attacks us, so be it."

"So be it," Antor agreed. "Here's what I was thinking. It's a huge gamble, but if we lead them to Earth and turn over Red, I have a feeling they'll destroy us rather than let us fly away."

"And by destroying us, they destroy themselves and all knowledge of Earth's location," Zenga finished. "Earth is saved and we're saved."

"That's the idea." Antor restored the star map and glanced at Holly. She was thinking about how huge a gamble it was to lead Inferno to Earth. Zenga and Teef followed Antor's lead and looked to Holly, awaiting her opinion or decision. Earth was her home world, so it was her responsibility.

312

"It is risky, as you said, Antor." Holly focused on the dot that was Earth, feeling overwhelmed by the pressure of deciding the best course of action, possibly the future of her whole planet, and every single person on it.

"Holly?"

She looked up into Antor's warm brown eyes. The expression in them was particularly earnest. "I think the plan has a very strong chance of succeeding. You've met Red. He won't let Zenga and I, and Teef now, leave Earth knowing its location. He wants it to be his secret treasure trove of singers. And we did get the best of him, and chained him up. He is going to try and destroy us."

"And that's a good thing?" Holly murmured.

"In this case, it is."

"But you're leaving it up to me?"

He squeezed her hand. "Of course."

"Thank you, Antor. I appreciate that you're letting me decide, and at the same time, I don't, if you know what I mean." She slumped into her chair, feeling too drained to make major decisions. "And if we don't go to Earth, and just … fly around seeing the sights, what then?"

Antor and Zenga shared one of their looks. Zenga said, "The Comet Tail will breakdown eventually. Her coils are really worn. If she breaks down in space, the crew of Inferno will board us and try to force us to reveal Earth's location."

Holly knew how that would play out. They would all be tortured in some fashion, until one of them broke, probably to spare the others pain and torment. Antor had already endured more than his share of suffering to protect Earth. And he had faith in his plan, so she should, too.

She took a deep breath and said, "Home, James, and step on it."

"Who's James?" Zenga said.

"Step on what?" Antor asked.

"James is a classic name for a chauffeur on Earth, and 'step on it' means 'go fast'! Final destination—Earth." She pointed at the viewing screen and said, "Make it so." Suddenly chilled, she began to shiver.

"It will be okay, Holly," Antor said.

"Will it?" Even if everything worked in their favour, she would still be saying goodbye to Antor, and that wasn't okay.

"I'm going to have to stay on the bridge for now, to navigate through the maze." Antor kissed her and she nodded. He adjusted the ship's heading and warned, "The ride might be a little rough with all the wormhole hopping, so hang on, and let's hope the Comet Tail can hold together."

Holly stayed to watch the viewing screen as the little ship ducked in and out of wormholes, and created just a few of its own. The time inside

313

the worm holes was like no time at all, even though they passed through mind-boggling distances. The time outside the wormholes was real time, and slow by comparison, even though it was faster than light speed.

The Comet Tail held up valiantly, and when Holly's eyes drooped, she sought her hammock. Teef came to. It might be their last chance to talk, so as soon as they were settled, Holly asked, "What will you do now, Teef? Will you be in trouble, because of what happened to Nastos? Can you go home? And if you do, will your parents sign you over to some other domineering chauvinistic jerk?"

Teef smiled. "There you go again, with the questions."

"I have a lot more questions."

Before Holly could ask them, Teef said, "Nastos's disappearance will be difficult to explain. After my taste of life away from my planet, I'm not really in a hurry to return to it. Zenga made me an offer." She smiled with excitement. "If A-1 will promote her to Captain of the Comet Tail, now that Captain Hampelle is dead, she's offered to hire me as part of her crew. I think it would be fun. She said the Comet Tail could be refitted with new coils, which would keep her flying for a few more years."

"That sounds great, Teef." Holly imagined the Comet Tail with Zenga, Antor and Teef, continuing to have space adventures without her. It made her feel sad. She closed her eyes to hold back tears.

From overhead, Teef asked Holly about her life on Earth. Holly was happy to be able to speak freely and openly. She talked about her life on Earth, until they both drifted off to sleep.

41 Antor - Home

For hours, Antor concentrated on piloting the ship. He refused to think about never seeing Holly again. The Comet Tail's coils kept spinning, and Antor was careful not to push her. The Inferno called to complain about the slow pace, and to verify that Earth was their destination. Antor confirmed it, then hung up on them.

When Zenga turned up to relieve him, he was ready to stretch his legs. And he needed to talk to his prisoner. He visited Red in the cargo bay and sat down across from him, to enjoy the scenery. After all the suffering Red had inflicted, Antor appreciated seeing the fellow chained in his place.

"We'll reach Earth in about six hours," he said, gauging Red's reaction. "The Inferno is right behind us. They want us to hand you over when we get there. They promise they'll let us leave, unharmed. I'm not sure I believe them."

"They are my crew, they will obey me," Red said with his usual arrogance. "If you gift me Earth, I will keep my promise. Holly and her town will be left in peace, and the rest of you can continue on your way. You'll even get to keep your limbs, since Holly's winnings more than paid that debt, as well as footing the bill for my new ship. You can even keep this one. My gift to you. You're coming out ahead, Antor."

"Is your promise worth more than Hampelle's?" Antor demanded,

"Unlike your former Captain, I am a man of my word."

Antor didn't believe him for a second, which was good. Red acting like an honourable man would be disastrous. Antor rose and stretched. "Not long now, Red Belial."

"Good to hear. These quarters are so unpleasant, I almost feel bad that I chained you here for a week." Red smiled with all the appeal of a vypede. Antor was glad to get the heck out of the oppressive space. It was really starting to smell, too.

He returned to the bridge and flying the ship. When Holly turned up a couple of hours later, Antor was ready for another break, with her. "Zen, I've flagged the next few wormholes. Can you take over for a bit?"

"Take your time," she sang. There was no privacy on a spaceship.

Antor took Holly to his own cabin, the only place on the ship where they could be truly alone. "I'm almost home?" she said, not looking thrilled about it.

"You are." He reached into his duffle bag for the cell phone and said, "Do you want to call your mother, so she can expect you?"

"No, I'm home early so I'd like to surprise her. The phone calls haven't gone so well, have they?" She wrinkled her nose so adorably, Antor had to kiss it.

"That's true." He replaced the device in his bag.

"We're saying goodbye now, aren't we?" Holly said, studying his face.

"Yes." Antor pulled her as close as their bodies could fit together. He could feel her heart beating. He wanted to stop time, break the laws of physics outside a wormhole. Holly wrapped her arms so tight around him, she held him together when it felt like he was coming apart. "You'll be home soon, safe with your family." He clung to that thought like a lifeline.

"And you'll fly off into the sunset," she whispered.

"Not really, we'll leave the sunset behind. Your sun isn't that big, compared to other suns."

She smiled through tears that turned her eyes into pools of sadness. "I'll miss you, Antor. I'll miss you when you're gone. I'll miss you forever. I know it has to be this way, but it's still so hard."

"Earth humans mate for life, don't they?" Antor wiped a tear away with his thumb.

"Not really, but they try. Some manage it. You would have been my forever, Antor. Sometimes a girl knows these things, and you were the one for me. The other half of my heart."

"I never felt like I belonged anywhere, until I was with you." He was getting all choked up.

"Oh, Antor. You're trying to make me cry. There are so many things we never got to do together. I'll never know what it feels like to make love with you. And I never got to hear you sing, unless you want to sing for me now, and—why are we floating?"

Antor looked down. He had been so focused on Holly, he hadn't noticed his feet leaving the ground. "Zenga must have hit the wrong button. Some of them are still cross-wired. I did play with the gravity controls, in case I needed to float Red to the ceiling." Antor hugged Holly tighter as they levitated. He rolled them horizontal with Holly on top. "There's still time to make love. It might be interesting while we're weightless. And I think I've figured out condoms." The knife inside the sheath had clued him in. He was teasing Holly, but the possibility was enough to make his head spin.

"Sounds fantastic." Holly kissed him with lava heat.

Antor's brain turned off. He was lost in sensations, floating with Holly, kissing Holly. He raised her shirt to feel her skin against his. Zenga had disastrous timing. She figured out how to restore gravity.

316

Antor dropped like a rock. At least he was on the bottom, to cushion Holly's impact. It was a long way, from the ceiling to the metal deck. He landed on his back, with the weight of two. Every trace of breath was forced from his lungs in one big whoosh.

Once his head stopped vibrating, he asked, "Are you okay?" It came out as a groan.

"Yes. Are you, Antor?"

"So-so." Once he could breathe again, he hoped he would be okay. He felt broken, but that was probably just temporary.

His door opened and Zenga peered in. "Oops, sorry about the gravity. Are you both okay?"

"We fell." Holly jumped to her feet. Antor didn't try to move, but he did manage to drag in a whisper of air, now that Holly's weight was off him.

Zenga peered down at him. "Antor? Are you going to get up?"

"I might need help."

The girls pulled him upright. Antor managed a painful breath so he could say, "You're supposed to restore gravity in increments, not all at once." He sounded madder than he was.

Zenga got defensive. "Well, you're the one that messed up all the controls. It's lucky I could restore the gravity at all."

"Not lucky, Zen. Definitely not lucky. And if I hadn't messed up the controls, Red would still be in charge of the ship," Antor said through gritted teeth. He limped to the bridge to make sure no damage had been done, except to him. He claimed the Captain's seat and everything appeared to be running smoothly. He checked their proximity to Earth. "Only two more wormholes," he said. "Almost there. That was fast." Even faster than he had expected.

Holly moved to stand behind him and restlessly played with his hair. He steered the ship into the singularity of the smallest wormhole so far and in no time, they shot out the other end, with the Inferno almost riding their ass.

Within the hour, they were entering the last shortcut. They were spit out into the center of Holly's spiral galaxy. Antor used the terrific momentum to power their own mini-wormhole to end up in the solar system so many sought.

"Where's Earth?" Holly asked.

"Your galaxy is 100,000 light years across, and has a few billion stars. You can't see Earth quite yet, but very soon."

"Oh."

The Inferno hailed them. "Comet Tail, is this Earth's galaxy?" It sounded like Ephine was salivating. Eager greed was making his mouth water.

"It is. We're heading for the planet now, so relax. I'll let Red talk to you as soon as we're in orbit."

"You do that." It sounded like a threat, but maybe that was just the way he talked.

Antor didn't strain the coils. He coasted toward Earth and turned off the galactic map to see real space. He pulled Holly onto his lap and wrapped his arms around her, watching her profile.

"Is that my sun?" she said in wonder.

"That's it. Keep watching. There." Antor pointed to a small blue and white orb. "There's your Earth, your home."

Holly gasped. "It looks so different from in pictures. It's beautiful, isn't it?"

"It is." Antor wasn't lying. Most planets were brown or gray or dirt-red or cloudy with gases. Not many looked like garden green and water blue worlds. Not many at all. And there was one green world that the whole Universe of humans hunted for—the original Green World, where human life had been born before it spread out across the galaxy. Antor reflected on all the hidden wormhole paths to and from this green world, and truly wondered if Holly's Earth could be the womb of human life. The planet was old enough. In four and a half billion years, it could have reinvented itself many times over, and always come back to genetically producing the same species. It was a staggering possibility. And if Earth was the original Green World, Antor came from Earth as much as Holly did, more or less.

He steered the ship into orbit, less concerned than usual about UGS or revealing the spaceship to a restricted planet. The Inferno slid into orbit ahead of them. There was no immediate hail. Antor knew Ephine would be scanning the surface for human life, and he'd find more humans than should fit on a small planet. He would be listening in on the planets broadcasts and radio waves to hear what he wanted to hear, the Universe's best singers. He wouldn't be disappointed, not yet anyway.

They were all sitting tensely, waiting to hear from Ephine, when Zenga pointed at the viewing screen and cried, "Look!"

Something completely unexpected was happening, with no forewarning. The Inferno was shrinking, folding in on itself, over and over, until it was a lump of metal that was completely unrecognizable as a sexy, racy ship, except for a jutting bit of red fin.

Antor blinked in shock. "They tried to kill us. They fired the compacting weapon at us."

"Just like that. No warning, nothing," Zenga said in disgust. "They weren't going to let Holly go home. They didn't even care about Red."

"Not once they found Earth." Perhaps Antor should have expected it. Red himself had labeled Ephine as untrustworthy slime.

"They're gone," Holly murmured. It was taking time to sink in, for all of them.

"We're safe. Your planet is safe." A smile took over Antor's face. He hugged Holly and she beamed at him. Everyone cheered, except Willy. Antor told him he could cheer if he wanted to, but he didn't.

There was some celebratory leaping about on the bridge. Antor didn't join in, his body was too sore. He stayed on the sidelines with Willy, until the girls settled down. It took awhile. He had time to scan Earth's surface and activate the Gorka's tracer chips. They were north of where the ship had released them. The pair was still together, and alive. They were on the move.

Holly came over to see what he was doing. Antor brought the image up on the big viewing screen and said, "Those moving orange dots, they're the Gorka. They're heading north, probably seeking colder temperatures, since the land is seasonally warming."

"Can you zoom in on them, on Earth?" Holly was frowning rather fiercely.

"Very easily." Antor did, closer and closer until landmarks like lakes and roads were visible.

Holly cried, "Oh no. I don't believe it."

"What?"

Holly pointed to a cluster of buildings and roads. "That's my town the Gorka are heading for."

Antor studied the animals' trajectory. It did look like they were aiming toward the settlement, and it was the only one for about a hundred miles. "They won't get there for awhile," he said, trying to reassure her. "We should be able to intercept them. Only problem is, we'll have to land awfully close to your town to do it, and in daylight."

"I don't care. Those monsters have to be stopped." She squeezed his shoulder rather hard.

Holly was right, of course. "Okay, we'll start descending to land. Zenga, a little help please."

Landing the Comet Tail was a lot harder than ordering a shuttle, and Hampelle had been the experienced pilot, not Antor.

Zenga motioned him out of the Captain's chair. Antor shifted to the adjacent seat. "We want to land as close to the Gorka as possible, between them and the town," he said. "Just avoid the populated areas as much as you can."

She really didn't need Antor to state the obvious, and rolled her eyes. She pressed buttons and pulled levers. The ship began a controlled drop. Antor monitored the Gorka's position, trusting Zenga to bring them down intact. Holly kept a close eye on the live feed of Earth's surface and the superimposed orange blips.

"Holly, help me figure out where to land. You know this terrain a lot better than we do." Zenga slowed their plummet and all of them focused on the viewing screen, including Teef. They discussed possibilities and agreed on a low lying, bare field. It was directly between the Gorka and the town, if the purple monsters didn't deviate.

The field was too close to the town, but Antor didn't want to risk missing the beasts. The nearer the ship landed to the population, the better their chance of a successful interception and ambush.

While Zenga made the final approach, Antor dashed to get charged blasters. He was back on the bridge in time to see the Comet Tail touch down. He didn't feel a bump. Zenga had made an exceptional landing. "Beautifully done," he said, patting her on the back.

"Well, it's not like it's hard. Women have a more sensitive touch on the controls, you know." She was pleased, no doubt.

Antor handed Willy a blaster and said, "You're still linked to the main console, Willy. You'll leave the ship with us and I want you to keep me informed about where the Gorka are, in relation to our position. We have to catch them. That is our primary mission."

"Yes, Antor." Willy accepted the blaster.

Zenga grabbed one out of his hand, leaving him with two. Holly eyed the extra blaster and said, "I should get one. This is my home, I want to defend it."

Antor could understand that, even though he'd never had a home to defend. He handed the spare weapon to Holly, after making sure the safety was on. "Uh, just be careful when you shoot, and where you aim, and I'll try not to stand in front of you." Antor shut up when Holly glared at him.

"I learned my lesson, Antor. I almost put a hole through your face! Believe me, if anyone is going to respect blaster safety, it's me. I'm not going to shoot you again. I love you."

Antor felt warmth flood him. "I love you, too. That's why you got a blaster. If I didn't love you, I'd keep the blasters hidden and locked up so you couldn't get them."

"That's kind of sweet." Holly fell into his arms, forgetting about the blaster dangling from her shoulder. It was lucky the safety was on.

Being silly with the one you love was perfectly acceptable when you were alone. In front of others, it was simply embarrassing.

Zenga cleared her throat, pointedly. "Let's go. The Gorka won't wait. Teef, do you think you could monitor the bridge for us. Tell us what's going on in the area. Willy will keep us informed about any information you communicate. I don't want to leave the ship completely unattended on this planet."

"I don't mind. I would be happy to help from the ship." Teef settled in the Captain's chair, rather gingerly.

Antor depressed a couple of buttons. "There. The channel between you and Willy is opened, and it will stay that way. Willy will repeat anything you say. You can see what's happening on the viewing screen. Okay?" The screen had been imaged to show the whole field, and beyond.

"I understand, Antor," Teef said with a nod.

Antor checked where the Gorka were, in relation to the ship. "They're moving fast. We better get out there and establish a foothold." He opened the hatch and waited for Zenga and Willy to precede him. He stopped Holly. "Are you sure you don't want to stay on the ship with Teef? You would be safer."

"Antor, I want to stand on my planet, with you. Why should I be safe while you're risking your life for my world?" She didn't wait for an answer. "Let's go. We'll do this together."

They walked out into daylight. It was much milder than the last time Antor had visited Earth. It was almost balmy. Most of the snow had melted and the ground was squishy mud or wet compacted snow. Where the sun touched Antor's skin, it felt warm. He could smell soil and new growth. After a spaceship environment, it was tantalizing. He filled his lungs with the living air and felt rejuvenated.

"Willy, how far away are the Gorka?" Zenga asked.

"Less than two miles."

They all surveyed the terrain. Holly seemed distracted to be back on Earth. "I never thought I would see my planet again, but you brought me safely home." She faced Antor and studied him intently.

"What?" he asked.

"I wondered what you would look like on Earth, standing in the sunlight, and now I know. I'll be able to picture you here. You're even more beautiful than in space, even if you are in rough shape at the moment."

Antor was sure he wasn't a pretty picture, but he was glad Holly thought he was worth a second look. Holly, on the other hand, was so lovely in the sunshine, he wanted to gaze at her forever. He stroked her shining hair. It was more blonde than blue, now that the streaks had grown out or been blasted off. "And I'll be able to picture you here, where you belong."

Zenga stomped up. "You two are useless. This is war, not cuddly time. The Gorka are coming. Antor, take the east end of the field, Holly, the west corner. Willy and I will secure the middle. Move!"

"No, Zen. I don't think we should spread out like that. We need to hear Willy's updates, and Holly's not experienced with a blaster. She has to stay close to us. Willy, where are the Gorka now?"

The auto-mate processed the information and pointed almost straight across the field. "Seven minutes that way, Antor, if their speed remains constant."

Zenga winced. "Too close for comfort. Okay, let's stop standing in plain sight." They made for the edge of the field where a line of scrubby trees, the remnants of a fieldstone wall, and a hardy snowdrift provided decent cover. They spaced themselves along the wall, staying within calling distance.

"Willy, keep us updated about the Gorka," Antor said.

"Five minutes, Antor. Their direction is unchanged."

"Good." Antor's fear that they might veer off eased. He strained his ears to hear them, even though they were still too far away for that.

Willy said, "The Gorka are four minutes away."

"Closing fast, everyone get ready," Zenga hissed.

Antor crouched low and braced his blaster atop the stones. The rest of them did the same, watching the field, not making a peep of sound.

Except Willy. "Three minutes. How did you get out? Ouch, what are you doing? Help, help."

"What? Willy? Why did you say that?" Antor asked.

"I repeated what Teef said, Antor," Willy replied, without alarm.

Antor, by comparison, was extremely alarmed. He turned his gaze to the ship and cursed when two figures exited the Comet Tail through the bridge hatch. They started across the field, directly into the Gorka's path. Teef came unwillingly. She had no choice. Red had a dartgun poking her in the back. Antor didn't want to believe what he was seeing.

Red stopped at center field with Teef as his shield and called, "So this is Earth! And you've gotten rid of the Inferno. Impressive, Antor. I'll have to make do with the Comet Tail for now, but that's not a problem. I'll soon be rich enough to buy another ship. Why are you crouched behind that wall? Teef refused to say and I admit, I am curious. Come and talk to me, Antor, or I'll put a hole through the lovely Teef's heart and she'll never sing again. That would be such a shame, wouldn't it?"

"Stay down," Antor whispered and stood up alone. He climbed over the wall and took slow steps toward Red.

"Put down the blaster," Red growled.

The last thing he wanted to do was give up his weapon, when two flesh-eating monsters were in chomping distance, but he didn't have a choice. He laid it carefully on the ground, before he continued forward, straining his brain for a plan, any plan. He didn't come up with one and stopped in front of Red. "Are you okay, Teef?"

"Yes." Her voice was steady. She seemed to be holding up well.

"Red, let her go back on the ship. You have me now." Antor raised his hands in the Universal gesture of surrender. "You've found Earth, you have what you want, just let Teef go."

Antor wanted three things to happen. He wanted Teef out of harm's way, he wanted to stop Red, once and for all, and he wanted to survive—he wanted all of them to survive, excepting Red, of course. With the approaching Gorka, that was highly unlikely.

He was out in the open with Red. Up close, he could see that Red's arm was dripping blood. It was splashing on the muddy snow, scenting the air. One of his black horns was broken off at the tip and Antor put two and two together. Red had probably injured himself when getting free of his chains, using his horn to split the shackles. Maybe he had even benefitted from the interruption in gravity. It wouldn't have been painless, but Red wasn't the type to give in easily. His blood would draw the beasts to him like a magnet. Unfortunately, Red wasn't standing alone.

He thought he heard approaching movement. Zenga shouted, "One minute."

Red squinted in her direction. "Why did she say that?"

"I think she means you've got one minute to release Teef or she'll start shooting. You're a lot bigger than Teef and Zenga is one heck of a good shot. You'd be better off using me as a shield. I'm taller than Teef," Antor pointed out, squaring his shoulders and trying to look bigger.

"As a matter of fact, two are better than one. Get over here or I'll shoot you. We're going to back up toward the ship and you'll seal the hatch, and then you'll show me how to start the engines."

"He was going to leave you all here, except he couldn't figure out how to power up the Comet Tail," Teef explained.

"Oh. So you need me." Antor didn't waste time gloating. "Release Teef and I'll go with you, willingly. Otherwise I won't." He crossed his arms, standing firm. "Let her go, now!"

He heard a faint grunt from the nearest patch of forest. They were out of time. Red released his grip on Teef. She stepped away from him. Everything seemed to be happening both too slowly and too quickly, as if they were in a wormhole on Earth.

"Teef, get out of here, now! Go!" Antor had forgotten all about her wings. She took running steps, crouched and leapt into the air, arms spread. In five flaps, Teef was safely airborne.

Two purple bodies barreled out of the edge of trees behind Red. Gorka stand upright, unless they are chasing prey. This pair was bounding along on all fours, front and back legs a blur of overlapping movement. Gleaming fur rippled under the sun, muscles bunched and stretched in turn. The Gorka had thrived on Earth. It looked like they had grown.

323

There wasn't time to escape, yet Antor tried. He spun around. Before he could take off, Red grabbed him around the neck. "Let's go. The Comet Tail is waiting." He finally noticed the grunting and looked over his shoulder.

Red gasped and took desperate steps toward the Comet Tail, dragging Antor with him. Antor glanced at the stone wall and saw three blasters pointed his way. Willy, Zenga and Holly were standing up. All three looked as grim as their weapons. Unfortunately, they couldn't shoot Red without going through Antor. But they could target the galloping Gorka. Two barrels flashed red. Both shots missed. Three fired the next round. One of the beasts gave an enraged howl, but it didn't even break stride.

Red must have been more afraid of the Gorka than getting shot. He spun around so that Antor was between him and the teeth and claws. The beasts were so close, Antor could see flecks of foamy drool spraying off their long black muzzles.

Another round of blaster fire stopped the lead animal in its tracks. Red started to raise his dartgun, but Antor was in the way. The second Gorka hurtled over the body of its mate. It sprang forward with one great leap, at Antor. He couldn't escape, so he ducked as low as he could. Claws scraped his shoulders when Red took the brunt of the attack. Ripping flesh and crunching bone sounded as loud as Red's high-pitched keening. The Gorka sank its fangs into his face, putting an end to the horrible noise.

The three of them went down, locked together with Antor in the middle. He felt the impact of blaster fire rip through the Gorka's torso and a wash of warm blood soaked him. One blast was not enough to kill the beast. It kept clawing and biting. Red didn't die easily, either, not until the beast clamped onto his throat and crushed it.

Antor contorted and stretched to reach the knife in his boot. The Gorka released Red with a shake and turned its attention to live prey. Blaster fire skimmed by, removing a streak of purple fur. The beast ignored the interruption. Antor managed to yank the dagger out of both his boot and the sheath in one motion. Claws swiped his arm. He blocked the pain. When the long muzzle opened wide to eat his face, he stabbed with all his strength, not quite sure where the knife would end up.

He was more lucky than skilled. The blade buried deep in the beast's eye. It must have made it all the way to the brain, because the animal collapsed on top of Antor—deadweight, and the thing must have weighed more than six hundred pounds. Blood and gore sprayed Antor's face, blinding him.

Antor was pinned between the two corpses. Someone fired a last blaster round into the dead Gorka, which Antor didn't appreciate at all, since it winged his thigh. Everything went still and quiet. He couldn't move at all and waited to be rescued, fighting for air beneath the crushing weight of the Gorka. Everything got hazy.

Lots of footsteps approached, slow rather than fast. Antor tried to say, 'Help.' He couldn't speak.

"He's dead, isn't he? I think I shot him." Holly was sobbing.

"I'm sure it wasn't you, Holly. I think the Gorka got him." Zenga was sniffling. "Or Red got him. Or both."

Someone poked the Gorka. Antor felt the vibration. He tried to make any noise. He managed a sort of squeak. It wasn't very loud or manly, but it was heard.

"Oh, oh! Maybe he's not dead." Holly gripped his hand and he squeezed her fingers. "Antor's alive! Get that thing off him. Hurry, Willy."

The crushing deadweight tumbled off Antor. As soon as he was free, he dragged air into his deprived lungs and rolled off of Red's remains, coughing.

Lot of hands helped him to his feet. Everyone was talking at once, making a whole lot of noise. Holly flung her arms around him and held on tight. Considering that he was covered from head to toe in grossness, it was a brave act. Antor hugged her back, with all the strength in his arms, which was none.

"Oh god, Antor. I can't believe you survived that." Holly started crying in earnest.

Antor rasped, "I thought you only cried in Outer Space."

"Well, this is like Outer Space, with Gorka and Red and blasters, and the spaceship, and you almost dying. I'm surrounded by Outer Space. I thought you were dead and I thought maybe I shot you, so I'm allowed to cry. I might never stop."

Antor couldn't not smile. "You might have shot me if you fired the last blaster round, but it's just a scratch."

Zenga tried to check him over and gave up. There was simply too much blood and gore that belonged to others. She asked, "Antor, are you seriously injured? It's impossible to tell."

"A few scratches, but I'll live." He made a great effort to stand tall and succeeded. He was feeling pretty good, except for physically, about how everything had turned out in the end. Zenga passed him a handful of wet snow and he rubbed it over his face and eyes so he could see properly.

The view wasn't pretty. Red and the Gorka were a mess of bloody, steaming guts. Except for the patches of purple fur, it was hard to tell where one ended and the other began. Everything else was beautifully calm under the shining sun, with the fresh breeze blowing through the green trees.

It was hard to believe everything had worked out, but it had. Red was no longer a threat. The Gorka had been stopped. Holly was home, and her planet was safe. And now it was time to say goodbye. Nothing was happening in slow motion anymore.

"Time to clear up the evidence, before any Earthlings come to investigate," Zenga said, taking charge. "Willy, load the bodies onto the Comet Tail. Leave them by the rear hatch and we'll jettison them once we're out of this solar system."

"Yes, Zenga." Willy got to dragging.

Antor wasn't inclined to move, except to use a lot more snow to cleanse the rest of his skin. He found more claw marks than he'd expected.

"Oh, that was me, wasn't it?" Holly touched his thigh gently. There wasn't much left of his trouser leg.

"It's nothing, Holly." Antor hoped he had a pair of decent pants left. He was fast running out of clothes, and the ones he was wearing weren't fit for anything but burning. "Give me a minute. I'm going to change into something less gross." He didn't want to be disgusting to share their final farewell. That wasn't how he wanted Holly to remember him.

Zenga stopped him at the hatch. "Antor, don't you dare step on the ship in those clothes! They're dripping gut juice, and the Comet Tail is about to become a closed environment again. Take them off, bury them, and wash up properly in that snowdrift." She sounded like his keeper, but she made a good point.

"Toss me a towel, if you're not going to let me on the ship."

"I'll get it," Holly offered.

Zenga let her in. Holly wasn't nearly as disgusting as Antor. Her lesser gore was only secondhand—by association.

Antor aimed for the wall where the thickest snow had accumulated. He peeled off clothes and cringed at how much blood had soaked through his garments. Wearing his briefs and his boots, he had a thorough icy scrub, including his hair. When he felt properly freshened, he turned back to the ship and scanned for Holly and his towel. He was feeling exposed, and cold.

She was approaching, and she'd taken the time to change into more of Zenga's clothes. She certainly couldn't have hiked home to her mother, looking like she was either a serial killer or the victim of one.

Holly's eyes were fixed on him, hungrily. There was no denying the heat in her expression. She stopped in front of him and said kind of breathlessly. "I think I'll remember you exactly like this. Is that a … Speedo bathing suit?"

"No, just underpants." Antor reached for the towel, shyness taking over. Holly didn't release it until he tugged. If Antor wasn't mistaken, Holly found underpants in the snow as scintillating as he found her in broom closets. If only they weren't parting forever … but they were. He cleared his throat. "I better go get dressed. Maybe I can walk you partway home."

"That would be nice, Antor." Holly smiled so sadly, it felt like his heart broke right then and there.

"I'll be quick. Don't move." He hurried toward the ship. Her eyes followed him, he could feel their touch. In his cabin, he found one pair of respectable trousers, and his warmest shirt. He wrapped Holly's scarf around his neck, hoping she would let him keep it. He was going to need some tangible memory of her, something he could touch and hold, when he couldn't touch and hold her. Maybe he could even keep her phone and call her on occasion, and then he could look at their imaged picture every single day.

He opened the door and found Holly waiting in the passage with a packsack, all ready to leave and looking as miserable as he felt. Her Universe Idol crown was sticking out the top. Antor had never seen her wear it, except on TV. He took the pack out of her arms and placed it on the ground. When he opened his arms, Holly stepped into them.

Antor swallowed the huge lump in his throat. "I will miss you forever." His chest felt wet. "You're crying again, aren't you?"

Holly nodded. "Don't Outer Space guys cry?"

"Not if we can help it."

"Just like Earth guys." Holly wiped her eyes. They filled up again immediately.

Antor pulled her tighter. They were interrupted when Zenga summoned them to the bridge, sounding urgent.

"What, Zen?" Antor asked, as soon as he sat down and pulled Holly onto his lap. He wasn't going to let her go, not until he had to, and maybe not even then.

"Everything is cleared up outside. And we need to leave now," she said.

"Why? What's the rush?"

"A whole lot of those land cars have parked on the nearest road. I think our descent was seen in town, and I think a whole bunch of Earthlings are coming over to investigate the aliens. Maybe the entire town is on its way."

Antor closed his eyes in pain and held Holly tighter.

As if she was apologizing, Zenga said, "Holly, Antor, we really need to launch now."

"I know, Zen. I guess I can't walk you home," Antor said in Holly's ear.

"I guess not," she whispered.

He opened his arms and Holly left him.

327

Teef and Zenga said their emotional farewells to Holly at the open hatch. Antor didn't move. Holly picked up her little pack and left the ship without a word to him. He understood. They had said goodbye twice already. A third time would probably kill them.

He thrust out of his chair and ended up in the galley, rather than his room, where he could still smell Holly's flowery scent. For want of something to distract him, he opened the first aid kit and stuck healing bandages on the worst of his claw wounds, and his blasted thigh.

That done, he sat and stared at a bowl that had been left on the table. The space rations stared back, like little brown, white and green eyeballs. Antor wanted to hurl them across the room. He hated space rations. If he never ate space rations again, it would be too soon. He and the space rations were at a standoff when Zenga walked in. "Hatch is sealed. I need your help on the bridge to take off."

"Willy can help," Antor said, unmoving and uncaring. She patted his shoulder and left. The ship began to shake, the coils were speeding up. Antor closed his eyes when tears burned hotly. He didn't see or hear Zenga return. Suddenly, she was just there, sitting beside him, looking at him.

"Who's piloting?" Antor asked, almost curious. He wasn't even embarrassed about the tears.

"No-one yet. This isn't easy for me to say, Antor, but why don't you stay here."

"Here? In the galley?"

"No. On Earth, with Holly. Holly is as sad as you. Why don't you stay with her?"

"Huh?" He still didn't get it.

"You look Earth human. You've always wanted a home, why not Earth?" She raised her eyebrows questioningly.

Antor lowered his in confusion. "Stay here? On Earth? With Holly?"

Zenga rolled her eyes. "That's what I said. You and Holly … I know you come from different galaxies, but you're made for each other. You belong together. If you leave, you'll be miserable, Antor. So will Holly."

Not once had Antor ever considered the crazy idea, because it was so crazy. "It's a restricted planet, Zen. A planet. It's not a … spaceship. Earth doesn't even have real spaceships." He was making lame excuses, he just wasn't sure why. "And Holly might not want me to stay," he added, which might have been his real reason for not considering the idea.

Zenga took his hand. "Antor, when we were getting your towel, Holly told me she wanted to come with us, and she doesn't like Outer Space, at all."

"She did? That's great! She can come with us."

"I told her that I didn't think it was a good idea," Zenga said, before Antor could take off running to bring Holly back.

328

"But … why did you tell her that, Zen?"

"She wouldn't be happy living this life, Antor."

Inside, he knew it was true.

"My point is, Holly was willing to give up everything to be with you, so don't be stupid and say she might not want you to stay on Earth with her. Why won't you even consider it? Are you scared?"

He was, he simply hadn't clued in until Zenga said it aloud. "What if Holly realizes she doesn't love me, and she's stuck with me, because I'm stranded on Earth. There's nothing special about me, Zen. No-one has ever loved me before, and there's got to be a reason for that. Even my own parents didn't want me."

"Oh, Antor. That's so not true. I love you, you know that. And you don't know why you were abandoned on the Falling Star. There could have been so many reasons." She squeezed his hand. "Holly isn't going to stop loving you. You should have faith in her. Imagine how much faith she had in you, to be willing to give up everything for you, to let you lead Inferno to her planet, believing you would save it. She thinks the Universe of you, Antor."

"It sounds like you're trying to get rid of me," he said, wishing he had time to think, to decide.

"I want you to be happy, Antor, and I think you'll be miserable without Holly, and she'll be miserable without you. Earth isn't such a bad place," she said lightly.

"It might be the original Green World."

"What? No!"

"Think of all the wormhole chains that lead here. I think we might be on the lost Green World right now. I think we found it."

Zenga looked as dumbfounded by the possibility, as Antor felt about being stranded on one small planet, even if it was Holly's planet. He stood up and paced. He paced all the way to the bridge and looked through the viewing screen. Teef and Willy were in two of the chairs. Zenga would have company if Antor left. At the edge of the field, Holly stood alone. She was hugging her little pack and watching for the Comet Tail to leave forever, carrying Antor away.

"You have to decide now, Antor, before the coils overheat," Zenga said.

Willy had vital information. "The coils are overheating, Zenga."

Holly kept watching the ship, unmoving. She wasn't even crying. She looked too sad to cry, and as alone as Antor felt without her—and he knew. He knew Holly was his home. He'd known it the first time they met. And everyone should have a home. Antor realized there was no decision to make, or it had already been made.

"I'm going to stay," he declared.

329

"Finally. Make it fast."

He ran to his cabin, stuffed the little he owned into his duffle bag and rushed back to the bridge. He opened his mouth to deliver last minute instructions about the ship. Zenga cut him off. "I'll be fine, Antor. We'll be fine." They hugged hard.

"Teef, you can have my cabin. Don't forget to water the plants. And Zenga, don't forget to divert that meteor before you leave the galaxy, the one that's headed for Earth," he reminded her.

"Right. I won't forget. And maybe you can find out why so many aliens visit Earth, and why the planet has such advanced technology, and who's importing Outer Space entertainment broadcasts." It was a tall order.

"Maybe I can." Antor dug into his bag for the cell phone communicator. "Here, you can call me, every week. Press this button and you'll reach Holly's mother. Ask for me."

"I'll call." Zenga embraced him again. "Now go!"

He hugged Teef and even Willy, and wished them well.

Without any prompting, Willy said, "I will miss you, Antor."

"I'll miss you, too, Willy."

Zenga almost booted him out the hatch. The exterior of the hull was glowing molten orange. "Take off, Zen, before the ship explodes," Antor shouted, backing away fast. The hatch slammed closed and the Comet Tail shot straight up in a flare of sizzling light. In ten heartbeats, the ship was gone from sight.

Antor felt abandoned and quite terrified, until he turned around and saw Holly. He walked toward her and her expression transformed from disbelief to pure joy. She ran toward him and he caught her against his chest.

"You stayed. You stayed for me! Oh, Antor! I love you." She wrapped her arms so tight around his neck, he was almost strangled. It felt wonderful, except she was crying again.

"Holly, are you sure it's not me that makes you cry?" He had to ask.

"Positive." She smiled through her tears. "I can't believe you're here. We don't have to say goodbye ever again."

"No, we don't." Antor's heart felt full and whole again, instead of empty and broken. He leaned down and kissed Holly, and she kissed him. They only parted when they heard distant voices. It sounded like an excited crowd.

"We're about to have a lot of company," Holly gasped. "It sounds like the whole town has come to welcome me home. I wonder if my Mom is with them."

"Too bad you can't wear your crown and tell everyone you're the Universe Idol." He couldn't stop smiling.

"It is too bad. I guess I'll have to win my country's singing contest next year." Holly seemed to be suffering from the same smile-stuck-on-face affliction.

"I have no doubt you will," Antor said.

"And you'll have to try out, too, of course, so we can sing together," Holly added.

Antor considered that for a moment. "Maybe I will," he said, surprising himself.

"At least my townsfolk won't find a spaceship." Holly glanced back to where the Comet Tail had been. There was a gigantic, clear and deep impression in the wet mud. It was still steaming and ringed with charred vegetation. "Uh-oh, that looks just like a crop circle. We need a cover story. We'll say we just flew back from Europe, and we were hitchhiking home from the airport in the city. We didn't see anything and we know nothing about that suspicious mark. We didn't even notice it, or the big puddle of blood with ... is that clumps of purple fur? I thought Zenga said everything was cleaned up."

Antor hoped most Earthlings were a lot more gullible than Holly, or no-one was going to believe a word they spoke. "So it's okay to lie?" he checked.

"Yes! We're going to have to tell a whole lot of lies in the next few minutes. We'll have to say we got married in Europe, so you can stay with me until we get our own place. At least the gigantic jewels in my crown will make us rich enough to buy our own place, probably our own mansion. My Mom won't be mad, don't worry, or not too mad."

"Your mother didn't seem to like me when we spoke on the phone," Antor mentioned, and he was worried.

"She'll like you once she gets to know you. I'll have to tell her you're not a gangster or a biker, though. You're so beat up that you look like you fight all the time, and your hair is really long, like a biker, not to mention the leather pants, but I'll tell her you're not a biker. It will be okay, Antor. Facing my Mom is nothing compared to being attacked by Gorka, or tortured by Red, or having your ear blasted off by Nastos." Holly didn't mention her own name in regard to any ear blasting, and from the way she was babbling, she was seriously freaked about bringing him home.

In an odd way, it made Antor feel steadier, and confident about what he was about to face—his new life on Earth. With Holly by his side, he could face anything, even her mother.

"Holly, we're together, and I've never been happier. Don't worry, your mother won't scare me away. I'm looking forward to meeting your family."

"They'll be your family now, too," Holly said.

"They will?"

"For better or worse, my family is your family." She smiled and touched his cheek tenderly.

"I've always wanted a family, and a home," Antor confided.

For some reason, that brought tears to Holly's eyes. She cried as much on Earth as she did in Outer Space, it seemed. "Does that make you sad?" he asked.

"No. Yes and no. I'm sad that you never had those things, and I'm so happy you'll have them now, with me."

It sounded like a crowd was almost upon them, but Antor barely noticed. "Me too, Holly." He pulled her close enough to feel her heart beating in rhythm with his, and kissed her hello, instead of goodbye.

The End

www.ingramcontent.com/pod-product-compliance
Lightning Source LLC
Chambersburg PA
CBHW020904200626
46814CB00001BA/170